THE BLACK LIFE

Wealthy jeweller Eliezer Samuel contacts half Greek half Scots PI Alex Mavros after his Uncle Aron is spotted in the streets of Thessaloniki in northern Greece: but that's impossible – Aron Samuel perished in Auschwitz more than sixty years before. The case takes an even stranger twist when Mavros, accompanied by Eliezer's enigmatic daughter Rachel, travels to Thessaloniki to question the elderly witness. Ester Broudo denounces Aron Samuel as a traitor and a murderer. Was he really a Nazi collaborator? Mavros' investigations will uncover tragic and terrible secrets from the war and its aftermath, resulting in devastating present-day consequences.

THE BLACK LIFE

THE BLACK LIFE

by

Paul Johnston

Magna Large Print Books
Long Preston, North Yorkshire,
BD23 4ND, England.

British Library Cataloguing in Publication Data.

Johnston, Paul
　　The black life.

　　　A catalogue record of this book is
　　　available from the British Library

　　　ISBN　978-0-7505-3952-4

First published in Great Britain by Crème de la Crime,
An imprint of Severn House Publishers Ltd.

Copyright © 2013 by Paul Johnston

Cover illustration © Mohamad Itani by arrangement with
Arcangel Images

The moral right of the author has been asserted

Published in Large Print 2014 by arrangement with
Severn House Publishers Ltd.

Magna Large Print is an imprint of Library Magna Books Ltd.

Printed and bound in Great Britain by
T.J. (International) Ltd., Cornwall, PL28 8RW

To J. Wallis Martin
excellent friend, writer, editor and example

Author's Note

How I handle aspects of Modern Greek in English:

1) Masculine names ending in -os and -is lose the final -s in the vocative case: 'Yiorgos and Makis are having an argument'; but 'Yiorgo and Maki, stop fighting!' Mavros becomes Mavro when he is spoken to in Greek. Some names (e.g. Apostolos) retain the older form -e (Apostole) in the vocative.

2) The consonant transliterated as 'dh' (e.g. Ayia Tria*dh*a) is pronounced 'th' as in English 'these'.

3) Feminine surnames differ from their male equivalents – Christos Papakis, but Marika Papaki.

Prologue

Wittersdorf, north-west of Munich,
September 30th 1946

They waited until the woman and children had gone inside. A solitary light shone from the upper floor of the wood-built house. A few minutes later the man came out and walked with long strides to the shed. Every evening he chopped logs for half an hour, adding to the tiers of winter fuel against the wall.

The leader nodded to the others. They moved out from the line of conifers, Zvi to the left and Shlomo to the right, as usual. All three were carrying Walther PPK pistols that had been bought from the Americans, as had the list of names they were working their way down.

The door to the shed was half-open. There were regular thwacks as the heavily built man split logs with pinpoint accuracy.

'Drop the axe,' the leader said, in coarsely accented German. 'Now.'

The man looked at the three men and their weapons, then let the heavy implement fall to the sawdust-strewn floor.

'Who the fuck–'

'You are SS-Unterscharführer Ernst Moss-feld, with three years' service in Auschwitz-Birkenau.' The leader smiled humourlessly. 'Or

13

rather, you were.'

The German blanched. 'No ... I...'

'No, you are not Klaus Weiss. That identity is false. Your papers were obtained from a supposedly secret old comrades' organisation in Munich after you were detained for a paltry six months.'

Mossfeld's eyes bulged. 'Please, my wife ... my children...'

'Ah, you are sensible to mention them. Their fate is in your hands. If you do as I say, they will be unharmed. Otherwise...' The tone of the leader's voice came from the realm of dust and ashes that all four men had inhabited.

'How ... how can I trust you?'

Zvi laughed quietly. 'The same way the thousands you drove to the gas chambers trusted you. "Hang your clothes and shoes on the peg and make sure you remember the number. When you've had your shower you will reclaim them."'

Mossfeld was staring at the leader. 'I know you. You were in the Sonderkommando.'

'Yes, I was. You hit me hard and regularly.'

'I ... there were orders...'

The three armed men exchanged glances.

'And where would the Nazis have been without people who obeyed their orders?' said Shlomo. 'But now you're going to follow ours.'

The German took a step back as a coiled rope was thrown in front of him.

'Unfortunately,' the leader said, 'the fact that you don't have a car means that we can't gas you. And shooting is too quick, though you shot many of our brothers and sisters. So, slow strangulation at the end of that rope is what you get.' He pointed his pistol at Mossfeld's groin. 'Unless you want to be strung up with your cock and balls removed.'

'Put the noose round your neck, you subhuman piece of shit,' said Zvi.

After a time the German complied.

Shlomo stepped forward and tightened the knot. 'Now, on the chopping block.' He helped the big man up, his lips twisted in distaste.

Zvi had thrown the other end of the rope over the crossbeam above and was securing it to a post.

'Ernst Mossfeld,' the leader said, 'you are guilty of crimes against innocent men, women and children. May the devil take whatever soul you possess.'

Zvi and Shlomo wrestled the chopping block away and ducked the SS man's desperate kicks. He started to scrabble at the noose.

The three men watched him die. It took twenty-one minutes.

ONE

Mavros woke to the smell of freshly brewed coffee.

'I thought that a *sketo* would pull you out of whatever filthy dream you were having. That or grabbing your flagstaff and I haven't time for that.' Niki Glezou handed him the small cup of unsweetened coffee and ran her fingers through her tousled, highlighted hair.

'What time is...' Mavros looked at the clock. 'For the love of God.'

'Who you don't believe in. Normal people in Athens get up before seven, Alex. Normal people go to work.' Niki's tone was sharp, but she was smiling.

'What do you mean? I've got an appointment today.'

'Oh yes? What time?'

'Eleven.'

'I rest my case.'

Mavros downed his coffee, hiding that it wasn't strong enough. Still, maybe he'd be able to get another hour's sleep after she'd gone.

Niki's expression turned sombre. 'Remember we have the fertility specialist this evening.'

Mavros nodded. 'Seven-thirty. I'll be back long before that.'

'You'd better be.' Niki took his cup and saucer from the duvet and twisted his nose. 'We're getting to the bottom of why I can't conceive if it costs all my salary.' She lowered her head and kissed him on the lips. 'It isn't as if we don't try often enough.'

He watched as she walked to the door, swaying her hips seductively. The old Niki wouldn't have done that except in self-mockery. It seemed that a year of on-off living with Mavros had changed her priorities.

'Oh, and if you see the Fat Man,' she called from the hall, 'tell him that last *baklavas* was solid enough to build a bridge on.'

She still had her abrasive edge though. Then

16

again, Niki was under a lot of pressure. She was a social worker specialising in immigration issues and her workload had increased hugely. In her late thirties, she was also obsessed with getting pregnant. In the past they had split up because she didn't think Mavros was committed to them having a child. Over the last year he had done his best to show that he was. They had been brought close again partly because of the threat they were under. An ice-veined killer known as the Son was on the loose and had nearly done for Mavros the previous year. To throw him off their trail, Niki had sold her flat in the southern suburbs of Athens and they had moved to the top floor of a modern block halfway up Mount Lykavittos. A politician lived two floors below, so there was additional security. The rent was ridiculous, but Mavros's ageing mother helped. He didn't feel good about that. At least he was within close range of her place round the hill, as well as his friend the Fat Man's in Neapolis below.

He tried to go back to sleep without success. After a work-out on his exercise bike and rowing machine, he took a shower and investigated the contents of the fridge. Niki was only barely housetrained and all he found was a pot of her low-fat yoghurt. That did it. Breakfast at the Fat Man's was unavoidable.

'You're lucky. I just pulled a *galaktoboureko* out of the oven. Give it a quarter of an hour and we'll be in paradise.'

Mavros took in Yiorgos Pandazopoulos's sweat-dripping features and rounded belly. 'Ever

17

thought of changing that apron?'

'Ever thought of kissing my arse?' The Fat Man dropped his bulk into a battered armchair. 'Thought not. So, how's the lovely Niki?'

Yiorgos was banned from the flat on Lykavittos in case the Son followed him there. Mavros took circuitous routes to and from the place, but he couldn't expect the Fat Man to do the same. It was just as well. He and Niki got on like a volcano on fire.

'Worried about not getting pregnant,' Mavros said.

'I'd have thought another generation of–' The Fat Man broke off. 'Sorry, I know you want to make her happy.'

'And make you the atheist father of a bouncing mini-Mavros.'

'I bet Niki would be keen on that. What's going on workwise?'

Yiorgos had been involved in several of Mavros's missing-persons cases and acted as his sidekick and record-keeper.

'Not a lot. Cutting ties with Kriaras maybe wasn't such a good idea.'

'He's an arsehole and a lackey of the rich. Plus he almost got you killed. What else could you do?'

Nikos Kriaras was head of the organised crime squad, a fixer with connections to many of the super-rich who pulled the politicians' strings. He used to put clients – especially foreign ones with problems the police didn't want to deal with – Mavros's way.

'Well, I could have killed him,' Mavros said,

scratching his stubble.

'I'd have helped.'

'No doubt. But I'm not a murderer, remember?'

'You've come pretty close.'

'But never crossed the line.' Mavros gave him a meaningful look. 'Which is important.'

Yiorgos shrugged. 'Depends who the target is.' He went into mockery mode. 'At heart you're just a screwed-up foreigner with different-coloured eyes who doesn't really fit in Greece.'

Mavros laughed, as much at the truth of the statement as the tone. His father, Spyros, long dead, had been a senior member of the Greek Communist Party, while his mother came from a bourgeois Scottish family. There were brown flecks in his left eye, while the right one was pure dark blue. For some reason women found that attractive, though maybe his shoulder-length black hair helped. Or his innate charm. Or his imagination.

'Nothing from the Son?' the Fat Man asked. He was a longstanding communist too and had been close to Spyros, though his allegiance to the party had faded in recent years.

'You mean any special-delivery packages full of heads or spleens? No. Maybe he's busy killing people in another country.'

Yiorgos heaved himself up and headed for the kitchen. 'Which doesn't mean he won't be back.'

'You are using the alarm system I got for you?'

The Fat Man reappeared, carrying an oven tray of perfectly browned custard-filled pastry. 'Of course. And there are sharpened knives all over the house.'

Mavros knew those wouldn't be enough to keep the assassin and torturer at bay for more than a few seconds.

'I've also invested in a shotgun and an old but serviceable Makarov. One of the comrades helped me.'

'Did he also teach you how to use them?' Mavros asked acidly. He could handle firearms, but hated the sight of them.

'I did a bit of target shooting with the pistol, yes.' Yiorgos grinned as he cut a large slice of the pastry and dumped it on a plate. 'Hardly seemed necessary with the shotgun. Aim in general direction and pull trigger.'

Mavros took his portion, shaking his head. Then he bit into the *galaktoboureko* and was transported to a simpler, sweeter world.

After taking the trolley-bus to Omonia Square and losing – he hoped – any potential tail in the backstreets, Mavros headed for the Grand Bretagne Hotel on Syndagma Square. Although it was early November, the sun was shining strongly and his leather jacket was almost too much. The yellow parliament building – the former royal palace – stood on the rise to his right. It was filled with wheelers, dealers and thieves, with a few, very few, notable exceptions. There were tourists about though the season had ended; the buzz from the Olympics the year before still made Athens an attractive destination, even for people who only went through the motions with the Acropolis and the museums. The uniformed men on the door gave Mavros suspicious looks, but he didn't care. His jeans were clean and his T-shirt had no logo. Not many pairs of biker boots entered the city's premier hotel and that made him proud. Whether it would impress his potential client was another matter.

He walked across the wide space of marble. 'I have a meeting with Mr Eliezer Samuel,' he said, in English, partly because he was unsure how to pronounce the names and partly because he liked to play with his dual nationalities.

The receptionist, an attractive woman with what looked like genuine blonde hair, pulled tightly back, tapped on a keyboard. 'Your name, please?'

'Mavros.'

'Alexander?'

'Alex.'

She smiled primly. 'Yes, Mr Samuel is waiting for you, sir. Suite 542.'

He used the stairs and was pleased to find that his breathing was relatively unaffected by the five flights. He found the door and knocked.

It was opened by a tall young woman with a stern face and gleaming black hair that reached her shoulders.

'Mr Mavros?' she asked, the 'r' coming from the back of her throat in the French way.

'That's me. Obviously you aren't Mr Samuel.'

'No,' came a male voice from further inside. 'I am.'

'It's Sam-oo-eel,' the woman said softly, as she stepped aside.

Mavros moved into the sumptuously appointed

21

suite and was confronted by a well-built man with white hair, whose unwrinkled face suggested he wasn't as old as he might have been. He wore an expensive-looking dark blue suit, white shirt and red silk tie.

'Mr Mavros,' he said, extending a hand and squeezing his visitor's tightly.

'The same. That's quite a grip.'

'I play squash three times a week.' Although the man's English had French notes, it was fluent. 'Please sit down. Rachel will bring us coffee.'

Mavros was about to object, having sunk another *sketo* at the Fat Man's, but decided against it. Negativity was never a good idea at the beginning of meetings, especially when you needed the work.

Samuel picked up a file from the glass-topped table. 'I have a collection of your press cuttings here, Mr Mavros.'

'Alex, please.'

'Very well, Alex. Your career has been most impressive.'

'I've had my moments.'

'Modest, too. I like that in a man. The French ambassador tells me that some of your biggest cases have not been reported in the media.'

He knows the French ambassador, Mavros thought. How much does the French ambassador know about me?

'That's true.'

'Good, because what I'm going to ask you to do must remain confidential.'

Mavros sipped the coffee, which was nothing like as good as the Fat Man's. 'I'm always strict about client confidentially, but I can't guarantee that the people I have to deal with will keep their mouths shut. Inducements can be applied, of course.'

Samuel looked at Rachel, who had joined him on the sofa. 'You mean money?'

'Not necessarily. Everyone has a weak point.'

'Ah!' The Frenchman smiled. 'I like your style. Let us begin. First, tell us what you know about me.'

The initial contact had been by email. Mavros had checked Eliezer Samuel's background as a matter of course. Apart from professional thoroughness, he had to be careful – the Son could be lurking.

'You own and run Samuel and Samuel S.A.,' – he got the pronunciation right – 'one of the largest jewellers in France. Based in Paris, but with retail branches across the country. Last year the company made a net profit of over 60 million euros. You are sixty-three years old and are married to Nicole Pintor, your first wife Naomi having died in 1967. My commiserations.'

'Thank you. It was ... a terrible blow. She was hit by a car.' Samuel looked at Rachel. 'But Nicole has brought me great joy, as well as Rachel and her brother.'

'David, born 1972, who is your partner in the business.'

'What year was I born, Mr Mavros?' the young woman asked.

'January 14th 1977.'

'Touché.' She smiled briefly.

'I'm impressed, Alex,' Samuel said, lighting a

medium-sized cigar. 'Anything else?'

'You have an apartment in the seventh arron-
dissement, a country house near Tours and a villa
in Antibes.'

Samuel puffed out smoke. 'Very good. More?'

'Are you sure?'

He nodded, though his expression was grim.

'All right. Your parents were Sephardic Jews
from Thessaloniki. They, your elder brother and
sister, your grandparents and the rest of your extended family were killed in Auschwitz-Birkenau
after being transported in 1943.'

Eliezer Samuel had put down the cigar and was
looking straight at Mavros. Rachel took his hand.

'You have done your homework, Alex,' the
jeweller said.

'If I may, how did you escape?'

'My parents smuggled me out of Thessaloniki
not long after my birth. I was fortunate enough
to end up with a Jewish family in Canada.'

Mavros looked at the daughter. In profile, her
eyes on her father, she was very striking, her
cheeks high, her nose straight and her unpainted
lips full.

'I'm sorry,' Mavros said lamely. 'That must
have been very difficult for your parents.'

'I imagine so, though they didn't have long to
live with it.' Samuel picked up his cigar again. 'I
grew up in Montreal, but moved back to Europe
in the late 60s. With the passage of time and the
growth of the family business, I found ways of
living with the facts you stated.'

Mavros noticed the tense. 'Found ways? And
now?'

The Frenchman looked at his daughter, whose hand was still over his. 'And now our world has been turned upside down.'

Mavros waited, aware that questions were unnecessary. Samuel hadn't told him what the job was when he phoned to confirm their meeting. Now he would do so unprompted.

'I need some more coffee.'

Rachel refilled her father's cup from the cafetière. Mavros shook his head.

'This is what happened. I never returned to Thessalonique, as the French call it. That would have been too painful and I preferred to remain in a state of ignorance about the place where my family lived. But I provide funds for several Jewish organisations and have contacts there.' Samuel emptied his cup. 'Ten days ago I was contacted by Rabbi Savvas Rousso. One of the elderly women in a home I partly finance – her name is Ester Broudo – saw my Uncle Aron in the street.'

'Your Uncle Aron? I thought all your Thessaloniki relatives perished in Poland.'

'We did too.'

Mavros looked from Eliezer Samuel to Rachel and back again. 'So you want me to look for a dead man?'

Samuel nodded. 'Or that even rarer thing – a man who has come back from the dead.'

'That's ridiculous,' Niki said, as she and Mavros left for the fertility clinic. 'How can you find a dead man?'

'Presumably he wasn't really dead. Or the old

25

woman who saw him is dotty.'

'Those poor parents, giving their baby away. Or rather, those unbelievably harsh parents.'

Mavros tightened his grip on her hand as they passed the police guard outside the apartment block. Predictably, she had zeroed in on that part of the story. He shouldn't really have shared it with her, but client confidentiality didn't include Niki and the Fat Man. Someone had to sound the alarm if he disappeared on a job.

'It was good that they did, considering what happened to the family.'

'Yes, but how could a mother separate herself from her child – how old was he?'

'Six months.'

'My God,' she said, in anguish. 'I can't even begin to imagine what that must have been like.'

Shivering in the unexpected cold, Mavros stopped a taxi on the Lykavittos ring road and directed the driver to the clinic behind the Hilton. They could have walked, but the lurking threat of the Son meant they rationed that activity. They still didn't use a car, though. Mavros had never had one because he'd always lived in the centre of the city. Niki's Citroën was under a tarpaulin in the parking area on the ground floor of their apartment building. He didn't want the Son tailing her when she was on her own.

He squeezed her arm. 'They correctly guessed what was going to happen to the Jews of Thessaloniki. Besides they had two other children.'

Niki turned on him. 'That's supposed to excuse them, is it? They already had kids, so they could dispense with the third one?'

Mavros knew she was at high tension over the doctor's appointment. 'Look, Eliezer Samuel survived. He's got two kids of his own. That was what his parents would have wanted.'

Niki flopped against him. 'Yes, I suppose so.' She took his hand. 'Alex, if I get pregnant and it's a choice between me and the baby, you will take our child, won't you?'

'There's a couple of pretty major "ifs" there.'

'Answer,' she said, her fingers digging into his skin.

'It's totally hypothetical,' he objected. 'Besides, there would be medical advice to follow.'

'Coward,' she muttered, turning away.

Mavros kept hold of her hand but it was limp now, the attack of nerves having passed. That was just as well. He still hadn't worked out how he was going to tell her about the arrangements he'd agreed with the Frenchman.

TWO

My life wasn't always black. I still remember the blinding blue skies over the Thessaloniki I grew up in; the glinting waves in the bay and the green fields at the edge of the built-up areas. But things were already changing for the Jewish community. When the city was liberated from the Ottoman Empire by the Greeks in 1912, Sephardic Jews descended from those expelled from the Iberian peninsula in the late fifteenth and early sixteenth centuries made up the largest population group. That changed in 1922, when the exchange of populations meant that the Muslims left and Greeks from Asia Minor flooded into Macedonia and its capital. They resented the wealth of the Jews, though many of our people were poor dock workers and carters.

'My son, why do you care for those unfortunates?' my father would ask. 'I donate money to their representatives. You have no need to feel guilty.'

So he thought. The family had been jewellers for centuries and he had four shops in the wealthier parts of the city. My elder brother Isaak had started working at weekends when he was still at school, but I refused. I was always contrary. I got that from my mother. Despite the restrictions of bourgeois Sephardic culture, she ran our home like an empress – a short one, like the English Victoria, but much louder, I would guess.

'I don't care if you don't want to work in the shops,' she would say, 'but at least get out of that room. It isn't as if you're studying for school.'

That was true. My parents didn't approve of what I was taking in. They were comfortably off, but they never read anything but the Torah and the local newspapers. From an early age Shabbat was torture for me, though the Greeks forced all shops to open on Saturdays, so it was possible to escape. I don't know why I never believed. Like many young Jews at the time I saw myself as Greek first and Jewish second, but that didn't restrict my reading.

'Who is this Marx, this Engels?' my mother screamed, when she and my father decided to investigate my books. One of the maids must have put them up to it. We had a house on the shore beyond the White Tower and it was too large for my mother to look after without help. 'Lenin? He was a monster!'

'Marx was a Jew,' I replied.

'You're so clever you'll lose your nose,' she said, seizing the said organ with short but strong fingers.

'Communism,' my father said, as if his burgeoning belly had been punctured by a pin. 'Never had any time for...'

'I'm educating myself,' I said piously.

'You're fourteen years old,' Father said. 'You go to school for education.'

'As if they teach anything useful there.'

Mother twisted my nose. 'They teach scripture and obedience.'

'And arithmetic,' Father added. 'Essential for business.'

'I don't care about business,' I shouted back. 'I don't want to sell overpriced trinkets to the wives of men who exploit the workers.'

That stymied even my mother, who thankfully let go of my nose.

'Overpriced ... trinkets,' repeated Father, as if I'd slapped him in the face with a particularly rank herring.

At this point my brother Isaak stepped in. He was five years older than I was and had an enviable serenity about him.

'Leave the boy,' he said, with a soft smile. 'It is

29

good that he reads without supervision. Soon he will understand there is no future in communism.'

I would understand no such thing – not for several years – though I did know that being a communist was dangerous. There had been a dictatorship in Greece since 1935 and, although there were no particular policies against the Jews, anti-Semitism had been building up in Thessaloniki. Jewish Communists had been arrested and sent to prison or remote islands.

Dinner that evening was an unusually silent affair. My sister Miriam, twenty-one and newly married, was across the table with her skinny husband Albertos. They made a strange couple as Miriam was a similar shape to our mother, though less bulky.

'What's happened?' she asked, looking around the table.

'Your fool of a brother thinks Lenin is a god,' Mother said.

Miriam stared at Isaak, then realised I was the one in question. She laughed. 'Come, everyone knows he killed the Tsar and his family.'

'Good for him,' I said.

'His policies also led to the deaths of millions of the Russian poor,' Albertos said. He had been to university in Paris and was a lawyer.

'They're not called Russians any more,' I pointed out. 'Besides, Comrade Stalin isn't a dictator, unlike Hitler and Mussolini. Or Metaxas.'

People glanced around anxiously, as if agents of our own fascist leader were under the table or behind the curtains.

'That's enough of such talk,' Father said. 'I have made a decision. The boy may keep his books, but he must lock them in the cupboard. We can't have the servants looking at them again.' He turned to me. 'My boy, you know that Communists are atheists.'

I nodded enthusiastically.

'But you had your bar-mitzvah last year,' said Mother indignantly.

I shrugged. 'Did you give me any choice?' I moved my gaze round the table. 'Any of you?'

Isaak laughed. 'Our little revolutionary. Every family needs one.'

He was right about that.

THREE

The fertility clinic appointment was a disaster. Mavros had provided a sperm sample earlier – having declined Niki's offer of assistance – and the results were back: there was no shortage of little swimmers. That put the onus on Niki. The doctor had found nothing obviously amiss, but she had to do more tests. Apart from that, it was a question of ensuring they made love on fertile days and various strange postures that she should adopt immediately afterwards. They went home feeling less like messing around than a pair of eunuchs.

'Next Thursday's the beginning of my fertile time,' Niki said, coming out of the shower with a towel covering not much of her.

'Ah,' Mavros said.

Niki was immediately on the alert. 'What does that mean?'

'I'm going to Thessaloniki on Monday,' he mumbled.

'What?'

He repeated the words more clearly.

'That's just great, Alex,' she said, eyes blazing.

'How long for?'

'Em, I don't know.'

'Of course you don't.' She sat down beside him on the bed. 'Look, do you really want us to have a baby?'

Mavros sighed. 'Yes, I do. I've said so often enough.'

She looked at him sceptically. 'You can never say it enough.'

'I just did – again.'

Niki put the towel over her head. Mavros wasn't sure if the display of her very attractive body was deliberate. Given that she wasn't fertile, he suspected not – then berated himself for the disloyal thought.

'So you're going to look for a long-dead Jew?' she said from behind the curtain of cotton.

'The money's good and we need it, especially with these medical bills.'

There was a muffled 'hmph'.

'Besides, I might track him down quickly – or rule out the sighting as a mistake – and be back in time.'

Niki's face reappeared. 'Well, that would be uncommonly decent of your majesty.' She smiled emolliently. 'Sorry, I'm being a bitch.'

Mavros pulled her towards him. 'No, you aren't. I understand.'

'Do you?' she asked, then stopped resisting.

She may not have been fertile, but they had an unexpectedly good time.

The next morning Niki let Mavros sleep. He woke up around ten. There was a text message on his phone: 'Confirm funds sent 2 yr a/c. Rachel S.'

That cheered him up. Still, the truth was he didn't particularly fancy going to Thessaloniki on a wild ghost chase. He liked the city well enough, though it held some painful memories, but it was a long way just to talk to an elderly woman. That reminded him. He wanted to pick his mother's brains.

As he took the long way round Lykavittos, slipping down narrow streets and looking out for a tail, Mavros considered the condition of the job that was likely to cause him the most grief. Eliezer Samuel was already back in Paris, but his daughter had remained in Athens. She was following up leads to her great-uncle via the Jewish Museum. The plan was that she and Mavros fly to Thessaloniki together. He was on the horns of a particularly buttock-piercing dilemma. Should he tell Niki about that? If so, would it be better if he described Rachel as a dowdy woman in her forties? One thing was certain: Niki had a track record of extreme jealousy. As he approached his mother's apartment block, he put the decision off. Procrastination was the mother of lies.

Mavros nodded to the private guard that his mother had agreed to pay for after the Son's threat to the family over a year ago, then pressed the buttons on the entry pad. They were changed every week, much to the other residents' irritation, even though the increased security was appreciated by some of them. Kolonaki was central Athens' wealthiest area and burglaries were common. He ran up to the sixth floor, as usual the last flight of stairs making his lungs burn.

The outer door to his mother's apartment had been replaced with a heavy steel panel. He had keys but he preferred to keep her on her toes, so he pressed the buzzer and mugged to the camera on the ceiling.

The door opened.

'Alex. How nice of you not to call in advance.' Dorothy Cochrane-Mavrou's voice was only slightly sharp. She knew her son was testing her. 'Hold on while I get this stupid chain off.'

Mavros embraced his mother when the door was closed again, feeling how frail she was. She'd had a stroke a few years before and, although she was back living on her own and running her small publishing company, she had aged rapidly. Then again, they had celebrated her eightieth birthday earlier in the year so she was doing well enough.

'Don't listen to me. It's always a joy to see you, dear.' Dorothy kissed him on both cheeks. 'Come and have some tea.'

Mavros followed her into the kitchen and

opened the box of shortbread. His Scottish genes had donated him a sweet tooth or thirty (he had two caps). His mother smacked him lightly on the hand.

'You'll end up like your overweight friend.' Dorothy would never use as vulgar a nickname as the Fat Man.

Mavros carried a tray into the spacious living area. The French windows gave a view to the Acropolis and the sea beyond the southern suburbs. The water was grey-blue in the autumn wind and the jagged lines of the mountains in the distance were blurred.

'So, how are you and Niki?' Dorothy knew about the fertility clinic appointment.

Mavros filled her in.

'Poor girl. I feel for her. I was so lucky with you three.' Her brown eyes took on an extra lustre. 'Spyros and I never had to worry about fertile days.'

Mavros couldn't help glancing at the photos on the dresser – his father with his powerful gaze and clipped moustache, his sister Anna with husband Nondas and their two kids, and, at the rear, partly obscured, his brother Andonis, caught in time with an eternal smile.

'Let them rest in peace,' Dorothy said, smiling sadly.

'I know.' Mavros looked away. Spyros had died when he was five and he had few memories of him, but Andonis was another matter. His handsome, outgoing brother had been eleven years older and was his childhood hero. Andonis had got involved in the student opposition to the

Colonels' dictatorship and had disappeared when Mavros was ten. For years he had tried to find him, but had finally accepted that there was no hope, despite the fact that the main reason he'd got interested in missing persons was to locate his brother. Then the bastard Son had told him that Andonis was still alive. He'd been on tenterhooks for months, hoping that the killer would get back in touch despite the danger that would entail. But he hadn't and Mavros had decided that it had been a cruel joke.

'Besides, as long as we remember them they're still here, aren't they?'

Mavros was surprised by his mother's words. She had spent years talking him out of continuing the search. Now it seemed she'd never stopped thinking about her lost husband and son.

'I know, I know,' Dorothy said. 'But you must understand, Alex. I had to make you get on with your own life. Living in the past is for old people, not young tearabouts like you.'

Mavros laughed at that characterisation. He was forty-three and, despite the leather jacket, boots, jeans, long hair and stubble, his tearabout days – such as they were – would soon be over. Eating three pieces of shortbread wasn't exactly starting a revolution.

'I wanted to ask you something, Mother,' he said, wiping his mouth.

'Anything, dear.'

'That book *Years in Hell*.'

'Oh yes.' Her curiosity was piqued.

'Can I have a copy?'

'Of course. I'm sure there are some left. It didn't sell well. I should have done a translation into English. Not many Greeks wanted to read about the fate of the Thessaloniki Jews.' She got up stiffly and went over to the bookcase that filled one long wall. 'Here you are.'

Mavros took the volume from her. He remembered flicking through it when it came out in the mid-90s, but the truth was he hadn't been very interested either. Now he was and he ran his finger down the index.

'Looking for something in particular?'

Mavros raised his eyes. 'A family called Samuel.' He used the pronunciation that his client's daughter had whispered.

'I can't say I remember them. Common name, I should think.'

He found an entry and went to the page. "Samuel, Yosif, jeweller and owner of several shops, known for his generosity to less fortunate Jews. Transported to Auschwitz-Birkenau with all his close family in 1943. None returned to Thessaloniki." Hm.'

'Helpful?'

'Sort of' He told Dorothy about his new case.

'How extraordinary, especially if the witness turns out to have been correct. You should read the whole book. There were several cases of people coming back years after the end of the war. In fact, you should talk to the author, Allegra Harari. I'm sure she's still active. A very forceful woman.'

Mavros looked at the back of the book. A plump-faced, middle-aged woman with piercing eyes stared out at him, her expression suggesting strong will.

'She was an independent researcher back then, though she may have got a university job. I must have her number and address somewhere.'

'It's all right. I'll find her on the Internet.'

'Go on then.'

Mavros stared at his mother. She used a computer for editing texts, but had always sworn that the Internet was the work of the devil – a very haphazard devil at that.

'I've been converted. Anna finally made me see the benefits.'

'Uh-huh.' That didn't surprise him. His sister was a fashion and gossip columnist, though she preferred the term 'lifestyle'. She'd been an early champion of new technology and could bore for Greece on the latest mobile phones.

He logged on and quickly discovered that Allegra Harari had her own website, which had a contact email address including the letters 'th', showing that she was in Thessaloniki. He noted it down. A quick viewing of the site suggested she knew a huge amount about the city's Jews and their history.

'See?' Dorothy said. 'Wonderful thing, the Internet.'

'I have actually been using it for some time, Mother,' he said, with mild irritation.

'I know, dear.' Dorothy's eyes twinkled. 'Sometimes you take yourself a bit seriously.'

Mavros took a deep breath. His mother didn't witness the perma-clowning that took place between him and the Fat Man, but maybe she was right. Since the reappearance of the Son and the concomitant disruption to all their lives, plus the resumption of his turbulent relationship with Niki, he probably hadn't been a bundle of charm and wit.

'What is it you're working on now, Mother?' he asked, looking at a jacket proof. '*The Athens Olympics – Boom or Bust? An Economist Writes.*'

'It's a very good book and a timely one,' she said.

'Yes, but how many jokes are there?'

'Silly boy,' Dorothy said, realising what he was up to. 'Go and clean your flat. I'm sure that'll cheer Niki up.'

'I'm sure it would,' Mavros said, getting up to leave. Seeing the Fat Man would cheer him up more.

'So you're going to the co-capital?' Yiorgos said, using the term that was meant to make the northern city feel it was the match of Athens.

'On Monday.'

'Want some company?'

Mavros told him about Rachel, describing her appearance.

'You lucky bastard. What does Niki think about that?' 'Em...'

'You haven't told her? I didn't realise she'd taken both your balls.'

'Very funny. It's a... sensitive time.' Without going into detail, he told the Fat Man about the fertility issue.

'Oh, right.' Yiorgos was all at sea. He'd lived with his mother till he was in his late fifties – for convenience as much as anything else – and had very limited experience of the opposite sex; apart from female cadres, who were not encouraged to share their favours. 'So what are you going to do?'

'Search me. Nothing, probably.'

'That usually works. If she calls, I'll be sure not to mention the gorgeous Rachel.'

'I bet you will.' Mavros picked up a book from the cluttered coffee table. '*The Jews of the Greek Communist Party*? Since when did you care?'

The Fat Man shook a can of beer to see if there was anything in it and then drank. 'Just a bit of background reading. You never know what might come in handy.'

Mavros had told his friend about the Samuel case by phone the previous evening, but was taken aback by his friend's dedication. In the past it had been known to lead to disaster. 'Look, it's probably just a case of mistaken identity.'

'Doesn't matter. It's interesting. I knew a couple of Jewish cadres back in the Sixties. They were very dedicated. They felt they had even more to prove than the rest of us.'

Mavros was impressed. There weren't more than a few thousand Jews in Athens. The only one he'd met was a landlord back when he worked in the Justice Ministry. Mr Sabbetai was the only property owner he'd ever dealt with who was both fair and responsive to problems.

'Anyway, if you're up in the north, you'll need someone to hold the citadel here.'

Mavros looked around the chaotic room. The Fat Man's mother used to keep it immaculate, but now there were pizza boxes and beer cans everywhere and the paintings of the area around Sparta where the family originated were hanging crookedly. Dust would soon take over the maisonette. At least that would be a form of the collective ownership espoused by the party.

'The citadel?'

Yiorgos followed his gaze. 'Well, the rubbish dump.'

There was an outburst of hilarity, then they sent out for more pizza.

'Here, why don't you cook something?' Mavros demanded. The Fat Man wasn't only an expert at sweet delicacies. 'Don't answer. You have one major character flaw – you're lazy as a pig in shit. And you're a glutton.'

Yiorgos laughed. 'So what? At least I can count.'

FOUR

I was fifteen when the Italians invaded Greece through Albania at the end of October 1940. By then I was a member of the Communist youth, which was a proscribed organization like the main party. Everyone in my family thought I spent the evenings at woodwork classes: I had some ability with my hands and occasionally provided them with models of ships and buildings. In fact I was taking messages between cadres, distributing leaflets, and sticking anti-government posters on walls and shop windows. I often had to run faster than the icy Vardharis wind to save my skin. Uncle Avram, my father's younger brother, arranged for his six-month-old son Eliezer to be smuggled out of the country. Even in the circumstances, we thought that was an extreme step. Aunt Rachel never got over it, although she had two older children.

My brother joined up the day after Prime Minister Metaxas's famous refusal to allow Mussolini's troops into Greece.

'Are you crazy?' my mother screamed. 'This war has nothing to do with you.'

'Yes, it does,' Isaak replied. 'I'm a Greek.'

'But first you are a Jew, my son.'

He shook his head. 'You think the Christians look at it that way? First comes the fatherland.'

My father shook his head, but I could see he was proud of Isaak: proud and frightened.

Miriam's Albertos was a reserve officer so he went straight to the front in the snow-covered peaks of Epirus with the rest of the Greek Army. Isaak was posted to the end of the railway line at Kalambaka, where he unloaded supplies that were sent onwards by mule and on the backs of men and even women. Soon the returning trains were filled with the wounded and frostbitten. But the line held and the invaders were beaten back into Albania. Victory was heralded as a miracle.

Initially the comrades, those who hadn't been imprisoned, thought the war was a bad joke – two fascists beating their chests at each other. Then they mobilised too, sensing that, win or lose, there would be opportunities for the party despite the

Molotov-Ribbentrop Pact. Many of them took their places in the ranks and died alongside bourgeois officers.

My sister moved home after Albertos left. She was four months pregnant and wandered about the house like a tormented spirit, face pale and arms crossed over her abdomen.

'You'll do the infant harm,' Mother said. 'Sit down, girl. There are potatoes to be peeled.'

Our servants had vanished when the war started. I had the impression they'd been waiting for an excuse. Anti-Semitic groups had been targeting the more obvious homes of Jews. Our downstairs windows had been broken and dog shit rubbed on the door. But Father's shops were making even more money as departing soldiers bought rings and proposed to their girls.

'I want to go to the fighting,' I said to Kostas, the cadre who oversaw us.

'You're too young,' he said, running his eye over me. 'Though you're almost big enough. There's plenty to be done here.'

So I went on with what struck me as minor work, paying little attention to my schooling. Now that the spaghetti-gobblers had been dealt with, the talk among the more forward-looking party members was of the future. If the Germans intervened to save the idiot Duce's face, Thessaloniki would be the first Greek city to be hit. But Hitler's hordes were still no further south than Austria so there was time to build defences. Not that anyone really believed they would hold.

We heard nothing from Isaak and Albertos for weeks. The newspapers gave some idea of the chaos that reigned and wounded men had appeared at the railway stations, before being carried off in ambulances to the overcrowded hospitals. Miriam was almost out of her mind and even my endlessly supportive mother struggled to comfort her. They cooked and sewed, their voices low in the kitchen. It was the only warm room in the house, fuel having become hard to find.

Then one day there was a knock on the door. I happened to be in the hall and opened up. I was confronted by what I first took to be a beggar with a beard, his clothes torn and filthy, with one foot wrapped in blood-stained rags. I reached for a few coins from the bowl my father kept by the door.

'This ... this is the ... Samuel house?' the man croaked, in our tongue, Judezmo.

I looked back at him and was knocked flat as he collapsed on top of me. My parents heard the noise and came running.

'Are you all right, my son?'

'Yes, Mother,' I said, sliding from beneath the unconscious vagrant. Then I saw the mud-coated brass buttons on his shoulders and realised he was wearing an army great coat. I immediately knew something bad had happened. Looking over to the kitchen door, I saw Miriam, her eyes wide and her mouth open in a silent scream.

The man came round after a few minutes and we took him to the stove. He drank a cup of hot milk and held it out for more. Then he ate a whole loaf of bread, panting like an animal. All this time, Miriam was standing at his side, whiter than an unused bridal sheet.

44

'Alalouf,' he finally said. 'Dario Alalouf. Lieutenant.' He avoided looking at my sister, his gaze resting for some reason on me.

'You have news?' I said, when nothing was forthcoming.

'I have ... bad news.'

'My son!' Mother shrieked, falling into Father's arms.

Dario stared at me, then his eyes dropped. 'Albertos ...

My mother's cries ceased, to be taken up immediately by Miriam. Father let go of his suddenly restored wife and went round the table to embrace my sister. He managed to get her on to a chair and calmed her enough for the stranger to go on.

'He ... we counter-attacked them south-east of Himarra. Albertos was ... was very brave. His men worshipped him. We ... we had them on the run, when...' Dario broke off and gave in to violent sobbing, which Miriam echoed.

I felt a curious excitement, a need to know my brother-in-law's fate. 'What happened?' I said, my voice inappropriately loud.

That broke through the emotion. Dario gave me a sharp look and turned to Miriam.

'I'm... sorry. Albertos told me about you ... and the child you are carrying.'

'What happened?' I repeated.

The officer glanced back at me. 'A final shell from the enemy battery on the outskirts of the town. He... It was a direct hit.'

'But Albertos,' my sister said. 'Where is he?'

'He was a hero,' Dario said. 'They're going to

give him a medal.'

'Where is he?' screamed Miriam.

Lieutenant Alalouf got to his feet with a struggle and bent his right arm in a painful salute.

'Albertos is ... is nowhere,' he said. 'He went into the earth and the wind and the sky.'

Mother started wailing, though I knew she was relieved that Isaak hadn't been the victim. It was left to Father and me to tend our women. Albertos's comrade took his leave, head bowed, but it wasn't the last time we saw him.

A month later we were informed that Isaak was in one of the hospitals. He had contracted pneumonia after being injured, but he gradually got over that. Losing his right hand and forearm, crushed by an artillery piece that suddenly rolled off a flatbed truck, was much harder for him.

FIVE

Eliezer Samuel had wanted Mavros to go to Thessaloniki earlier, but the investigator refused. He knew he'd need to spend the weekend with Niki, given that he didn't know how long he'd be away. He went to the Fat Man's on Friday morning and consumed too much *kataïfi*, the shredded wheat drenched in honey sitting heavy on his stomach.

'When were you last in the co-capital?' Yiorgos asked over the top of *Rizospastis*, the Communist daily. He wasn't close to the party any more, but he was still a member.

Mavros thought about that. 'Must be over five years ago.' He swallowed a laugh.

'Oh yes?' The Fat Man was instantly suspicious. 'What happened?'

'The wife of a dried-fruit trader from Corinth ended up there.'

'And you gave her a shoulder and other things to lean on?'

'Actually, no. I was with Niki then.'

'So what was the drowning man's laugh for?'

Mavros emptied his glass of chilled water. 'She'd run off with one of her husband's brothers.'

'Keeping it in the family, eh?'

'Exactly. The thing was, the guy in question had the worst wig I've ever seen. The remains of his hair were brown and he'd gone for a red top that made him look like a clown. There were plenty of tears.'

Yiorgos raised an eyebrow.

'When I told the husband, he went off with the clown's wife.'

'Peloponnesians!'

Mavros grinned. 'You're pretty dull by comparison.'

'I'm a Spartan. We don't mess around.'

'I noticed. Too scared of supposed hunting accidents?'

The Fat Man brushed crumbs off his shirt. 'No, too concerned about the moral high ground.'

When they'd stopped laughing, Mavros picked up the book about Communist Jews. 'Getting anywhere with this?'

'Well, there's no mention of anyone called Aron Samuel.'

'That would have been too easy.'

'No doubt. There were the usual party organs up there during the pre-war period and there was organised resistance during the occupation, even though most of the cadres were in the mountains.'

Mavros had been reading *Years in Hell*. 'The party didn't help the Jews very much.'

Yiorgos shrugged. 'They did what they could. Don't forget, Metaxas and his cronies had caught a lot of our people.'

'True. When were you last up in Thessaloniki?'

'Em...'

Mavros smelled a rodent. 'Spit it out.'

'What, the *kataïfi?*'

'Only if it's absolutely essential. Come on. The story.'

The Fat Man looked seriously abashed. He made a mess of folding his newspaper, then started to get up.

'The story,' Mavros insisted.

'It's classified.'

'What, by the comrades who wanted to take a cut of your card games when you had the café? The same comrades who used you for decades and then turned their backs on you.'

'I still have friends,' Yiorgos said sulkily.

Mavros realised he'd gone too far, but he'd been suspicious about his friend's interest in his latest case from the moment he saw the book on Jewish Party members. 'I know you have. Ask yourself this question. Do you know something that might help me ... us ... in this case?'

48

'Oh, now it's "us", is it?' the Fat Man said. 'You'll be up north on expenses with a fancy piece and I'll be scratching my arse in this dump? Very "us".'

Mavros had known he wouldn't get away with such a blatant appeal to his friend. 'Seems to me that a shower and a general clean-up would solve both your problems.'

'Ha ha.'

'Then you'd be able to concentrate on providing me with the backup I can't live without.'

Yiorgos was suspicious, but couldn't resist the idea of being cut into the case. 'All right, but keep it to yourself. It was fifteen years ago, anyway. I was sent on the train to put the fear of Lenin up a young cadre who'd lost his grip. He'd been arrested and had laid into the cops. They were sweating him for stuff he shouldn't have known and our lawyer wanted–'

'The line laid down by one of the party's known enforcers.'

The Fat Man grinned. 'Was that a compliment?'

'I mean, gutbuckets.'

'Do you want to hear this or not?'

Mavros kept quiet.

'I did what I had to without any problem – told him what would happen to his family if he squealed. One of the local comrades had been ordered to put me up for the night. This was after the end of the dictatorship and we were legal again, but they wanted to save on a hotel bill. The cadre who met me in Aristotelous Square was a Jew.'

Mavros listened more carefully.

'Young chap, couldn't have been over thirty. It was a Friday. I had to take part in the special dinner they have.'

'Shabbat.'

'Something like that. He didn't believe, of course, but his wife did and she wanted the kids to grow up in the faith. Afterwards he–'

'What was his name?'

Yiorgos scratched his sparsely covered crown. 'Shimon something ... an Italian painter...'

'Shimon Caravaggio?'

'No.'

'Shimon Michelangelo?'

'Uh-uh. I've got it – Shimon Raphael. What was I saying? Oh yes, he took me to his office under the flat – he was a customs broker – and started telling me all these stories about the Jews during the war. His father, who was about seventeen when the Nazis invaded, was sheltered by an Orthodox family and didn't go outside for over two years.'

'Shit.'

Yiorgos shook his head. 'That isn't the worst. A week before the Germans left, they came looking for him. He managed to get out the back. They shot the couple and their young kids on the spot. Apparently Shimon's father lost it completely. He disappeared for five years and never talked about where he'd been or what he'd done. But listen to this.'

Mavros leant forward.

'He wore a string of human teeth round his neck, night and day.'

50

'Jesus.'

'I don't think he was much in evidence.'

Mavros sat back. 'Well, thanks for that. Sets me up nicely for the trip.'

The Fat Man handed him a piece of paper. 'Here's Shimon's address and number. He's still alive and well – he called me on my name day this year. Maybe he'll be able to help.'

'Thanks. Hang on. You knew his name all along. What was that game with the artists' names?'

His friend laughed. 'I wanted to see who you came up with. Caravaggio? Interesting...'

Mavros extended both hands violently, fingers spread, and sent Yiorgos straight to the underworld.

Rachel Samuel was sitting on the balcony of her room in the Grand Bretagne. Although the wind was a chill northerly, she was in the lee of it and the sun was strong enough to give her pleasure. Paris in November was much drearier, not that she spent all her time there. In the last two years she'd been on trips to different parts of the world, working only part-time for her father. She had gained expertise in fields that he suspected, but had been careful not to ask about. He knew she'd become 'a competent', though, and it angered her that he'd insisted on employing the investigator who looked like an ageing rock star. Still, she could never be angry with her father for long. He had the kind of soul that wasn't satisfied with starting his own company from scratch and making it into a great success. He was generous to charities – not only Jewish ones – loved music from opera (apart from Wagner) to bebop, collected Fauvist art, and was devoted to his family. Rachel didn't spend much time with her brother David – he didn't approve of her activities – but she was close to their mother, who had suffered a stroke and lost the use of one arm and leg.

'Ah, Maman,' she said in a low voice, 'what would you think of me if you knew? Your parents escaped the transports from Paris by hiding beneath a barn in the Auvergne. They suffered cold and hunger, but they went unnoticed on the high plateau. It cost them all they had to buy the locals' food and silence, and Papi carried messages for the Résistance. A heavy price was exacted even from the Jews who survived the Nazis. Maman, you have lived in your husband's shadow, but you are wiser than him. He closed his mind to past horrors and fashioned a new world for himself and for us. Now, late in life, he is driven to confront what he has always avoided. If his Uncle Aron is alive, what story will he have to tell?'

If, she thought, pulling her skirt up her thighs and feeling the skin tingle in the sun – *if* he is alive; *if* it really was him who had been seen; if Alex Mavros could find him. She hadn't been impressed by the missing-persons specialist, despite the fact that he had done his homework – that was hardly difficult on the Internet. She was frustrated that she'd had to wait till Monday to fly to Thessaloniki. Her father had told her to go earlier if she wished, but she had spent her time in Athens profitably. She had gathered information – though none was of direct help regarding her great-uncle – and she had arranged for a weapon. Her contact had been helpful and the supplier a model of efficiency.

There was also the fact that she wanted to keep a close eye on Mavros from the minute he started work in Thessaloniki. She had read the file her contact had provided, which was considerably more detailed than what her father's secretary had put together. She knew Mavros's long-dead father had been a leading Communist and that he had indirect access to the party, even though he seemed to have no political allegiance. That might prove useful. She was also aware that Mavros was deeply unpopular both with organised criminals, though he seemed to have steered clear of them in recent years, and with the murky elite that ran Greece. That suggested he was his own man.

The question was, would he become *her* man on the search for her elderly relative? To guarantee his loyalty, she might have to get close to him. That didn't worry her, though she wondered if he would be circumspect. He had a long-standing lover. She had seen Andhroniki – known as Niki – Glezou's photo. The woman was attractive enough, but no serious competition. Mavros would be as easy a conquest as other men.

Rachel Samuel, under her own name and others, had done that and worse in the past and she felt no remorse. The cause was all.

'Have you seen this?' Niki asked, waving the Sunday paper at Mavros.

53

He was only half awake. 'Which rag is it?'

'No, this story about the Nazis in Thessaloniki.'

'Nazis?' he mumbled, his mouth dry from the previous night's beer, wine and brandy. There was another taste he couldn't immediately identify.

'The Phoenix Rises.'

'Oh, those tossers. Em, did we ... did I...'

'What?' Niki watched him tentatively licking his lips. 'Yes, you did, thank you very much.' She smiled. 'It was wonderful, though I won't get pregnant that way. And if you make that joke about little girls and anchovies...'

'Don't need to now.'

She dug her elbow into his ribs. 'Listen to this. "The Phoenix Rises' leader Makis Kalogirou said that party members in Thessaloniki had acted in self-defence when illegal immigrants attacked the organisation's local office. The police are questioning witnesses. Meanwhile, three Iraqis and a Sri Lankan remain in extensive care and twelve others have been treated for less serious injuries." Bastards. As if immigrants ever start trouble with steroid-addled skinheads in black shirts and big boots.'

Mavros nodded. Every week Niki saw the results of unprovoked attacks on her clients. 'Those lunatics have always been around. I read that some of them carry photos of Papadopoulos, as well as using the Junta's phoenix symbol.'

'Not just the sadly deceased dictator. They actually worship Hitler and his mad sidekicks.'

'Excuse me while I take a shower. I suddenly seem to be covered in phoenix crap. As well as–'

'Don't mention fish of any kind.'

'My lips are ... scaled over.' A pillow hit him as he went to the door.

Later they went for a walk to the top of Lykavittos, having gone through the back streets before starting on the hill.

'I'm sick of all this skulking around,' Niki said. 'What if I do get pregnant? Am I supposed to walk in circles before I wheel the buggy to the park?'

Mavros remembered the damage the Son had done to his numerous victims. 'We'll work something out,' he mumbled.

'We? It's your fault that madman's in our lives.'

They stopped at the road end and looked over Athens. The air was clear and the island of Aegina with its triangular peak seemed to be within arm's reach.

'And now you're going to leave me on my own.'

He squeezed her arm. 'It won't be for long. Maria will pick you up for work every morning, won't she?'

'And bring me home, yes. She's very good about it, but I hate imposing.'

'She's your friend. You could always give her some petrol money.'

'She won't take it.' Niki blinked away tears. 'Alex, this is no life, especially not to bring a child into. If I ... if I even can.'

He put his arms around her. 'Of course you can. The clinic will sort things out. Nothing can stand in the way of Mavros sperm.'

She laughed and dried her face. 'Delightful.' Then she frowned. 'If you so much as touch one of those sultry women up north, I'll chop it off.'

'That would rather defeat the object.'

'It would, wouldn't it? But my honour would be avenged.'

'Yes, my lady.'

They continued up the concrete pathway to the small church on the summit. The Greek flag was cracking in the wind. Mavros took in the panorama of the capital, mountains to east, west and north enclosing the packed conurbation. All things considered, it was as well he hadn't told Niki that the stunning, if not exactly sultry, Rachel Samuel would be with him in Thessaloniki.

'You'll call every day?' she said, clutching his arm.

'Of course,' he replied, aware that he'd often failed to do so in the past.

Niki looked at him dubiously then kissed him on the mouth.

'I love you, Alex.'

'I love you.' Her body felt slight, a vulnerable frame of breath, flesh and bone. He couldn't stop himself shivering.

'Yes, it's chilly up here,' she said, moving towards the church wall. For a moment he thought she was going to enter the building. Had her longing for a baby reawakened the long-lost religious devotion that her foster-parents instilled? But she stayed outside, clenched in her thin coat.

Mavros was on the point of calling off the case – Niki needed looking after. But she was ahead of him.

'I'll be all right. Get the job done, take the

money and come back as soon as you can,' she said, with a smile that he suspected had been hard for her to summon up.

He nodded, not for the first time feeling inadequate and boxed in. 'Let's have a drink,' he said, turning to the café.

'In that overpriced tourist trap? Forget it. You can make me something hot at home.' She smiled again, this time with little reserve. 'And bring it to bed.'

There was no arguing with that.

SIX

It wasn't till 1942 that the Germans really showed their yellowing lupine teeth in Thessaloniki. Previously they'd made our lives difficult by shutting down Jewish papers and encouraging anti- Semitic activities, as well as looting synagogues. There were some executions, supposedly of Jewish Communists. The party knew the men were only the former.

I had been developing my skills as a clandestine operator, sneaking around the streets avoiding Germans both in uniform and in plain clothes that were much better quality than any Greek's. My brown hair and pale skin meant I could pass for a gentile. I was sixteen and still at school, though I paid little attention to lessons and frequently played truant. The teachers told my parents.

'How are you going to be a doctor if you don't study hard?' my mother demanded, when she was ladling out the soup one evening. Food was scarce and my father had to use all his contacts to obtain even basic supplies.

'Who said I wanted to be a doctor?'

'Oh, so clever, my son. What about a lawyer or a professor?'

I glanced at my father.

'You can work your way up in the business,' he said, almost apologetically.

I didn't favour the suggestion with a reply.

'Albertos was a lawyer,' my sister said. She was only partly in contact with the real world and had little interest in Golda, the daughter she'd given birth to a year earlier. My mother and her sisters took care of the cheerful little mite.

Dario Alalouf, whose parents were dead, had become a regular at our table. 'And a very good one, from what I heard,' he said, smiling at Miriam tentatively. It was obvious to everyone except my sister that he was head over backside in love with her. He limped because one of his feet had failed to recover from wounds sustained in the Italian war.

'There's nothing wrong with the jewellery trade,' my brother said. He was working as a salesman, though his missing hand put some customers off.

'Really?' I said, with no doubt irritating petulance. 'The Nazis take what they want without paying and all's well?'

'We... get by,' Isaak responded meekly. Since his injury, he'd gone into himself. Mother had to get him up in the morning and make sure he washed.

In my arrogance and innocence I thought I knew it all. The party was doing what it could against the occupiers – the defeated Italians were present too – and the resistance movement EAM had spawned an armed wing called ELAS. Many older comrades had slipped away to the mountains to fight and I was waiting to be given permission by the youth organisation. Yes, I was full of myself, but I soon found that my imagination was limited. At dawn on Saturday July 11th (the Shabbat, of course – the Germans were masters at arranging things on their victims' significant days and festivals), all Jewish men between eighteen and forty-five were ordered to report to the Freedom Square (a carefully chosen location) for registration. Father was in his early fifties and I was too young, but Isaak and Dario had to go, despite their medical incapacities. I followed them, slipping into the large crowd of Christian Greeks that was gathering to watch. It was already hot and our men were ordered to remove their hats another blow against Jewish tradition on the Shabbat. I later heard that there were over ten thousand men and they were made to stand in lines for many hours. Those who collapsed were beaten and had water poured over them. Then German soldiers demonstrated physical exercises, forcing their malnourished victims to follow suit. I saw Dario crumple to the ground and receive several kicks. Eventually he got back to his feet. It was then that a tall Christian in a good suit and hat near me started to laugh.

'Beat the shit out them!' he yelled. 'The Yids are lice on the skin of Greece.'

People around him cheered.

I saw red, but managed to keep a grip on myself. When our men were finally dismissed, I pushed my way through the crowd to help Dario and my brother. As I passed the man, I managed to plant my elbow in his groin. His breath was expelled in a loud vocal fart. Looking back, I see that as my first act of revenge.

I helped Isaak and Dario back home, struggling with the weight, thin though they were. They collapsed in the hall, croaking for water.

'What have the animals done to them?' Mother shrieked, as she ran to the kitchen.

Miriam stood halfway down the stairs in her usual distracted state. Then she seemed to come back to herself and moved to help Dario. From that moment they became close and a few months later were married. You could say that was one good thing to come out of the mass humiliation. But the Germans didn't stop there. Our men were sent to work on roads and other building projects. Doctors that my father knew managed to get Isaak and Dario declared unfit – I don't know how much he had to pay. Many of the workers died. Those who survived did so only because the Jewish communities in Thessaloniki and other cities raised an enormous ransom. I realised then that the Nazis – masters of the world in their own eyes – were common thieves. But that wasn't all.

Although the city authorities had been trying for years to take over the huge Jewish cemetery to the east of the centre, no one expected them to act suddenly. The Nazis stiffened their spines and soon acres of marble tombs were bulldozed, the stone carted away for reuse.

I didn't want to visit the family memorial after it had been destroyed, but Father insisted. He knew Mother and the older women would be hard to control. My widowed grandmothers lived together in advanced age and infirmity, though they visited us every week. That cold day at the end of 1942, we gathered round the fragments of our ancestors' resting places. The gravestones had been knocked over and the slabs covering the bodies smashed.

'His hair!' my maternal grandmother gasped. 'His face!' She staggered against Isaak and then fainted.

I looked down at the blackened remains of my grandfather. He had played with me when I was small, his thin fingers moving model soldiers and horses around the drawing room carpet. There were remnants of skin on his skull, though the eyes had dissolved and the white hair I remembered as shiny was stained and filthy. The shroud was ragged, the head poking through and a frightening rictus beneath the collapsed nose. The old man's teeth were still attached though his flesh on his gums had gone.

The women were wailing, tears drenching their cheeks, as they offered up prayers. We were never a very religiously observant family and my involvement with the party meant I hadn't recently participated in synagogue visits and the like. Raising my head from the horror and taking in the uncaring beauty of the grey-blue gulf, with snow-wreathed Mount Olympus in the distance, I knew for certain there was no god.

But there were plenty of human devils and their work had only begun.

SEVEN

Mavros met Rachel Samuel at the airport outside Athens before six in the morning. They checked in without delay.

'I thought you weren't going to make it, Mr Mavros,' his client's daughter said. She was wearing a dark blue trouser suit and white blouse, with no jewellery. There was a hint of eye shadow, but no other make-up.

'Sorry, early mornings aren't my thing. Call me Alex.'

She turned her piercing brown eyes on him. 'Very well. And you may call me Rachel, but only when we're alone. I don't want people getting the wrong idea.'

Mavros was tempted to ask what the right idea was, but let it go. Half an hour later they were in a Boeing as it taxied towards the runway.

'Am I right in thinking you aren't a very good flier?' Rachel asked.

'That obvious?'

'You're as twitchy as a teenager on his first date.'

'While you've seen it all before.'

She raised an eyebrow. 'I've amassed a lot of air miles, yes.'

'Within France?'

Rachel smiled briefly. 'I didn't want to point it out when you met my father, but your research was incomplete. We've opened stores in New York, Shanghai, Hong Kong, Sydney and several European cities in the last five years.'

Mavros felt like a jackass.

'But don't worry,' Rachel said, accepting a sweet from the stewardess. 'We're in partnership with Middle Eastern interests who, for obvious reasons, don't want the name Samuel to be used. There's no link on our site to Luxury Jewels of the Orient.'

'That's a relief.' Mavros gripped the arms of his seat as the pilot gunned the engines and asked innocently, 'What are you? A travelling sales-woman?'

Her expression – supercilious with the slightest trace of flirtation – didn't change. 'If you like.' She glanced at him as the plane rose into the air. 'I represent the family company too. Apparently I'm an acceptable face.'

Mavros returned her look. It was true, she didn't look particularly Jewish – she could easily have been Lebanese or Jordanian, not that he had much knowledge of those countries or the region in general. She was certainly a lot more than acceptable, but he disliked her haughtiness. He once had a brief relationship with a French-woman. It foundered on her objection to what she called 'Mediterranean brio'. Like his employer's daughter, she was from Paris.

'So, Alex, how do you intend to start?' Rachel raised a finger at the stewardess and asked for tea with lemon. There were only three other people in the business-class section, but she wasn't going to wait her turn.

He shrugged. 'Simple things. Interview the woman who says she saw your great-uncle. Talk to a research contact I have. Ask around in the Jewish community.' He could have done with a brandy, but he wasn't going to ask for one in front of his stern companion.

'I'll be able to help with the first and third of those.'

Mavros was already unhappy about being lumbered with an overseer. If the money hadn't been so good he'd have declined the case. The one time he'd taken a client with him on an investigation had ended in mayhem.

'Couldn't you look into opening a store in Thessaloniki?' he asked.

Rachel Samuel's laugh rang out like a knife striking a glass. 'That isn't why I'm here and you know it. Besides, how will you converse with an elderly Jewish lady? I'm prepared to bet she doesn't speak English.'

'And you speak Greek? Or Ladino?' Mavros was pleased with himself for finding out the name of the language spoken by Sephardic Jews.

'The correct term is Judezmo. It's a complicated issue, but Ladino specifically refers to Hebrew or Aramaic text translated into Judaeo-Spanish, and is not a spoken language.'

'Oh. But you speak it?'

Rachel's gaze wavered. 'No. In fact, I don't even

speak Hebrew. My father's the same. He left Thessaloniki as an infant and he could never face learning the old family language. That may change if our search is successful.'

The word 'our' grated on Mavros. He made the mistake of looking out the window and his stomach somersaulted. The pyramid peak of Mount Dhirfris on the island of Evia was approaching. He was keeping Shimon Raphael, the Communist customs broker, as a personal source. In his experience, clients who wanted to be involved frequently had ulterior motives – though he couldn't think of an obvious one that would account for Rachel Samuel absenting herself from her high-powered job. He had done Internet searches for her great-uncle and found nothing. That wasn't necessarily a bad thing. He'd once located a former policeman on the World Wide Web: his client had nearly beaten the man to death because he'd killed his son during the dictatorship.

He thought about the man he was looking for. Aron Samuel would be eighty years old now. Even if he had survived the death camps, why would he return to his birthplace? A sixty-year case of amnesia? A man who had been so damaged that he'd been in mental institutions for most of his life? Neither was very likely. Perhaps the best bet was that he'd hidden himself away, perhaps on another continent, and had only returned when he sensed death was near.

He put that to Rachel.

'We have considered those possibilities,' she said. 'Sephardic communities around the globe keep in close touch, especially since the advent of new technology. My father submitted the names of his entire family to on-line groups everywhere, but no one has responded. None of my relatives was issued a death certificate, as you can imagine. The SS kept lists of numbers, but they are incomplete.'

'You are sure that they were all transported to Poland?'

She nodded. 'The Jewish community in Thessaloniki has those lists, or at least the ones with my relatives' names on them. Once people arrived at the Auschwitz complex, there was only one way to leave.'

Mavros had read Primo Levi. 'There were some survivors.'

'A few.' She turned away.

Suddenly Mavros felt the weight of responsibility the case had placed on him. He'd handled investigations that had ended in multiple deaths, but this was different – this concerned the enforced end of a 50,000-strong community.

Rachel Samuel's eyes were on him again. 'You look even worse.'

'I'm OK, thanks.'

Then the plane dropped into an air pocket and he clutched her arm, gasping loudly.

'Sorry,' he said, removing his hand.

'That's all right,' Rachel said, smoothing her sleeve.

It was only as the plane turned away from Mount Olympus towards Macedonia International Airport that Mavros recalled how her forearm had felt: like tightly twisted steel cable. He watched the coastline come closer, spotting the beach at Ayia Triadha before the plane touched down with scarcely a bump. A few passengers behind them applauded.

'How quaint,' Rachel said, closing her laptop bag.

'You should have seen it when I was young. Everyone crossing themselves and cheering as if the pilot was a superhero.'

They were off and through the terminal quickly, both having only hand luggage. Niki had told Mavros to buy more clothes and put them on expenses if he had to. He wondered if he'd be able to get that past his client's daughter.

'Shall we hire a car?' she asked.

'Not for the time being. The traffic in the centre's a nightmare. The hotel can arrange one if we need to go further afield.'

The taxi took them through outskirts full of stores and business properties. The post-Olympic boom, based on apparently inexhaustible credit, was still in full swing. It was only when they approached the centre that Rachel began to look more animated.

'What are those buildings?' she asked.

'The Aristotelian University – biggest in the country.'

'I thought so. I've been doing research too. You know it was built on part of the old Jewish cemetery?'

'No, I didn't,' Mavros replied, feeling guilty. He'd visited friends at the institution several times when he was on vacation from Edinburgh University.

'Yes, there are pieces of gravestones embedded

in the walkways.'

He'd never noticed that. He decided to keep his familiarity with the campus to himself.

'There's the White Tower,' he said, as the taxi turned towards the seafront. 'Maybe Venetian, maybe Ottoman.'

'And rather beige.' Rachel looked at the faded circular building that was capped with a smaller round fortification.'

'The symbol of the co-capital.'

'Strange they couldn't find something more Greek.'

'The Archaeological Museum's back there,' Mavros said, looking over his shoulder. 'It's full of Macedonian gold from the time of Alexander the Great.'

Rachel had turned her head to the water on the other side of a wide pavement. It was blue, but the sun created rainbow tints from oil on the surface. There were several cargo ships anchored in the bay.

'Yes,' she said, 'but were the ancient Macedonians Greek?'

Mavros laughed. 'That's a bit of a hot issue.'

'There are others that no one gets worked up about. Such as, were the Jews of this city Greek?' Her voice had hardened. 'Their papers showed they were, but very few people seemed to care when fifty thousand of them disappeared during the war.'

Mavros hoped the driver's English wasn't up to following the conversation. He seemed oblivious as he pulled up outside the Electra Palace, one of the best hotels in Thessaloniki.

'Am I staying here?' Mavros asked.

'Of course. We need to be in close touch.' Rachel paid the driver and strode ahead, pulling her wheeled case.

Was there a hint of innuendo in her words, he wondered. Then he remembered her stern look. Behave yourself, idiot. And remember the woman you love is waiting for you back home.

He padded into the luxurious reception area and registered. They both had rooms on the fourth floor. The clerk handed a rectangular package about the size of a desk-top keyboard but thicker to Rachel. He waited when she answered her phone till she waved him away, signalling that she would call him. He took the stairs as his bag wasn't heavy. The room was large, overlooking Aristotelous Square and the bay beyond. He wondered what Aristotle would have thought of his name being used in the city. As far as he remembered, the philosopher was born some distance away and the city was founded after his death. When he was tutor to Alexander the Great, he would have been at the Macedonian capital of Pella, half an hour's drive to the north-west. Still, that was close enough for the municipal council. He remembered what Rachel had said about the Jews. Every Greek knew something about Aristotle and Alexander, but next to nothing about the people who had comprised Thessaloniki's biggest population group for centuries. Their cemetery may have gone, but he suddenly felt the presence of a myriad ghosts.

The room phone rang.

'Shall we go and see Ester Broudo?' Rachel

said, the question more like a command.

'Who?' Mavros said, playing dumb. He'd never been good with authority. 'Oh, you mean the old lady who saw your great-uncle? Whenever you're ready.'

'Downstairs in ten minutes.' The call was terminated.

'Make that eleven,' Mavros said. He washed his face and hands, then called Niki on her mobile.

'Semen Supplies.'

'Very funny, Alex.'

'You sound harassed.'

'It's a normal day at work, so yes, I am. You survived the flight.'

'More or less. Now we're off to see a woman about a man.'

'We?'

Mavros froze. 'Um, yeah, didn't I say? The Fat Man's got a friend up here who's going to show me around. Shimon's his name.' It wasn't a full-blooded lie.

'No, you didn't mention that. I've got to go. The Phoenix Rises tried to burn down a flat full of Afghanis near the museum last night.'

'Scumbags.'

'Fortunately no one was hurt but the place was gutted, so I've got to find them alternative accommodation. Call me tonight. Love you.'

'Love you too.' As he headed for the door, Mavros thought about Niki's dedication to her job. She worked much harder than most of her colleagues and liaised with NGOs about illegal immigrants. Could she be too run down to conceive? Her blood tests had been OK, though her iron count was rather low. The issue might be psychological, in as much as that could be separated from her body. Was devoting so much emotional energy to society's unfortunates adversely affecting her physical condition? He needed to talk to her and the doctors about that.

He came down the last flight of stairs in a rush. As he'd expected, Rachel looked at her watch.

'Scottish-Greek time,' he said. 'If I was fully Greek, you'd have had to wait even longer.'

She didn't grace that with a reply, leading him to the main doors. Her heels, medium height but still enough to elevate her slightly above him, clicked over the marble. By the time he joined her, she was already getting into a taxi. The vehicles were blue and white in Thessaloniki, less garish than the Athenian yellow.

'Here,' she said, handing him a slip of paper.

He gave the address to the driver, who knew it and drove east.

'A football stadium?' Rachel asked, as they passed a concrete mass.

'Toumba, the home of PAOK.' Mavros wasn't a football fan, but one of his friends had dragged him along when he was visiting. 'The club was set up by immigrants from Constantinople after the exchange of populations.'

'Is that so? Academics must go wild over Thessaloniki's anthropological complexity.'

'Have you ever met a wild anthropologist?'

She glanced at him. 'Several. The discipline seems to attract oddballs.'

Mavros was about to ask where she had learned her unusually formal, almost Queen's English,

71

but the taxi stopped outside a pink villa surrounded by a high fence. He got out and looked
for a name plate – Rachel had told him earlier
that Mrs Broudo lived in an old people's home –
but there was none.

'Well, well.' Rachel was standing on the other
side of the gate. A swastika had been spray-
painted on the stone column.

'Bastards,' he said.

'Probably not. I'm sure our artist was baptised
into the Orthodox Church like every Christian
Greek.' She rang the bell.

'Not me. Then again, I'm faithless. But you
know what I mean. I hate neo-Nazis.'

She smiled tightly. 'Not surprising, given your
father's politics. You had a run-in with some of
them on Crete, didn't you?'

'How thick is that file you've got on me?'

'It's a memory stick.'

'Miss Samuel?' said a middle-aged man in pass-
able English. He wore a dark suit and blinked
from behind thick round glasses on the other side
of the steel-barred gate. There was a skullcap on
his thinning black hair.

'Rabbi Rousso, I presume.'

He nodded and smiled, then looked at Mavros.
'And you are?'

Rachel was too quick for him. She gave his
name, glancing at him as if he were a necessary
villain. 'My ... assistant.'

The rabbi took in his hair and clothes with a
degree of bewilderment, then pressed a button.
The gate swung back.

'Welcome to the Molho Home,' he said, leading

them up the slope to the villa. 'The house and grounds used to belong to a cotton merchant. They were donated to our community by his grandsons.' He dropped his gaze. 'The two of them were the only members of the family to survive the Shoah. They emigrated to the United States in the 50s.'

They followed him through an entrance hall that had seen better days. It was spotlessly clean, but the unmistakable odours of institutional food and elderly bodies prevailed. The place was also colder than it might have been. The rabbi took them down a corridor lined with paintings of bearded men in sober suits then earlier ones in ornate robes, their wives and offspring gathered round them.

'This is the sun room,' he said.

The eyes of old men and women in thick cardigans were raised, initially those of the former to Rachel and the latter to Mavros. He could almost see the words 'beauty' and 'beast' floating up.

Rousso introduced them in their language, then Mavros heard the name 'Ester'. A short, crumpled woman pulled herself up with a Zimmer frame, refusing help from the rabbi. Although her movements were slow, her unclouded blue eyes were agile. They were led to a room on the left.

'I'm afraid I'll have to interpret,' Rousso said. 'Mrs Broudo knows no English or French.'

They sat round a table. Mrs Broudo immediately took Rachel's hand and talked at speed. The rabbi struggled to cut her off, eventually taking her other hand. There was some rapid muttering and he imposed order, stopping the old woman

73

after each lengthy sentence.

It transpired that the residents had been taken in a bus to the Monasterioton synagogue in the centre to attend a wedding a week earlier. It was as she was waiting to be helped up from her seat that Mrs Broudo had seen the man she was sure was Aron Samuel. He was on the other side of the street from the place of worship and his face was in profile. That was how she recognised him. He had what Rabbi Rousso translated as 'imperious' features and a long, completely straight nose.

Rachel pre-empted Mavros again. She asked how the old woman could be so sure it was her great-uncle after six decades. Ester Broudo smiled briefly when the rabbi translated. She said she had a crush on Aron when she was a teenager, even though she only ever saw him across the school playground. He never paid any attention to her. He had a reputation as a rebel who didn't care about lessons. But she spent many intervals between classes staring at him and she wouldn't be moved from the certainty that it was him she had seen. She added that he still had a fine head of hair, though it was pure white now.

'Did she see anyone with him?' Mavros asked, determined to play some part in the interview.

The answer was negative.

'What was he wearing?' Mavros continued.

A brown suit, very well fitted – Ester Broudo's husband had been a tailor and she knew about male clothing – and a scarf with magenta and white stripes.

Rachel leaned forward. The old woman's hand

was still on hers. 'Why did she insist that the rabbi urgently contact my father?'

There was a long silence after Rousso had translated the question. Mrs Broudo's head dropped and she started to sob. After a while she started to speak, her croaking voice filled with what seemed to Mavros to be heartfelt passion.

The rabbi's mouth hung open when she finished and Rachel had to prompt him to speak.

'I'm sorry,' he stuttered. 'Ester ... Ester says that your great-uncle was ... a traitor in Auschwitz. She says he was a murderer. He was ... he was responsible for the deaths of her grandfather, grandmothers, father, mother, sisters and brother. She wants your family to know that, even though she has nothing against you.'

'Ask her what she means by responsible,' Rachel demanded, extracting her hand from Mrs Broudo's grip.

The rabbi did his best, but the old woman would not say any more. Eventually Rachel got up and nodded brusquely to Mavros, then turned and walked out of the room. He shrugged at the rabbi and smiled at Ester, but she took no notice of him.

Mavros found Rachel outside the entrance hall. She was very pale and had her phone in her hand. The rabbi arrived, panting.

'I'm ... I'm very sorry, Mademoiselle Samuel,' he said.

'Does Mrs Broudo have any history of mental illness?' Rachel asked coldly.

'Not that I'm aware of.'

'Have you ever heard her talk about the Samuel family before?' Mavros put in.

'I asked the superintendent that very question. She said not. Ester has become frustrated by her physical decline, but she is a kindly soul.'

'Did anyone else on the bus recognise my uncle?'

Rousso shook his head at Rachel. 'Ester didn't mention what she'd seen to anyone until she came to me as the group was leaving. I was very surprised. I knew nothing of your family's past, but she was insistent that I call your father. I had his number, of course. Your family's donations are much appreciated.'

Rachel thanked him, then started to walk down the drive. He and Mavros followed.

'What's your feeling, Rabbi?' he asked. 'An elderly lady – she must be around eighty – recognising a man who's shown no sign of life since the end of the war. Do you believe her?'

'Yes, I do,' he said, with surprising certainty. 'I've known Ester for over twenty years. She was a teacher and a very good one. Her mind is as sharp as it ever was and her eyesight is unusually good. Not only that, she's changed since she saw him. It's as if ... I don't know... as if she'd been waiting for him.'

'Does she have any relatives or friends outside the home?'

'None, I'm afraid. You heard what happened to her family, and her husband died in the 60s. They had no children.' He lowered his voice. 'We searched her room too. There were no letters or anything from Mr Samuel.'

Mavros was unimpressed by the intrusion into the old woman's privacy, but he didn't let it show.

'What do you think she meant about Aron Samuel being responsible for her family's deaths?'

'I really can't say. I've checked the records and memoirs. There is nothing to suggest any such thing. But...'

Mavros waited as his companion's pace slowed.

'But there were Jews who collaborated with the Nazis, both in Thessaloniki and in the camps.'

Rachel had her back to them, waiting for the gate to be opened.

'Why would one of those come back?' Mavros asked. 'And why would he show himself in the vicinity of a synagogue, especially when people were arriving for a wedding?'

He got no answers to those questions.

EIGHT

As 1943 progressed, the Nazis got smarter – or rather, those in Greece started to use methods that had been successfully applied in other countries. There were Jewish police and they oversaw the removal of families from different parts of the city to ghettos. In February a curfew was imposed, then we had to wear the notorious yellow star. I got my mother to fit hooks on mine – 'What are you thinking? They will punish you, foolish boy!' I almost told her about my activities for the party, which were why I wanted to have freedom of movement, but that wouldn't have been fair. The family shops and all the stock had been confiscated. My father was told he would be recompensed. Not even he believed that.

I gave up going to school and went about party business all day. There was some danger, as I could have been betrayed as a Jew who wasn't wearing a star – enough people knew me. The law now said that Christians couldn't even talk to us. I spoke to the cadre who allocated my jobs. He told me to leave the city and go to the mountains, where I would be welcomed by comrades in the resistance. I thought about it, thought about it hard. If Thessaloniki hadn't been surrounded by relatively flat ground I might have gone, but it was a long trek to the heights in the west and there were enemy patrols and checkpoints. I asked Isaak for his opinion.

'Go, brother, go while you can. Life here is only going to get worse.' He looked around the almost empty room. We had been forced to sell furniture and ornaments at ridiculously low prices to buy food. At least we had a few things to sell; many Jews didn't.

'What about the others?'

'I'll look after Mother and Father, and Dario will be with Miriam and Golda.'

I stared at him. 'You've only got one arm and Dario's limp is getting worse.'

'So what?' Isaak said, with unusual spirit. 'Do you think we're going to have to do circus tricks for the Nazis?'

'Nothing would surprise me.' I'd heard stories from comrades about mass shootings in villages that had resisted and people being laughed at by their executioners.

'See? That's why you have to go.'

I slept on it and still couldn't make my mind up. It was easier to go on dodging our enemies every day. There was no shortage of them now. Apart from the Germans – soldiers and SS men – there were the Greek police, the Jewish police (the worst of all for me, traitors and collaborators), vigilante groups of anti-Semites and ordinary citizens who had no love for us. I only occasionally heard of Jewish children being taken in by Christians. And I was busy. The few comrades left in the city who had escaped arrest were resisting every way they could – disabling vehicles, stealing and redistributing food, printing and putting up posters and declarations. There were even attacks on the enemy, though they were restricted because the cost in innocent lives was high. I grew more and more angry, and decided to act on my own.

There was a Jewish policeman called Zakar, a heavily built former labourer who liked to throw his weight around. Several times I narrowly escaped being grabbed by him when I wasn't wearing the star. I saw him savagely beat an old man – one of his own people – who was struggling to carry large bags to the Baron Hirsch camp near the railway station. A few nights later, I followed him to his home near the port. I had an iron bar under my coat and I intended to break his arms with it so he wouldn't be able to hit people any more. I raised my scarf so that only my eyes were visible.

The foolishness of my plan only became clear

when he was struggling to get his key into the lock: I wouldn't be able to immobilise him simply by striking his arms. Even if I hit one, he'd be able to pull out his truncheon and defend himself. So I decided to go for his head. He was wearing a shabby cap that was meant to make him look authoritative. I swung the bar, but he must have sensed my presence. He turned and took the blow on his shoulder. Then he moved much more quickly than I expected. His weight drove me on to the road and he scrabbled at my scarf.

'Fucker,' he gasped, breathing ouzo fumes over me. 'You're Samuel's boy.'

I was in a state of panic. Not only had he pinned me down, but he knew who I was. Somehow I had kept my grip on the bar. I managed to slip my arm from his grasp and crack him on the side of his head. He yelped and rolled off me. I pulled away and peered down in the dim light. He had one hand over his right eye and was making a mewling sound.

'I'll break ... your back ... you little shit.'

I looked around. The street was deserted and there no lights in the windows.

Zakar got to his feet and tried to grab me. I brought the bar down on his left arm and heard a satisfying crack. He screamed and took the other hand from his eye. There was a lot of blood on his face. I broke his right arm too. He dropped to his knees, moaning like a child, but I knew his innate savagery would reassert itself. I beat him on the side of the head until it was a pulp and he had stopped breathing. Then I ran down to the waterfront and threw my weapon in the harbour. It was only as I approached home that I realised I was neither horrified at what I'd done nor afraid. I got into bed and fell asleep immediately.

My mother woke me, muttering about the clothes strewn across the floor. I shot out of bed and obstructed her in case there was blood anywhere.

'What's happened to you?' she asked. 'Normally a rhinoceros couldn't drag you out of bed.'

'You manage every morning.'

She glared at me but backed away, probably because my morning glory was at half-mast. 'You be careful, clever boy. This city isn't safe for any of us. Someone killed one of our policemen last night.'

Jewish papers had been closed down, but the gossip system had always been more efficient. I showed no interest, though I was concerned the occupiers would strike back. They didn't, probably because they didn't care, but the Jewish police became even harsher. We found that out when we were forced to leave home and tramp to the Baron Hirsch camp soon afterwards. My father took a blow to his back when he stumbled.

'You can still slip away,' Isaak whispered, as we hauled the heavy bags Mother had packed.

I shook my head. 'I'm staying with the family.' I grinned at him. 'Someone will have to keep us alive.'

We looked over our shoulders at our parents. Mother had wept for a whole night when we'd got the notification, but Father had accepted it equably. He seemed to know things were all up for us in Thessaloniki. Miriam had the baby in her arms and Dario was trying to keep up – we'd only let him take a medium-sized case.

The camp was surrounded by a high fence, SS men with dogs standing outside. It was already packed and we struggled to find shelter. The stench of human waste and unwashed bodies hung over the place like swamp gas. There was a distribution of soup, but the first evening we ate the food we'd brought with us. I saw a boy much younger than me slip through a gap in the fence. He was immediately set upon by a Jewish police-man and beaten unconscious. Women screamed, men groaned and babies cried.

I thought we were in hell, but I had no idea.

NINE

Mavros and Rachel Samuel walked down the hill towards a main road. There were interesting old houses on both sides, some in bright colours and with elaborate balconies and turrets. Between them were modern concrete blocks, their only decoration the fronds of plants. The cars on the roadside suggested the area was inhabited by people with more money than taste.

'What did you think of that?' Rachel asked, her eyes on the cityscape ahead.

'It wasn't exactly what I expected.'

She laughed once, then her face composed itself. 'Me neither.'

'There's nothing in the family story about your great-uncle being a ... turncoat?'

She glanced at him. 'There is no family story, haven't you realised that? We thought he died with everyone else.'

'Well, there's the beginning of a story now,' Mavros persisted. 'I can put those accusations to my expert.'

Rachel stopped and ran a hand across her forehead. 'I suppose you have to. They may be rumours or malicious lies.'

'Maybe. Hang on, Mrs Broudo lost all her family in the camps. That means she must have heard about Aron's alleged behaviour herself, either when she was in Auschwitz or after she returned. We need to go back and ask her which.'

'Please.' Rachel suddenly leaned against him. 'I ... I don't feel up to that musty place again. Besides, do you really think she'll say anything else to us?'

Mavros put his arm round her back. 'Do you want to sit down?' There was a step nearby.

'No, I'm all right. The smell in there...' She shook herself free and walked on.

'You could call the rabbi and ask him to try her.'

Rachel gave him a dubious look.

They reached the junction and hailed a cab.

'Where's your expert?' she asked.

'I haven't had a chance to fix a meeting yet,' he said. 'How about some lunch?'

She didn't look keen, but agreed. The taxi dropped them at a restaurant the driver recommended near the White Tower.

'Byzantine specialities?' Rachel said, looking at the board outside.

'Means Turkish.'

'Looks generically Middle Eastern to me. Why not?'

They took a table by the window. Rachel didn't want to drink alcohol, so Mavros followed suit. They ordered Smyrna meatballs, Greek Fire (lamb in a hot sauce) and the Emperor's Salad. Before the food arrived, she asked him to call the researcher and arrange a meeting, preferably that afternoon. He did so. Allegra Harari sounded friendly and organised. She was free and gave him an address in the city centre.

'Help,' Rachel said, when the salad arrived.

Mavros examined the vegetables, some standing upright like trees and others arranged like lines of flowers. 'It's the Emperor's country estate.'

They made nothing more than small talk while they ate. Rachel gave little away about herself. The lack of rings suggested she wasn't engaged or married, but her stern air put him off asking. Not that he cared. She was a client like any other. He stopped himself. He hadn't ever had a client as beautiful as her.

'Right,' he said, when they'd done as much as they could with the Emperor's property and the other dishes. 'We've got an hour before our date with the historian. Do you want to go back to the hotel?'

'No, it's all right.' She took out her laptop. 'I'll sit here and catch up on my mail. Give me the address and I'll meet you there. I've got a map.'

Her tone made it clear that he was being dismissed. He tried to pay but she waved her hand. He was happy to go because he had calls to make. On the seafront he rang Shimon Raphael. The customs broker would meet him that evening. Mavros decided he'd call Niki now in case it ended up a late night.

'On your way home?' he asked, after greeting her.

'Yes, we just left the office.'

'You sound tired.'

'The usual crap.'

'Strange, because I got up two hours earlier than you.'

'Idiot. How often has that happened?'

'There's a first time for everything.'

'That's very true,' Niki said disconsolately.

He realised she was thinking about her failure to get pregnant. 'Hey, chin up. Have a nap when you get back.'

'Hm. What's happening with you? Found the dead man?'

'Not even I am that fast. We ... I've made a start.'

'You and your local sidekick?'

'That's right.' He felt like a heel, but telling Niki about Rachel would be a recipe for catastrophe. They talked for a few minutes.

Mavros walked on. Any blank wall had been sprayed with the words 'The Phoenix Rises – Are You with Us?' Often enough 'NO!' had been added beneath in a variety of colours, but 'YES!' appeared with worrying frequency. The far-right group didn't have anything like that amount of visibility or support in Athens. He'd have to ask

Shimon about its presence in Thessaloniki.

Then it struck him. How was he going to get away from Rachel? As he approached the hotel, he considered his options. All of them included falsehoods and he felt bad about that. Deceiving one woman was bad enough, but two was a disgrace. He laughed guiltily and called the Fat Man.

Rachel Samuel checked that no one was on the other side of the restaurant window. It was clear. She accessed the encrypted site, entering her password. She reported on what Ester Broudo had said and added that more information might be available later in the day. After a few seconds, she received a reply.

'Target status confirmed. Are you prepared?'

'Affirmative,' she typed. 'Tonight we pay a call.'

'Approved. Confirm.'

She acknowledged the order and signed off in the normal way.

A few minutes later she paid the bill and zipped up her bag. On her way to the researcher's office, she thought about Alex Mavros. He was keeping something from her, she was sure. Leaving him on his own later wasn't ideal, but she had no choice. He'd have to live with his disappointment. Lover back in Athens or not, she could see he liked the look of her. He wasn't unattractive himself – which would make things easier if she had to get full value from him.

Mavros watched Rachel walk down the crowded street. Her legs were lithe and elegant, and she moved between people both gracefully and with great nimbleness. He wondered if she'd ever played football, then dismissed that with a smile.

'What's the joke?' she asked.

He had to think on his feet. 'Look at that,' he said, pointing to an ancient Citroën Deux Chevaux with horses' heads painted on the doors. 'If those are on the doors on the other side, it'll be a Quatre Chevaux.'

Rachel ignored that. She was looking at the Phoenix Rises graffito. Under the bird emblem was a bit of Greek key pattern like a swastika. 'What is that?'

He explained, adding that the scrawl beneath was some wit answering 'Are You with Us?' with the question 'Are you paying?'

'That's exactly the problem,' Rachel said. 'Fascist organisations always bribe their supporters. Who are these people? Do they have any real power?'

Mavros led her inside. 'They put some immigrants here in intensive care last week. But, no, hardly anyone votes for them.'

'Yet.' Rachel shook her head. 'Look what happened with Le Pen in France. He was in the presidential run-off.'

They took the lift to the sixth and top floor.

'This lot are stronger in Thessaloniki and the north, I think. They take a hard line on the former Yugoslav Macedonian Republic.'

'Hard line as in?'

'They want to seal the border.'

Rachel stared at him. 'That wouldn't do Greek business much good.'

'Which is partly why people don't vote for them. Oh, and they want illegal immigrants to be put in barges and towed into international waters, preferably without food or water.'

'Delightful.'

Mavros found the door, which had been freshly painted, and rang the bell. It was answered by a woman he recognised from the photo on her site, though she had put on weight and her hair was greyer.

'Mr Mavro?' she said, in Greek.

'Alex.'

'Allegra.'

He introduced Rachel in English.

'Shalom,' Allegra Harari said, with a smile, then continued in Greek.

'I'm afraid she doesn't speak English,' Mavros explained. 'You don't know Russian? Or Polish? Or German?'

Rachel shook her head, her lips pursed. 'None of those languages has any appeal to me, especially not the last.'

Mavros translated.

'Believe me, I didn't learn them for pleasure,' Allegra said, leading them in. 'But you can't work with the Lager records and the research into them if you don't know those languages.'

'Oh,' said Rachel, taking in the comfortable sitting room, 'she lives here.'

Their hostess answered at some length.

'Her father was bought the flat with the money he received in compensation. He came back from Auschwitz to find the family house had been assigned to a Greek, who refused to give it back.

The court case lasted nearly ten years.'

'Disgraceful,' Rachel said, sitting on the sofa indicated by Allegra. She and Mavros both declined coffee. 'Tell her who we're looking for and ... what the old woman said.'

Allegra Harari listened carefully, taking notes. 'So,' she said, when Mavros finished. 'First of all, I know Ester Broudo. I agree with Rabbi Rousso. She is not a fanciful person and certainly isn't one to make something like this up.'

Mavros translated.

'But she could still have made a mistake,' Rachel said.

'If you think that, why are you here?' Allegra asked, with a knowing smile.

Rachel didn't respond.

'Next,' the researcher continued, 'I am aware of your family. Yosif Samuel, Aron's father, was quite an important figure in our community before the war – though his lukewarm attitude to religious affairs earned him enemies among the faithful and his lack of interest in Palestine as the Jewish homeland annoyed the Zionists. Like many Thessaloniki Jews, he saw himself as a Greek, although men of his generation were less outspoken about that than the younger ones.'

'That's interesting,' Rachel said, her expression suggesting otherwise.

Mavros wondered how much she knew about her great-uncle. He'd quizzed her on the plane and had been given the impression that he was a faceless ghost. Her questions to the Jewish community in Athens had apparently produced nothing useful.

'Of course, I can do detailed research,' Allegra said.

'I'll pay,' Rachel said.

'We'll talk about that later.'

Mavros took out the book his mother had published. 'There's a brief mention of the Samuels in here.'

Rachel stared at him and took *Years in Hell* from his hand.

'No,' Allegra said to him. 'To be frank, I don't remember coming across much information about them. But that was nearly fifteen years ago and many archives have opened up since then. Many are also on line. How is Dorothy?'

'Ageing but generally well.'

'What is this?' Rachel asked.

'A book of extracts from Auschwitz survivors' memoirs, edited by Allegra. My mother published it before the turn of the century.'

'Really? You didn't mention it.'

He smiled. 'I assumed your high-capacity computer stick contained everything there is to know about me. Your family isn't mentioned in the book.'

She handed it back. 'Very well. Please ask her to carry out a full investigation into my great-uncle, paying particular attention to today's allegations about him. I will give her a deposit.'

Allegra Harari declined the latter with a hurt look and told Mavros she'd start immediately. Rachel gave her a card with her email address on it. He handed over his.

As they were preparing to leave, he asked about

the Phoenix Rises graffiti.

'Ach, those idiots are everywhere. They paint out the sign in the Square of the Jewish Martyrs and make a mess on the Holocaust Victims' Monument. We ask the police and the municipality for help, but nothing happens. I've had personal threats too.'

'What did the police say?'

'Not much. They took photographs of what was sprayed on my door and put them in a file.'

'What threats were made?'

'The usual filth – "We'll Burn You, Jew Bitch", "Prepare to Be Made into Soap" and so on.'

'When was this?'

'Over the last three months – the latest was a week ago.'

'You should get a steel door.'

'And let them know they've frightened me? No, thanks. I have nephews who come quickly. They almost caught the cowards once.'

Back on the street Rachel asked, 'What was that about?'

Mavros told her.

'I don't like it,' she said. 'Are you sure she's safe?'

'Search me. I didn't know the Phoenix Rises were into making threats against Jews.'

'Yes,' Allegra said to him. 'There wasn't much information about them. She should have her nephews there all the time.'

'Probably not practicable.'

'Neatly put. OK, I'm going back to the hotel.'

Mavros nodded. 'Me too. Em, I'm afraid I've got something on tonight.'

Rachel gave him a searching look. 'Something personal?'

'Old friend.'

There was a pause before she responded. 'Don't worry, Alex, you aren't tied to my apron strings.'

'Is that an apron?'

She laughed. 'Witty too. Or so you think. Don't worry, I have work to do. I'll be staying in.'

As they approached the hotel, they passed a gaggle of uniformed police in the street. They were smoking and drinking coffee, their laughter and back slaps filling the air.

'Off duty?' Rachel asked.

'I doubt it.'

'No wonder this city isn't safe for minorities.'

Mavros shrugged. From what he'd been reading in *Years in Hell*, the co-capital had a distinctly chequered history in that department.

Rachel opened her laptop as soon as she entered her room and went on to the encrypted site.

'Request covert guard on Allegra Harari.' She added the address. 'At least at night.'

'Reason?'

'Threats from avian bonfire.'

'Status?'

'Potentially serious. Subject is source.'

'Acknowledged.'

Rachel signed off and exited the site. She looked at the diamond watch her father had given her for her eighteenth birthday, then took it off. The evening's work would require her to be as inconspicuous as possible.

TEN

We had heard rumours about trains full of Jews leaving the city and the comrades had told me to run or hide, but I had committed myself to my family. I'm still not sure why. Of course, loyalty to family is a central tenet of our community, but I had spent most of my early years rebelling. I think the killing of Zakar had a lot to do with my decision. It wasn't that I was afraid of his colleagues tracking me down. Beating one of the enemy to death, even one of our own, gave me confidence; it increased my innate arrogance. I actually believed I could protect my relatives from anything the Nazis had planned.

Not that it was obvious what those plans were. Cunning was to the fore, as always with the SS. We were made to exchange our Greek currency for zloty, which we would be able to use in the work camps in Poland. It was a convincing trick, one that enabled the enemy to pocket our dwindling funds as well as reassure us about our future. Even I believed that what lay ahead was labour. In that, at least for me, I was correct.

The grandmothers were lying in the corner of a ramshackle hut that had been vacated by a family that left on a train shortly before we entered the Baron Hirsch. They were living corpses, only their fleshless faces visible beneath layers of clothing. Mother was bustling around, cooking soup on a fire fed by coal I'd managed to steal from another tumbledown house.

'That I should have a son who is a thief,' she groaned.

'That I should have a mother who is an ingrate,' I replied.

She was outraged but Isaak and Dario laughed, and even my father raised a smile. He had aged ten years in recent months and refused to eat, passing his portions to my sister.

Little Golda was at the breast much of the time. Isaak was embarrassed and turned away. I did too, but not without catching the occasional glimpse of Miriam's blue-veined flesh and the dark skin of her nipples. I had little knowledge of the other sex and used my imagination to relieve my teenage lust. There was a girl in the youth party who I liked, though romance was not encouraged and she turned away when I stared at her during the lengthy speeches the cadres read out. She was nominally a Christian and I got the feeling she didn't like what I was, despite the party line of no religious discrimination. We were all atheists in theory, though plenty of older comrades still baptised their children.

'Come on,' Dario said, pulling my arm. 'Let's see what else we can lift.'

We moved through the crowded, filthy lanes of the camp. People were sweating in the May sun, but no one took off their clothes. They would have disappeared immediately. The trading of food was going on, brought in illicitly or stolen from elsewhere in the Hirsch.

'We need knives,' my brother-in-law said,

94

limping half a pace behind me.

'What?' I said, looking at the heavily armed SS and Jewish policemen on the other side of the fence. 'To fight them?'

'No, to be ready for whatever awaits us where we're going. Do you think the Poles are going to welcome us with open arms?'

He had a point. I whispered to him to act the decoy. He was good at it, playing the part of an official and rattling on about the importance of cleanliness. Soon I had a pocketful of table knives, two of which had a decent edge. At our last stop I managed to palm a wooden-handled kitchen blade with a vicious point. I nudged him and we strolled away.

'Did you hear what that man said?' my brother-in-law asked.

'My attention was elsewhere.'

'The transports. Apparently they're made up of cattle trucks. There are no seats and no toilets. Peopled were crammed into the last train.'

Something about the word 'cattle' made my stomach somersault. Cattle would only be transported by rail when they were going to the slaughter.

'Keep that to yourself,' I said. 'There's no point in scaring our people. When our turn comes, make sure you stay close to Miriam and the baby. I don't know if my sister is strong enough for this.'

He nodded. Neither of us had to say anything about the grandmothers. They might not even last the night.

I was wrong there. They were alive the next day

95

and we had to manhandle them on to the cattle truck when our names were called by the guards. The vehicle stank, with minimal ventilation and a leaky can in the middle for us to relieve ourselves. Males and females were supposed to be separated, but Isaak, Dario and I managed to form a wall around the others in one corner with our cases. The grandmothers were propped up against the wooden sides, and Miriam and Mother sat in front of them. They did what they could to comfort little Golda. Father tried to help us, but he dropped to his knees before the train started to move. When it did, he fell forward and almost smothered my maternal grandmother. I pulled him back.

'Thank you, my son,' he said, his voice cracked. 'How long do you think the journey will last?'

'Three days at most,' Dario said confidently, but I knew he was lying.

How can I describe what it was like? The great writers – Primo Levi, Elie Wiesel – have set it down in words that will last as long as human beings read. But you want to hear my version, don't you? Well, to do anything was close to impossible, even for a relatively strong young man like me: inhaling the fetid air, standing as the carriage jolted and bucked, supporting each other with our arms, pushing through the mass of people to the shit can, helping our women use it with our coats opened around them, eating the last of our food. We had little water and were rarely given any. People went mad, screaming, punching, fainting. Others died, mostly the old and the very young. My grandmothers already seemed to be in another world, with no awareness of the horror we were living, but they were still breathing. On the second day Miriam started to weep, at first quietly but soon inconsolably loud. We let Dario get down beside her. She didn't seem to recognise him. Then I heard her say 'Albertos'. She went on repeating her first husband's name for days. Dario looked broken. At least Miriam let him caress Golda. It wasn't my sister's fault that her spirit was broken, but Dario deserved better.

Isaak was at the side of the cattle truck. He started digging at the wood with one of the knives I had stolen. Soon the blade broke. He took another. It was a mistake. At one of the frequent stops – we were never allowed out when the cans were emptied and the dead removed – an SS man saw what he was doing from outside and smashed the butt of his rifle against my brother's hand. He cried out, dropping the knife through the gap he'd made. Blood came from his shattered fingernails. I thought some of the bones were broken. Now both his arms were useless.

What more can I say? We were parched, the sun beating down on the train as it clacked across interminable plains and through gorges. Apart from the mad ones, no one wasted breath on talking. We concentrated on surviving. In periods of lucid thought, I was assailed by doubts and fears. If we were being taken to a work camp, why were we being debilitated in this way? Why weren't we being given more water? Or bread – most people's food ran out after a few days. I traded use of my sturdiest blade to open cans, taking a portion for us. We were all still alive, even the grandmothers.

97

The men without beards now had thick stubble and the skin on the women's faces was shrinking, their cheekbones more prominent.

The voices outside became louder and coarser every time we stopped. Looking through the slats, I could see more SS men, their jaws extensions of the coal-scuttle helmets they wore. Some of them had whips in their belts, others held on to straining dogs that barked as if our smell was offensive. Which it was, of course. The shit can often overflowed and we stood in our own waste matter. But those dogs with their slavering jaws weren't infuriated by the stench of faeces and urine. They had been trained to direct their aggression against Jews. Even the animal kingdom was against us.

'My son,' came a desperate voice.

I bent down. 'Yes, Mother.'

'You have a knife still?'

'Yes.'

'My son, you will need expiation, even if you do not believe the sacred writings.'

I leaned closer, struggling to catch her words. 'Why?'

'You must kill them,' she said, nodding towards the grandmothers. 'They will not even notice.'

My knees gave way and I fell on top of Mother.

'Do it!' she said into my ear. 'Do it now!'

I rocked back and looked up at my father. His eyes were closed and he was being held up by Dario.

'I can't ... I can't do that to his mother without telling him,' I hissed.

'Please, my son, I beg you. There is nothing left for them. Please.'

I took in the old women's deeply lined faces. Their eyes were shut and their hands beneath their coats. They looked like Egyptian mummies, but it wouldn't be as easy as Mother thought. I would have to open their clothing and that might wake one or both of them.

'I can't!' I pleaded. 'I can't!'

Then I realised the train was braking hard, its whistle blowing. The howling of attack dogs started and harsh voices rang out.

I had missed my chance. It was too late, too late for all of us.

ELEVEN

Shimon Raphael got up from his table when I walked into the restaurant in the famous Ladhadhika area near the port.

'Alex Mavros in the flesh,' he said enthusiastically.

'The same,' he said, shaking the hand he'd extended. 'How did you recognise me?'

'Yiorgos emailed me some of the press articles about you.'

'Oh yes?' He wondered what else the Fat Man had sent. 'He didn't by any chance tell you I like female to male transsexuals, did he?'

Shimon laughed uproariously, silencing even the noisy clientele for a few seconds. 'Not exactly. There was something about sheep, though.'

'You didn't believe it.'

'Of course not. I haven't seen Yiorgos for years, but obviously he hasn't changed.'

'I don't know. Imagine all his character faults and multiply them by a hundred.'

The customs broker bellowed again. 'He's a character, all right. He says he works with you.'

Mavros raised the glass of wine that had been filled for him. 'Not on this case. At least not on the spot. That can be ... risky.'

'I imagine you don't have quite as large an appetite as our friend,' Shimon said. 'Even I don't. Let's go for quality rather than quantity. I know what's good here.'

Mavros listened as various starters and a baked fish were ordered.

'So, cheers and welcome to Thessaloniki.'

'L'haim,' Mavros said, as they clinked glasses.

'Very good. Not that there's many of us left here to say that nowadays.'

'How many?'

'About twelve hundred.'

Mavros looked around the restaurant's understated décor. 'And fifty thousand died in the camps.'

Shimon's face was grim. 'A bit under that, but the numbers can't be exact.'

'Including Aron Samuel.'

'As far as the community knew – until you told me otherwise.'

'You know Allegra Harari?'

'Of course. Her brain is a thing of wonder. She's been offered jobs in American universities, but she won't leave the city – says we have to fill the space left by our ghosts as best we can.'

The waiter brought small dishes of octopus, meat balls, beans and cheese.

'You know she's been threatened by the Phoenix Rises?'

Shimon's hand stopped between plate and mouth. 'So have I. And others.'

'You take it seriously?'

'Sure. Fireproof doors on my home and office, CCTV, alarms. Listen, Alex, don't get the idea that this is anything new. There have always been far-right lunatics. Some of the most hot-headed local nationalists fought with the Serbs in Bosnia – brothers in Orthodoxy, eh? All that bollocks about the Yugoslav Macedonian state's name back in the 90s didn't help. The scumbags went to Kosovo too, not that the Muslims took any shit from them.'

Mavros ate a piece of octopus. 'Mm, this is good. They don't seem to be interested in standing for parliament.'

Shimon grunted, his mouth full. 'There's no point. They get about one per cent in the local elections. Their leader, Makis Kalogirou, is the opposite of a vote magnet. He's about as eloquent as a septic-tank hose.'

'They were organised enough to mess up those immigrants.'

'Beating the hell out of people's one thing they can do. Another's defacing walls and monuments.' The customs broker soaked bread in the remains of the bean sauce. 'Anyway, enough of those wankers. You want me to dig up what I can about Aron Samuel.'

'I do. Rachel's got Allegra–'

'Rachel?'

Mavros explained who she was, adding a physical description. 'She sounds interesting.' Shimon grinned. 'I didn't know you had company.'

'I'd have thought the Fat Man would have spilled that ASAP.'

'Strangely, no. Probably jealous he's not up here stuffing his face with us and his eyes with her.'

'Very likely.'

'So Allegra's doing the archive work on Samuel.'

'That's right. I thought you might know ... some different stones to look under.'

Shimon guffawed. 'Different stones? I like that. Maybe I do. Acting as a middleman between clients and the customs does put certain information my way. In this case, I don't have any of that, but I do have some potential sources. Leave it with me.'

'Thanks. You'll be paid, of course.'

'Of course.'

Mavros smiled. 'I'll tell you one thing you might be able to help me on without excavation work. Ester Broudo claims she saw Aron on Thursday November 3rd. Do you happen to know whose wedding was taking place at the main synagogue that day?'

Shimon answered immediately. 'I was there, all my family was. Ilias Tsiako married Stella Vital.'

'That was easy. Could you see if there's a link between any of them to the Samuel family? Aron may have been paying his respects or the like without going inside.'

'Good thought. Yes, I'll check it.'

'And the Broudo family? What do you know about them?'

'That they were almost annihilated, like most of us. My parents knew Ester, but I haven't seen her for years. Do you want me to check her too?'

'If you can do that without creating any waves.'

'Ha! I'm overweight but surprisingly light on my feet.'

The small plates were removed and a large platter was set between them.

'The chef's a master at this,' Shimon said. 'He stuffs it with parsley, oregano and garlic and then adds a touch of genius to the sauce.'

Mavros sniffed. 'Mint?'

'Close. Spearmint. Sounds weird, but wait till you try it.'

The fish was magnificent. They gave their full attention to it and only when he was finished did Mavros broach the subject he thought might be awkward.

'You were in the party, Shimon?' he said.

The customs broker nodded happily enough. 'Since the youth organisation. Pissed my parents off in a big way. In fact, it was one of the reasons they left for Israel.'

Mavros gave him a sympathetic look.

'No, don't worry. They'd been ready to go for years. My old man was in Auschwitz and he never settled here when he got back. It wasn't easy for our people.'

'So I've been reading. Properties illegally handed over to non-Jews, businesses stolen...'

'And worse. Male survivors of the camps were called up for service in the Civil War. My old man wasn't a Communist, but he was no royalist either. Two of his friends were killed alongside him in the final offensive on Mount Grammos.'

'So why did you stay?'

'The party, mainly. Then they got upset when I took over the company – the guy I worked for dropped dead. Accused me of being a class traitor, a profiteer and a money-grabbing Jew. I had a wife and kids then and I didn't need the hassle.' Shimon caught Mavros's eye. 'No offence. Your father was a hero.'

'None taken. I don't think he'd have liked the party as it's become. They look after their own like the other political groups. They're part of the problem.'

'Ah, but those ideals. How come you weren't seized by them?'

Mavros poured the last of the wine into their glasses. 'Bad timing. I was five when the old man died, not long before the Colonels came to power. And I was ten when my brother disappeared.'

'Another hero.'

'He was to me. After he'd gone, I turned against what he'd fought for.' He shook his head. 'A kind of betrayal.'

'From what I've heard of him, he wouldn't see it that way. After all, you're alive and well.'

'It's not knowing what happened to him that kills me. I don't let it define my life like it used to, but I'm still tortured by the need to find out.'

Shimon stretched a hand across the table. 'Life is torture, my friend. I lost eleven family members in the camps and there isn't a day when I don't look at their photos. And now I have to walk past spray-painted swastikas.' He shrugged. 'Not that there's anything new about that. The collaborators did what they wanted in Thessaloniki since the Germans ran the city. They were well connected.'

'Really?'

'Their sons and grandsons kept that up. Makis Kalogirou is one. His grandfather made a fortune out of Jewish businesses he got cheap from the Germans.'

Mavros sat back, a worm of doubt wriggling into the topsoil of his mind. Jews and neo-Nazis, the threats to Allegra Harari, Aron Samuel's long-delayed return to the city – if Ester Broudo hadn't been mistaken – and attacks on Muslim immigrants in the former Ottoman city. Was he being drawn into a world of violence with long and infinitely twisted roots?

'I'll stay overnight, Niki,' Maria Orfanou said, as she pulled up outside the apartment block. 'You need company.'

'No, I'm all right.'

'You don't look it.' Maria was a no-nonsense fifty-five year old whose devotion to her immigrant clients was as great as Niki's. She was long divorced and lived with a homely Albanian woman in the northern suburbs. Driving Niki home was a big detour, but she did it because she wanted to. 'Come on, at least let me get you inside.'

Niki assented wordlessly. They'd been for dinner in an old-fashioned taverna, but she'd eaten little, leaving Maria to hoover up the rest. Overeating was her colleague's only vice.

Once they negotiated the politician's night guard, the code pad, the lift and the various security devices that protected the flat, Niki flopped down on the sofa.

'Go,' she said. 'I'm just tired.'

'Really?' Maria asked dubiously. 'All right. Make sure you lock up after me.' She leaned forward and kissed Niki on the cheek. 'I'll see you tomorrow morning.'

'I'll get a taxi. Don't worry, we have a reliable one.'

Maria looked around the darkened flat as if monsters were lurking in the corners. 'Will Alex be happy about that?'

'Never mind what Alex thinks,' Niki replied waspishly. 'He's having fun in Thessaloniki.'

'He's a good man,' Maria said.

'Maybe.' Niki gave her an anguished look. 'But he isn't here when I need him.'

'Oh, darling,' her colleague said, sitting next to her. 'Trust me, there aren't many like him. You know that perfectly well. You want to have his child.'

'Yes ... I do,' Niki sobbed. 'But ... but I can't.'

'You will,' Maria said, in a tone that brooked no argument. 'If you don't, you'll have me to answer to.'

Niki smiled and then pushed her gently away. 'Yes, ma'am. Now get the fuck out of here.'

Maria laughed and did as she was told. She turned at the door and said, 'No taxi, though. I'll pick you up as usual.' She and her partner had two cars, one ending with an even number and one with an odd, so she could enter the congestion zone every weekday.

Niki got up after she'd gone to triple-lock the door, apply the chains and set the alarm. Then she went to the bedroom and lay down in her clothes, taking off only her shoes. She could smell Alex on his pillow and the duvet.

'Bastard,' she said. 'Why aren't you here?'

Sleep finally took her in the small hours.

Rachel was in a black Mercedes E-Class with her contact. He had flown in a week earlier and familiarised himself with the city and the target.

'Quiet around here,' she said.

'That's why we're in this stolen Panzer. Less likely to stand out.'

She pressed keys on her laptop. 'This photo is a couple of years old. Maybe they'll have given him plastic surgery.'

'The Russians? He's not that useful to them.'

'So why are they keeping him here in luxury?'

'Because they can get him over the borders to Macedonia and the other Balkan countries easily. He was rabble-rousing in Kosovo during the summer. Gives the Vladimirs something to posture against, as well as scare NATO.'

'I've read the file,' Rachel said. 'I don't understand why they're flying in caviar weekly. Presumably the vodka is for his guards.'

'The bastard's got a gut on him. Anyway, they like to keep people sweet, especially when they've got something they want.'

'And the target's valuable because he's helping them disrupt the region. Don't they realise he was in a Jordanian al-Qaeda cell?'

'Of course. The intercepts suggest they think he's given up on that. Maybe he has.'

'But we haven't given up on him. Fourteen people killed and thirty-three injured, including three blinded, in Tel Aviv by the suicide bomber he trained and indoctrinated.'

'That was the worst incident, yes. There were at least five others.'

Rachel nodded. 'Our masters have presumably taken into account the chaos this will cause in Greece. Let alone with the Russians.'

'Presumably.' Her companion's tone was studiedly neutral.

She looked at her watch. 'Five minutes, if they stick to the schedule.'

'They've done so every night I've been here.'

'The Russians obviously think he's safe in restaurants.' She checked her weapons: two Taser X26s and the Glock 19 that had been delivered to the hotel. The order was that she use only the former, as well as the spray can in her jacket pocket. The agent beside her was the designated executioner. He was screwing the silencer on to his Glock.

'One minute,' Rachel said.

They pulled down their black balaclavas.

The steel street door opened thirty seconds early, but they were ready, having already checked that the street was deserted.

The Jordanian was wearing a voluminous dark-blue coat that failed to disguise his distended lower abdomen. The pair of Russians was also in coats, their hair cut very short. They looked around and then walked towards a grey BMW Sport Wagon at the roadside.

The Mercedes moved forward quickly. Rachel took down both guards with the Tasers from her open window. As they lay jerking on the road, her colleague got out and caught up with the target, who was running back to the street door. The first bullet hit him in the rear of his left thigh. He collapsed with a cry. The agent slammed his head into the ground, then kneeled beside him.

'Many souls are waiting for you,' he said, in Arabic, after glancing around to be sure no one had appeared in the vicinity. Then he shot the Jordanian twice in the back of the neck. Getting up and walking backwards to the car, he watched as Rachel sprayed a red swastika on the dead man's back and another on the steel door beyond him.

Then the Mercedes and its two occupants disappeared at unremarkable speed into the chill November evening.

TWELVE

The wagon doors were unlocked and pulled open. We were in the corner on that side, so the wave of clean air washed over us immediately. Except, although it was much fresher than the stink of shit and piss and unwashed bodies, some of them dead, it wasn't clean. There was a dark sweetness to it, like meat that had been caramelised. I helped my grandmothers up, unable to look them in their pale eyes. I still had two knives, but I was even less able to use them than before.

The brusque orders were translated by the few of our people who knew German.

'Everyone out!'

'All the luggage on the ground!'

'Get in line!'

Figures in dirty grey-blue striped suits were pulling people's bags out of the way. Some of them were Greeks.

'Quickly!' one said to us. 'Don't worry, everything will be fine.'

I looked into his bloodshot eyes and knew he was lying, though perhaps not unkindly.

'Can we all stay together?' I asked.

He turned his head and then quivered as a man in mismatched uniform tunic and trousers hit him on the back with a short whip.

'Just do what you're told,' he said hoarsely.

I got out of the cattle truck and helped my mother down. Isaak and my father handed down the grandmothers, while Dario and Miriam slid out, Golda in her mother's arms. The uproar meant we could hardly speak to each other. The occupants of the train, many of them in much worse condition than us, were funnelled by heavily armed SS into a narrow space. Greek-speaking helpers were now pulling dead bodies out of the carriages and loading them on to trucks. There was a pretty station building with flowers to our right, which calmed some of our people. Maybe this was a work camp after all.

But what was being made here? Was it a canning factory producing supplies for the German forces fighting the Soviets?

Without warning, the women were separated from us. My mother started to wail, then controlled herself because she and Miriam had to hold up the grandmothers as well as Golda. We watched their line move quicker than ours, splitting at some kind of junction ahead. With every breath we took in as much dust as air. Isaak's missing hand was not obvious and he had regained some movement in his recently injured one. Despite the heat, he was wearing his coat. I kept mine on too as I didn't want to lose it. We were told by the Greeks that our luggage would be brought to us later.

There were SS officers in well-cut and clean uniforms, standing on raised platforms ahead. One of them was smiling as he moved his hand to left and right. People were pushed in the appropriate direction. I saw trucks on the left side, old men and women and young children being lifted aboard. I had a bad feeling, in part because the sky to the left was covered by a thick black cloud.

'Don't limp,' I said over my shoulder to Dario, having seen a young man with a crutch sent to the trucks.

My father was behind me. We were both directed to the right. An officer had already sent my mother that way. I watched as he signalled that Miriam and Golda be separated from the grandmothers and sent to the right as well. The old women were carried to the trucks by rough-handed men. I didn't know what to do. There was nothing I could do. I felt sick. Then I heard a shout and looked over my shoulder. Dario had been sent to the left, his limp obviously detected. I later learned the officer making the selection was a doctor. I waited to see what happened to Isaak and was struck several times about the head and back. I only moved on when I saw that my brother was following.

'What will become of the others?' Father asked. He had aged even more in the last hour.

'They probably have an old people's home,' I said, aware of the keenness of his stare.

'And Dario?'

'There are plenty of jobs he can do.'

Isaak had caught up with us. 'More than I can,' he said.

There was a revving of engines and we watched as the trucks drove away with their human cargo.

'Kaput!' shouted one of the uniformed men, cracking his whip at us. 'Alles kaput!' He pointed at the lowering sky.

We didn't know German but his meaning was clear, even if we didn't yet know what caused the cloud. It wasn't long till we found out. A Greek in stripes told us when we were queuing for delousing.

'They burn them,' he whispered. 'After they've been gassed.'

The others started moaning and crying, but my face remained dry. I was thinking about the knives, which I had dropped as we got out of the cattle truck, frightened by the weapons and stony faces of our captors. If I'd had the courage I could have saved the grandmothers. I could even have given Dario a friendly death. I would never be able to expiate that failure of nerve, whatever my mother thought. I glanced around. It was nearly dark and we had no idea where the women had been taken.

'Do you think Mother and Miriam and Golda are still together?' Isaak asked.

I shrugged.

'I'm sure they are,' Father said, trying to convince himself as much as us.

Then we were told to strip. My brother was no longer able to disguise his foreshortened arm. He was pulled out of the line by an SS man. I went to help and was floored by a blow that filled my eyes with colours that ran into each other. My father was wailing, then he too crashed to the ground. That was the last we saw of Isaak.

We were dragged to our feet and shoved forward. I remained dazed for hours; in fact it was days till I became fully aware of our surroundings. We were without hair on our heads and bodies, wearing the vertically striped clothes, fighting for the bread and soup ration, as well as for tins and spoons to put the latter in. Some of the Thessaloniki community helped us. We slept crammed together in tiered bunks. It was suffocatingly hot at night and the more experienced men, the majority not Greek, told us to be quiet in languages that were easily comprehensible even though we had never heard them before. The capos, fellow prisoners given benefits to keep us in line by force, and the block master – ours a round-bellied Pole – were quick to strike at men who spoke out of turn or talked at night. Father and I had been separated,

113

but I saw him several rows away; and at the roll calls, which often lasted for hours; and on the work details – scrubbing floors, marching at fast pace to dig pits and carry stones, toiling to the brink of consciousness.

Until I and several other young men were pulled out of the hut one morning without warning. I turned and caught a glimpse of my father. He waved, but I could see the film of tears on his eyes.

Outside we were lined up.

'You're going to love this,' the capo said. He was one of our own, but he had successfully transformed himself into a lackey of the SS. He was said to have beaten several prisoners to death. 'And volunteering is good for the soul.'

'I'm not volunteering for anything,' I said, as he passed. That earned me a punch in the belly and a knee in the face.

An SS man watched as I got up. He berated the capo, telling him I was the Reich's property and that the Sonderkommando needed men in good condition. I had picked up a fair amount of German in the weeks I'd been in the Lager, but I didn't know what a Sonderkommando was.

A couple of hours later I found out. As we were marched out of the main camp, I had a hallucination, not for the first time. I thought I saw my mother behind a window in one of the command buildings. Her head had been shaved like ours and her cheeks were damp. Unlike my father, she didn't wave and her shoulders were bowed, as if they bore the weight of nations.

I still don't know if I imagined it or if she really was in that building.

THIRTEEN

Mavros thought about calling Niki. He decided against it because he didn't want to wake her. It was after eleven when he got back to the hotel. He looked up at Rachel's room. There were no lights. She must have finished working on her laptop and turned in. He ran upstairs, immediately aware that he had eaten and drunk too much, but determined to burn off at least some calories.

He had a shower and lay on the bed, but sleep wouldn't come. He got up and went to the window. The lights of the square below were still on and there were plenty of people around – the cafés and bars on the seafront would be open for hours. He looked out to sea. The lights of the ships at anchor shone dimly through the thin mist rising from the water. The suburbs around the bay to his left were bright nearby, but soon faded to a blur.

Beyond the airport was the beach resort of Ayia Triadha. He'd seen it when they came into land, but had managed to push the memories back. Now, after Shimon Raphael's mention of Andonis, he couldn't block them out any longer. Mavros had been nine and his brother twenty when the family had stayed in an old comrade's house in Ayia Triadha for a month. It was the summer of 1971. Their father was four years dead and the dictatorship still in power. The train journey from

Athens had been uncomfortable, his mother in particular out of sorts because of the heat and other passengers' sweat. His sister Anna, fourteen at the time, had her nose permanently in the air to discourage the attentions of boys, not that any had risked coming close. They took a taxi from the railway station in Thessaloniki to the village, Dorothy saying 'hang the cost'.

What followed was a golden summer for them all. Back then Ayia Triadha wasn't developed – as Andonis pointed out, it had been founded as a refugee village after the exchange of populations in 1922 – and the beaches weren't busy. The comrade and his family were in the Peloponnese and had left a rattly old Fiat that Andonis used to take them further afield. Mavros remembered jumping with his brother from rocks on the shore, while their mother read manuscripts and Anna fashion magazines. He recalled late lunches at deserted tavernas, fresh fish and salads, his first sip of wine passed to him by Andonis when Dorothy wasn't looking. Then Anna met a boy she actually liked and they capered around on the beach like much younger kids. Andonis and Alex built sandcastles, threw balls at each other, had swimming races that his brother often let him win, even read books together. Andonis usually pored over illicit tomes of Marxist theory, but he liked adventure stories and they went through *Treasure Island* aloud, doing the accents. Dorothy insisted they speak English for at least a couple of hours every day.

Then there were the excursions into the city. They visited the sites – the Roman and Byzantine

116

remains, the church of the city's patron Saint Dhimitrios, and the narrow lanes of the upper town. They even had a look at the old fortress of Gedi Koulé at the summit of the defensive walls, still in use as a prison. Many Communists had been executed there during and after the Civil War. Andonis stared at it with a mixture of wonder and revulsion. On the way down he told Alex to wait at a corner, returning a quarter of an hour later.

'Don't tell Mother,' he said, with conspiratorial smile. 'Ice cream?'

Alex ran after him, excited to be part of his brother's secret activities against the regime. Under a year later Andonis was gone, whether taken by the security police or responsible for his own disappearance nobody – least of all Mavros – knew; or was telling.

And here he was back in the co-capital again. Andonis's feet had walked these streets. The same applied much more in Athens, but somehow that was different. To his shame Mavros had got used to the ghost of Andonis there. Here in Thessaloniki his brother seemed tantalisingly tangible.

He looked out over the square again and his heart skipped a beat. Walking towards the hotel in a dark jacket and trousers was Rachel Samuel. Where, he wondered, had she been? A nightcap after a long evening at the typeface? She didn't strike him as the drinking kind, either solitary or in company, and she certainly wasn't dressed for it.

'What's going on up there?' Niki sounded out of sorts.

Mavros wiped the phone with the edge of his towel. 'I've just come out of the shower. I know nothing.'

'Turn on the TV.'

He did as he was told. 'Martha the talking dog?'

'Idiot. Find a channel with news.'

He pressed buttons on the handset. 'Ah.'

'Ah?'

'I see what you mean. "Jordanian man shot dead in Thessaloniki". That's shocking – if not exactly germane to what I'm doing.'

'Still, it'll make things livelier in the city. And no doubt keep you away from me even longer.'

Mavros was at the window. It was raining and people were walking quickly across the square. Dark-skinned men selling umbrellas were on several corners. 'I don't see why it should. You're having a hard time, aren't you?'

'You should retrain as a psychiatrist, Alex.'

'I was going to call you last night, but I thought you'd be asleep.'

'I wasn't. I wish you had.' She let out a sob. 'Alex, I can't handle this. I don't know what I'll do if I can't get pregnant.'

'Come on, my love. There are plenty of therapies if they find something irregular. It's too early to get down about it.'

'I know ... I know. It's just... Oh, there's Maria. I have to go. I love you.'

'Love you too,' he managed, just before the connection was cut. He cursed himself for not calling the previous night. He should have known

118

she'd be awake worrying.

His mobile rang again.

'This is Rachel Samuel. Were you busy at work?'

'What? Oh ... yes. Checking something.'

'Why don't you join me for breakfast and tell me about it?'

He agreed and rang off, looking around for his clothes. With a clean T-shirt underneath, his denim shirt had another day in it, he reckoned. On his way out of the room, he rang the Fat Man.

Rachel was sitting in a corner table, the remains of a continental breakfast in front of her. She had her laptop open.

'Have you seen this?' She turned the screen towards him.

Mavros looked at a Reuters article about the shooting.

'I checked the map. It happened only a kilometre from the home where Ester Broudo lives.'

'Really? Is that significant?'

She looked at him coolly. 'Should it be? I was orienting myself. Go and get something to eat.'

He did as he was told, picking up croissants, jam, yoghurt and juice from the buffet and ordering a Greek coffee from a passing waiter.

'It says here that swastikas were sprayed on the dead man and a nearby door.'

'Bloody fascists. That should put the Phoenix Rises right in the spotlight.'

She closed the computer. 'So, what were you working on so early in the morning – by your standards, at least?'

119

He had a story worked out – in fact, he'd already put it into action. 'I was asking my colleague in Athens to see if there's any reference to your great-uncle in the Communist Party records.'

Rachel raised an eyebrow. 'Why would there be? There was never any mention of him being a member.'

'There was never mention of him at all, according to you and your father. Besides, we have a contact, so why not use him?'

'Why not indeed?'

Mavros nodded to the waiter as his *sketo* appeared. 'How was your evening?' he asked. 'Work, work, work?'

She looked straight at him. 'Until ten or so. Then I got bored and went for a walk. The seafront was pretty.'

'Pretty chilly, I would think.' He was impressed by her directness, but two things bothered him: the vagueness of 'ten or so' and the fact that when he saw her she was coming from the back streets across the square, not from the front. Then again, maybe she stopped being a robot when she'd finished work.

'Chilly? I didn't notice.' She dropped her gaze. 'Do you have an agenda for today?'

She had him there. He took a large bite from a croissant.

'Only,' Rachel continued, 'I have the name of an elderly gentleman who knew my father's family. He survived Auschwitz. That's all my father said, but I have the address and he's expecting us this morning. Well, me, but I'll need my trusty translator.' She smiled briefly.

120

Mavros concealed a sigh of relief. Short of suggesting they visit the Jewish Museum, he was out of ideas till Shimon, Allegra and the Fat Man reported back.

They took a taxi that passed the White Tower and headed south-east.

'There are some amazing buildings here,' Rachel said, pointing at a run-down villa surrounded by apartment blocks. 'Hang on.' She looked at her guidebook. 'That one was built by a Jewish merchant. It became a school after the war, but it's been empty for thirty years.'

'Shame.'

'Mm. I wonder what happened to the owners.'

Mavros let that go unanswered. From what he'd read in *Years in Hell* and Shimon had said, the few Jews who returned from the camps were not treated well. Maybe the man they were going to interview could expand on that. His name was Baruh Natzari. Mavros took the anthology of memoirs from his shoulder bag and checked. He hadn't contributed.

The taxi dropped them in a narrow street not far from the seafront in the southern suburb of Kalamaria. A plane was visible on its way to the airport.

'Here it is,' Mavros said, pointing to the name in Greek letters. He rang the bell.

There was a squawk and then a high-pitched voice asked who was there. Mavros explained and the entry buzzer rang.

'It's the fourth floor,' he said, looking at the list of residents in the hall. He inclined his head towards the stairs. 'Shall we?'

Rachel kept ahead of him all the way.

'Impressive. You work out?'

'I swim. Half an hour every morning and evening.'

'Except when you're on business trips.'

'I always stay in hotels with pools.'

'Of course.' Mavros rang the bell.

The door opened as far as the chain allowed.

Mavros nudged Rachel forward. She introduced herself in English. The old man replied in a different language and she shook her head.

'Another Judezmo speaker,' she said. 'Over to you.'

The chain was removed and they were welcomed with old-fashioned warmth, their host smiling and bowing. Baruh Natzari was small and shrivelled, his head completely bald and the skin brown. The loose clothes he wore were clean and ironed, and he moved with surprising agility. He turned to them in the well-appointed living room that smelled of old books and floor polish, dark eyes twinkling.

'What can I offer you?' he said to Mavros in Greek. 'I usually have a brandy about now.'

Rachel shook her head, but Mavros wanted to keep the old man company. He watched as glasses of brandy and water were filled with a steady hand. A bowl of pistachios was pushed towards them across a low table.

'Sit down, sit down,' their host said. 'I like to stay on my feet. Don't let it bother you.'

In fact, his constant movements were a distraction. Mavros tried to ignore them as he consulted

Rachel about what to ask.

'Mr Natzari,' he said, 'Miss Samuel–'

'First names,' the old man said, with a cackle. 'I am Baruh, she is Rachel and you are...'

'Alex.'

'Proceed, Alex.'

Mavros smiled. 'You weren't by any chance a lawyer, were you?'

'Indeed. My forensic manner is so obvious?'

'To me, yes. But then I see a lot of lawyers.'

'Too bad. But you don't want to know about my former profession.'

Mavros shrugged. 'I always find it useful to hear as much as possible from the people I interview.' He glanced at Rachel. 'I'm not sure about my client.'

There was another cackle as Baruh Natzari looked at the card Mavros had given him. 'Missing-persons specialist? You are a private investigator like in the old noir films?'

'Of sorts. I drink too much on occasion, but I've given up smoking and short-lived love affairs. And I don't have a gun.'

'Ha! I think I like you, young man. And who are you looking for now? I received a message about the Samuel family. I must admit I haven't thought about any of them for decades.'

Rachel stared at Mavros and he realised he hadn't translated for some time. He did so and she told him what to say.

'Mr ... Baruh, the Samuel in question is Rachel's great-uncle, Aron.'

The change in the old man was immediate. He stopped hopping about and moved to the sofa, sitting down as if his strings had been cut.

'Aron... Aron Samuel?'

Mavros and Rachel exchanged glances.

'But Aron Samuel has been dead since Auschwitz-Birkenau was evacuated.'

'You're sure of that?'

This time the laugh was sardonic. 'We, the prisoners, could be sure of nothing. The Germans were the ones who kept detailed records.'

'Many of which were destroyed, although we are looking through recently discovered ones now.'

'And why is that, may I ask?'

'Do you know Ester Broudo?'

Baruh nodded. 'A good woman. We were never close, but we often met at community events over the years. Still do, although she doesn't get about much these days.'

'Did you attend the wedding of–' Mavros looked at his notes – 'Ilias Tsiako and Stella Vital the week before last?'

'Of course. I am a distant relative of Ilias.'

Mavros translated and saw Rachel's eyes widen.

'Mrs Broudo said that she saw Aron Samuel outside the synagogue. She is quite certain of it. I don't suppose you saw him.'

Baruh Natzari's eyes were suddenly glazed. 'Saw a dead man? How would that be possible?'

'How can you be sure Aron died in Auschwitz?'

The old man was the distracted one now. Mavros repeated the question..

'Never mind... never mind that. What else did Ester tell you?'

Mavros translated, then asked Rachel if he

124

should repeat the old woman's words. She nodded, her lips tight.

'She said that Aron Samuel was a traitor and a murderer, and that he was responsible for the deaths of her family. She didn't – wouldn't – explain what she meant.'

'I'm not surprised... I mean, although she has always meant well, Ester never got over the loss of her relatives, especially her mother, whom she doted on.'

It was clear that Natzari was prevaricating.

'Did you see Aron in the camp?' Mavros pressed.

'We called it the Lager. Not ... not often.'

'He wasn't in the same hut or on work details as you?'

'You seem well informed about events that took place years before you were born, Alex Mavro.'

He held up the book his mother had published.

'Ach, *Years in Hell*. I have read it, of course. You think the so called eye-witnesses tell the whole story? They were the lucky ones. Not only did they survive, but they escaped the worst of it, the true Gehenna.'

'Ask him to explain,' Rachel said, leaning forward.

But the old man's lips remained firmly closed.

FOURTEEN

'The good news is that you get more food, better clothes and more comfortable beds.'

We stared at our new capo, a Jew from Ioannina called Valais. We had been marched to the rear of the Lager, where flames and oily black smoke were spewing from the squat chimneys. None of us had it in him to ask what the bad news was. We found out soon enough.

Valais pointed to the gate in the high barbed-wire fence. 'The trucks bring them through there.' He led us to a low building and down steps to an open door. The smell inside was more disturbing than the burnt-meat stench outside; here it was almost alive, the warm stink of unwashed bodies. Members of the Sonderkommando – the special unit – were taking clothes, men's, women's and children's, from hooks, piling up pairs of shoes, many tied together in pairs, and running their fingers over cuffs and hems. Jewellery and coins were tossed into cans, though I saw some items being slipped into the men's pockets.

'They think they're going to have a shower,' Valais said, outside a steel door with a small glass peephole. It was unlocked and he pulled it open.

Now the odour that filled our nasal passages and lungs was miasmic, worse than anything on the trains: excrement, urine, vomit, blood, and something non-human, a faint chemical bite that

126

infected everything else.

And then we saw them. We knew our people were being killed, even though we had hidden that in the deepest recesses of our minds. Now we could no longer ignore the truth. Men of the Sonderkommando were dragging naked bodies from tangled heaps to a lift at the side of the white-tiled building. There were pipes and showerheads under the ceiling. A passing SS man saw the direction of our gaze.

'Letzte dusche für Juden!' he shouted, grinning widely. 'Save us, O God,' started one of my companions.

'None of that in here,' the capo ordered, swinging his length of rubber hose close to the man. He seemed to have gone mad in the space of minutes – hands over his ears, thumbs closing his nostrils and eyes tightly shut. Moaning, he sank to his knees.

Valais squatted beside him. 'Do you want to join them?' he said, forcing open the prisoner's eyes. 'Go on like this and you will, I promise.' The capo thought he was malingering.

I and the others couldn't help staring at the bodies. They were covered in blood and shit, the oldest and smallest at the bottom of the heap. Their mouths were open and their eyes bulging. Many had scratches and deeper wounds all over them.

Valais tried to haul our companion to his feet. The SS man came back and laughed. He gave orders to the capo and together they dragged the man outside. There was a muffled shot a few seconds later.

'There is your warning,' Valais said, returning alone. 'Knaus is an unforgiving swine. Follow me.'

We went towards the heap of bodies, stepping over them to get to the rear door. Then we followed the capo up a narrow stair and found ourselves in an enclosed courtyard. The roar of the furnaces was deafening. Three bodies – an emaciated old man, a woman with a recently shattered arm, and a small girl – were arranged on a steel plate and then slid into one of the ovens, the door slamming shut. The men immediately went over to the mound of bodies that had been brought up from the gas chamber and dragged out another three.

'Loading the ovens is skilled work,' Valais said. 'You won't be doing that for a while.' He took us into a side room.

Another of my companions let out a groan, but immediately silenced himself. Men of the Sonderkommando were wrenching gold teeth from the mouths of the recently killed with steel pliers. Nearby, others were cutting off the hair of women and girls.

'They came straight from the train,' Valais said. 'The Germans use the hair, I don't know what for. They melt down the gold from the teeth, of course.'

'Where...' My mouth was drier than it had ever been. I had a flash of my grandmothers and Dario. Had the three of them been placed together in the same oven? Had their mixed ashes been raked out, as I'd seen other grim-faced men doing? Had Isaak been burned here too?

128

'What?' Valais demanded, leaning closer.

'Where will we work?'

'You start at the beginning. It's easy enough. You help our people on their last journey.'

Help them, I thought. No honourable man can do that. Then I remembered our short-lived companion. There was only one choice to be made here. This was the end of the world: you either lived or you died. I wanted to survive.

We stood around watching until the twelve-hour shift ended, then joined the rest of the men. We were marched under guard to a hut wired off from the rest of the Lager. People on the other side stared at us. Their eyes were full of hate and I couldn't meet them after a few looks. In the more spacious accommodation we were told to exchange our striped rags for whatever fitted from a heap of suits, shirts and underclothes. Some were filthy, but others seemed to have been deloused. By the end of the process we looked like scarecrows, few of the garments being narrow enough for our half-starved bodies, but incongruously well-clad ones.

The soup and bread arrived. It was true, the helpings were larger. I ate beyond the point that my guts started to protest. I had to focus on my own body. Only it matters, I told myself. I couldn't do anything for our people here. I hadn't been able to save my grandmothers and my brother-in-law, let alone my brother. Then I dropped the lump of bread. I had suddenly realised. My mother, my father, Miriam and Golda. Would they pass through the final gates too? Was I to 'help' the remaining members of my family die?

'What is it?' asked Anjil Gerson. He had been with me on the tour. I didn't know him before, but he was also from Thessaloniki and a couple of years older than me. He was unusually well built. His father was a docker and had got him a job in the port when he was fourteen.

'Nothing,' I said, giving him a cracked smile. 'At last my belly's full.'

'I could get used to this,' he replied.

'Listen to the new boys,' said a mocking voice from the bunk above. 'He says he could get used to this.'

The men around us started to laugh. Unlike in the other huts, the block commander stood by without laying in to them to restore order.

'They haven't even ushered a crowd into the changing room and they think they're kings of the Lager!' shouted a man with a deep scar on his cheek.

We could only wait until the noise died down.

'Listen, son,' said the man who'd started the rumpus. 'Nobody lasts more than four months in the Sonderkommando. You think the SS want witnesses to what goes on here?' He grunted. 'If you're lucky you'll have the honour of loading my corpse into the oven.'

No one was laughing now.

Anjil hunched over, his chin pressed to his chest, but I stood up and walked to the latrine, my head held high. I wasn't proud that something inside me wanted to stay alive so badly, no matter the cost in terms of human decency or civilisation, both Jewish and Western. I couldn't save anyone except myself and the only way I could do that was to become like the animals in the SS. At least there was no shortage of examples.

FIFTEEN

'That was helpful,' Rachel said, in the taxi back to the centre.

'Confirmation of sorts, I'd say.' They'd been ushered out by the old man after his refusal to speak further about Aron Samuel. 'There does seem to be a dark side to your great-uncle.'

'Seem being the operative word. How would we never have heard about it?'

'Maybe people didn't want to burden you. Besides, your father was long gone from Thessaloniki. I doubt his existence was even remembered.'

'Until he started donating to the community.'

'True. When was that?'

'I'm not sure. Ever since I can remember.'

Mavros thought about that. If Ester Broudo really had seen Aron Samuel, perhaps Baruh Natzari had been in touch with him; even met him.

'What?' Rachel asked, grabbing the front seat as the taxi hit a deep pothole.

He told her, adding, 'What if Baruh was covering for your great-uncle? He didn't actually say anything against him. In that case, I should keep an eye on his building – see who comes in

131

and goes out. It isn't as if there's anything more pressing to do until Allegra and ... Allegra and my Communist contact get back to us.'

She was watching him carefully. 'All right.'

Mavros told the driver to turn round, responding to his swearing with some of his own.

'You know,' he said, 'there's one thing I don't understand. If Aron's been alive all these years, why hasn't he got in touch with your father?'

'You answered that question before – he didn't know where he was.'

'He could easily have found out he was in Paris. The company is large.'

Rachel looked out to the seafront. 'I suppose so. Maybe he never knew that a Samuel runs it. Or he's senile.'

'There are numerous possibilities,' Mavros admitted. 'Stop here,' he told the driver. 'I'll talk to you later. Don't give him a tip.'

'I wasn't intending to.'

Mavros got out and walked away. He'd met some icy women in his time, but Rachel Samuel took several boxes of luxury French biscuits.

He found an Internet café with a view of Baruh's block and settled down with a newspaper and a *sketo* that was nowhere near the Fat Man's standards. The murder of the Jordanian was all over the front page, with a photo of a red swastika on a green steel gate. The police spokesman was tight-lipped, saying it was too early to make statements beyond the victim's name and age – Tareq Momani, 42, a fully legal immigrant – and that he was shot three times at close range. As yet no witnesses had come forward.

Mavros paid for the use of a computer, keeping an eye on the old man's street door, and entered the dead man's name in a search engine. There were a couple of links that referred to an older and a younger man, and then one that made Mavros sit up straight. It led to an article in a periodical published by expatriate Arabs in London over a year ago – 'Why Don't the Jordanian Authorities Arrest This Man?' According to the writers, Tareq Momani was a noted dissident, one they didn't approve of at all. He was suspected of being behind several suicide bombings in Israel, as well as having connections with al-Qaeda. Could it be, they suggested, that the Jordanian secret police were using Momani for their own purposes?

A middle-aged woman entered Baruh Natzari's block, her hair covered by a dark brown scarf. Mavros found the *Jerusalem Post*'s website and entered the victim's name. Nothing came up. He tried other Israeli newspapers that had sites in English. Zilch. Then he saw the woman emerge across the street, the old man beside her. Mavros paid for his coffee and made for the door. He stayed on the other side of the street from the couple, about five metres behind them. Neither spoke and the expression on the woman's face was one of bored resignation. It didn't look like she was related to or friendly with Baruh. Was she some kind of Jewish community volunteer? That impression gained credence when they went into a supermarket. Mavros crossed the road and stood outside. He caught glimpses of his targets as they passed between the aisles. The old man paid and they returned to his block, the woman carrying two bags to his one. A few minutes later she was back on the pavement, heading towards the seafront.

Mavros was about to go back to the café, having crossed the road, when he saw Baruh reappear, reflected in the window. The old man raised his arm and got into the taxi that stopped. It continued down the one-way street.

Another blue and white cab drove up and Mavros waved to it.

'Follow that cab,' he said.

As usual the instruction provoked laughter. Mavros was amused too. It was the closest he ever got to playing Humphrey Bogart. The taxi in front turned right on to a wide avenue.

'Are you a betting man?' the elderly driver asked. 'Five euros they're going to the airport.'

'You're on,' Mavros replied. Baruh Natzari was carrying no luggage, not even an umbrella.

They approached the airport, but the taxi ahead drove past the road that led to it.

'Double or quits?' the driver asked.

Mavros laughed, then recognised the lie of the land: the sea a few kilometres to his right; the marshland of the Axios and Aliakmonas river deltas across the water; and the great peak of Olympus in its snow-capped glory to the south-west.

'Ayia Triadha,' he said.

'A good choice. I'll have to go for Peraia.' A few minutes later the driver groaned as they drove through the latter village.

Mavros struggled to recognise the outskirts of

the resort. It was much larger than it had been in 1971. Then they reached the seafront and he instantly had a flash of his mother in a deckchair, Anna and her boy splashing each other, and Andonis and he racing along the hot sand.

'He's stopping by that taverna,' the cabbie said. 'What do you want me to do?'

'Go past and turn round about a hundred metres further on.' Mavros watched with his head lowered as Baruh Natzari got out and walked spryly into the restaurant.

'What do you want me to do?' the driver asked.

'Stay here, please. Forget the ten euros.'

'A bet's a bet. Besides it's a good day for a walk.' The grizzled man handed Mavros a card. 'Call me if I'm not here when you get back. I won't be far.'

'Right.' Mavros was pleased that he'd fallen in with an honourable taxi driver. He walked back towards the place Baruh had entered, slowing as he got close. The taverna had clear plastic sheets around its outside tables and gas burners were warming the few customers.

The Auschwitz survivor was sitting opposite a much younger man, who had medium-length curly black hair and heavy features. Mavros took several photos with his phone on maximum zoom. They were nothing better than average in quality, but might come in handy later. He stepped behind the wall of a tourist shop that was closed. He wasn't able to hear them, but there was something he could do. He pressed buttons on his phone.

'Allegra? It's Alex Mavros.'

135

'Hi. I haven't got anything substantive for you yet.'

'Don't worry, I didn't expect you to have. There's someone else I'd like to ask you about.'

'Go ahead.'

'Baruh Natzari.'

'Ah, Baruh. He's a character, all right.'

'I know, we met him earlier. He clammed up about Aron Samuel. Any idea why that might be'?'

There was the sound of keys clacking. 'Hold on while I check my archive. Baruh is one of the last from the Lager still in Thessaloniki. My grandfather knew him and I remember meeting him when I was young. He was unusual because he was funny in a restrained kind of way. Like all who came back, he was carrying a burden.'

'There weren't too many jokes this morning, though I liked him well enough.'

'He knows death is near. Imagine what it must be like to have been young and seen so many of your community murdered or starved or weakened into catching the most disgusting diseases. Now his own death is close, he's struggling to take it in. He doesn't come to community gatherings any more.'

'He was at the Tsiako–Vital wedding.'

'Was he? I didn't see him. Here we are. Natzari, Baruh, born in the city on February 16th 1925, Auschwitz-Birkenau survivor, parents and all close family killed there, returned 1947, avoided conscription into the National Army because of chronic dysentery, fought for return of family home and eye-glass dispensary (case 178/2901/

1950), awarded compensation, March 9th 1956; established antique shop in Kalamaria, 1957. Deeds passed to Jewish Community, September 25th 1992. Weekly visit from JC volunteer since 2003.'

Mavros had been taking notes. 'Interesting, but not informative about any link to Aron Samuel.'

'Hold on, I'm checking the transports to Auschwitz. No, they weren't on the same one. I'll run his name through the Lager archive and see if I can find a connection.' Allegra Harari paused. 'You know, Alex, this is hardly likely to help you find Aron. I mean, so many years...'

'Give me your email address. I'm going to send you a photo.' He fiddled with his phone and managed to dispatch one of the shots he'd taken of Baruh and his companion. 'Tell me if you recognise the young man.'

After about a minute Allegra replied, 'No. It's a bit blurred, but I'm pretty sure he isn't a member of our community.'

'All right, thanks. We'll be in touch.'

Mavros watched Baruh and his companion. They were having an animated conversation. Then the waiter was called. It looked like the bill had been asked for. He rang the driver.

'Can you come now, please? About twenty metres before the taverna?'

'Yes, sir, right away, sir,' came the reply, in English. Like many Greeks, the cabbie had spent time in the US; or had a predilection for old movies.

Mavros got in when he arrived. A few minutes later a new midrange Peugeot drove up, another young man at the wheel.

'Follow that car?' the driver asked.

'Go, go, go,' Mavros replied, in English.

They went.

The Fat Man waited for his old friend and comrade in a café in Victoria Square, about a kilometre
north of Omonia. He never tasted the coffee made
by his former competitors, but couldn't resist
cakes. He was on his second piece of *sokolatina*
when the familiar figure approached.

'Yiorgo.'

'Apostole.'

The other man, in his late sixties and with an
extremely wrinkled face, sat down opposite and
offered his hand. 'That chocolate sludge will kill
you.'

'Not as quickly as those.' The Fat Man pointed
his fork at the foul-smelling cigarette between
Apostolos's yellowed fingers.

'See you in hell.'

'But we don't believe in it.'

'Sure we do. It's where we meet up with the
great comrades of the past and kick the shit out
of the rich.'

Yiorgos beckoned to the waiter.

'Orange juice,' his friend said.

'It's too late to get healthy.'

'Thanks. That's what I told the wife, but she and
the doctor don't agree. Of course, they didn't
spend five years in the mountains or ten in prison.'

'Not forgetting the three on Makronisos.' The
Fat Man had miraculously escaped being sent to
the notorious prison island off the coast of Attica

138

during the dictatorship, but he was in hiding for its seven-year rule. 'They were what turned your face into a shrunken pomegranate.'

'Hm,' Apostolos said, screwing up his eyes as he took a sip of the freshly squeezed juice. 'Yeurch.'

'I should have thought the nicotine engrained in your mouth and throat would hugely improve the taste.'

The comrade extended an arm, fingers spread apart, to send him to Hades' realm as he drained his glass. 'So,' he said, lighting another cigarette, 'why the sudden interest in Jewish party members?'

Yiorgos knew he couldn't get anywhere without satisfying Apostolos's curiosity, even though the archive search had been unofficial.

'That Aron Samuel who was supposed to have died in Auschwitz? Someone saw him in Thessaloniki last week. Reportedly.'

The comrade was almost invisible behind acrid smoke. 'What do you care?'

'My friend Mavros is working the case.'

The smoke was waved away. 'Spyros's boy?'

The Fat Man nodded. 'He could do with a haircut, but his heart's in the right place.'

'I hope so. Because Aron Samuel is on the hyper list.'

'What? Why?'

Apostolos coughed harshly. 'You know how the system works. It was hard enough for me to find the first of those out. Why he's hyper is well beyond my abilities.'

Yiorgos regretted eating the two pieces of cake. When someone was classified as hyper – as in hyper-not to be talked about – it meant one of two things: either the subject was or had been engaged in top-secret work for the party; or he or she had been cast into the deepest of outer darknesses. Whichever was the case with Aron Samuel, it was bad news for Alex.

'I told you that stuff was poison,' Apostolos said, blowing out another pollution cloud.

The Fat Man had an exaggerated coughing fit and then called Mavros.

SIXTEEN

The next day, those of us new to the Sonder-kommando were woken in the grey Polish dawn. We were given bread and margarine, the latter a rare sight in the Lager.

'Don't eat too much,' Valais said, leaning against a bunk. 'Your stomachs are going to be tested today.'

Anjil's mouth was full of bread. 'I thought we had to work up to the worst jobs,' he said, spraying crumbs over his grey suit jacket.

'You think there's anything pleasant here?' Valais turned away. 'Come on.'

He marched us through the enclosed area around our huts. Ahead, the smoke from the chimneys was less dark and the air clearer.

'There's a transport from Greece coming in,' the capo said.

Anjil and I exchanged glances.

140

'What will we have to do?'

'What I told you yesterday. Help them into the changing room and get them undressed. They're to have a shower, right? They all have to take their clothes off. The women will be embarrassed, but you have to talk them into it. If they ask about the chimneys, tell them that prisoners' old clothes are being burned.'

I didn't feel as bad about it as Anjil, who was gasping for breath and muttering prayers. Then it struck me that I might see people I knew. Would I be able to lie to them about their fate?

We were lined up near the fence inside the extermination compound. Apart from the machine-gunners in the towers, most of them well into middle age, there were SS men moving around. Knaus ran a steely eye over us and then grinned as he talked to Valais.

'The sergeant hopes you enjoy your first day at work,' the capo said brusquely, his back straight; but there was pity in his eyes, I could see that.

The SS men stiffened as a truck containing officers came through the gate. I recognised the smiling doctor from the selection at the station. He walked with a pair of other officers to the low wall near the steps that led down to the changing room. Their uniforms and boots were spotless, as were those of their guards, who were armed with machine-pistols.

In the distance I heard the sound of engines, several of them, grinding along under heavy loads. Without thinking I looked over my shoulder and instantly received a blow from Knaus's short whip. He glared at me and then sniggered manically. Valais shook his head as if he was disappointed in me when the SS man walked away.

The trucks arrived. As they drove into the compound, I saw they were packed with standing prisoners; old men with long ringlets of hair below the brims of their hats, women and children – what had happened to Miriam and Golda? – and people who were clearly beyond physical labour. SS men signalled to them to move forwards till they were tightly packed outside the building.

Knaus bellowed an order and Valais nodded to us. We followed him to the front of the changing room. After more trucks deposited their exhausted cargoes, the doctor stood up on the wall and started to speak, his voice loud but reasonable. Valais translated.

'Welcome to Auschwitz-Birkenau, where you will find satisfaction in work and well-earned repose. But first you must have a disinfecting shower. It is unfortunate that the conditions of your journey were so difficult – for that, you must blame the Greek railway system. They failed to supply sufficient carriages and those used were fit for animals.' He smiled widely as Valais got his message across to the masses: there must have been between two and three thousand in the compound by now. This false concern and readiness to blame others were standard features of the way the SS gulled their victims into co-operating in their own execution. And it worked. People listened intently and did not complain, though the SS men and their dogs nearby played a part.

'As you proceed to the changing room and showers, you will find helpers of your own kind. Please follow their instructions and move quickly. There are many of you and we don't wish to cause you further discomfort.'

A hum of voices speaking Judezmo started. Valais got down from the wall and sent some of us down to the changing room. Anjil was placed at the top of the stairs. His eyes were wild and I saw Knaus watching him.

Then the flow of people started. They were almost all from Thessaloniki. I directed them into the long room, telling them to hang their clothes on the numbered hooks.

'But we can't undress with men present,' said an elderly woman, her bloodshot eyes wide.

I steeled myself. 'But you must, madam. There is no time to separate you. Please, is this your daughter? She will help you.'

My words rang hollow, but the women did as I said, moving to the far end of the cavernous chamber. I realised that I had power over them, even if it was false and evil. The truth was, I liked that power. I didn't even bother trying to persuade myself that I was making death easier for them.

The children started wailing, frightened by the crush and the sight of aged limbs and shrunken abdomens. Their mothers did what they could to calm them, some putting even their older offspring to the breast.

'Tell me this is true,' one of the women demanded. 'Promise me no harm will come to my children.'

143

'I promise,' I said, without hesitation. 'You will have your shower and come back here to get dressed again.'

'But our clothes are filthy.'

'You will be issued with clean ones later.'

'You promise? As one of us? You are from Thessaloniki, yes?'

I nodded.

'What is your name?'

'Aron Samuel, son of Iosif.'

'The jeweller?'

'Yes. He is in the camp too.' That wasn't a lie, at least not a knowing one. He could have been dead by now.

'Swear on the name of your mother – what is it?'

'Sophie. She too is working here.' Again, I was guessing.

'Swear on her name that you are not deceiving us.'

I did as she asked and she moved on with her children. My heart was beating no faster than normal. Perjury and oath-breaking were meaningless in that hell.

After what seemed like an eternity, the last of the naked people went into the gas chamber. The SS and others of us formed a line behind them. The doubters had managed to stay to the rear, but they were swept up, this time with little pretence of decency. There was a loud hubbub in the chamber beyond, people pointing at the pipes and shower heads.

'Do not believe them!' one old man shouted. 'They will kill–' He went down as an SS man bludgeoned him from behind. Anjil, his lips trembling, and I were detailed to shove the motionless body past the heavy door.

Knaus looked around. 'All in? Very good, seal the chamber.'

The door was slammed to and bolted.

'You new men,' Valais said. 'Stay here.' A couple of SS men hung back, their weapons pointing in our direction.

I heard the sound of another vehicle outside and caught a glimpse of a truck with a Red Cross on its side. I soon found out that was another SS ploy. The Zyklon B granules were transported to the gas chamber in a vehicle that supposedly brought succour to the suffering. No doubt Nazi leaders found the irony amusing.

Knaus returned from the entrance, almost salivating. He spoke to our capo excitedly.

'The sergeant hopes that you enjoy the show,' Valais said stolidly. 'He wants you to pay special attention to the sounds.'

We waited in line, Anjil's whole body quivering and twitching, even after one of the SS men kicked him hard on the back of his leg. The only symptom of potential concern that I displayed was a dry mouth, but that was standard in the Lager and may not have been due to the impending spectacle.

Then the screaming started. There was pounding on the other side of the door, both from hands and lowered shoulders.

'Look!' Knaus ordered, pointing to the viewing panel. 'Look!' No translation was necessary.

When my turn came, I watched writhing bodies and mouths gaping to take in some small part of the poisoned air that was still pure. Eyes were protruding and men tried to climb over the children and elderly in the mistaken belief that there was clean air under the ceiling.

Anjil lasted a few seconds at the spy-hole before he collapsed. Valais went to help him, but Knaus drew his pistol. He placed it a few centimetres above the nape of Anjil's neck and fired. The shot was hardly audible, though the noise from within was subsiding. I felt only relief – that Anjil had been spared further horror but, more important, that I had survived.

Knaus grinned at me. I had passed the test.

SEVENTEEN

The taxi driver stayed about fifty metres behind the Peugeot as it headed in the direction of the airport.

Mavros's phone rang. 'What news from the city of fat?'

'Charming.' Yiorgos didn't sound put out. 'Have I got bad news for you.'

'Oh, great. Spill your – no, on second thoughts just spell it out.'

'Your Aron Samuel's a hyper.'

'What?'

'You heard me.'

'Is that it? Have you any idea why?'

The Fat Man laughed. 'Not even your father would have been able to squeeze that information out. Though he might have known, of course.'

'So was Aron pro or anti the party?'

'First-name terms now, eh?'

Mavros watched as the Peugeot went past the airport and joined the ring road. 'You know how it is – you get close to the people you're looking for.'

'Close to a dead man? Nice. You realise he could be long dead. Hyper classification continues after death. Or have you found something out up there that suggests otherwise?'

'Not really.'

'Predictably vague. Have you seen Shimon Raphael?'

'Yes, he sent his best. He's following up the party angle here.'

'You know he won't find anything. When Samuel was hypered, his name would have been removed from the files in all the offices.'

Mavros grabbed the seat in front. 'Jesus.' The Peugeot had suddenly rocketed away. 'Can you keep up with him?'

The elderly driver shook his head. 'One, this heap is no racing car and, two, I'm not breaking the speed limit.'

'Shit!'

'What's going on?' Yiorgos asked.

'We're in the process of losing the car we're tailing.'

'You see, if I'd been with you, that would never have happened.'

Mavros laughed, looking at the next exit but seeing no sign of the Peugeot. 'No, because you'd have lost him a long time ago.'

'What are you going to do?'

'Good question. I'll call Shimon and tell him about the hyper. Talk to you later.'

The cabbie looked at him in the mirror.

'Where to now?'

Mavros sighed. 'Back to the centre – the Electra Palace.'

'Nice.'

'If you like that kind of thing.' He decided to pick the driver's brains – he'd often found out useful things in taxis, especially in towns and cities outside Athens. 'Did you hear about that foreigner who was shot?'

'The Jordanian? Probably taken out by one of his own.'

The cab slowed as the traffic increased nearer the city.

'What makes you say that?'

The driver laughed. 'Because they're animals.'

Mavros took a deep breath. The guy hadn't struck him as a racist. 'You mean Muslims?'

'No! I don't give a shit about what they get up to if they're honest. I'm talking about gangsters. The Arabs here are into drugs, whores, whatever you like.'

'Don't the local outfits take exception?'

'Yes, but the Arabs have got connections in the Middle East and they've got big money.'

'You know there were swastikas sprayed at the scene?'

The cabbie gave him a suspicious look over his shoulder. 'What are you, a cop?'

'No, I just watch a lot of American TV.'

'Uh-huh. Anyway, they're an obvious blind.'

148

Mavros leaned forward. 'How do you mean?'

'Think about it. They're trying to put the blame on the Phoenix Rises.'

They turned off the ring road and went down a narrow Street between apartment blocks towards the city centre. It wasn't long before one of the neo-Nazi group's graffiti appeared on a wall.

'The Phoenix Rises did put several Muslims in hospital,' Mavros said. 'And there's a swastika-like shape at the bottom of their symbol.'

The driver sighed. 'Yes, but the swastika itself isn't used by them. They're too chicken.'

Mavros had been about to ask him if he was member of the Phoenix Rises. It now looked like he might be something even worse. He decided to raise the temperature.

'Fifty thousand Jews from Thessaloniki were murdered in the death camps. What do you think of that?'

The cabbie's eyes were in the mirror again. 'What do I think of it? The city became Greek at last.'

'I suppose you liked the Colonels too.'

'Until they lost their grip, yes, I did.'

Andonis's smiling ghost rose before Mavros. He managed to restrain himself, but decided he'd deduct the ten euros he'd won from the bill to mark the founding of his very own Scottish-Greek Jewish Solidarity League.

Rachel Samuel had been on the encrypted site again. Her instructions were to monitor the reaction to the hit and report. To that end she contacted the assassin, who had a source in the local Jewish community. As the hours went by, more information was put in the public domain, and more people and agencies commented. She had little interest in what the Greek government and parties in parliament said. They all uttered the usual platitudes about regrettable violence and, depending on their position on immigration, its either unacceptable or inevitable results. She had to wait until mid-afternoon until the Phoenix Rises released a statement.

In opposition to the supposedly popular parties, who bribe voters openly and under the table, we shed no crocodile tears at the passing of the notorious Jordanian gangster Momani. The real scandal is why he was granted residence in Greece. He was rich and no doubt paid off high-ranking people. But let no one dare suggest the Phoenix Rises had anything to do with his murder. There have already been insinuations that the presence of the swastika incriminates us. We strongly deny any involvement. Even if we had wished to remove the parasite from Greek society, we would hardly have been foolish enough to point to ourselves in this way. Some have said we deliberately avoided using our own emblem, but could not resist making reference to the Third Reich. Let the proof be provided. We would never use the sacred symbol of Nazism in such a crude way, not least on the body of a Semite. Though let it be remembered that the Reich had healthy relations with the many Arabs opposed to international Jewry.

In order to protest our innocence and repeat our core beliefs, the Phoenix Rises will this evening rally in Eleftherias Square, where leader Makis Kalogirou will speak.

150

Are You with Us?
Long Live Greece, purified of all contamination!
Long Live Freedom!

Rachel went to the bathroom and washed her face. Anger and loathing were coursing through her veins, but there was no evidence of them on her features. She had been well trained. Still, she needed an outlet and decided to call her father. They spoke in French, but their version of the language would only have been fully understood by the Jews of Paris. She told him about the little that she and Mavros had discovered.

'This Ester Broudo, you still don't know why she said those things about Aron?'

'She could be deranged, though Rabbi Rousso thinks not.' She described Baruh Natzari's refusal to talk about her great-uncle.

'Strange. Maybe there really is something for you to investigate.'

'I think there is and so does Alex Mavros. He's following the old man as we speak.'

'How is the long-haired detective doing?'

'He is ... competent. And he hasn't told me everything.'

Her father laughed. 'You'll get it out of him. More money will convince him, though only if that's strictly necessary.'

'I'm not sure that will work. There are other ways.'

Eliezer Samuel paused. 'I leave that to your discretion.'

Rachel told him about the Phoenix Rises' proclamation.

'Disgusting animals. Stay away from them. There are always anti-Semites, no matter where you go. You'd have thought they've achieved their end in Thessaloniki, with only a few hundred of our community left.'

'We aren't their only target,' she said, 'even though they make threats to the local Jews. There are many more Muslim immigrants, legal and otherwise.'

'Stay away, I tell you. Uncle Aron can have nothing to do with them.'

'All right, Papa. We'll speak again soon.'

'I love you, my little girl.'

Rachel cut the connection. She was used to her father's displays of affection, but she couldn't reciprocate. If she loved anyone, it would be him. But she didn't think she had that ability – it either wasn't in her nature or had been expurgated by the things she had learned.

She called Mavros. His number was engaged.

'What?' said a surprised Shimon Raphael. 'Hypers are pretty rare.'

'They are.' Mavros had stopped the taxi at the White Tower and was walking back to the hotel, phone to his ear.

'It may explain why there's nothing in the official files here. I asked a former comrade to look. But I've still got other sources on the job.'

'What do you think about the killing of the Jordanian?'

The customs broker grunted. 'I thought you'd ask me about that. What, you reckon Aron Samuel shot him?'

The idea hadn't entered Mavros's mind, but now it was there he tried to process it. 'He'll be eighty if he's alive.'

'But the swastikas are interesting.'

'Swastikas on a Muslim. Is it true the dead man was a gangster?'

'Not that I've heard. Some people are bound to say so.' Mavros was still wrangling with the idea. 'Why would Aron be involved in a murder like that?'

'You're the investigator,' Shimon said, with a loud laugh. 'I just toss in off-the-wall ideas.'

'Thanks. Did you get anywhere with the Tsiako–Vital wedding?'

'Kind of. The Vitals don't seem to have had any connection with Samuel – they're originally from Florina and only moved here ten years ago. The Tsiakos are more interesting.'

Mavros felt the faint tug on the end of the line that sometimes came out of nowhere to break a case. 'In what way?'

Shimon exhaled loudly. 'Well, it's a version of the old story. The only person who escaped the Holocaust was his grandmother. She was sheltered by a Christian family and later married another survivor, a Zvi Tsiako. But get this. He was the same age as Aron Samuel and he attended the same school.'

'That *is* interesting. What happened to him?'

'He was in Auschwitz-Birkenau and then in various displaced-persons camps until he finally made his way back to Greece in 1947. He missed the Civil War and built up a decent business as a cloth wholesaler, before he died of a heart attack

153

in the 90s. His son Yitzhak, Ilias's father, runs the company now and the bridegroom is a junior manager.'

'Do you know Yitzhak?'

'Yes. He's a good sort. Very keen on chess.'

'Can you arrange a meeting for me? Don't mention Aron Samuel. Say I'm a historian.'

'All right, I'll let you know. Listen, I have to go. The bastards from the Phoenix Rises are having a demonstration in the square near my office this evening and I'm shutting up early.'

'That wouldn't be Eleftherias Square, would it?' Mavros was looking at his map and saw the place's proximity to the port.

'The place the Nazis humiliated the Jews in 1942 – yes, it would.'

'Lovely. How do they get a permit from the council?'

'A good question, the answer to which involves rectangular, coloured pieces of paper. The spirit of collaboration lives! See you.'

Mavros put the phone in his pocket and looked ahead. The square in question was to the right of the seafront, close to the cranes. He decided to take a look, but his phone rang before he got far.

'I want a report,' Rachel said. 'Where are you?'

'Close. Give me ten minutes.'

He turned towards the hotel. His client's daughter was as demanding as ever. She wasn't going to like the fact that he'd lost Baruh and his young companions one bit.

Mavros's phone rang again as he was washing his hands and face in his room.

'Alex, have you finished up there yet?'

'Niki, my love. I'm sorry. The case is beginning to drag.'

'What a surprise.'

'How are you?'

'How should I be?'

He groaned silently. This was the Niki who drove him round the bend. 'I don't know – tired after work?'

'Well, obviously. Try harder.'

He bit the dum-dum bullet. 'Em, worried about not getting pregnant?'

There was a peal of ironic laughter. 'Very good. You should take up darts.'

And throw them at your– Mavros banished the thought. 'No, thanks.'

'Fortunately my friend Maria is staying with me tonight.'

'Good.'

'Isn't it? Of course, you're one who should be here, not her. You, my lover, the father of my children to be.' She broke off and started to sob. Maria's voice could be heard in the background.

'I'll be back as soon as I can, Niki, honestly.' He knew how crap that sounded. 'Hang on, please.'

There were further moans and snuffles, then Maria came on the line.

'I'll take care of her, Alex,' she said sternly. 'But you owe it to her to get back. She's very shaky. Here, darling, say goodbye to him.'

'Bye, Alex,' Niki said sullenly.

'Bye, my love. I'll talk to–' The connection was cut.

'Bollocks,' Mavros said, in English.

155

Now he felt even less inclined to go and explain himself to the human chilblain down the corridor.

EIGHTEEN

We didn't only shepherd our people into the gas chamber. There were times when the crematoria couldn't take all the corpses. Then the SS had us dig pits. That was what saved me. It was a wet day and shovelling the black mud out was back-breaking labour. Even though we had better rations, we were still in poor physical condition, not least because of the twelve-hour shifts. After two days we needed long ladders to climb out of the great trench. The surface down there was treacherous. One of our number sank to his waist and we only got him out by tying a rope round him and hauling from the top. He screamed all the way. When we untied him, we saw why. One of his shoulders had been dislocated. Fortunately an SK member who had trained a football team in the life before the Lager managed to reset it. Otherwise the mud-covered man would have been the first occupant of the hole.

Knaus supervised our work, screaming at us when we paused to catch our breath. Valais followed his lead, but his heart wasn't in it. He'd been coughing for weeks and had begun to stoop. At last the SS man was satisfied. He sent one of the guards back to the compound. Soon more troops arrived, several with dogs, and formed a double column about two metres apart. Then, with screams and wailing, our people started to appear. They were naked, but no attempt was being made to hide their impending fate. Whips cracked and boots flew as they stumbled down the muddy path.

We were standing at the narrow edge of the pit, beside heaps of logs and barrels of fuel. I looked around, wondering if I could hide somewhere till night, then instantly dismissed the idea. I had to stay alive and that meant taking part in the horror.

Men and women of all ages, and children ranging from babies to teenagers, were brought to the long lip of earth. Their heads were shaved, so they'd been in the Lager for some time. A line of SS men stood in pairs. One pushed the prisoner to his or her knees, and the other fired a single shot from a small-calibre pistol into the back of their necks. Our people were then shoved into the trench and their places taken by the next victim. Knaus laughed as he fired, yelling to his men to speed the walking dead. Valais and I looked at each other. Our capo looked ready to drop. I suddenly thought of my family – my parents, Miriam and little Golda. Were they here? I forced myself to look. I saw none of them.

Many of those who had been shot were still alive when they hit the mud, their arms and legs twitching. One even raised her head – a young woman, who had tried to shield her breasts as she was pushed down the line.

'My baby!' she screamed in our tongue. 'My baby!'

SS men threw the small children straight into the pit – they weren't worth a bullet. They scrabbled around in the dirt, wailing piteously. Others in the SK closed their eyes, but I let the vision burn into my memory. It was the only way I could keep faith with my community – by witnessing its destruction. An idea gripped me. If I survived, I would avenge them.

Eventually a halt was called. Guards came to where we were standing and started pumping diesel over the victims. Then Knaus arrived, carrying several lengths of rough cotton. He lit them and handed them to us, speaking to Valais.

'Throw them in all over the trench,' the capo ordered.

We did as we were told without hesitation. The material burned quickly. There was a succession of thwumps as the fuel caught fire. The bottom of the trench turned into an inferno, the undead shrieking before they inhaled the burning air.

'Now the wood,' Valais said, trying to lift a log.

I helped him. The heavy pieces of wood slammed down on the bodies, and then the killing started again. It went on all day. Valais tried to follow the orders he was given, but his eyes were dim. It didn't surprise me when he threw himself into the flames after the third layer of bodies was ignited. He didn't writhe or struggle: a last demonstration of will before the death he craved or exhaustion?

Although I respected him, I was not moved. In fact, his sacrifice benefitted me immediately.

158

Knaus came over as I rolled one of the last logs into the pit.

'Valais was weak,' he said, his mouth close to my ear.

I had picked up enough Lager German to understand him.

'You're capo of these shithounds now.' He smacked me on the back and pointed to my eyes. 'I see what you are. You are like me.'

I gave him the smile he required. It wasn't as if I was lying. He was right. Fortunately there were no more prisoners in the line. A great cloud of greasy and foul-smelling smoke was blown over the fence.

I led my unit back to the compound. We were expecting to be sent to our hut, but the SS hadn't finished for the day.

'You see them?' Knaus asked.

I looked at the filthy men outside the changing room.

'You know them!' the SS man said triumphantly.

And I did. They were Sonderkommando men, those who'd been in service when we were drafted in. Heads lowered, they filed down the steps unsteadily.

'You don't need to help them,' Knaus said. 'They know what awaits them.'

Guards followed them in. I heard a solitary shout, then a burst of machine-pistol fire. One – only one – of our people had resisted. Soon they were all in the gas chamber and the door closed. We were sent round the back. I remembered the tough guy from our first night and wondered if I would find myself taking his body to the furnace.

After fifteen minutes the fans started to run. Soon afterwards the door on the crematoria side was opened. My men and I put on gas masks and went inside. The place of death was sparsely filled. SK men were executed separately from ordinary prisoners in case they incited resistance. I picked my way over the bodies. One man rolled over and gasped, his tongue extended like a gargoyle's. I gripped his head by the ears and smashed it against the concrete floor. I'd seen enough people go into the flames alive that day.

We buckled leather straps around each man's neck and dragged them to the lift. I hardly recognised any of them, so changed were they by the gas – no longer human beings, just pieces of filth-covered flesh to be disposed of. That was how the Nazis referred to prisoners. We were 'pieces', tattooed with numbers, our names erased before we were.

'Pinhas,' I mumbled, when I saw a fellow Thessaloniki Jew. 'I will remember you.'

And, as you hear, I have. A few hours later, they were particles of smoke and ash drifting over and into the chill waters of the Vistula. I was still a prisoner, but the beasts had made a mistake. They had given me more power. In the eyes of many people I would abuse it, furthering the ends of the SS; I would abase myself and collaborate – but I would stay alive. Now I had a motive even stronger than personal survival. I would make the executioners of my people pay.

NINETEEN

In her room Rachel interrogated Mavros in detail, breaking off to examine the photo of Baruh Natzari and the young man.

'Did they see you from the restaurant?' she asked, looking into his eyes.

'It's always possible when you have to hang around on your own. But I don't think so.'

'What about on the road from the seaside place to the dual carriageway, when there were three of them?'

'Maybe. I had the driver keep his distance, but there wasn't much traffic. Then again I was in a taxi, which is more anonymous.'

'And on the ring road?'

'There was much more traffic – cars, trucks *and* taxis.' Mavros didn't enjoy being put on the spot. 'It's perfectly possible that the driver decided to put his foot down for another reason. Maybe they had an appointment.'

Rachel's stare intensified. 'Do you really believe that?'

'Er, no. I think they spotted us. But that doesn't mean Baruh recognised me. I sat low down in the back.'

'That's something, I suppose.' She looked at her open laptop. 'What is this "hyper" classification you mentioned?'

Mavros explained, breaking off to take bites

from a room-service sandwich.

'So my great-uncle was either a Communist who had to be protected or who was an enemy of the party?'

'Mm. He could have been a member who turned on the comrades. Traitors were always treated like non-people.'

Rachel sat back in the sofa. 'So this is a dead end.'

'For the time being.' Mavros still hadn't told her about Shimon Raphael and the Tsiako connection. There was something about her he didn't fully trust, employer or not. 'Maybe Allegra will be able to make something of it.'

'Have you told her?'

'Er, not yet.'

She gave him an irritated look. 'Do it now.'

He called the researcher. She was interested, but doubted she'd be able to use it. The Communists were a closed book to her. She promised to give them an update on her work tomorrow.

'How do you suggest we proceed?' Rachel asked. Not for the first time, he wondered if she'd learned her English from 1950s text books.

He cast around for a way to satisfy her. Again, she had a suggestion of her own.

'The Phoenix Rises,' she said. 'I heard they're having a rally tonight.'

'Really?' Mavros wondered how she'd found that out.

As if she'd read his mind, she added, 'The concierge told me to stay away from Eleftherias Square this evening. Isn't that where Jewish males were forced to assemble during the war?'

'Good of the neo-Nazis to rub that in.'

Rachel nodded, tight-lipped. 'I want to go.'

'You what?'

'You heard me.' She stood up. 'I want to see the people who spray swastikas on the gate of our old people's home, as well as the other hateful muck around the city. And who threaten Allegra Harari.'

Mavros got to his feet. 'I really don't think that's a good idea.'

She gave a sudden laugh. 'Calm down, I don't have a Star of David flag with me. You're not scared, are you?'

'Of a bunch of iron-pumping morons in steel-capped boots? Of course I'm scared, though as much of your father's reaction as of them. Formally he's my client, which makes me responsible for you.'

Rachel headed to the bedroom. 'I can look after myself. I'll see you in the lobby in ten minutes.'

Mavros went to his room further down the corridor and found the scarf he'd thrown into his bag. It was red tartan, which would hardly make him fade into the background, but at least he could partially cover his face. He hoped Rachel had something similar. If not, there was always the hotel boutique. He decided to ring Shimon.

'She must be crazy,' the customs broker said, after he'd heard Mavros's story.

'I don't get that impression. Rather the opposite. Anyway, I just wanted you to know where we were in case something happens.'

'Something?'

'You know what those arseholes are like.'

163

'Only too well. Talk her out of it.'

'I'll try again.'

'Call me later, OK?'

Mavros agreed and rang off. There was a bitter taste in his mouth. He'd attended enough demonstrations in Athens over the years, in particular the annual march to the American Embassy on the anniversary of the student uprising that was crushed by the Colonels in 1973. The Phoenix Rises would muster a tiny percentage of attendees and the police would no doubt be there, but things could easily turn nasty if the Communists or other antifascists turned up.

He saw Rachel by the main doors. She was wearing jeans that displayed the lower part of her figure to advantage, and a loose black woollen jacket that did nothing for the other half. He was glad to see she had a beret and a scarf, both dark blue. As he got closer, he noticed her footwear.

'Are Doc Martens big in Paris?'

She glanced down at the black boots. 'I bought them this afternoon. The other shoes I have aren't for walking. Shall we go?'

He followed her out, trying to recall what she'd had on her feet before. High heels in Athens, certainly, but nothing too crippling in Thessaloniki. Maybe she was a punk rocker in her spare time.

They walked along the seafront, the lights from the ships bobbing up and down. The wind had got up and he shivered in his leather jacket.

'The Vardharis,' he said. 'That's what the northerly's called here. The Vardhar is another name for the Axios River, which rises in and runs

164

through much of the Former Yugoslav Republic of Macedonia and meets the Aegean not far west of here.'

Rachel turned her head towards him. 'You're a bottomless pit of information.'

He smiled. 'Ah, but it's relevant to what we're about to see and hear. After Yugoslavia fell apart in the early 90s, Macedonia's constitution contained claims to Greek territory – it's a landlocked country and, like Bulgaria, has always wanted direct access to the Mediterranean. Of course, there wasn't much they could do against a much larger and better-armed country, and eventually the constitution was changed – but not before a huge outbreak of nationalist zeal, particularly in Greek Macedonia, i.e. here. The Phoenix Rises is still rabid about the issue, especially the flag. Originally it was a blatant use of the star of Greek Macedonia, and the extreme right still sees the watered down version as an insult.'

'I thought the ancient Macedonians weren't Greek.'

Mavros looked around. 'Don't say that. I told you it's a hot issue.'

'My guidebook says the southern Greeks thought they were barbarians.'

The sound of martial music was audible, as well as chanting. Some of it was against the Phoenix Rises.

'There's much more to it than that, though Demosthenes did insult Alexander's father in that way. I'm not a historian but, as far as I understand, they were Greeks who spoke a dialect of the

165

ancient language. I wonder if Aristotle thought Alexander the Great was a barbarian before he started tutoring him.'

'A fine job he did,' Rachel scoffed. 'Alexander was a monster like Napoleon. Nothing mattered except conquest and death.'

'It's a point of view,' Mavros admitted. 'Right, listen carefully. There could be mayhem ahead. Do what I say without question if anything happens. Are you sure you want to see these scumbags in action? It's not as if you'll be able to understand what's said.'

'That why you're here, isn't it?' she said, striding on.

Mavros shook his head and caught up with her. A group of Communist youth was screaming abuse from the seafront, while a militaristic anthem was blasting out from speakers at the opposite end of the square. Riot police with shields and batons stood in a line. Rachel stepped through and wasn't stopped. Perhaps they thought she was a fascist, Mavros thought. His long hair attracted disapproving looks, but they let him proceed. The monument to Jewish victims of the Holocaust, a bronze tree of flames, was almost obscured by flags and the people holding them.

There were about a hundred people standing in front of a platform covered in Greek flags and olive wreaths. A large red banner hung from the covered dais, the word 'Counter-attack' written in black letters, the Greek letters adapted to resemble Gothic ones.

'These people really are idiots,' Rachel said, her

mouth close to his ear.

Mavros glanced around. It didn't seem that anyone had heard or, if they so, that they understood English.

'Fraktur, the old German script, was banned by the Nazis in 1941 on the grounds that it was Jewish.'

'We're not talking about Nobel prize-winners, Rachel. Pull up your scarf and for God's sake don't take any photos.' Mavros looked to the front and made out Makis Kalogirou, the party leader. He was of medium height and almost square in shape, wearing a shit-brown jacket adorned with badges and what looked like medals. There was also a red band on his upper left arm. Mavros couldn't make it out, but he suspected there was a white circle with a black phoenix spreading its wings.

Rachel moved closer. 'Who is he? What's he saying?'

Mavros identified the speaker, whose voice was high and grating. 'He's ranting about the media bias against him and his gang. Although they have no time for Jordanians or other non-Aryans, they had nothing to do with the murder. They do not use the swastika.'

'What's that on his arm?'

'I'm guessing a phoenix. They don't use it on graffiti or posters because they get criticised so much for harking back to the dictatorship. Those fools were fond of the bird that rises from its own ashes too.'

'He doesn't look like much of an Aryan.'

'I think they trace their Aryan descent via the

Goths and Huns, who passed through Greece in the late Roman and early Byzantine periods.'

'I thought you weren't a historian.'

'I have an interest in the past. Where would we be without it?'

Rachel glanced around the square. 'The bastards these animals worship left my family without a past.'

Kalogirou had stopped speaking to gulp down water and this time Rachel was heard by a tall skinhead to her left.

'Who you call bastards? Who animals?' he said, in English, looming over her. He was wearing combat trousers and a black shirt.

Mavros moved between them, but he was too late.

'The Nazis were bastards and the Phoenix Rises are animals,' Rachel said, enunciating the words clearly.

The skinhead pulled his right hand back, then squealed as Rachel's right boot caught him hard between the legs. As he went down, she raised her left knee so that his chin cracked on it.

A scrum of bodies immediately surrounded them. Mavros tried to pull her away without success. She laid out another pair of Phoenixes, then lowered her head and drove it into the belly of a third. Mavros grabbed her lower abdomen and pushed her forward. People scattered on either side of them. The uproar behind grew even louder. They were about twenty metres from the nearest riot police, not that they would necessarily be favourable.

'This way!' Rachel yelled, her beret gone and

her scarf loose round her neck. She raised her arm and slammed it into a black-clad man's throat.

'I can't do that!' Mavros shouted back, shrugging off the grasping arms of another fascist.

'No, I mean follow me.' Rachel handed off a skinny youth in the face, doing serious damage to his acne, and then veered left, heading for a gap in the police line. A narrow street at right angles to the square gave them a potential escape route.

Mavros felt hands seize both his arms. He brought his forehead down on one of the men's noses – a trick he'd learned from a university friend in Edinburgh – and elbowed the other in the gut. Then he sprinted clear and followed Rachel down the street. They kept going at speed until the next junction. As they turned the corner, they looked to see if anyone was in pursuit. The police had finally got their act together and blocked off Eleftherias Square.

'Jesus!' Mavros gasped.

'Keep walking,' Rachel ordered. 'We need to get back to the hotel ASAP.' She pulled his scarf off and dropped it in a rubbish bin.

'Hey, my mother gave me that.'

'She can get you another one.'

'Are you all right?' He couldn't see any wounds on her face.

'Yes. You?'

'Miraculously, I am. Where did you learn to fight like that?'

She shrugged. 'Assault protection classes. I had a friend at high school who was raped.'

Mavros's breathing was almost back to normal.

'They teach you all that?'

'The instructor said I had an aptitude for it.'

'He was right.'

'It was a she.'

Back at the hotel they walked upstairs together.

'Well, that was interesting,' Rachel said. 'I'm going for a swim and then I have to work. I trust you'll be staying in this evening.'

'That would be prudent.'

'Good night, then.' She swivelled away and strode to her door.

Mavros had a shower and ordered dinner from room service. He was starving, his hunger fuelled by the excitement of what Rachel had literally kicked off. What was she up to? He hadn't expected an ice-cool woman like her to spring into action like a whirling dervish. Her feelings about her Jewish heritage were obviously stronger than he'd realised. Then he had a thought. Had she gone to the rally with the intention of causing trouble? He turned on the TV and found local a news report. After they'd got away, the Communist youth had broken the police line and laid into the neo-Nazis. The over-made up harridan on screen lamented the violence and disorder on the streets of the co-capital, but she didn't condemn the Phoenix Rises' policies. There had been rumours that Kalogirou's mob was funded by the super-rich, who had an interest in inciting chaos so the government could justify clamping down on civil liberties. They also owned much of the media.

None of that explained Rachel's actions. He

considered calling her father, but let the idea go. He didn't fancy being frozen out by her.

Which reminded him. He rang Niki.

'Yes?' she said faintly, when he was about to ring off.

'It's me. How are you?'

'I was asleep.'

Mavros raised his eyes towards the ceiling. 'Shit, sorry. I'll let you go.'

'No, it's all right. I didn't even make it to bed. I dropped off on the sofa. Not enough sleep since you left.'

'Sorry.'

'Stop apologising. Have you made any progress?'

'A bit.' Recounting the riot that Rachel had instigated wasn't on the cards. 'Hope to make more tomorrow.'

'Oh, Alex. It's not long till the weekend. You will be back by then?'

'I'm sure I will,' he said, not convinced. 'Are you ... are you feeling any better about ... you know?'

'Was your degree in beating about the bush?'

He took a stab at ribaldry. 'I did have quite a lot of girlfriends, actually.'

Niki laughed, prompting him to clench his fist in triumph. 'I hope you aren't drooling over those steamy Macedonian women?'

'No, miss. Not at all, miss. Well...'

'Ha! See? We can have fun together.'

She was right. They did laugh, though there hadn't been much of that recently.

They talked for a while longer and then she

yawned audibly.

'Go to bed,' he said. 'On the way brush your teeth and do whatever else you do in the bathroom. I'll talk to you tomorrow.'

'All right. Love you.'

'Love you too.'

Shortly afterwards Mavros stretched out on the comfortable bed. He felt his eyes close, then he was fully awake again. He should have gone to sleep thinking of Niki, but the person who was trying to get into his dreams was Rachel Samuel. She scared him and that was a definite turn on.

TWENTY

I was seduced by the power invested in me as a capo, though I only beat my men when SS guards were in close proximity. When I explained what was expected of them – they were all new to the SK – most of them buckled down. One got himself machine-gunned when he ran towards the fence and another was shot by Knaus for breaking down. The rest, a mixture of Poles, French and Greeks, took to the work without appetite but driven by their will to keep going. Inevitably I spent more time with my countrymen. Two were from Rhodes and another, to my surprise as the transports from Thessaloniki had ended, was an old schoolmate. Zvi Tsiako was taller than me – as you can see, I'm taller than average – and there was still some muscle on him.

'Will you look after me?' he whispered one morning, as we were on our way to the crematoria.

I gave him the hard stare of the capo. 'Why? What can you give me in return?'

'Support,' he said, the over-long sleeves of his new jacket flapping. 'We know each other.'

That was hardly true. I hadn't seen him for years and he had no idea of my involvement with the party. Still, I had noticed that prisoners with friends lasted longer.

'Do what I tell you without question or hesitation and I'll think about it,' I replied. 'And roll those sleeves up. You'll set yourself on fire.'

That day my group was filling and tending the crematoria. I had it easier, but I'd spent many shifts doing what they had to do – loading the corpses in threes on to the steel trays and pushing them into the flames. They also had to maintain the temperature, clear blockages from the drain that drew off the melted fat, add coke at the right time: they were the worst jobs, not least because your face and hands got scorched.

They did well enough. Unlike me, they had to go straight to work at the furnaces. The SS had killed almost all of the old SK members after an abortive revolt in one of the other compounds. It was months in the planning and I'd been aware of it. From the outset I knew it was doomed to failure and stopped my men discussing it. In the end hundreds were killed at the cost of a few SS men's lives – one thrown alive into the flames – and the destruction of a single crematorium. Now they are seen as heroes, but I think they were simply unable to face the cycle of extermination. I lived from day to day, never worrying about my future. As far as I was concerned, the present was all.

Zvi proved to be good at his work and I allowed us to become closer. He talked of his family, some of whom he knew had passed along what the SS called 'the road to heaven'. He didn't seem unduly concerned. The others in the unit looked at him with suspicion. He didn't care about that either.

After a month we were rotated off crematorium duty and returned to the front compound. Some days were difficult, especially those when long-term occupants of the Lager selected for execution arrived. Most were emaciated, skeletal figures, their heads bowed and their legs incapable of anything more than shuffling. They were known as 'Muslims' in the argot of the camps, I don't know why. Perhaps it was another Nazi joke, reducing their Jewish victims to followers of the prophet Mohammed. Sometimes, however, there was resistance. Even disease-ridden, downtrodden slaves can fight to the last. The guards fired on them whenever necessary. Our job was easier once they were in the changing room. Many removed their tattered clothing and staggered to the gas chamber with relief.

I was standing in the middle of the crush one day. The walking dead were experienced in the ways of the Lager and flowed past me as if I were a rock in a stream. They knew what capos were capable of. Still, one naked man contrived to walk into me and I turned on him, club raised.

'My son?' came a querulous voice. 'You are alive?'

I stared at him and eventually recognised my father. He was half the weight he'd been when I last saw him, his ribs visible and streaks of excrement on his legs. Dysentery. I pulled him over to the wall, keeping my mouth away from his.

'You ... you are alive,' he repeated, his faint voice scarcely audible above the slap of bare feet on the concrete. He smiled, revealing toothless gums. 'Soon I will not be ... thank God.'

I struggled to speak. 'The others?' I asked, the words forcing themselves out. 'Mother? Miriam? Golda?'

He sobbed and tried to lean against me. I backed away, afraid of contagion and only going close again when he slumped against the wall.

'I heard that ... your sister ... and your niece were sent here from the experiment block in the summer. You did not see them?'

I shook my head, struck by his avoidance of their names. Perhaps he thought the words were too pure for the place, especially if their bodies had been subject to the Nazi doctors' brutality.

'And Mother?'

'I don't know.' He looked at me with eyes that were already lifeless. 'No one in the huts I've been in knows.'

The words did not affect me. I was sure my mother was dead. None of them had been mentally strong enough. I looked round. The SS men were shouting and my men were lining up behind the prisoners.

Father grabbed my arm with claw-like fingers.

175

'Stay alive,' he said. 'Stay alive for us all ... tell the world.' Then he let go and walked into the crowd, suddenly energised. He wanted the death that had been waiting for him for months.

After the door was closed behind them, I supervised the SK men as they gathered up the pitiful clothes and wooden shoes. My father wanted me to tell the world about what had been done to the Jews. I had no interest in that, at least in terms of words and proclamations. What I was planning would have horrified him.

Zvi came up and slipped a gold coin into my hand. Some prisoners kept them till the end. I knew where it would have been secreted, but I didn't care. I was making a collection of tarnished money and battered jewellery. We would need funds.

The end of the Lager came with bewildering speed. Yes, we had heard the Soviet guns getting closer. The SS did nothing, their faces as steel-stupid as ever. Then we were set to destroying the gas chambers and crematoria, our fingers and toes freezing in the winter wind. Capos joined in, eager to take part in the demolition of facilities that could have sent us after the rest of our communities. Not that order in the Lager disappeared. People were still shot all day long. Zvi and I only escaped by slipping out of the SK line and joining those prisoners who had been deemed fit enough to travel to camps further west. We survived the so-called death march, leaving behind many who collapsed on the snow and were dispatched by the guards. Our march to freedom was marked by the frozen corpses of those who had gone before.

We were chilled to the marrow in open railway trucks, moved from Lager to Lager and ending up in Buchenwald. Some of the prisoners there attacked the guards and killed them. Then the Americans liberated us, fresh-faced boys wandering around the mounds of corpses as if they were in an open-air but foul-smelling museum.

'What now?' Zvi asked, after we had been eating decent rations for two weeks.

'What now?' I looked into his pale blue eyes. 'The real war begins.'

TWENTY-ONE

Rachel Samuel woke at six. She had a coded text message that sent her to her laptop. There was a report on the encrypted site from her contact in Thessaloniki.

'Two shaven-headed young men in jackets with the Phoenix Rises emblems entered Allegra Harari's apartment block at 20.25 hrs yesterday evening. They were interrupted while hammering on her door and shouting. One has a broken left radius and the other a broken right humerus. The attackers were gagged and dragged down the stairs. Local operative on watch.'

That was probably my fault, Rachel thought, making a spectacle of myself at the rally. She had sent a report before she turned in. She was still waiting to hear from her controller, but he could hardly complain – one of her instructions was to destabilise the neo-Nazi group however she deemed appropriate. Then again, she and her contact weren't the only people with that aim. Baruh Natzari and the young men who had shaken Mavros from their tail might have had a similar agenda. But was there someone else involved?

Mavros rang Shimon Raphael.

'I saw you on TV!' the customs broker said.

'Oh, shit.'

'What happened? You were only on for a few seconds.'

'We ... got involved.'

'I noticed that. I take it the black-haired beauty with the useful moves is your client.'

'His daughter, yes. She got a bit carried away.' To put it mildly, he thought. Rachel must have spent her summers in a seriously aggressive kibbutz. Then he remembered what she'd told him about her assault-protection training.

'I hope Niki didn't see it. You're all right?'

'Yes, thanks.'

'Good. The Youth Party got stuck into the bastards and sent some of them home with sore heads.'

'I saw that on the news. Disgraceful behaviour blah blah blah from the talking heads.'

'Stooges of the special interests,' Shimon said dismissively. 'Listen, I've got something for you on Zvi Tsiako.'

'Hit me.'

'Can't on the phone, can I? When can we meet?'

'Let me get back to you. I don't know what Miss Karate and I will be up to today. Is what you've got hot?'

'Warmish, I'd say. Get on with whatever else you're following up.'

Mavros signed off. He looked at his notes – Tsiako, Baruh Natzari and his racing-driver friend, Ester Broudo's hard words about Aron Samuel; none of that led anywhere. The Phoenix Rises was a sideshow. Then he thought of the murdered Jordanian. He'd been taken out by someone who sounded like a professional, two shots to the back of the neck as well as one to the thigh that brought him down, the forensic surgeon confirmed; in Greece, those experts presented their findings to the media as soon as they finished the autopsy. An icy finger ran down Mavros's spine. He'd had dealings with a highly skilled hit man – none other than the Son, who had taunted him about Andonis the previous year, using that as a reason not to kill Mavros. Could he have been given the contract on Tareq Momani? Or could he have found out about the Samuel case and decided to make the waters muddier than those of the Axios delta?

No, Mavros told himself – that was just paranoia. If the Son had discovered he was in the co-capital, the bastard would have made his presence known much more directly.

His phone rang. It was Allegra Harari. After the usual exchange of greetings, she said, 'Something happened outside my flat yesterday evening.'

'More spray painting?'

'No, it was worse than that. Hammering on the

179

door, vile insults and threats.'

'Did you call the police?'

'No, I called my nephews. They were over in less than fifteen minutes.'

'Still, that's a long time to have your door pounded.'

'No, it wasn't like that. The sounds suddenly stopped. As you know, I don't have a peephole, so I could only rely on my ears. There were two loud cracks then screams that were quickly cut off. I'm sure I heard tape being ripped off a roll. After that there was scuffling and sliding in the direction of the stairs.'

'When was this?' Mavros asked.

'About 8.30. When my nephews arrived, I opened up and we looked around the landing. There wasn't much to be seen, only a few drops of blood.'

'Drops of blood? What did the police say?'

'They didn't come. They were too busy with the Nazi rally and its aftermath.'

Mavros thought about that. The interrupted door-knockers could have come from Eleftherias Square to take out their anger at the triumph of the young Communists on Allegra. But who had dealt with them?

'Any other sign of the intruders?' he asked. It sounded as if they had sustained serious injuries. 'Did people in the block see them?'

'No, everyone was keeping their heads down. But one of my nephews spoke to the pizza boy across the street. He said he saw two skinheads in Phoenix Rises jackets staggering away, clutching their arms, later in the evening. Their faces were bloody and raw.'

'Anyone else out of the ordinary?'

'No, he'd just come back from a delivery.'

'Maybe a group of Communist Youth caught up with them.'

'Maybe.' Allegra sounded doubtful. 'They would have made noise – shouting, that kind of thing – on the landing, wouldn't they? It was almost as if a ghost disabled them and got them out of the building.'

A ghost, Mavros thought. That was all he needed. The only person he knew with the qualities of a violent ghost was the Son. Surely he couldn't be taking such a close interest. Plus, his father had been a torturer during the dictatorship. It seemed unlikely the Son would sympathise with the Jews. Unless someone was making it worth his while.

'Alex?' Allegra's voice was shrill.

'Sorry, what?'

'I was saying, come round in the late afternoon with your young lady. I should have something by then.'

Mavros couldn't help smiling. If Rachel heard herself described in those terms, she'd go into fight mode. As would Niki. Then he remembered that she might have seen him with Rachel on the news.

After breakfast, Rachel and Mavros took a taxi to Kalamaria and rang Baruh Natzari's bell. There was no answer. The street door was open, so they went up to his floor. Ringing the bell and knocking had no effect, until a door down the

181

corridor opened. An elderly lady with blue hair came out in her slippers.

'Can I help you?' she asked, peering through thick glasses.

Mavros stepped forward. 'We were looking for Mr Natzari.'

The woman answered in a tongue Mavros had heard before in recent days.

'I'm sorry. Is that Judezmo?'

'You're not one of us? The young lady looks like she is.'

Mavros translated, saying that he would give her name and see where that led. Rachel nodded.

'This is Rachel Samuel,' he said, smiling at the woman. Her face was wrinkled beneath poorly applied make-up, but she had a ready smile.

'I knew a Samuel family. Please, come inside.'

Mavros ushered Rachel in after the old woman, glancing at the label by the doorbell. 'Mrs Catan, is it?'

'That's right. Aliki Catan.' She led them into a pristine sitting room, the furniture dark, but the fabrics bright white. 'I do it all myself,' she said proudly. 'I won't let a cleaner in here.'

Rachel sat down on the sofa. Mavros stood at a cabinet, looking at the photos. Some were faded black-and-white, others more recent – small children, smiling parents.

'My children, my grandchildren,' Mrs Catan said, with a smile. Then she turned to the older shots. 'My grandparents, my parents, aunts and uncles, siblings, cousins...'

Rachel appeared behind her and touched her hand. 'The lost,' she said, in a tone Mavros hadn't heard from her before. He translated.

'Yes, dear. Almost all of them.' Mrs Catan dabbed a tissue to her eyes. Then she pointed to a bull-chested man in a good suit, who was smiling expansively at the lens. 'That's my husband, Shlomo. Solomon,' she added to Mavros. Her forefinger wavered at other photos, showing the man getting older, the final ones with heavily ringed eyes. 'The cancer took him.'

Mavros and Rachel offered condolences.

'You know what my Shlomo always said? "Every day is a new life." He came back from Auschwitz, you see.'

There was a respectful silence.

'I grew up in Athens,' the old woman continued, 'and my parents managed to get us into the mountains. They worked for the resistance and I went to the schools EAM set up. After the war I trained as a nurse and moved up here to be with Shlomo. We met at a wedding down south.' She looked at Rachel. 'Are you one of the Toumba Samuels, my dear?'

'Remember the football stadium we passed on the way to the old people's home?' Mavros said. 'That area.'

'I don't think so,' Rachel replied. 'To be honest, I don't know where my family used to live.' He translated and explained about her infant father's departure from the city.

Then he decided to push the discussion forward. 'Did you ever hear of an Aron Samuel, Mrs Catan? He's Rachel's great-uncle.'

'Aron?' she repeated, brow furrowed. 'I don't think so. Baruh would know.'

183

'That's why we're trying to find him,' Mavros said. 'Have you any idea where he might be?'

'Since he isn't here, he'll be at his cottage.'

Mavros's stomach clenched. 'Ah. And where is that?'

'Outside the village of Exochisti on the slopes of Mount Hortiatis. You'll find it easily. It's the last house on the right on the way to Asvestochori.'

'Does he have a phone there?'

'No. It was his family's place and he's kept it as it used to be. Not that I've been there for many years.'

'Does he have a mobile phone?'

Mrs Catan shook her head. 'He doesn't hold with them. Neither do I. New-fangled rubbish. Why don't people talk face to face any more?'

Mavros stood, nodding to Rachel. They were out of the flat quickly and, after trying the old man's door again, on the street. He told her what the old woman had said.

'I presume we're going to this Exochisti place,' Rachel said, fiddling with her phone. 'Here's a map.'

'New-fangled rubbish,' he said, with a smile she didn't fathom. The village was about fifteen kilometres away, to the east of the city.

'We need some wheels,' Rachel said. She located a nearby car-hire firm on her phone. Twenty minutes later they were in a Jeep Cherokee, getting off the ring road and heading for Panorama. Rachel was driving a lot more skilfully than Mavros would have managed.

'This looks like a nice place,' she said.

184

'Where the nobs live,' Mavros replied, taking in the large, detached houses.

'What is a nob?'

He swallowed a laugh unsuccessfully. 'In this case, a wealthy person.'

'So I am a nob?'

He wasn't sure if she was teasing him. 'The word has two spellings and several meanings in the UK.'

'I'm French and I've only rarely stayed longer than a week in Britain. Enlighten me.'

'Your new-fangled rubbish will do that much more effectively,' he said, deciding against talking dirty. 'There's a sign to Exochisti.'

She followed the road indicated. It rose quite steeply and then traversed the mountain. There were views over the gulf and towards the city. Exochisti was a pretty village of red-roofed houses, with modern developments on the outskirts. They went in the direction of Asvestochori and reached the end of the village. The last house on the right was a single-storey building covered in bougain-villea and vines, the latter covered in withered leaves. There was no house door on the roadside, but a wooden gate stood between the trees. The nearest house was fifty metres or so away, on the other side. Theirs was the only vehicle close by.

Mavros breathed in the mountain air, feeling the chill of it in his lungs. He waited till Rachel had locked the car, then opened the gate. A path lined by oleanders led to the other side of the house, which had a stone terrace looking over a well-tended garden. Olympus was visible across the water.

185

'Pretty spot,' Mavros said. He walked to the French windows and looked in. One of them had a handle and keyhole. He knocked on the glass.

No one appeared.

Rachel joined him. 'What's that?' she said, her eyes angled towards the depths of the room on the right.

'Shit!' Mavros took out a handkerchief and tried the handle.

The door was locked. He saw a stone that was probably used to prop the door open and picked it up. 'Stand back!' Then he smashed the pane nearest the handle and stuck his hand in. 'Key's in the lock.' He turned it with some difficulty. 'Don't touch anything.'

Rachel held up gloved hands.

Mavros ran in, flicking a light switch as he passed it.

'It's him,' Rachel said, stepping past him.

A chair was lying on its side beneath Baruh Natzari, whose body moved slowly in the wind coming through the door. A rope had been slung over one of the wooden ceiling beams. The old man's head was bent to the right, a thickly wound knot under his left ear. Mavros touched his hand. It was colder than the stone he'd used to break in.

'Interesting choice of clothes for an Auschwitz survivor,' Rachel said. Her voice was level and Mavros got the impression this wasn't her first dead body.

'Pyjamas with blue-and-white vertical stripes,' he said. 'I see what you mean.'

She moved to the other side of the sparsely

186

furnished room and looked at the photographs on the ledge above the fireplace.

'Look at this,' she said, with barely suppressed excitement.

Mavros joined her and peered at the black-and-white image. 'Shlomo Catan,' he said. The husband of the dead man's neighbour must have been in his late thirties when the photo was taken. The short-sleeved shirt and shorts suggested a hot location, but the vegetation in the background wasn't Mediterranean. 'And Baruh himself.'

But Rachel wasn't looking at them. Her eyes were on the middle of the three figures.

'That's my great-uncle,' she whispered. 'I'm sure of it.'

Mavros examined the tall, thin figure, his hair combed back from a high forehead. He certainly resembled the pre-war shots of Aron Samuel he'd been shown. That wasn't the only thing that caught his eye. While the men to each side had only holstered pistols on their belts, he was holding what looked like an army-issue rifle. A machete or something similar had been stuck into the ground between his legs.

Rachel bent closer. 'Those aren't footballs, are they?' she said.

Mavros took in the glassy eyes and broken lips on the severed heads in front of the trio.

'No,' he said, glancing back at the hanged man. 'They're not.'

TWENTY-TWO

Zvi and I fattened ourselves up as the first spring of freedom blossomed in the land of the Thousand Year Reich. The Americans were generous. They were also nearly as bureaucratic as the Nazis. I had decided early on that my real name was of no more use to me. When the clerks asked for our details, I called myself Anjil Gerson after my doomed friend from the Lager and gave them a false date of birth. There seemed no point in changing my home city, especially as it was already apparent how few of Thessaloniki's Jews had survived. Like me, the people I spoke to either knew for certain that family members had been killed or had minimal hope of them turning up alive. I didn't mention that I had been in the Sonderkommando.

By summer, we had been moved to a displaced-persons camp near Frankfurt. On the way I was pleased to see that Germany's towns and cities had been heavily bombed. Some Greeks had already arrived. Zvi and I found a member of our community who had worked in the I. G. Farben chemical plant at Monowitz-Buna, originally a sub-camp of Auschwitz and later one in its own right. Shlomo Catan was still getting over dysentery, but there was a cold light in his eyes that attracted me. He was also wide-chested, though there was little flesh or muscle on him. I had already told Zvi what I intended to do and he was enthusiastic. When Shlomo was fit, in early September 1945, I started gathering together what we would need.

The basis of all camps – whether labour, extermination or rehabilitation – is commerce. The American soldiers, bored by their repetitive duties and desperate to get back home, had little interest in military discipline. What they wanted was money, valuables, souvenirs – anything to impress their families and help them get on after demobilisation. It took time, because initially we had little to trade, only the few coins we had been able to hide about our persons on the march. We didn't even know much English, though I quickly picked up the basics, as I had with German in the Lager.

'Is this really going to work?' Zvi asked, as we crouched beside the wire fence after lights out.

'Trust me,' I said. 'And think how easy it'll be compared with SK work.'

He nodded. We had left Shlomo behind in case his stamina ran out. After the sentries had crossed, we started to clamber over the fence. The Nazis had used the place for some nefarious purpose, so most of the strands were barbed. Some, however, had been replaced by ordinary wire and we had taken note of the locations on our daily exercise walks. Outside, we started to run. The nearest village was five kilometres away and I wasn't sure how long we would need.

We stopped to rest before the first houses. There were fewer lights than in the camp, which pleased me – good for what we were about to do and evidence that the Germans had limited electricity.

'Think of Knaus,' I whispered.

Zvi's expression changed to that of a savage. I imagine mine was similar – worse, probably. We crept up the path to the first building. The door was flimsy, no more than a row of planks held together by rusty nails.

'I'm going to break it down,' I said, lowering my shoulder. The barrier caved in. I didn't even notice the impact, so hard had I become in body as well as spirit.

'What's going on?' a middle-aged man said, rising unsteadily from a chair. He sat down immediately when Zvi put a sharpened table knife to his throat. The moon was low, casting its light through the windows.

I leaned over him. 'We are Jews,' I said, grinning to display my broken, discoloured teeth. 'We make a deal with you. In return for your life, we take everything worth carrying.'

There was a muffled squeal and then I smelled urine on his trousers.

'Anyone else here?'

'My wife ... my daughter ... please...'

I went to get them. Both were asleep in a double bed and woke in terror. I had a fork against one throat and a knife against the other. When they got up, I saw that the girl – seventeen or so – was pretty, though very thin. I pushed them into the front room.

The man groaned and repeated, 'Please,' over and over. He glanced at his daughter and I understood.

'Don't worry, we don't rape sub-humans,' I said. I can't tell you how much pleasure that gave me. Of course, it made them even more frightened. I turned to the woman, whose pouched cheeks were incongruous above her thin frame. 'Bring everything of value that you have – food, drink, jewellery, clothes.' I caught her gaze. 'We will search afterwards. Believe me, we learned all there is to know about hiding places in the Lager. For every item we find, your man loses an ear, an eye... Then we start on your daughter. No noise!'

She scurried around, opening drawers and emptying the contents on to the floor, then bringing out food – ham, cheese, bread, preserved fruit and vegetables. Then she went into the bedroom. I watched as she pushed the bed aside and took up a piece of floorboard. She sobbed as she handed me a box. In it were gold coins, two watches and her jewellery – none of it worth much, but it would serve our purpose. There were also three medals, one of them an Iron Cross. While she took clothes from the chest and wardrobe, I went back to the seated man.

'How did you get this?' I said, holding up the cross.

'I gave the fatherland part of me,' he said, picking up the empty left leg of his damp trousers. 'At Stalingrad.'

We had heard about the Germans' crushing defeat from Soviet prisoners, but all I could think of was my brother Isaak, dragged away to be killed because of his missing limb.

'What did you do?' Zvi asked.

'Saved two officers' lives.'

'Fool.'

He nodded. 'I wouldn't do it again.'

191

His woman came back with her arms full of apparel. Zvi put the best of it in a blanket, along with the jewellery and food. It made a large bundle that would need both of us to heave back to camp.

'Please,' the daughter said. 'Leave us something to eat.'

I laughed. 'Have you heard of Auschwitz?'

They all nodded, heads down. Allied propaganda had made it very clear to the German people what the Nazis had done in their name.

'Children starved, old people died of thirst – and that before they were gassed like rats and burnt in ovens. Now tell me you want food.'

They were silent. I considered killing them – I could have done it easily enough – but reminded myself of my plan. It took priority and I couldn't afford the risk of three irrelevant deaths derailing it.

'Tell no one in the village of this,' I said, as we left. 'Because we will be back and I will find out if the others have made preparations. Remember – ear, eye, nose, lip...'

It took us most of the rest of the night to get our loot back to the fence. There was no way we could get it over without help, so we gave the medals to the American sentries. They were happy and so were we. Our bank had opened.

TWENTY-THREE

'We need to go,' Rachel said urgently.

'Hold on.' Mavros was looking for a suicide note. He asked her to stick her gloved hands into the hanged man's pockets – nothing. He went through the door at the rear and checked the other rooms. The kitchen table was bare and there were no dirty plates or glasses anywhere. The two bedrooms, the walls of both lined by low oriental divans, were tidy and free of anything suggestive.

'Come on,' she said, when he returned to the living area.

Mavros had taken the photo of the three men and a couple of others that were less gruesome and in what looked like European locations.

'We really should call the police,' he said.

'And explain that we broke in?'

'Why not? We could say the door was like that when we arrived. We didn't leave any prints. Face it, the car may well have been spotted by a neighbour. Us too.'

She shook her head in irritation. 'It's not as if your hair is standard under-cover operative style – you stick out a mile. Anyway, they'll want to know what our interest was here.'

He shrugged. 'It'll be worse if we drive off and they track us down.'

'How about if I drive off and you stay here?'

At first he thought she was joking. 'And if you

were seen?'

'I'm sure you'll be able to cover for me.'

Mavros looked at her. 'All right. I'll make an anonymous call when we're clear of the area.'

They went back to the car, their heads bowed.

'So you think it was suicide,' Rachel said as they headed towards Asvestochori.

He shrugged. 'Hard to be sure without taking him down and examining the body. I didn't see signs of anyone else's presence.'

'All right, let's assume he killed himself,' she said, following a sign to Thessaloniki. 'Why? Do you think our visit upset him so much?'

'Mention of your great-uncle certainly stopped him in his tracks. But don't forget he was with one young man in Ayia Triadha yesterday and another drove them away. It seems a fair bet Baruh was brought to the house in Exochisti after they lost me.'

'How did the old man look in the restaurant?'

'He was talking with a fair amount of animation, as was his companion. I wouldn't say he looked suicidal.' Mavros took the photographs from his pocket. 'And then there's the question of the photograph. Baruh Natzari, Shlomo Catan and Aron Samuel.'

Rachel glanced at the images on his lap. 'Now we know for certain my great-uncle survived Auschwitz. When do you think those were taken?'

'Difficult to tell. They look to be in early middle age, don't you think? Your great-uncle was born in 1925, so he'd have been thirty-five in 1960, forty in 1965.' He raised one of the photos to the light. 'Actually, they all seem to be younger in

194

this. It could have been taken in the mid-50s.' He studied Aron Samuel. His face was lined and his expression intense. He looked like a man on a mission. At least there were no severed limbs in that shot. The men were wearing suits with open-necked shirts and standing in front of what Mavros thought were rhododendron bushes.

'You think they cut those heads off?'

'Seems likely. A display of trophies. You noticed that the dead men's faces were European, although sunburned?'

'Mm.' Rachel seemed distracted.

'What are you thinking?'

'That the war didn't stop in 1945.'

She didn't speak again until they were in the city. 'Are you going to phone the police, then?

'Yes. There's a public phone.'

He got out and used the phone card he kept in his wallet. Speaking in a clipped and high-pitched voice, he gave the basic information and location then rang off.

When he got back in, Rachel was looking at the map. 'I want to visit the Jewish cemetery,' she said, her voice low. 'You don't have to come.'

'No, I'd like to see it.'

'Direct me, then,' she said, tossing the folded map to him.

'You wouldn't prefer me to use your new-fangled phone?' She didn't bother to acknowledge that.

The Fat Man was stretched out on the sofa with a copy of *Rizospastis* over his face. He still picked up the party organ most days, though its hectoring tone and one-dimensional vision of the world got him down. He had consumed a light lunch – a six-egg omelette, a couple of country-style sausages and a salad – and was having his regular mid-afternoon doze.

He woke when the front door was smashed open, the alarm immediately blaring. A few seconds later came the crash of the first Molotov cocktail through the window. It hit the wall above the TV and sucked in all the air from the vicinity. A second bottle bounced off the sofa and rotated towards the armchair beyond, spewing a spray of flame that ignited the newspaper. A third smashed through the window. Yiorgos was already off the couch and heading for the kitchen. He pulled the pump-action shotgun from beneath the table and racked the slide.

'Come on, you fuckers!' he yelled, thundering out into the hall, which was already ablaze. A bottle with a flaming rag in the top smashed on the floor in front of him. The Fat Man tried to see beyond the flames, feeling his arms burn. He turned and saw that the *saloni* was an inferno. Flames were running up the stairs of the maisonette as well. The only exit was the front door. It was pulled shut by a figure in black, a balaclava over the face.

'Shit!' Yiorgos took a step back. Tongues of fire licked at his feet. He was struggling to breathe. He had only one option. Or rather six. He fired all the rounds at the door, ducking as air rushed in from outside.

The Fat Man lowered his head and, bull-like, pounded through the flames. He piled through the remains of the door and ended up on the other side of the street, his lungs and eyes stinging, and the shotgun still in his hands.

A car stopped and a young man opened the door. 'Get in!' he said. 'I'll take you to the hospital.'

Yiorgos was still gasping for breath, wiping his eyes with his sleeve. 'Fire ... brigade,' he gasped.

'Too late for that, my friend.'

'Other ... houses...'

'All right.' The driver made the call. 'They're on their way. How are you?'

'Fucking ... roasted.'

The driver sniffed. 'Pretty rare, I'd say.'

The Fat Man felt consciousness slip away. As his system shut down, he was struck by the idea that he'd met the young man before. Who was he? No, surely not.

Then his brain short-circuited and he plummeted, unknowing, into the fiery lower depths.

The new Jewish cemetery in the northern suburb of Stavroupoli was closed, presumably because of the risk of defacement. They stood at the gate and tried to see inside. There were monuments of marble, some of them large.

'According to this,' said Rachel, brandishing her guidebook, 'there's a memorial to the fifty thousand Jews of Thessaloniki who died in the Holocaust.'

Mavros looked at the photograph. It showed a tall rectangle of marble with lettering in Hebrew and Greek, a Star of David and what he presumed was a stylized, semi-circular menorah on top.

'Maybe it's just as well,' Rachel said, turning away.

'What do you mean?'

'Well, none of my ancestors are likely to be in here, are they? The Nazis and the city council destroyed the old cemetery to make way for the university.'

Mavros kicked himself in the brain. 'It's a peaceful place,' he said inadequately.

'Which means that the likes of my great-uncle and his friends have no place here.' She looked at him. 'Though I suppose Baruh will end up in his family tomb, if there is one.'

'Maybe you should talk to the Jewish community,' he suggested. 'I know Allegra Harari's doing our research, but there are bound to be people who knew Aron, or at least of him.'

'Like Ester Broudo, you mean?' she said waspishly. 'I don't need to hear that he was a collaborator and traitor again, thanks.' Her head dropped. 'That photo suggests she was right about him being a murderer, though.'

They stood around for a few more minutes.

'Come on,' he said. 'I'll take you to see someone before we go to Allegra's.' He'd decided that keeping Shimon Raphael and her apart was pointless.

They got into the car, Rachel taking the wheel again. He told her to head for the port. The Jeep was only fifty metres down the road when a black pickup passed them, going in the opposite direction. It was loaded down with skin-headed young men in black shirts, others wearing motorbike helmets. A Greek flag and one bearing the

Phoenix Rises' emblem flew from either side behind the cab.

Rachel slammed her foot on the brake. 'Oh no, you don't,' she muttered, slipping into reverse.

'What are you doing?' Mavros said, more alarmed than he wanted to show. 'We're out-numbered.'

'But we've got a lot more power.' Rachel completed her turn and rocketed back towards the cemetery gate.

The young men were preparing to get down, two of them holding spray cans.

'Hold on,' Rachel said, her eyes narrowed.

'No!' Mavros shouted.

The Cherokee hit the side of the pickup at about forty kilometres an hour. The occupants of the cargo bay went flying, while the men in the cab didn't jump clear in time. Rachel dropped into second gear and pushed the pickup, now on its side, towards the wall ahead. The impact was jarring.

Mavros looked around. Dazed young men were picking themselves up from the road. Rachel reversed towards them and they scattered.

'Jesus, you might have killed someone,' he said, surprised the airbags hadn't inflated. 'The driver and at least one other man are still in the cab.'

'Fuck them.' She opened her window and shouted after the scattering neo-Nazis. 'Stay and fight, you cowards! Morons! Animals!'

Mavros didn't translate. He got out, ran to the pickup and tugged at the door on the top. He could see two men inside. Both were conscious, one flattening the other. Neither were wearing seat belts.

'Are you all right?' he yelled.

They both said they were and that the bitch was going to die, before they saw who was speaking to them.

'Fuck you, hippy!' the nearer one yelled. He scrabbled for a set of brass knuckles.

Mavros went back to the Jeep. Rachel was on the tarmac, still screaming at the retreating fascists.

'Inside!' he said. 'Now!' He got in the driver's side. 'Now!'

Rachel climbed in the other side, but not before she'd picked up one of the spray cans and written the word 'Pigs' on the underside of the pickup.

'That was ... risky,' Mavros said, as he drove away, turning into the first backstreet he could find. 'Map reading, please.' He glanced at her. 'That's quite a temper you have under the ice-princess exterior.'

'Bastards,' she said, breathing heavily. 'Disgusting scum.'

'True. But you just took the law into your hands like them. They dragged you down to their level.'

She confined herself to giving him directions until they saw the masts and funnels of the ships in the port.

Miraculously he found a parking place and killed the engine. 'Not too much damage to the bumper.'

'Why do you think I got a monster like this?'

As they walked to Shimon's office, Mavros wondered about that. Had Rachel been planning on confronting members of the Phoenix Rises? Last night's performance at the square nearby suggested so.

The sooner he found her great-uncle, dead or alive, the better.

Mavros's phone rang as they were about to walk into Raphael and Company. He saw from the screen that it was Niki. His heart missed a beat.

'Excuse me,' he said to Rachel and stepped away, suppressing a groan. He did not need to be nagged at this juncture.

'Alex,' she said, when he answered. 'Something bad's happened.'

Did she mean the rally? No, it didn't sound like it. His gut clenched and visions of his mother, sister, Niki herself flashed before him.

'Are you OK?'

'Yes. Don't worry about me. It's the Fat ... it's Yiorgos.'

'What's he done?'

'It's not that. Alex, his neighbour Mr Kostas rang. He wanted you and I told him you were out of town and he didn't want to tell me and I said I couldn't give him your mobile number unless–'

'Niki!' he shouted. 'What happened to the Fat Man?'

'Sorry, darling. His house ... it's burned down.'

'What? Is he all right?'

'That's the problem. Firemen have put the blaze out, but they haven't found his body. They're still searching, of course. They say there was broken glass and petrol. It doesn't look like an accident. There was a report of shots being fired too.'

'The Son,' Mavros said, his heart hammering. 'The fucking Son.'

'We don't know that, my love. Yiorgos might be in one of the hospitals. Maria's ringing round.'

'It's him,' he said, inhaling deeply. 'Who else could it be?'

Niki was silent for a while. 'Are you coming back, Alex?'

He dropped into a squat, his mind racing. 'There are things I have to do. Talk to Mother and the others...'

'I've done all that. They're in emergency lock-down.'

'Really? Thanks for that. But, Jesus, where is he?'

'Get the first plane, Alex. I'm waiting for you.'

Mavros got to his feet and saw Rachel looking at him seriously. Yiorgos. Had his best friend been cremated, or could he have got out? Given how slow-moving the Fat Man was, the latter seemed less than likely.

TWENTY-FOUR

By the spring of 1946 we were fully recovered physically and we had what we needed – changes of clothing, good boots, gold coins, weapons (we bought Colt .45 automatics, grenades and combat knives from American soldiers whose quarter-masters were open to bribery) and, most important, information. The SS had been declared an illegal organisation and many of its surviving members were in camps undergoing the de-Nazification programme. A few, very few, were put on trial and some of the high-ranking officers would later be executed. But many of the low ranks had disappeared, back to their home cities, towns and villages where they either changed identity or lived openly, to the indifference or approval of the residents. The Americans caught many, but they were losing their appetite as it became clear that a new form of war with the Soviets was building up. For us, that was good. We got lists of SS men still at large. We also extracted names from mayors and other officials in small towns, sometimes leaving our terrified sources alive. It was pleasing to put them under threat of death – them and their families. Now they knew a little of what the Jews had experienced.

There were other groups of avengers operating throughout the former Reich, but we avoided joining them or infringing on their field of operations. Some had the shadowy backing of Zionist groups in Palestine. We were Greek Jews and saw what we were doing as retribution for our own community. When we had amassed enough victims, all three of us intended to return to Thessaloniki and rebuild our lives. An independent state for the Jews struck us as little more than a ghetto with a warmer climate. We had suffered enough for many lives, but we were still young and naive – not least in imagining that our lust for vengeance would ever be sated.

At first we were amateurish, killing men before

they had time to reflect on their deeds, injuring bystanders in grenade attacks – not that we viewed anyone in Germany or Austria as innocent – and allowing our fury to get the better of us. There was a corporal who had been in the Waffen-SS before being transferred to Ravensbrück as a guard because frostbite had taken some of his toes. He fought us to the death – his own – leaving Zvi with a knife wound to his upper arm and me with cracked ribs. Shlomo finally cut the swine's throat, which led to us all being drenched in blood. We burst into paroxysms of laughter as we sat around the body, gore dripping from our faces and hands. Then we agreed that we had to be more controlled.

'We do to them what they did to our people,' I said.

'Are you planning on building a portable crematorium?' Shlomo asked. He was the joker, even though his father had been beaten to death in front of him by a German criminal who had been put in charge of a sleeping block.

'I don't care about their bodies,' I said. 'I want them to die in full awareness of who killed them and why. So, we gas them in their cars. We hang them like they did the misguided escapers from the Lager. We tie them down and cut pieces off them like the bastard doctors did, without anaesthetic.'

'Good idea,' Zvi said solemnly. He pursued our goals with the dedication of a zealot. Soon that turned into full-blown religious devotion.

So we stole vehicles – usually American staff cars – and tied the former SS men down inside them, often after using our knives on them, but never injuring them badly enough that they lost consciousness. We told them who we were and what they were being punished for. Threats to their families usually meant that they went quietly, their trousers stinking. We ran a hose from the exhaust to the window and watched the murderers slowly choke, their eyes sticking out and their tongues swollen. Then we dragged them into the undergrowth, cleaned up the driver's seat and took the car back. The last thing we needed was the Americans turning against us. Sometimes we even found a helpful driver who let us pay for our transport; once a Jewish soldier came along for the ride. He shouted and swore as the victim died. Eventually Zvi had to knock him out. We were on the outskirts of a village.

After six months roaming and executing around Bavaria and western Austria, we finally got a sniff of Knaus. He was cunning and obviously had good connections. We had been paying a clerk in Munich to keep an eye out for him on the lists. Nothing. Then we struck lucky. American soldiers at a checkpoint caught a courier for one of the old-comrade organisations that had sprung up with such speed that they must have been planned during the war. Whether he was tortured by an enraged Jewish serviceman or whether he was just a coward – there was no shortage of those in the SS – he gave names. It turned out that his contact in southwestern Bavaria was Knaus, now calling himself Herr Entreis. We took special care with planning his end. Even Shlomo had heard of him, though he hadn't been in the SK.

He wasn't an easy man to isolate, this Gustav Entreis. He lived with his family of three – a blonde wife and five-year-old female twins – in the centre of a small town that no Allied bomber had reached; wooden buildings with steep roofs, a small park on the banks of a rapidly flowing stream, birds singing as if there had been no extermination programme.

'Why don't we burn the whole place down, turn it into a crematorium?' Shlomo asked, after we had reconnoitred. 'If he escapes the flames, we can take him out in the chaos.'

'We want him to go slowly and in full possession of his twisted mind,' Zvi said. 'We want him to die screaming insults at the Führer.'

'And he might get away in the chaos,' I said. 'We need to lure him out. We know he's trading on the black market. What have we got to excite him?'

Shlomo rooted around in his haversack. 'How about the jewellery?'

We had been robbing German homes between killings. Much of the loot went on bribing the occupation forces for information and supplies, but we had kept a stock.

'That'll work,' I said. 'He always struck me as the rapacious type.'

'As well as a murdering pig,' Zvi said, his eyes wide. He had the same memories of the compound and the execution pits as I did, only not as many.

'How do we approach him?' Shlomo asked.

'The safe way would be for you, the one he doesn't know, to go,' I replied, with a smile he didn't return. 'But I want to do it. He won't recognise me now I've put weight on and have normal-length hair. And if he does, I'll have his guts out before he can move.'

'I don't know,' Zvi said. 'Your German is all right, but it'll still make him suspicious.'

'Don't worry, I know what I'm doing. I'll go this evening. Wait for me at the edge of the woods above town, at the first bend in the road.'

'He won't go there in the dark,' Shlomo objected.

'If he's as greedy as I think, he will. Stay there till midday. If I haven't appeared by then, say Kaddish for me and burn the place down. You noticed the fuel tank by the town hall?'

They nodded dubiously, then let me sleep in the shelter of the trees to the west. I woke refreshed, a plan having crystallised in my mind. I put a pistol in my belt and a sheathed knife in my jacket pocket. The bag of jewels went in the other pocket. I was wearing a poorly cut suit and a Homburg hat that had seen better days.

'See you later,' I said, nodding to the others. I didn't offer them my hand – I was sure I'd be back.

The town, really an extended village serving the surrounding hamlets as a market, had a post office and some shops but not much else. There were more streetlights than was usual at the time, suggesting there was money to run generators. I saw men drinking beer in an establishment with deer and wild-boar heads on the walls. They didn't look as if the war weighed greatly on them. Knaus was among them. I waited across the street, then ran to catch him up when he came out.

'Sir, sir,' I said, breathing heavily as if I was exhausted.

'What is it?' he said, turning and eyeing me suspiciously. His hand went to the pocket of his jacket. Although he too had put on some weight, his expression was as it had been in the Lager – overbearing, vicious, selfish.

'A moment of your time, sir,' I said, playing the nervous bottom-feeding shyster we'd seen so many of. 'I have something that will interest you.'

'Who are you?' he demanded. 'Where do you come from?'

'Werth is my name. I am a Sudeten German, but now...' I shrugged.

He didn't look convinced. 'You sound like a Yid to me.' He drew a Walther P38. 'Give me a good reason not to shoot you. No one will care.'

I raised my arms. 'Left jacket pocket, Mr Entreis.'

'How do you know my name?'

'Marcus in Munich recommended you.' That individual was a former SS man, a big black-market player and an Allied informer.

Knaus relaxed slightly, then stuck his hand in my pocket. He opened the leather pouch and looked in. His lips twitched and he licked them.

'Very good,' he said, then laughed harshly. 'So kind of you to donate them.'

'But, sir, I have more.'

'Where?'

'I left my suitcase in the woods above town.'

He stared at me and for several moments I

thought he had recognised me. Then he looked away, calculating the odds.

'Keep your hands up and come with me,' he said, leading me to a narrow passage beside the town hall. He lived in the next building. When we were out of the direct light, he pointed the pistol at my groin. 'Take your cock out.'

My heart rate remained steady. I hadn't expected Knaus to be easily duped. 'So I must lower my hands,' I said, my voice uneven.

'One hand. The left one.'

I did as he said, extracting my member after struggling with the buttons.

'I knew you were a Yid,' he said, stepping closer.

I pissed at him and that distraction gave me the second I needed to whip the knife from my pocket and bring it down heavily. The blade hacked at least halfway through the bones of his right wrist and the Walther dropped to the ground. I cut his scream off by ramming the muzzle of my Colt into his mouth, hearing teeth break.

'Silence,' I hissed. 'Silence and I won't rape your daughters.'

I wasn't sure if the threat would work, as the SS man had only ever shown self-interest, but he bit his lip and I stuffed a rolled-up length of fabric into his mouth before he could react, tying another strip round the gag. Then I pushed him down the passage towards the fuel tank. The truth was, I had never intended taking him to the others in the woods. Knaus was mine.

I took off the second of the belts I was wearing and secured him to the pipe leading from the tank. Then I turned the wheel and let diesel flow towards his feet. Soon his trousers had absorbed plenty of it.

'And now it's time to talk,' I said. 'For me, that is. You only have to listen.' I stabbed him in the upper thigh. 'Understand?' He nodded vigorously.

I took off my jacket, having retrieved the pouch of jewels. It was only then that I noticed I was still exposed and put my penis away. I removed the grenades from the straps I'd tied beneath my knees and lined the four of them up next to the puddle of fuel. Then I pulled up my left sleeve and showed him my Lager number.

'Do you recognise me now, Sergeant Knaus? I was in the Sonderkommando at Auschwitz-Birkenau for many months.'

He started making sounds – no doubt trying to plead, offer me money, maybe even compliment me on my good service and my survival.

'The time has come for you to hear the judgement passed down by the thousands of souls you sent into the cold Polish skies. You beat people to death.' I clubbed him across the side of the head with the Colt. 'You shot them in the back of the neck in their hundreds. Don't worry, that's too quick for you.' Instead I ran the knife blade across his throat, watching the blood drip but not spurt. 'You drove people into the gas chamber.' I laughed, staring into his terrified eyes. 'Quite a lot of diesel fumes here, aren't there? You ordered their corpses to be burned. You *will* experience that, but with a difference – you'll burn alive.'

He whimpered through the gap, jerking his head from side to side. That stopped when I stabbed him through the other thigh. Blood flowed rapidly from the femoral artery and I realised time was short.

'You were also responsible for the deaths of the mutilated victims of the doctors.' I jabbed the point of the knife into his groin. 'Do you have anything to say before sentence is carried out? I thought not.'

He was desperately trying to communicate, looking up at the wall to his right.

'Your family?' I was disappointed he was concerned about them, then I realised he was using them for his own safety. 'Are they at home? That is unfortunate. Then again, think how many families you incinerated. Heil Hitler!'

Knaus struggled to get free as I pulled the pin from one of the grenades, kicking the other three into the diesel. I looked him in the eye and laughed, then dropped the grenade and ran for the end of the passage. I made it just before the explosion.

I walked quickly up the hill as people ran towards the blaze that had ignited the rapid series of blasts. No one paid me the least attention.

'What happened?' Shlomo asked.

Zvi glared at me and swung a punch, which I avoided. 'You did that deliberately, didn't you? Why couldn't you share him?'

I explained what had happened, but Zvi wasn't convinced. We were never as close again.

A few days later we heard that thirty-seven people, including nine children, had died in the fire, which was put down to an electrical fault. I felt, and still feel, no guilt.

When we parted Zvi told me I had become one

of them, a Jewish monster. The words meant nothing to me. They were men, I was a man, and we each had to make choices. I chose to survive and become an avenger. The Nazis were misguided. I don't think I was.

Do you?

TWENTY-FIVE

'What is it?' Rachel said.

'My ... my friend in Athens. His house was burned down. They don't know if he was inside.'

'Oh my God.' She clutched his arm.

Mavros was still squatting, holding the phone away from him as if it had dealt him a blow. Suddenly it rang again. Mavros activated the connection but was unable to speak.

There was a cough. 'Is that you ... half-Scottish tosser?'

'Yiorgo? You're ... you're alive. Where are you?'

'I'm – get off, I can take my trousers off myself, thank you – I'm in the General Hospital.' More coughing. 'With a nurse who seems ... to have an extreme interest in my privates.' A firm female voice could be heard in the background. 'Apparently I'm a–' this time the coughing lasted even longer – 'difficult patient.'

'What a surprise. Tell me what happened.'

'Bastards threw ... Molotovs.'

'But you got out.'

'Thanks to the shotgun. There isn't much left

of the door.'

It sounded like the Fat Man didn't know about the destruction of his family home.

'Are you hurt?'

'Some burns, I don't think ... they're too bad ... some minor cuts.'

'How come you disappeared?'

'This young guy picked me ... took me to the hospital. I passed out for a bit. The traffic was fucking ... awful so we got delayed.'

'Young guy?' Mavros asked, thinking of the Son.

'I had the feeling ... I'd seen him somewhere ... before.'

'Was it the Son?'

'No ... I don't think so. Blinded ... couldn't see properly.'

Mavros thought about that. Even if it wasn't the Son himself, he could have put someone else up to it. But why make a move on Yiorgos rather than him or Niki? Or his more vulnerable mother?

'Who would have burned ... tried to burn you out?'

'I'm taking them off... What? Burn me out? I don't know. You haven't made ... enemies up there, have you?'

A bony finger twisted in Mavros's abdomen. Shimon said he'd been on the TV news. Could some fucker in the Phoenix Rises have recognised him and tried to get him out of Thessaloniki by striking at the Fat Man?

'They're trying ... they're going to put a mask on me. Listen, Alex, don't come back for me ...

213

you hear? Unless you've ... finished up there. Do your job, all right? I'm in good hands. Well, quite good hands .... severe, really, but...' The connection was broken.

Mavros slumped against the wall and drew his arm across his eyes.

'Is he OK?' Rachel asked.

'So it seems.' He shook his head. 'His house was firebombed.'

'Shit. Who by?'

'Too early to tell.'

'Let's get a coffee,' she suggested. 'You look like you need several.'

Mavros let himself be taken to a nearby café, where he ordered a triple *sketo*. He felt better soon afterwards.

'Sorry, I need to make some calls.'

Rachel nodded and occupied herself with her own phone.

'Niki? Panic over. He's in the General.'

'Oh, Alex, thank God. How is he?'

'Cantankerous.'

'I meant physically.'

'Nothing too serious, though he's coughing like a bull in a, er ... bull ring.'

'I'll ring and see if I can visit.'

Mavros swallowed a laugh. Niki and the Fat Man didn't get on like any kind of building on fire. 'That would be ... nice of you.'

'Are you at the airport?'

He glanced at Rachel, who was sending a text, her long fingers moving like a pianist's.

'Not yet. Yiorgos told me to stay if I wasn't finished.'

There was silence.

'Niki?'

'I can't believe you, Alex. Never mind me, but your best friend is almost killed and you're still up there?'

'I don't know... I need to find out who was behind the fire.'

'And you can do that from the co-capital?'

'I can't do it from Athens either. I'm not an arson expert.'

'Arson?'

Shit, Mavros thought, then told her what Yiorgos had said. 'So it could still be you know who.'

'Or someone employed by him. The cops will look for witnesses once they take the Fat Man's statement and get the fire service's report.'

'You could be looking for witnesses now.'

That was true. 'Leave it with me, Niki. Please, I know what I'm doing.'

'Yes, you do. When it comes to yourself.' She rang off.

Mavros shook his head, then his phone rang again. The name on the screen made him feel even worse.

'My commiserations on your friend's ... problem.' Police Brigadier Nikos Kriaras, chief of the capital and surrounding area's organised crime unit, sounded unusually concerned. He distrusted mobile phones and spoke cryptically.

'Yeah, like that's why you're calling.'

'So hostile. I was hoping we could get over last year.'

'When you let the Son loose? I don't think so.'

'Do you think it's him?'

215

'Do *you?*'

Kriaras sighed. 'This is going nowhere. I called to ask if Pandazopoulos passed on any information we could use. I hear he's conscious.'

Mavros was immediately suspicious. 'Why are you so interested in a fire?'

'Anything to do with you interests me.'

Mavros told him what Yiorgos had said.

'Molotovs? Has the big man being throwing his Communist flab around? Antagonising the far right, maybe?'

Mavros let that pass. 'Will you organise a canvass? Maybe the slimeballs were seen.'

'Yes, sir. Anything else?'

'No.'

'Very well. Have a good time in Thessaloniki.' The connection was cut.

Bastard, Mavros said to himself. He might have known that Kriaras would be keeping tabs on him. He'd probably told his counterpart in the co-capital about his presence.

Rachel was still busy, so he made calls to his mother and sister. Both were pleased to hear that the Fat Man was alive and reasonably well, though neither of them were his biggest fans. They would maintain high alert in case the Son was involved.

'All done?' Rachel asked.

He nodded, although he'd had a worrying thought. If Nikos Kriaras knew he was in Thessaloniki, maybe the Son did too.

Mavros led her to Shimon Raphael's office.

'If you want to go to Athens, it's fine by me,'

216

Rachel said. 'Let's see how things down there and up here develop.'

'What about your ... woman?'

'What about her?' he replied sharply.

She didn't answer.

Shimon rose as they came in, the office being a single though large room. Clerks were working at computer terminals.

'Alex,' he said extending a hand. 'And you must be Ms Samuel.' He was speaking accented but fluent English. 'I saw you sticking it to those neo-Nazi fools on the TV.'

Rachel looked at Mavros coolly. 'I am,' she said, turning back to Shimon. 'You've evidently heard of me, but I know nothing about you.'

'Shimon is an old friend of the Fat ... my friend Yiorgos,' Mavros put in. 'He's been helping me with some background matters.'

The customs broker laughed loudly. 'Background, yes.'

'So, what have you got for us?'

'First of all, Ester Broudo.'

Rachel frowned.

'Everyone I've talked to says she's sharp as a tack and an upstanding member of the community. No dark secrets.'

'All right,' Mavros said neutrally.

Shimon unlocked his desk drawer and took out a file. 'As I said, I don't think it's major, but it's interesting.'

Mavros opened the file and ran his eye down the papers inside.

'You want to explain what this means?' he asked, struggling with the small print of the documents.'

'Sure. During the war the Germans set up an organisation called YDIP, the Service for the Disposal of Jewish Property. It was run by local worthies – so they'd have characterised themselves – but answerable to the occupiers. In fact, most of them were traitors, collaborators and thieves. They expropriated Jewish businesses and homes, not to mention personal possessions. The people closest to the Germans enriched themselves hugely, as did those who were able to bribe them.'

'Didn't they have problems when the Jews came back?' Mavros asked. 'I read there were court cases.'

'Which dragged on for years and often resulted in limited return of property and compensation. Many claimants emigrated rather than wait.'

'And in any case there weren't many of them,' Rachel put in. 'How many came back? Three thousand?'

Shimon nodded. 'It's difficult to be sure, but well under ten per cent.'

Mavros could tell there was more. 'So, what have you dug up?'

Shimon looked at Rachel. 'Your great-great-uncle, Yosif, owned five shops as well as the family home. All were obtained by the same person.' He paused. 'Efthymis – Makis – Kalogirou.'

Mavros's head jerked back. 'As in...'

'Makis Kalogirou the neo-Nazi wanker. Efthymis was his grandfather.'

'That's ... interesting,' Mavros said. 'And possibly more significant than you imagine.'

'Wait a minute,' Rachel said. 'You're saying that

218

the grandfather of the Phoenix Rises' leader owned my family's property.'

Shimon nodded. 'And that Makis – a.k.a. Efthymis, he has his grandfather's name, may he rot in hell – is the current owner.'

'God,' Rachel said. She looked queasy.

'There's something else. Old Kalogirou went missing in August 1948, towards the end of the Civil War. There was no trace of him and his body was never found.'

Mavros had a flash of his brother Andonis. 'What happened?'

'According to the newspapers, he went out for dinner with colleagues – meaning other right-wing extremists – and never showed up. It was assumed an aggrieved employee got to him. He was a notorious exploiter, working his staff hard and paying them as little as he could get away with. He'd also made several people redundant recently. Someone – no doubt another collaborator – removed everything he could from the YDIP files about the Samuel properties.' He tapped his nose. 'I have a special source.'

The customs broker turned to Mavros. 'I've got something on the "hyper" issue,' he said, in Greek. 'Do you want me to share it with your client?'

'Is it good or bad?'

Shimon raised his shoulders. 'It's confirmation.'

'Go on, then. She could do with something to take her mind off the Nazis.'

'I've been checking into Aron Samuel's background,' Shimon said, in English. Rachel immediately perked up. 'He was a member of the

Communist Youth Party here. His file has been – how can I put it? – purged. I don't know when.'

'So he was a Communist.' Rachel looked shocked. 'We ... my family has no sympathy with the left.' Her eyes narrowed. 'What happened to his file?'

'I don't know. I used to be a member of the party – I'm sorry if that offends you – but I can't find out that kind of information.'

'He was either a traitor or a valuable operator, probably undercover,' Mavros explained.

Rachel's face was pale again. 'Well, those are tempting alternatives. What else do you know?'

Shimon dropped his gaze. 'That's it, I'm afraid.'

Rachel got up, nodded to him and headed for the door.

'She didn't take that well,' the customs broker said. 'It's not as if Communists are lepers.'

'They are for some people, especially Jewish Communists.'

'True.'

Mavros extended his hand. 'I'll be in touch. I owe you dinner.'

Shimon grinned. 'And a research fee.'

Mavros laughed. 'Don't worry, you'll get it. And if you hear anything else...'

'Don't worry, my friend. I have your number.'

As he walked away, Mavros suddenly remembered what had happened to the Fat Man. He went back and told Shimon.

'Fuck. But he's OK, you say.'

'Apparently.'

'Who would throw Molotovs at Yiorgos's place?'

220

'Good question. Does the Phoenix Rises have a track record of that up here?'

'Off the top of my head, no. They prefer fists and boots.' He smiled crookedly. 'Besides, they wouldn't fancy something named after a leading Soviet official.'

Mavros shook his head, but couldn't resist smiling.

'Aren't you going back to Athens?'

'He told me not to. I'll see.'

'Oh, I almost forgot. Yitzak Tsiako will see you at the Noufara Café on Tsimiski Street at nine. He'll be finished his evening's chess by then.'

Mavros looked at his watch. He'd forgotten about the family whose wedding Aron Samuel had been seen outside of. He needed to get a grip.

Allegra Harari was as cheery and bustling as she'd been on their last visit. Her experience the previous evening didn't seem to have affected her.

'Oh, that,' she said dismissively. 'The neo-Nazis are cowards. I think it would have been as you said. Some of the anti-fascists must have seen them and scared them away.'

Mavros was less inclined than she to dismiss the 'ghost' she'd mentioned. Only a trained operative would have been able to take out head bangers so silently; only an experienced professional would get them out of the building so efficiently. The sole person he knew with those qualifications was the Son. Was he dogging their footsteps in Thessaloniki? Who would have put

221

him up to that? The obvious answer was Nikos Kriaras. Was the policeman acting on behalf of the privileged groups that controlled the politicians and ran the country from behind the scenes? What would their interest in a supposedly long-dead Jew be? Or were they more interested in the Kalogirou family? His mind was spinning. Then he had another thought. What if the Son was working on his own account? But if he was in the co-capital, he couldn't have petrol-bombed Yiorgos's house – unless he'd subcontracted that job.

'Alex?'

Mavros came out of his reverie and looked up at Allegra.

'I was saying that Rachel should refrain from taking the fight to the Phoenix Rises, even though they're vile and ignorant animals.'

Mavros translated, adding, 'I quite agree.'

Rachel gave him a cool look.

Mavros told Allegra what they had learned from Shimon Raphael, stressing that it was in confidence.

'Don't worry, I won't tell anyone. Shimon's a good man, especially since he saw the light about the comrades. They've lost their way. They'll be rehabilitating Stalin soon. Besides,' she said, looking down at a page full of notes, 'that chimes with what I've found.'

'Really?' Mavros was surprised. How could a non-Communist have discovered anything revealing about a member?

'Yes. As you know from the book I put together for your mother, several survivors of the death camps wrote private memoirs about their experiences. Others tried to forget, of course. And others ... well, others were never the same again.'

Rachel looked at her curiously after the translation was made.

'Meaning?' Mavros asked.

'Meaning that their minds were damaged by what they went through. I interviewed all of them – those who hadn't been taken to Israel or elsewhere by their families – and I kept notes. Something nagged at me about Aron Samuel from the start and I finally tracked it down.' She held up a transparent file filled with handwritten pages. 'Haim Rosenberg. Twenty-five when he was put on the fourth transport to Auschwitz-Birkenau. Returned here in November 1945. Lost everyone except his sister Rula, who was hidden by Christian Greeks in a village outside Thessaloniki. Haim lived with Rula and her husband and children till they all left for Israel in 1995.' Allegra fell silent.

'What did he tell you?' Mavros prompted.

'I'm still not sure if I believe him – he was prone to hallucinations. Anyway, he said he saw Aron Samuel here several times during the Civil War. He was unclear about dates.' She shook her head. 'But no one else did. I really don't know if his testimony is reliable.'

Mavros kept Rachel up to speed, aware that Allegra was uncharacteristically nervous.

'Haim couldn't work so Rula used to send him to the shops. They lived in the centre, near the Arch of Galerius, so he went past a lot of offices and cafés every day. He said he saw Aron waiting around, looking in windows, and once following a man who came out and walked down the street.'

'Why did he remember that?'

'Because of the look on Aron's face. Haim said it terrified him, gave him nightmares for months ... because it reminded him of the guards and the worst of the capos in the Lager. "Death had eaten him and spat him out alive", he said.'

Mavros translated.

'You think the man he followed was Kalogirou?' Rachel asked. 'You think my great-uncle made him disappear?'

Allegra heard the Greek name. 'What has the Phoenix Rise's idiot leader got to do with this?'

'You know about his grandfather?' Mavros said.

'Oh, you're talking about the collaborator. Of course. He got a lot of Jewish property at low prices from the Nazis, via the YDIP. You've heard of that?'

He nodded. 'Including the Samuel family's.'

The researcher looked surprised. 'I didn't know that.'

'Apparently the records were tampered with.'

'There was a lot of that. Did you know that some of the collaborators in this city became government ministers during the 50s?'

Mavros nodded. 'The Merten trial proved that.'

'Indeed it did.'

'My father was a lawyer. He worked with the prosecutor.'

'Good for him. It was a disgrace what happened.'

Rachel nudged him and he translated.

'I'll tell you about Merten later.' He looked at his watch. 'We have to go. Thanks for this. Have you made out a bill?'

The researcher shook her head. 'This was a public service. But be careful. The link to the older Kalogirou is worrying. It means the Phoenix Rises might be involved. They might have found out that Aron Samuel was spotted.'

'How?'

'Not only Christian Greeks were collaborators. There was a Jewish police force that helped the Germans in the war. If a poor member of our community was tempted by money...'

Mavros asked Allegra about the old man they had found hanged, but got no further information on him. He told her they were going to visit Yitzak Tsiako and asked what she knew about his father, Zvi – no more than Shimon, it turned out.

Mavros and Rachel took their leave. Before he explained to her about the Merten trial, he had a worrying thought. The special interests served by Nikos Kriaras and innumerable others no doubt included people whose ancestors had been black-market operators and collaborators. It wasn't at all unlikely that some had ties to the far right in general and the Phoenix Rises in particular.

Was it a coincidence that the pickup full of skinheads had arrived at the Jewish cemetery gates when they were leaving?

TWENTY-SIX

We killed many of them, the beasts of Auschwitz-Birkenau and other Lagers. Some were women, but I had no pity for them. If anything, they were worse than the men – hard-faced blondes who spat at us and swore till their last moments, never pleading for their lives. The poison of Nazism ran deeper in their veins, while many of the men had it sucked out of them on the Eastern Front along with their aggression. Only SS guards who had never seen combat escaped disillusion.

Gradually our work became harder. The Americans and British had tolerated the killing of SS members in the aftermath of the war. As battle lines were drawn against the Soviet Union, we became an embarrassment. More than once we had to shoot our way out of confrontations with Military Police units, although we always aimed high. By the beginning of 1947, Shlomo and I accepted Zvi's argument that we return home. That proved to be difficult as the British monitored the movements of Jews in order to control those trying to get to Palestine. We spent several months in a camp in central Italy. We weren't captured, but walked in voluntarily, having run out of food. Also, we were in desperate need of rest.

The problem was, we weren't allowed to leave when we recovered. At least we were supplied with clothes and shoes. The guards weren't like the SS men and we could have staged a breakout, but we had matured. Killing was no longer a good idea, so we waited, Shlomo and I playing cards and backgammon, while Zvi devoted himself to the Torah. He rapidly became a very Orthodox Jew and regarded us as little better than gentiles. He had been shot in the shoulder by an American patrol and had played only a small part in the last executions.

Eventually, along with other Greek Jews, we were shipped home. We wanted to disembark at Igoumenitsa opposite Corfu, but the Civil War was being fought in the northern mountains of the mainland and we had to go to Patra and then Athens. We were treated with suspicion, despite the papers we had been issued with in Italy. Members of our community in Athens helped us find a fishing boat that was going north. There had been fewer of them than in the northern cities, but more had survived because of the good work of their chief rabbi, the help of Christian Greeks and the proximity of the mountains. When they heard we were from Thessaloniki, they clutched our arms and commiserated with us. Later we found out that they didn't tell us all they knew.

It was a bright morning in the autumn of 1947 when we sailed past Mount Olympus on our way to the Gulf of Thessaloniki. I found myself weakening as I approached my home city, as if the steel in my bones was melting despite the chill breeze. My close family members were all gone, but there would be people I knew, maybe more distant family members. We would not be the only ones to return.

Zvi started praying aloud as we came into the enclosed waters. Shlomo and I moved as far away as we could on the cramped vessel.

'Will he talk?' my comrade asked.

'And if he does? We have taken eyes for eyes and heads for heads, as in the holy writings.'

He shook his head. 'You still have a devil in you, Aron.'

'While you do not. Never fear, I'll tame the beast. So will you.'

But we didn't. From the moment we set foot on the concrete wharf, we were treated like outsiders, unworthy of consideration let alone the rights of other Greeks. The city was in effect under martial law because of the war against the Communists. I had no interest in the party any longer – what I had been through was so much deeper than class politics that I avoided all contact with the few old comrades who had remained in the city. Zvi went to the synagogue and was soon a leading light in the long beard and ringlets faction. He even found a wife to set up home with. For Shlomo and me it was different. His family home had been knocked down and there was only wooden scaffolding over a hole in the ground. He spent his days in the City Council and Jewish community offices, trying to establish his claim.

I went to our house on the seafront the day after we arrived. I tried the first day, but I was sick and had to bed down in a hostel provided for camp survivors by some American charity. As I walked by the water, I felt purged, cleansed, though the weight of the Lager was always on my shoulders. The old building was still there, the shutters open and a much brighter blue than they had been. I walked up the path. It was a Sunday and I could hear voices from inside children's and adults'. I knocked on the familiar door, also freshly painted. Heavy steps sounded on the tiles.

'Yes?' asked a solidly built man, running a critical eye over me.

'This is my house.'

I was taken by surprise, for all my combat expertise. The man punched me hard in the face, sending me sprawling down the steps. He came after me, kicking me in the ribs and groin. I protected myself as best I could, unable to fight back. As I lay with my lips to the earth, I was back in the Lager, a helpless victim.

'Listen, you Jewish swine,' the man said, lifting my head by the hair. 'This is my house, you hear? Bought and paid for, all the papers in order. What the fuck are you doing here? Why didn't they make soap out of you?'

I heard a wave of laughter. Through the blood that was running into my eyes I saw a crowd of people outside the door – teenage children, middle-aged men and women, and grandparents.

My attacker lifted me by the scruff of my neck and my belt and carried me to the gate.

'Never come back. If I see you again, I'll kill you,' he said, then threw me into the road.

There was a horn blast and a jeep swerved, the driver shouting.

I crawled away, suffering from shame as much as from the blows, which were no worse than the many I had suffered from the capos and SS men. Not only had the bastard stolen my family home, he'd beaten me like an unworthy slave. I got up and stumbled off. Eventually I found a ruined house and took refuge in the basement. It stank of sewage and rat piss, and was no more than I deserved.

In the following weeks I avoided contact with anyone in the Jewish community. I did not feel I belonged with them any more. They had survived and were rebuilding their lives. I had been in the Sonderkommando and they would see me as a traitor, especially because I would seek no atonement. I had not asked to join the unit and once I was in it, it was impossible not to follow orders. Zvi no doubt impressed people by his religiosity. I had no such crutch and no desire to obtain one. I knew then that what we had been doing in Germany and Austria was right. And the fascists, whatever their nationality, were still at large in their thousands.

Stealing food had become second nature in the Lager and I kept myself alive in the city without too much difficulty. I had a single aim – to bring down the man who had stolen my birthright. Shlomo was the only person I saw. He found out what I needed during the days he spent pressing his claim to the hole that had been his home. Soon I knew all about Efthymis Kalogirou, son of Petros. His father had joined one of the most violent ultra-nationalist groups after the Germans occupied the city. Somehow he had escaped the violent retribution his fellow fighters suffered at the hands of the resistance and had worked to increase the family wealth after the war ended. He should have been shot as a traitor, but the Civil War meant that old sins were disregarded – all that mattered to the government, first backed by the British and then the Americans, was the eradication of the Communist fighters. Efthymis Kalogirou should have been executed too – there were many stories of him cosying up to the Germans and paying them for Jewish property with stolen gold. He had been a personal friend of Max Merten and had benefited from that connection.

I waited before striking because I wanted to see what happened with Shlomo's case. But by the summer of 1948 it became clear he was wasting his time. He had no money for a lawyer and the man who had bought the property was a leading local politician with connections in Athens.

'We will kill them both,' Shlomo said.

'No, we won't,' I replied. 'I'll deal with Kalogirou on my own. It's the only way I'll get my self-respect back.'

He laughed. 'Self-respect after the SK? That's a joke.'

'Do what you want,' I said. 'If you can, take his money. That's what I intend to do with my fine Christian.'

'It'll be better if we help one another.'

'No, that's for the future. This job I do on my own.'

And I did. I followed Kalogirou, taking care he never saw me. I kept my head down when anyone from the Jewish community came near and I don't think others recognised me. By high summer I knew his daily movements in precise detail. I also knew exactly when and where to pick him up.

On Thursdays, after eating with friends, he went to a brothel and returned home after one in the morning. I'd been observing the house and saw the room he went to; it used to be my father's study, at the rear on the ground floor. The lights were out in the other rooms when I reached the back balcony. The shutters were closed, but I flipped the catch with a switchblade I'd stolen from a stoned gambler. The window hadn't been replaced since our time and there was enough of a gap between the edges of the frame to accommodate my blade. I climbed in and settled down behind the large leather armchair. I was struck by the smell of the room, unchanged despite the passage of the years, but I kept a grip on myself. Steel had filled my veins and bones again.

It was a simple job. The collaborator came in and crashed down into the armchair. I knocked him out with a good-sized stone I'd picked up and tied his hands behind his back. Then I gagged him as I'd done with Knaus and waited for him to come round. I thought his eyes were going to pop out of their sockets when he recognised me in the single light I had turned on.

'So, traitor thief,' I said, blade against his neck. 'You're going to open that safe.'

He made a series of muffled noises, and then went silent as the knife point pierced the skin of his throat. I encouraged his cooperation by telling him what I would do to his family if he resisted. He complied with alacrity. From my observations, I knew he was a loud-mouthed bully. They always crumbled quickest.

The safe was a treasure trove. Not only was there a large number of gold coins, mainly British sovereigns, but there was a Luger Parabellum pistol and six eight-round magazines. I pushed one in and fed a round up the spout, then closed the safe.

'You're coming with me,' I said, pushing him to the door. I already had his house keys in my hand. I got him outside with no trouble and locked the door behind us. As far as his family would be concerned, he had never come home. We walked along the darkened seafront – no vehicles passed – and I told him what I was going to do with him. He quivered and tried more than once to run away, but I held on to the rope round his wrists. I also stabbed him repeatedly in the arms and legs – not enough to disable him, but to maximize the pain. By the time we reached the building site I had identified earlier, he knew exactly what was ahead. The cement foundations of an apartment block had been laid that day. I stood him by the side of a still soft trench and used the knife all over him. But he was still alive when I pushed him into the concrete. When he stopped struggling I smoothed the surface and sat watching as the dawn's first slivers appeared. Efthymis Kalogirou had gone to the underworld.

'He disappeared like our people,' I said to Shlomo on the boat south next day. 'His family will never know what happened to him. They'll live with a cruel hope that will eventually turn into despair and desolation. That's justice.'

'Justice would be getting our property back,' Shlomo said lugubriously. His target hadn't shown up where he had lain in wait, so his family was unavenged.

I put my arm round him as the city vanished into the mist. 'My friend, there are plenty of Nazis for us to kill. By now they'll be all over the world. And they don't know we'll be on their trail. We also have enough funds to start operations again.'

'But there are only two of us. It'll be harder.'

'Someone will turn up.'

I was right. We found Baruh Natzari in Italy. He had been in Auschwitz and was the only survivor of a vengeance squad that had been pursued in Bavaria. His need for justice was still great.

We followed the Nazis to South America and turned their new world into a living hell.

TWENTY-SEVEN

'We may as well walk,' Mavros said. 'Finding parking places is a nightmare in this city.'

'What was that name I heard you mention to her?' Rachel said. 'Merton?'

'Merten, Max Merten. He was the German civilian administrator of Thessaloniki during the war. He was involved with the setting up of the YDIP and made a fortune from it.'

'What does he have to do with my great-uncle?'

'Nothing that I'm aware of, but he would have known the elder Kalogirou, the collaborator who got your family's property and grandfather of the Phoenix Rises' leader.'

The evening air was chill and Rachel's features had taken on a spectral look. 'What happened to Merten?'

'He made the mistake of coming back to Greece in 1957, was arrested on the orders of a sharp-eyed prosecutor and accused of war crimes. My father worked on the case – not as a defence lawyer, I hasten to add. There were all sorts of political shenanigans behind the scenes. Merten accused Greek ministers in the Karamanlis government of being collaborators. He was sentenced to twenty-five years but was whisked out of the country soon after and set free after a couple of months in a German jail. As you can imagine, that didn't go down well in the Jewish community worldwide.'

'Why are you interested in this sidebar to my great-uncle?'

Mavros decided to be straight with her. 'The Phoenix Rises is only a surface-level manifestation of the interest groups that pull the strings in this country. The roots of those people's fortunes were either in the war – collaboration, assisting the Germans financially, black-market activities – or in the Civil War that followed. The ship-owners flourished in the post-war years. The super-rich are quite happy when the far right struts about, but they like it less when terrorists kill business-men, as has happened in the past. They also aren't keen on people like me, especially when I turn the media on them as I did last year.'

The Noufara Café's sign was ahead.

'You think they burned your friend's house down?'

Mavros shrugged. 'Their minions, maybe.'

'So this case is about you, not my great-uncle.'

'I'm beginning to suspect it's about both. They may be interested in locating Aron too.'

'But why?'

'Maybe we're about to find out.'

Niki took a deep breath and went into the twin-bedded room. Only one was occupied, though the large figure could have done with a double.

'Hello,' she said, in a low voice.

The Fat Man's eyes shot open. He had an oxygen line in his nostrils and there were dressings on his arms.

'What are you... I mean, it's good of you to visit.'

'I wanted to see how you were,' she said, unwrapping a bowl of fruit and putting it on the bedside locker.

Yiorgos gave the fruit a dubious look. 'I don't know why they're ... keeping me in here. I'm perfectly ... all right.'

'You don't sound perfectly all right.'

'Smoke inhalation ... no lung damage.'

'That's good. What about burns?'

'First degree, all of them. I got out in time.' He paused. 'How's the house?'

Niki looked him in the eye. 'I'm sorry. Only the exterior walls are still standing. The roof collapsed and everything inside is ... gone or unusable.'

The Fat Man turned away, blinking repeatedly.

'I know,' Niki said. 'It was your parents' house, you lived there all your life...' She leaned forward. 'What?'

'Fucking bastards,' he said, then started coughing. 'I'll ... tear their ... balls off.'

'Did you see anyone?'

'In that smoke? No chance. Someone ... in black ... face covered.'

'So how do you know there was more than one person throwing the Molotovs?'

He looked at her as if she were stupid. 'Because they came in quick succession through the door and the windows. I don't suppose the cops have found anyone.'

'Not that I've heard.'

Conversation dried up. A nurse came in and took the patient's blood pressure and temperature.

'Can I get out ... of here now?' Yiorgos demanded.

'That's up to the doctors. They'll be round tomorrow morning.'

'Marx and Lenin, another night in this dump.'

The nurse gave him a supercilious look and departed.

'You ... you can stay at our place when you're discharged,' Niki said.

The Fat Man stared at her. 'Really?'

'Of course. But I need a favour from you.' She smiled. 'I know we haven't always got on–'

'Understatement ... of the millennium.'

'Well, yes, but we do share an interest.'

'You mean the half-Scottish long hair with the

237

weird eye?'

'I mean Alex, yes.' Now she couldn't look at him. 'Yiorgo, please, tell him to come home. He listens to you.'

'Does he ... really? That isn't a major ... feature of our friendship.'

'Yes, it is. Please, will you do that for me? I ... I need him.'

He watched her as she dabbed her eyes with a tissue. 'Look, I know you're having ... a hard time right now. But it's early days. The doctors will work things out.'

'No, they won't,' Niki said firmly. 'I ... I know I can't have children.'

'What do you mean? That's not what Alex told me.'

'I feel it like a ball of ice inside me. I ... I can't.' She broke down.

The Fat Man tried to take her hand, gasping as a dressing snagged. 'Come on, Niki. It's not that bad.'

She stood up, unaware of the movement he'd made. 'I have to go. Just tell him, Yiorgo. I need him home. Make him understand. Please.' Then she gave him a tremulous smile, turned on her heel and walked out.

He lay back, swearing under his breath. The truth was, he wanted Alex back too. He felt lost without the house, the structure and substance of his life cremated and ruined. His friend should be there for him and for Niki.

But he couldn't do it. When Alex was on a case, he couldn't be restricted, especially not by the people who loved him. When he was ready to come back, he would. It would be a betrayal to plead with him.

The Fat Man thought about Niki. She had dressed well as usual, but she was a wreck. Someone needed to take care of her, but he was the last person to do that. He struggled even to take care of himself. As he thought of the house and his possessions – the photographs of his father and mother, the latter's beloved kitchen equipment, the furniture that had been there for decades – he did what Niki hadn't: he started to wail inconsolably.

A solitary man was stooped over a chessboard on a table in the far corner of the café.

'Mr Tsiako?' Mavros said.

'Yes, yes.' The seated man got to his feet. He was in his fifties, stout and completely bald. After the introductions were completed, he beckoned to them to join him.

'Miss Samuel doesn't speak Greek,' Mavros said.

'I have English,' Tsiako said. 'This helps?'

'It does,' Rachel said, with a smile.

A waiter appeared and they ordered coffees.

'I must say, I am intrigued. Shimon said you were a historian, Mr Mavros.'

'Alex, please. Of a sort. I'm assisting Miss Samuel–'

'Rachel.'

'Rachel, with enquiries into a family member.'

Tsiako looked at her more carefully. 'Are you a Thessaloniki Samuel?'

She nodded. 'My father is Eliezer, but he ended

up as a small child in Canada during the war.'

'I have no knowledge of him.'

'My great-uncle Aron was the son of Iosif Samuel, the jeweller.'

The chess player's eyes opened wide. 'Aron Samuel,' he said, shaking his head. 'I hoped not to hear that name again.'

'Why?' Mavros asked. 'What did your father tell you about him?'

Yitzak Tsiako turned to him. 'You have been doing your research,' he said, his tone sharp. 'Despite the fact that you are not one of us. What else has that loud-mouth Shimon told you?'

Rachel leaned forward. 'Please, Mr Tsiako, I have heard bad things about my great-uncle. If necessary, I will make recompense.'

'Ha! What recompense!' He rose. 'There can be no recompense for what Aron Samuel did.'

Mavros got to his feet and put his hand on the other man's arm. 'Please stay,' he said simply. 'The young woman has a right to know about her family.'

Yitzak Tsiako eyed him suspiciously and then sat down. 'It is true, I suppose. How will future generations make a better world if they don't understand the mistakes made by their ancestors?'

Rachel nodded. 'Please tell us about your father.'

After a pause, Tsiako began to speak in a low and monotonous voice, as if he were reading a religious text aloud. 'My father was in Auschwitz-Birkenau with your great-uncle. You know what is the Sonderkommando?'

They both nodded.

'After the war, some Jews accused them of collaboration. This was unfair because, like anyone else, they wanted to stay alive. My father told me the stain of this work would never be cleaned from him, but he didn't regret what he had done. He wanted to survive so that the family would continue – as indeed it has. My son was married recently.'

Mavros and Rachel exchanged looks.

'But he didn't only work in the Sonderkommando. After the war, he and Aron Samuel killed many members of the SS, including guards from Auschwitz. They wanted to make revenge for the thousands of our community who were lost.'

Mavros considered mentioning Shlomo Catan, the third avenger, but decided against sidetracking the speaker.

'But my father, he lost appetite for this killing. He persuaded the others – there was another Thessaloniki man in their group – to return to Greece. My father became very devout. In fact he devoted the rest of his life to studying the holy books and educating those of the community in their complexities. He told me he separated from your great-uncle and the other man in Athens after quarrelling with them.'

'Do you know why?' Rachel asked.

'Yes.' Tsiako said no more.

'Please,' she said. 'I need to understand everything.'

'Young woman, this is not a burden you have to carry. Your great-uncle killed Nazis, as did my father. Aron never came back. You must imagine that he made his own peace with his conscience

241

and with God.' Yitzak Tsiako got to his feet again.

Rachel stood up quickly and grabbed both his arms. 'I must know,' she said, her eyes on his.

'You must know, you must know! Why?'

Rachel sobbed – Mavros wasn't completely convinced – and said, 'My father is dying. He's been searching for Aron all his life. He deserves this knowledge, whatever it is, before he takes his last breath.'

Tsiako's brow furrowed. 'Very well,' he said, but he remained upright and picked up his coat. 'After the war Aron Samuel was solely responsible for the death of an SS sergeant called Knaus in a small town in eastern Bavaria. In the resulting fire thirty-seven people died, including nine children. As far as my father was concerned, your great-uncle had become the same as the enemy – a killer and a beast, who took pleasure in his work. You can say that the Lager made him that way, but not all survivors of the Sonderkommando behaved like that after liberation.' He raised a hand. 'Yes, I know my father was also an avenger. But his character was strong enough for him to stop and spend the rest of his life atoning. I'm sorry, Miss Samuel. Your family is tainted by Aron's actions.'

'He continued, didn't he?' Mavros said.

Yitzak Tsiako put on his hat. 'I heard so, though it isn't common knowledge.'

'Shlomo Catan told your father.'

'You are well informed.'

'Where did they go? South America?'

'Yes. Excuse me, I must get home.' Tsiako turned away without shaking their hands.

242

Mavros glanced at Rachel. Her head was down.
'We didn't ask him if he saw Aron at the wedding,' she said. 'I think he would have mentioned it. In fact, I think he would have pushed your great-uncle in front of a car.'

She nodded. 'So Aron was one of the Nokmim, the Jewish avengers. They were not few.'

'How many of them burned children to death?'

She walked to the exit. 'I'll see you in the morning,' she said, when he caught up. 'I need to be alone.'

'I presume your father isn't really dying.'

'Of course not.'

Mavros watched as she went down Tsimiski in the direction of the hotel, wondering if the hardness in her was a genetic link to Aron or the result of her own experiences, whatever they might have been.

'Alex?'

'Yiorgo! How are you?'

'In pain and pissed off ... more of the latter than the former.'

'Hang on, let me turn the TV off. What's up?'

'They won't let me out of the General Incompetence Hospital.'

'I bet you're the ideal patient.'

'Huh. Guess who came to visit?'

'That old comrade you go eating with? Apostolos?'

'No, that tosser hasn't turned up – which ... now you mention it, is interesting.'

'You don't think the party's behind the fire.'

'Of course not. But they might know who is.'

'Bloody hell.'

'Exactly. If I'm lucky, they'll be going after the bastards.' Mavros shook his head. 'Violence breeds violence.' Yitzak Tsiako's story about Aron Samuel was still fresh.

'They burned my house down!'

'You can stay with us.'

'That's what Niki said.'

Mavros almost dropped the phone. 'What? She ha ... she doesn't like you very much.'

'That's a two-way street. But she visited me.'

'Amazing.' Mavros hadn't expected Niki to go through with it.

'Yes. There was a cost attached, though.'

'Meaning?'

'She wants me to ... convince you to come back to Athens. We both need you.'

'Christ.'

'No, it's true. You already know she does. And I... Alex, what am I going to do? All my stuff, Mother's things...' The Fat Man started to sob.

'Come on, Yiorgo, we'll sort out a place for you,' Mavros said, feeling out of his depth. Although he and Yiorgos had faced death together more than once, he'd never seen or heard his friend in tears, even when his strong-willed mother, Kyra Fedhra, died. 'You ... you have kept up the insurance payments?'

There was a series of gulps. 'Yes ... but that won't pay for the place ... to be rebuilt, let alone for my personal belongings.'

'Listen, stuff can be replaced. Obviously not your mother's things, but you can buy new kitchen equipment in her memory.'

244

The Fat Man got a grip on his breathing. 'I suppose so,' he said listlessly.

'And if you need more money I'll find it for you.' Mavros had no idea how, but he was feeling guilty. The attack on his friend's house was aimed at him, he was sure.

'Oh, that'll be all right then,' Yiorgos said ironically. 'Super Alex flies to the rescue. I can sleep soundly now.'

'Come on...'

'No, you come on ... back here on the first flight tomorrow, OK?' The connection was cut.

Mavros leaned against a wall, phone in hand. That was the comparatively easy part. Now he had to talk to Niki.

TWENTY-EIGHT

The heat. Thirst. The insects. Sweat. The runs. Water-purification tablets. The food. All that was easy enough to live with after the Lager. Finding our targets in South America was difficult, even though we had money to bribe officials. How did we have money, you ask? There were prominent Jews in most countries and they were keen for Nazi escapers to be dealt with. They supplied us with identities and even arranged for Spanish lessons. We also robbed our victims and their helpers.

We started in Argentina, where Perón had been an open supporter of Hitler and welcomed his followers. Anything can be bought anywhere, especially in South America, but it was almost impossible to obtain the new identities of SS men. Security was tight in the port of Buenos Aires when ships from Europe docked – we had been dropped on a deserted beach by a Greek captain, who was well paid – so we couldn't spot the enemy arriving. Even our paymasters struggled, despite the fact that Perón was not hostile to their community and even appointed Jews to his cabinet. Finally an official with big gambling debts was identified and we got our first names.

Initially the Nazis were kept in the capital city. After we and other groups had hanged some and thrown others out of their windows, they were moved into rural areas. It took us time, but we tracked them down. One hit, on a doctor who had worked with Mengele, needed three months of planning, though the execution only lasted two hours. He would have begged for his life, but we cut out his tongue. He would have wept, but we removed his eyes. You are shocked? Horrified? Remember what they did in the camps. Remember what the SS doctors did in Auschwitz, probably to my sister and niece. Be a man.

Eventually it became too dangerous for us in Argentina and we went north. Paraguay was a good hunting ground. We were there several times over the years. It was comical to see Germans from big cities trying to run farms and logging businesses, despite the privileges they were given by the government. We became inventive, rolling tree trunks over our victims –

after they'd heard the speech Baruh wrote, enumerating the sins of the German people and the Nazis and SS in particular. He became a fine orator and even Shlomo, whose inclination was more towards action, listened intently. I watched the effect of the words on the men pinned to the ground. They voided their bladders and bowels, they cried for their mothers, they begged for their families to be spared. I let their people live if they had married native women. I even let a German wife go because she showed genuine contrition. You wonder how I know it was genuine? I removed three of her fingers. I had learned in the Lager how to distinguish lies from truth. There is something in the timbre of the voice, the stance people take, the way their eyes move. If I knew that, why did I cut off her fingers? Why not? They took our people's entire bodies by the million.

Brazil, Chile, Peru, they were all profitable for us too, counting profit by deaths, of course. As the 50s progressed, however, we became aware that people were on our trail. Not just the Nazis and their friends – we were always too quick and cunning for them; but our own kind, members of the recently formed Mossad. The first meeting we had was in a suburb of Santiago – three of us and three of them.

'The state is grateful for your work,' the leader said. Even though it was a hot night, he was wearing a woollen pullover. Black, of course.

'We are grateful for the state's approval,' I said, watching his right hand. There was a pistol in his pocket.

'But your orders now are to cease operations and go home.'

Shlomo took a step forward, but I caught his arm.

'You have authority over us?' Baruh asked quietly.

'I have authority over all Israeli personnel in South America.'

'Congratulations,' I said, with a smile. 'But we aren't Israelis.'

'You are Jews, Mr Samuel.'

The conversation was in German, the only language we shared. How the guards in the Lager would have laughed.

'Yes, we are Jews,' Shlomo said. 'Sephardic Jews from Thessaloniki. We don't take orders from anyone. Why do you want us to stop slaughtering the bastards?'

'That does not concern you.'

I moved closer, watching his hand as it moved towards the butt of his pistol. 'The state of Israel has powerful sponsors,' I said, in a calm voice. 'They do not want a trail of bodies. I imagine your victims disappear.'

'While yours – at least more recently – are left in full view as examples.'

Baruh laughed. Like us all, he had become inflexible in the pursuit of the enemy. 'Examples to farm hands and native working men. We haven't worked in cities for years.'

'What will you do if we refuse?' Shlomo demanded. 'Shoot us?'

The leader took out his weapon in a blur of speed and pointed it at my chest. 'I hope it doesn't come to that, but if we have to...'

His comrades were pointing machine-pistols at the others, who responded by drawing their side arms. It was an Israeli stand-off, except that I raised my empty hands. It was obvious the time had come to move on.

'Put your guns away,' I said to the others.

'What?' said Shlomo.

'Jews killing other Jews is the wet dream of every Nazi,' I said. 'Back off. We'll leave it to the professionals.'

The others stared at me in astonishment and then complied. Baruh looked like he had understood.

'Again, your work is appreciated.' The Israeli took a package out of his other pocket. 'Passports and funds. Be aware that your friends will no longer supply you. Go to Washington DC – separately – and visit the Israeli embassy. You will be reimbursed for your actions. But they must cease forthwith. Is that understood?'

I nodded. The others backed away into the darkness.

Shlomo turned on me. 'What are you doing?'

Baruh laughed softly. 'Always the bull in the marketplace. Aron has played them consummately. We take their money and get on with our work.'

I shook my head. 'No, we do as he said. I know you still have the appetite for vengeance – so do I – but we need to build other lives.' I put my arm round Shlomo's shoulder. 'Don't worry, we will still track down the murderers. But we will be more careful. I for one want to live to a great old age.'

'Methuselah,' Shlomo muttered. 'The Nazis will grow old too.'

'Not all of them,' I said.

So we went to the US by different routes. The passports were American and seemed to be genuine, which showed at least that not only Nazi rocket scientists and medical researchers were given citizenship by that country. I used the large amount of money I was given to set up a jewellery business in Brooklyn – that would have been some comfort to my father. I sold it for a large profit after five years and played the stock market carefully, using trusted advisers. By the early 60s I was very well off. Shlomo and Baruh both went back to Thessaloniki and studiously avoided each other. Of course, Mossad had changed strategy by then and pulled off the sensational abduction of Eichmann in 1960. That made me smile. Every summer the three of us met in a different country and executed Nazis that I had gathered information about. We did what the leader who warned us off had done – disposed of the bodies and left no evidence: for our own safety as much as anything else. Remember Zakar, the Jewish policeman I killed in Thessaloniki? I had no desire to be the victim of a young zealot like the one I had once been. As for the Communists, I had no interest in them. Stalin had proved to be little better than Hitler and I needed no command structure.

What's that? How did the beheaded men fit the modus operandi? Ali, that was in Paraguay in the late 50s. We were lucky. An SS man we were targetting – a former medical officer at Auschwitz – was joined by two men at the weekend in his ranch house outside a village. He worked part-time as a village doctor and was still carrying out experiments. We saw one child with a shaved head covered in scars. Anyway, his visitors, despite their tanned faces and country clothes, had a bearing that made us suspicious. We burst in on them when the native servants had left. The trio was drinking schnapps and smoking cigars.

After we'd tied them to their chairs, I started the interrogation. The other two swore at me until Shlomo and Baruh used their knives. Then they gabbled out their stories. One had been in an SS-Sonderkommando behind the lines during Operation Barbarossa, shooting Jews in their thousands in White Russia and the Ukraine. The other had been a guard at Treblinka. They were cowards and soiled themselves. The doctor was another kind, arrogant and pleased with what he had done and continued to do.

'The non-Aryan races are sub-humans,' he said, his voice high and unwavering. 'You think that because you have weapons you are superior to us. No! A Jew is never more than an animal.'

Shlomo stepped towards him, but I raised a hand.

'Cut off the SK man's head,' I said.

Shlomo did so, slowly.

When he'd finished, I said, 'It seems to me, Herr Doktor, that your friend has been slaughtered like an animal.'

He was less sure of himself, but still held his head high. The Treblinka guard started to plead, falling silent only when Baruh brought his knife to his throat.

'You Jews,' the doctor said. 'Only good for shepherding your own people into the gas chambers and pulling out their shit-covered bodies.'

I told him I'd been in one of the Auschwitz-Birkenau SKs.

'Why are you alive?' he screamed. 'You should be smoke and ash like the rest of your kind!'

I nodded to Baruh, who decapitated the second Nazi, dropping the head on the table in front of the doctor.

'What do you want from me?' he shrieked.

'Not much,' I said. 'I will let you live if you curse Hitler and Himmler, deny the validity of the so-called ideals of the Nazi state, and beg for your life.'

It took time, but eventually he did all that, almost passing out from loss of blood. We bound the worst of his wounds so he was fully conscious when the sun rose. Then I sawed his head off with leisurely strokes of my blade.

The photo was a memento, one of few we took or had taken. It meant a lot to all of us.

TWENTY-NINE

'Alex,' Niki said warmly. 'I've been thinking about you.' She paused. 'I'm in bed and I'm only wearing my knickers.'

Mavros felt a twitch in his groin. 'Lucky you. I'm on the street and the bloody Vardharis is freezing my nuts off.'

'No, no, not that! Wrap them up well. When does your flight land?'

'What?'

'Aren't you coming back tonight?' Her voice was suddenly hard.

'Em, no...'

'I don't understand. The Fat Man said he was going to talk to you.'

'He did.'

'So what are you waiting for? We both need you.'

Mavros thought about it. He could cut and run, but it went against the grain professionally. Plus, the Samuel case was progressing. Maybe he could just go down for a day.

'Look, I have to talk to my client.' He remembered in time not to mention Rachel. 'I'll try to get an early flight tomorrow.'

'You'd better.'

He didn't like being threatened, especially where his work concerned. 'I said, I'll talk to my client, Niki,' he repeated. 'There are certain protocols...'

'Don't give me that bullshit!' she screamed. 'I need you, end of story. Either come or fuck off!'

'You're being unreasonable,' he said. 'Hang—'

There was a buzzing in his ear.

The young man with dark hair was twenty metres behind Mavros, watching as he spoke on the phone. He could tell by the way the subject handled himself that he was a skilled operator. The information he'd been given suggested that the investigator didn't carry a weapon and wasn't particularly good with his fists. All to the good. There were enough violent fools in the city. But Mavros had been asking questions, too many questions. He and the young woman were opening doors that had been sealed for decades, digging up old bones, getting too close to the mother lode. It was his opinion that the Scottish Greek should be snatched and given a stern talking to, perhaps some pain as well. That hadn't been approved, but tailing him was deemed appropriate. But what would the benefit be if all he did was return to the hotel and stay in for the rest of the night?

Then again, the young woman might reappear, as she had done on the night they lost her. Her sidekick was a professional and had left them standing by turning right before a light changed to green. There was definitely more to her than met the eye, though a 'hands-off' policy on her had been ordered too.

He thought back to the meeting he'd had with Baruh Natzari in Ayia Triadha. The old man hadn't seemed to be suicidal. Had someone else got to him? He had been about to check the house the next day when he saw the Cherokee roll up and Mavros and the woman go in. After they'd left he jumped the gate and saw the hanging body. He called it in and was told to touch nothing and get out, after taking all the photos. He didn't find the one that was required.

Mavros was gesturing as he talked on his phone and had moved towards the side of the road. It happened before his tail could react. A black car drew up, the back door opened and the investigator was pulled in. A few seconds later the car – a Lexus RX330 – had disappeared into the traffic.

Fuck! His heart pounding, the young man made the call and prepared himself for a verbal battering.

'What the–' Mavros doubled over in the back seat as a fist was driven into his abdomen.

'Shut up, Jew-lover. And keep your fucking head down!'

Mavros had caught a glimpse of the man who grabbed him. His head was shaven and he was wearing a speckled green combat jacket. Now he could see only high-laced cherry coloured boots.

'We're going to have fun with this one,' the gorilla said to the men in front.

'Hope so,' came a voice from the passenger seat. 'You shouldn't get your long hair on the TV, fuckwit.'

Mavros presumed an answer wasn't required and concentrated on getting his breathing back to normal.

'You know what we do to people like you?' said the man beside him, pulling his hair. 'Kneecapping, for a start. Tarring and feathering. Duelling scars, not that you'll get a sword. Oh, and a long truncheon up your arse, without a drop of lubricant.'

Mavros held his tongue. These men were foot soldiers, not that any real army would take them. He could only hope that someone higher up the neo-Nazi feeding chain would get involved. No, that would be even worse.

After about fifteen minutes, the car slowed and took a sharp left turn, ascending a slope and then stopping abruptly. A balaclava was put over his head, the eye and mouth holes to the rear. He inhaled hard to draw air through the wool.

'Come on, hippy.'

He was pulled out roughly and frog-marched across a level floor. Doors opened ahead and he was eventually pushed down into a seat. His hands and ankles were chained to the metal supports. He could hear two men in the room, talking in low voices; he thought both had been in the car.

Suddenly the talking stopped and boots stamped together.

'Sir!' one of them said. 'Jew-lover, long-haired Communist half-Greek Alexander Mavros, as ordered, sir!'

A chair was pulled across the floor. Mavros felt warm breath through the wool over his right ear.

'You've been very foolish, my friend.'

Mavros recognised the voice immediately. It

belonged to Makis Kalogirou, the Phoenix Rises' leader.

'Not as foolish as you. Kidnapping is a serious offence. Ah!'

His hair had been pulled back again.

'Would you like me to cut your throat, smart-arse?'

He felt cold steel on his skin.

Showing weakness to fascists was not an option he was prepared to consider. 'Killing defenceless people is what you people are good at,' he said, heart pounding.

'Would you like to fight me on equal terms?' The tone was mocking. 'Choose your weapon.'

'How about toothpicks? They're about the size of your dick.'

That earned him another punch in the abdomen. He was hauled back up and felt a sharp edge cut through the balaclava and into his cheek. He managed to confine his reaction to a gasp.

'You've got an active tongue,' Kalogirou said, his mouth close to Mavros's ear again. 'How about I hack it out?'

'Feel free. You think I haven't sent a report about you and your pathetic followers to Brigadier Nikos Kriaras at Athens police HQ?'

'Why would he be interested in me? I haven't left Thessaloniki for months.'

'Maybe, but you've got supporters down there. Some of them firebombed a friend of mine's house.'

'You can't prove that.'

'Wait for the forensics report.'

There was a pause.

'What are you and that Jew bitch doing in my city?'

'Kicking the shit out of your witless sidekicks.'

'And wrecking a pickup. Some of those men were badly injured.'

'Men? They looked like blowflies to me.'

His hair below the balaclava was pulled back again. 'How about I set some more of them on you?'

'Do what you like. It's just a power trip for inadequates, the Phoenix Rises. Didn't it occur to you that giving your rabble a name referring to the Colonels' junta isn't exactly a vote winner?'

'People are coming round to our ways of thinking.'

'And what are those? Hitler was a hero, the Third Reich will rise again, foreigners are responsible for all the problems in Greek society, and the Left are traitors?'

'You're very well informed,' said the invidious voice in his ear. 'Maybe you'd like to join. No, I forgot. Your father was a senior Communist and you're working for a Jew.'

Mavros couldn't resist, spurred on by the mention of his old man. He jerked his head sideways and felt his skull crunch into Kalogirou's nose – a lateral Glasgow kiss. It cost him, though. His belly took more blows and his face was punched hard several times. The blood from his nose made it difficult to breathe.

'That was ... foolish.' Kalogirou's voice was muffled, presumably because he was staunching the blood from his nose. 'Tell me what you're doing here, now!'

'Looking for a Jew. Will that get you off my back?'

'What Jew?'

'One who's been dead since 1945.'

'Name?'

'Fuck off.'

He was pummelled again.

'Fuck off,' he repeated, after clearing the blood from his mouth.

'Shall we give him the full treatment, sir?' said one of the gorillas.

'Maybe later. I need to check something.'

Footsteps moved away and Mavros was left where he was.

'You're dead,' said the man who had grabbed him from the pavement. 'No one hits the chief. You're fucking dead.'

Mavros kept quiet, wondering what Kalogirou was doing. Calling Kriaras? Anything was possible.

After a time the footsteps returned. 'Listen to this warning. You'll hear it only once. Take your Jewish cunt and get out of Thessaloniki. If I see either of you again, you'll end up in the municipal dump, minus dick, eyes, nose, tits, the lot. Understand?'

Mavros nodded slowly.

'Get him out of here.'

'Yes, sir. Where shall we take him?'

'He's at the Electra Palace, isn't he? Dump him a couple of hundred metres away in a back street.' There was harsh laugh. 'I wonder if they'll let him in the way he looks.'

Mavros was hit about the face again, then taken to the car and pushed in. The traffic noise gradually increased as they drove. By the frequent stopping and starting, he could tell they were in the centre. Eventually, after a couple of tight turns, the car pulled up and the door was opened.

'Throw him in that rubbish,' the driver said.

He was propelled through the air, landing in an evil-smelling mass.

'Remember, run away to your own city like a good little rat.' The big man laughed.

When the car had reversed away, Mavros pulled the balaclava off. He folded it inside out and put it in his pocket in case DNA samples were necessary, then stumbled on to the road. Wiping the blood from his eyes, he saw the seafront. As he headed for the hotel, he made the decision.

The Phoenix Rises was interested in him and Rachel, and its leader had obviously been told to let him go after warning him off. Why and who by? There must be a link to Aron Samuel. He was staying in Thessaloniki till the case was over, no matter what Niki and the Fat Man said.

Rachel looked down at Aristotelous Square from the window seat in her room. Her laptop was beside her and she had filed her daily report. Her contact had been keen to proceed that night, but she had declined. They needed more information before striking. He had gone to carry out surveillance from a concealed position.

She found herself thinking about Alex Mavros.

The investigator was smart and dogged, but she didn't fully trust him. She was hamstrung by her lack of Greek and Judezmo, and she wasn't sure he was telling her everything. Then again, he had included her in the visit to the customs broker, his hitherto secret source. She was also puzzled by the Communist angle. Why would Aron have got involved, especially when he was so young? And why had his file been hyper-classified? Then there was the fact that Mavros's friend's house in Athens had suffered an arson attack. Was that connected to what they were doing up here? The fact was, they were no nearer finding her great-uncle, even though they had dug up a fair amount about him, most of it unpleasant. Had he really been a vicious killer both in and after Auschwitz? It looked that way. And if he was in the city, what was he doing? She called her father and gave him a summary. He took it in and told her to stay on the investigation. She said that Mavros might have to go back to Athens. That was to be avoided at all costs, she was told. Eliezer felt they were getting close.

From the window she saw a familiar figure moving in a less than straight line across the square. One hand was over his forehead and the other was extended as if he expected to fall at any moment.

Rachel grabbed her phone and ran to the door.

Mavros walked down the corridor to his room, Rachel by his side. He had declined her support as his abdomen hurt too much.

'Come to mine,' she said. 'I've got a first-aid

kit. You stink.'

'Sorry.'

They went in and Mavros looked at himself in the mirror, shrugging off his jacket and pulling up his shirt. He prodded gently, grimacing.

'Let me,' Rachel said, 'I've been trained.'

'On a kibbutz?'

She stared at him. 'How did you know?' She pulled on latex gloves and pressed her fingers over his abdomen. 'Your ribs aren't cracked,' she said, after a while.

'No, they aimed lower.'

'That's a problem. You might have ruptured something. Does this hurt?'

'Yes!'

'This?'

'Yes, but not as bad.'

'You need to check for blood in your stool and urine.'

'OK. Has that cut on my cheek stopped bleeding?'

Rachel put her hand behind his head and brought it slowly forward. 'No. It needs stitches.'

'Shit. Going to hospital now is the last thing I need.'

'Come to the bathroom. You can't have a shower, but I'll wash you. Get those clothes off.'

Mavros let her clean him up with wet cloths, keeping only his underwear on. The experience was about as sexually arousing as a being scrubbed by a wire brush.

When Rachel had finished, she took him to the bed. 'Sit down.'

A quarter of an hour later, she finished dealing

with his wounds. Although she'd used an anaesthetic spray, they still hurt like hell.

'There, that dressing on your cheek will be all right until morning. Don't sleep on that side.'

'I doubt I'll be sleeping much.'

'At least your nose isn't broken.'

'It feels like it is.'

'And none of your teeth are loose. I think that cut above your eye will heal without stitches. We'll see tomorrow.' She smiled. 'Well, I'll see. You're going to have two swollen and black eyes.'

'Oh, great.'

'Do you want to tell me what happened?'

'The Phoenix Rises. That scumbag Kalogirou.' He filled her in.

'So are you leaving at first light tomorrow?' she asked.

'Am I buggery.'

'Pardon?'

He smiled, wincing as his lips stretched. 'No. We're stirring things up. I don't react well to threats.'

Rachel stripped off her gloves. 'Neither do I,' she said, lying back on the bed. 'Would you like to spend the night here? Purely from a medical point of view. You might take a turn for the worse.'

Mavros looked at her, trying unsuccessfully to read her dark eyes.

'I'm not sure that will be necessary,' he replied.

But he stayed all the same. The bed was wide.

THIRTY

So it went on through the 60s and into the 70s. We got older and less fit, Shlomo especially, so we reduced the number of targets each summer. The Nazis were dying of old age and disease too. Eventually I continued on my own, realising that my comrades were in need of peace. At the later killings Shlomo attended, he turned away from the final act. He hadn't got religion like Zvi – we three were long past the temptations of faith – but he had reached the end of his abilities. There was no shame in that.

You might wonder what happened in the rest of my life. That is of little significance, but I recognise curiosity when I see it. In my forties I met a much younger woman, who saw something in me that had been buried by decades of harshness and deception. She teased it out, my Gavriella, and nursed me back to the world of feeling. We married and moved away from New York; I had made enough to support us for many lifetimes. Besides, it was getting unsafe in that hive of Jews. We moved to the mid-West and, swathed in love, I suspended my summer trips for several years.

But like the vampire after centuries in the tomb, I found my tainted soul still needed blood; and that others were banking on that being the case. Our house and land were a few miles outside a medium-sized city whose name I will keep to myself. One Saturday in the late 60s I was on my way back from the shops – my wife having never learned to drive – when I saw a man standing in the middle of the road that led only to our place. I was immediately suspicious and leant over for the pistol I kept in the glove compartment, racking the slide. Then I drove closer. The window was already rolled down. The man, who was dark-haired and thin, was wearing a coat that was too thick for late spring and his face was covered in sweat.

'Keep your hands out of your pockets,' I said. 'What do you want?'

To my surprise he answered me in Greek. 'Mr Samuel, I have been sent by the comrades.'

He meant the Communist Party. Now I really was shocked. How had they found me and what did they want?

'Are you on your own?' I asked, still holding my weapon.

'Yes. And I am unarmed.'

I wasn't sure about that, and if he was a trained operative he could cause me serious problems with only his hands.

'The comrades have a proposition for you,' he continued. 'We must talk.'

I looked beyond him. The house was still out of view.

'All right. Let me park.' I left the car at the side of the road and led him into a small wood.

'What do I call you?'

'How about Frizis?'

As you may know, Mordecai Frizis was a Jewish lieutenant colonel in the Greek Army, who died heroically leading his men in an attack on the Italians during the Albanian campaign.

'You are one of us?'

He shook his head. 'But, like all comrades, I grieve for your people's unjust fate.'

'Words are worthless. What are you doing here?'

He offered me a cigarette, which I declined. After the Lager I had stopped smoking – that activity was forever part of the horror. 'Comrade Samuel–'

'Why do you call me that? I have had no connection with the party for over twenty years.'

'Once a comrade, always–'

'No,' I said, touching the gun in my jacket pocket. 'I am no longer interested in the revolution. Your Stalin was little better than Hitler.'

He shrugged. 'Things have changed.'

'No, they haven't. I repeat, what are you doing here?'

'You are aware of what is going on in our country?'

'You mean Greece? It is no longer my country. I'm an American now.'

Frizis laughed coarsely. 'Once a Greek... Besides, what the comrades want is not confined to our homeland.'

'What the comrades want? Of me?' It was my turn to laugh. 'They are in no position to make demands.'

He raised his hands, then took out a filthy handkerchief and dried his face. 'Hear me out, Mr Samuel. The dictators in Athens have many supporters in the USA. They raise funds, talk to politicians – not that the Americans need much persuading, as the CIA has been running our country for two decades – make money out of tourism and so on.' The comrade gave me a hungry look. 'Some of these men could profitably be ... removed.' He paused. 'Such work being a speciality of yours.'

I took out my weapon and pointed it at him. 'What do you know about my work, as you put it?'

He rolled off a list of our victims – incomplete, but largely accurate.

'Where did you get that information?'

The comrade raised his thin shoulders. 'There's always an intelligence trail. It's just a question of who shares what with whom.'

I thought about that. Had Zvi, Baruh or Shlomo been talking? It was unlikely, particularly with the last two. Zvi might have been persuaded, seeing the trade-off as part of his atonement. Then there was Mossad. Could they have passed information to the comrades? They'd warned us off in South America. Maybe they'd had second thoughts. There was also the KGB. They did deals with whoever furthered their aims.

'No,' I said. 'I don't work for anyone.'

'There will be no chain of command. We will pass you data on potential targets and you will decide what to do.'

'Really? And if I don't.'

He wiped his face again. 'Better not go into that. Besides, the comrades back home do not want to coerce you. They feel that you will want to be involved. These people in America have

267

links with former collaborators in your home city. You remember the Merten trial? He was sneaked out of the country because the Greek government was scared that ministers' unsavoury pasts would be unveiled.'

I remembered Kalogirou, the pig who had taken our house and family business. Killing him had taken only part of the weight from my shoulders. I felt the blood course rapidly through my veins.

'You are interested, I can see,' the comrade said.

I pointed the pistol at his groin. 'There was an implicit threat in what you said earlier.'

His eyes opened wide. 'If you kill me, the full force of the international comrades will be directed at you.'

'An open threat now.' I raised the gun to his chest.

That made him shut up, though his mouth was wide open.

'Very well,' I said, after letting him sweat for several minutes. 'But I give no guarantees that I will act against the targets you select.'

'When you read their files, you will.'

'And I want all mention of me, present and past, removed from the party archives. There is a top-secret classification, is there not?'

'The "hyper", yes. We already had that in mind.'

'Go, then.' I pointed to a fallen tree. 'On the third of every month I will look under the trunk.'

He nodded. 'Thank you, comrade. Do you think ... do you think I could have something to eat?'

I stared at him. 'I will not break bread with you. We are not comrades or friends. And find another codename. Frizis was a Jewish hero and is off limits for the likes of you.'

He shuffled away. I knew he would have transport and probably backup in the vicinity, so he would not suffer. I was angry that my whereabouts had been uncovered, bitter that I would be working, even indirectly, for a totalitarian regime that I despised, but I was also excited. The taking of guilty blood was still my raison d'être.

Three months later I flew to Philadelphia, where I stole a car and drove to the most significant target's weekend home. The good thing about wealthy Americans is that they compete with each other over everything. He who has the most comfortable yet out-of-the-way country place wins. This man, Aristotle Pappas, was driven to his so-called cottage – you could have housed ten poor families in it – where he entertained businessmen, politicians, media personalities and even the odd Hollywood star. They all left on Sunday afternoons and he spent the evenings with high-class prostitutes, after sending away the servants. The job was almost too easy, though I had to shoot a large dog that launched itself at me near the back door. I had a suppressor on my pistol, so the occupants of the house heard nothing.

I watched through the window, wondering what to do about the girl. She was tall, blonde and ridiculously statuesque, but she didn't deserve to die. In the event, I pulled down my balaclava and knocked her out while she was giving her client a blow job. He screamed as I tied him up, blood dripping from his groin.

'Be quiet,' I ordered, shoving the suppressor into his mouth.

Pappas complied.

'Confirm to me that you met these individuals on your recent trip to Athens.' I spoke the names of most of the Colonels and their sidekicks.

He nodded.

'And you provided them with funds.' I pulled the pistol back slightly.

'Yes,' he said, in Americanised Greek. 'Investment opportunities … abound.'

'Are you doing business with the following…' The party had provided me with a list of Thessaloniki businessmen, known Nazi collaborators or sons of the same, to make sure I would act.

He nodded again.

'You realise that all of them obtained Jewish property at minimal cost after the war and threw people who came back from Auschwitz on the street?'

He glared at me. 'And I should care?'

I shot him three times in the mouth.

THIRTY-ONE

Mavros woke to find Rachel doing push-ups. She was wearing tight grey gym gear and there were sweat stains in abundance.

'I thought you preferred swimming,' he said, wincing as his abdomen reminded him what had been done to it.

'In ten minutes,' she said, her breathing easy. 'How do you feel?'

'I need drugs.'

'I checked your wounds while you were asleep. They're in reasonable condition. There are painkillers in the bathroom, but don't take more than two – unless you want to spend the day in bed.'

'I definitely do not,' he said, getting up stiffly. 'I'm going back to my room.'

'All right. See you for breakfast in half an hour. You can borrow my robe.'

Mavros put on the white towelling garment, gathered up his clothes and left. In the mirror in his bathroom he saw the discoloured swellings around his eyes. Children would take him for the bogeyman.

Getting dressed was impossible, given the state of his clothes. He phoned down to the hotel shop and asked for a selection of trousers, shirts and pullovers to be brought up. His leather jacket needed cleaning and he didn't want to impose on

Rachel's generosity by buying another. With basic apparel, he could find a cheap coat in the backstreet stalls. There wasn't much he wanted from the clothes that appeared, but he settled on a pair of black trousers, a blue shirt and a black sweater. His boots were wearable.

Before going down, he called the Fat Man and told him what had happened.

'Fuckers!' his friend said. 'Shouldn't you be in hospital?'

'I'll survive. Rachel patched me up.'

'Did she now? I won't tell Niki.' There was a pause. 'Look, Alex, I'm sorry about last night. They're letting me out of here today and I'll be all right. I'm going to stay with Apostolos for the time being. Don't come back for me.'

'Thanks, I appreciate that. Though I doubt Niki will see it that way.'

'May your Marx and Lenin go with you.'

Mavros rang his lover.

'Have you landed?' she asked.

He recounted the previous evening's events, up to the point where he went to Rachel's room.

'That's awful, Alex,' she said. 'Even more reason to come back.'

He sighed. 'Listen, I know you're feeling down and I know I don't pay enough attention to you—'

'But?'

'But ... I've got to sort things out up here. I'm not letting the Phoenix Rises get away with it.' He played his last card. 'Don't forget they're organised down there too. They might come after us. They may even have torched the Fat Man's house.'

'You just don't get it, do you, Alex?'

'Get what?'

There was a frustrated scream. 'I love you. I need you here. If that's beyond your comprehension, then forget it.' She put the phone down.

Mavros shook his head. There were times when he couldn't communicate with the woman he loved. Maybe she was right. Maybe his work was more important than anything else in his life.

Rachel raised her eyes from her laptop when he reached the table in the restaurant. 'Man about Thessaloniki. I presume I'll be paying for that outfit.'

He shrugged. 'Only if you think it's a reasonable expense.'

She smiled. 'Of course. You'll need a jacket too.'

Mavros couldn't help thinking how easier it was to deal with her than with Niki. After eating, they went to the shop and Rachel bought him an Italian leather blouson that was well beyond his price range.

He mumbled his thanks, feeling awkward. He wasn't used to being treated by a female client in that way.

'OK,' she said, as they walked into the reception area. 'What are we doing today? Leaving Thessaloniki like the Nazis said?'

He shook his head. 'No chance. I'm going to strike back. The Phoenix Rises has a reason to scare us off. I want to know what it is. You don't have to come along.'

'After what happened last night, you need a bodyguard. I'm going to brush my teeth and then

273

I'll be down.'

'I suppose I'd better do the same. But I'm taking the lift.'

'See you shortly.' Rachel set off up the stairs at speed.

Mavros cleaned his teeth, then consulted the phone directory. Predictably, the Phoenix Rises had an office near the church of St Dhimitrios, the patron saint of the city. There was no guarantee that Makis Kalogirou would be present, considering he had a company to run, but he would soon hear of their visit. Long experience had taught Mavros that drawing out an opponent made them prone to mistakes. Then again, there would probably be plenty of skinheads in heavy boots around. He came up with a plan to deal with them. It involved his toilet bag, a tube of toothpaste, containers of deodorant and shaving cream, and his alarm clock. Professional security personnel wouldn't be fooled, but blockheads might.

'What's that under your jacket?' Rachel asked when they met in the hall. She was wearing the black clothes and boots she'd had on at the rally, and carrying her laptop case as usual.

'A bomb.'

'What?'

'Not a real one. A dummy for dummies.'

She smiled. 'I like the sound of that. Car or walking?'

'The latter.' Mavros led the way.

'If I liked churches, I'd be impressed by this one,' Rachel said, taking in the long basilica with the uneven towers.

'Ayios Dhimitrios.'

'No dome, for a change.'

'What have you got against domes?'

'I prefer straight lines to curves.'

He glanced at her. 'I don't.'

There was a hint of amusement on her lips. 'Is that it?' she asked, pointing at a first-floor balcony festooned with Greek flags and the Phoenix Rises' emblem.

'You could hardly miss it.'

'Plan?'

'Let's play it by ear.'

'What?'

'See how it goes.'

'My life is in your hands.'

Mavros remembered the fight she'd put up at the demonstration. 'Ditto.'

They went into the building. There was a shop selling lingerie in the small arcade, which made him laugh.

'I'll bet they're all transvestites.'

'I'm not taking that.' She looked around. 'There's a curious lack of men with no hair.'

'They must all be upstairs. Or maybe they don't work in daylight.'

They walked slowly to the first floor, taking in the surroundings. There was a strong smell of fresh paint. The door at the end of the corridor was open, it and the frame bright blue. There was large image of a phoenix rising from the flames on the far wall.

'Still no one on guard,' Rachel said, right hand in her bag.

'I'm not complaining. Ready?'

They walked past the 'Wet Paint' signs and into the outer office. A middle-aged man in a black shirt was at a desk. He was wearing a Phoenix Rises cap and an incongruous multicoloured woollen scarf.

'What is it?' he asked, with a sniffle.

'Bad time of year for colds,' Mavros said.

'What happened to your face?' the man said suspiciously.

'Fucking Commies.'

'You were at the rally?'

Rachel and Mavros both nodded.

'I've got a delivery for the chief. Is he in?'

'Er...'

Mavros smiled at him patiently.

The man pressed a button and the steel door to his rear opened. A skinhead with bulging biceps looked out.

'You!' he said, staring at Mavros.

'Bomb!' Mavros yelled, holding up his toilet bag. 'Get back!'

Rachel slammed the man at the desk's head down, knocking him out.

'Fuck you, dick,' the gorilla said, stepping closer and raising a fist.

'What is it, Kosta?' came Kalogirou's piping voice from within.

'That Mavros wanker. He says he's got a bomb.'

'What? Close the door, then.'

'On the floor!' Rachel ordered.

Mavros looked to his left and saw the black pistol she was pointing at the skinhead. Jesus, he thought, what have I uncaged?

The bodyguard thought about it, but not for

276

long. Rachel clubbed him. across the back of the head as he was getting down and he crashed on to the parquet floor.

'No!' Kalogirou said, his voice more like a squeak now. 'No, I can explain!' He was on his feet, his short, square frame in front of a poster of Metaxas, the pre-war dictator. There was a bust of Hitler on his desk.

Mavros looked over his shoulder. Rachel had stayed at the door and was facing the main entrance.

'Only one gorilla for the party leader? That's a bit careless.'

'There are more. They'll be back any minute.'

'Uh-huh. Well, this won't take long. Let me just fix the timer.' He unzipped his toilet bag and showed enough of the clock to convince the quivering fascist.

'Five minutes,' he said, smiling. 'Though of course I can detonate it by hand if anyone gets too close. And it'll go off if anyone who doesn't know what they're doing touches it.'

'You're ... you're insane.'

'You would know. Actually, I was fine until last night.'

Kalogirou sat down heavily. 'That ... that was a misunderstanding.'

'You're fucking right it was. You've got a simple choice. Either you tell me what I want to know or I blow you and your pathetic headquarters to tiny pieces. You've got good, secure windows, I see.' Mavros pocketed the keys from the frames. 'And a solid door, which I'll lock from the outside – leaving you with Comrade Semtex.'

277

'What ... what do you want to know?'

'Don't worry, it's not advanced calculus. Who did you call last night? Who told you to let me go?'

'I ... I can't...'

Mavros walked backwards and put his toilet bag on the floor by the door. 'Send my regards to the Führer.' Rachel turned to him from the entrance. 'The fool prefers to be liquidised.'

'Fine by me. Come on, then.'

'No...' Kalogirou's scream was ear-splitting. 'I'll tell you... I'll... Oh God... It was Nikos Kriaras.'

Mavros stared at him and then nodded slowly. Then he took the key from the door, walked out, and closed and locked it.

'That should give him a bowel-shredding few minutes.' He stared at Rachel. 'Is that gun real?'

'That would be telling,' she said, stepping over the still comatose skinhead.

There was loud banging on the door behind them.

'Time to go,' Mavros said, leading her out. 'You owe me toiletries, a nice leather bag and an alarm clock.'

There was the sound of pounding feet below.

'Let's settle up later,' Rachel said, handing him the laptop bag and raising her weapon.

'Shit,' Mavros said, stuffing the keys into his underwear. 'Should have dealt with his phones.'

'Merde, indeed.' She smiled and inclined her head to a Greek flag on a pole. 'You might want to grab that. Perhaps they won't sully it with their filthy hands.'

Mavros laughed. 'Yeah, right.'

'It's me, Dorothy,' Niki said, looking up at the camera outside the heavy door.

After a lot of rattling and clunking, Mavros's mother opened up.

'Come in, my dear. Oh, what's the matter?'

Niki had started crying and Dorothy put a thin arm round her shoulders.

'Sit down and I'll make us some tea. That always helps.' She was speaking Greek, although Niki's English was good and they often conversed in that language. When Alex's long-standing girlfriend was emotional, she always reverted to her mother tongue.

Dorothy brought a tray into the *saloni* and found Niki with her head in her hands. She sat down beside her and asked, 'What's my errant son done now?'

'He won't ... he won't ... come back to me.'

'What do you mean?'

'He's ... completely wrapped up ... in a case ... in–'

'Thessaloniki. I know, dear. How is Yiorgos?'

'Better. He was lucky.' Niki dried her eyes. 'That's the thing. He asked Alex to come back too. But he ... he won't.'

Dorothy stroked her back. 'My son can be stubborn, I know. But remember that he does important work. My husband was the same. He'd get involved in court cases or party business and I wouldn't see him for days, often weeks. But I had faith in him. I believed he was doing the best he could for the unfortunates of this world. You have faith in Alex, don't you?'

279

Niki sobbed, and then looked at the older woman. 'That's ... that's the problem. I don't ... I don't know if I do ... any more.'

Dorothy was about to argue, but she hung back. Alex had endangered the people he loved; he was still doing so. Maybe you had to be related by blood to accept that, as even the fiery Anna did. Niki had been through some terrible experiences because of Alex's tenacity in uncovering the monsters behind the façade in Greece. It looked like she'd reached the end of her tether.

'Come on, drink your tea. It'll be good and strong by now.' She patted Niki's arm. 'I know you're worried about getting pregnant, but you have to give yourself a chance.'

Niki looked at her uncomprehendingly and let out another desperate sob.

Four skinheads in combat jackets, trousers and shining boots stopped halfway up the stairs, their eyes on the pistol Rachel was pointing at them.

'It's that nosy fucker and his Jew bitch,' one of them said, licking his lips.

'Excuse me,' Mavros said, brushing past Rachel. He raised the flagpole like a spear and rammed the end into the neo-Nazi's belly. He crashed backwards, taking two of his friends with him. 'Keep still!' he shouted, as he and Rachel picked their way over the sprawling men. The fourth turned tail and headed for the street.

'Go on, Alex,' Rachel said, backing away. She kept her weapon pointed at the upended men.

Mavros held on to the flag in case more

Phoenix Rises troopers arrived. He peered round the corner of the lingerie shop. There were only ordinary people in the vicinity. He dropped the flag.

'Get a taxi!' Rachel said, as she approached.

He did as she said. When one stopped, he got in and held the door open for her. She stuffed the pistol into the belt beneath her pullover and joined him.

'Just drive!' Mavros said.

The young man at the wheel pulled away.

'Do you speak English?' Mavros asked.

The driver shrugged. 'You are very bee-oo-ti-fool. Dance with me?' Then he rattled off a list of largely American product names. 'And Deer-eh Stra-eets,' he concluded.

'Dire Straits,' Mavros translated. 'A rock band,' he added, seeing Rachel's puzzled expression.

'So what was it the head Nazi told you?' she asked.

'Last night he called the head of the Athens Organised Crime Unit to ask what he should do with me.'

'What?'

'Well, I have history with that individual. But not much future.' Mavros leaned forward. 'Take us to the Archaeological Museum,' he said, glancing at Rachel. 'We might as well absorb some ancient culture as we plot the destruction of the present-day Greek state.'

'That bad?'

Mavros nodded grimly.

THIRTY-TWO

I combined dealing with Junta supporters in the US with tracking down Nazis throughout the 70s. Even though the dictatorship ended in 1974, there were plenty of targets – second- and third-generation Greeks who had taken on the worst aspects of their new country. I hadn't gone back to the party, but I found myself disgusted by the arrogance of the rich, both those who had inherited and self-made men. Because the FBI was a more formidable opponent than the police forces in South America and most of Europe, I resorted to methods that pointed towards accident or suicide. So, several fascist sympathisers hanged themselves from trees on their estates and some went off the road when their brakes failed. I had become a competent mechanic over the years.

If Gavriella had any suspicions about what I was up to during my often lengthy absences, she kept them to herself. Because I didn't go out to work, spending my days talking to my broker and banker, I saw a lot of my sons as they were growing up. Yosif, the elder, who bears my father's name, was always a handful, racing around the house like a dervish and prone to falling out of trees. As you have probably noticed, he's still impetuous. The scar under his hairline is evidence of that. Isaak, named after Gavriella's father and my long-lost brother, is the other side

282

of the coin – a rationalist and a sceptic. He would prefer you weren't here, but I don't run a democracy. Even if I did, Yosif and I would have prevailed. We need a witness.

In the 90s, when Shlomo's health began to break down and Baruh became more of a planner than an executor/executioner, I began to make use of the boys. Initially, they did research and ran errands. But from the start I felt they had to know what I was doing. They only thing I asked of them was that they never said a word to their mother – or to anyone else, of course. Also, they could back out at any point without recriminations or bad feeling. Neither of them did. Of course, they had learned about the Nazis at school and from war movies, comics and so on. They were aware that they were Jews, although we rarely attended synagogue or kept company with the local members of our community – they were few and tended towards the orthodox, as if the prairies and the open skies brought out something atavistic in them.

I gave my sons books as they grew older, encouraging them to read widely about Judaism. I even discussed the works of Holocaust-deniers with them. They gave those fools short shrift. When Yosif was nineteen and Isaak seventeen, I played them Claude Lanzmann's nine-and-a-half-hour film, *Shoah*. We split it into five parts, discussing each afterwards. When we got to the end, there were surprises all round.

'We've already seen it, Father,' Yosif said.

'Last summer, when you were away,' added Isaak.

I was impressed by their interest and self-motivated study. They were – still are – serious boys. I judged the time was right to tell them my secret.

'I was in Auschwitz,' I said.

'We guessed,' Isaak said. 'You wear long sleeves to cover them, but we've both seen the numbers tattooed on your arm.'

'And what did you think?'

'That you must be a hero to have survived,' Yosif said, putting his hand on mine.

I laughed bitterly. 'A hero? You know what the Sonderkommando was?'

He nodded, but Isaak shook his head. I told him, then described my life in the Lager – as I have to you.

There was silence when I finished. Then both of them put their arms round my back.

'You are still a hero,' Isaak said. 'You did what you felt you had to and we would not be here if you'd given up.'

I was gripped by the self-destructive impulse that had driven me since liberation, and 'd them what I did when I was away from h... – what I had done in almost every country in Europe and South America. I expected, this time, that they'd be revolted, their father a multiple murderer, a serial killer as the phrase in vogue had it.

Again they surprised me.

'Now I see you really are a hero,' Yosif said, bowing his head. 'There should be statues of you in Thessaloniki and all over the world.'

Even Isaak – ever the stern young man – smiled

at that. 'Come, brother, he may be our hero, but you can't expect the offspring of murderers, collaborators, profiteers and cowards to admire him.'

'What about in Tel Aviv, then?' Yosif had been to a kibbutz the previous year. 'There are plenty of memorials to Jewish heroes in Israel.'

I laughed. 'Memorials are for the dead.' I looked at them and judged that the moment had come. 'Besides, I'm still operating. Would you ... help me in the field?'

Neither hesitated for a second.

At the outset I set them to reconnoitring and surveillance duties, on targets in the US far from our home. They knew what the result of their efforts would be, but I kept them away from the executions until I was sure they could handle them. My experience in the SK and after was that some men, no matter how well prepared and apparently determined they were, could not face death at close range. I would never had subjected my boys to the ultimate challenge of taking another human being's life – no matter how low that person was on the scale of humanity – unless I was sure they were up to it.

Yosif was first. I had trained them in what the CIA and KGB would call fieldcraft, but for me was the practical knowledge I had accrued in action rather than in a classroom. One of the dictators' main supporters was a second-generation Greek who had become a major drug-dealer in Florida. We discovered that he liked to go fishing in the Everglades and had a cabin there. The problem was, he never went alone. We watched him and his trips always involved at least four vicious-looking guards, whose weapons were easy to spot. Prostitutes were also taken along.

'I don't think we should kill the women,' Isaak said.

'Why not?' demanded his brother. 'They're worthless trash that no one will miss.'

'Wrong,' Isaak replied. 'They have pimps – we've seen them. They'll ask questions.'

'True,' I said. 'Besides, innocent lives shouldn't be taken.'

Yosif stared at me. 'What about the women and children you killed immediately after Knaus?'

I held his gaze. 'That was a long time ago. I hope I've learned better.'

'There were no innocents in Germany and Austria,' Isaak said. 'This is different.'

Yosif eventually nodded in agreement.

'So how's it to be?' I asked. 'He's never on his own and neither is his car. That makes kidnapping him and tampering with the vehicle difficult.'

'Leave it to me,' Isaak said.

I looked at his brother, then nodded. 'You've got twenty-four hours.'

Yosif and I kept up surveillance. In the evening the drug boss – I don't want to soil my mouth or your ears with his name – went with his henchmen to eat in a restaurant with a large parking lot. As normal, one of them stayed with the car. We watched as a convertible with the top down rolled up and a stunning girl wearing very little leaned over to talk to the foot soldier. A few seconds later, he got in and the girl drove to far side of the lot, behind a truck and trailer.

Isaak knew where we were. He looked towards us as he rode up on a small motorbike, dressed as a pizza-delivery boy. He broke into the car within a minute and then worked away inside. My heart never beats faster than normal during operations, but I could see Yosif was nervous. Finally Isaak got out, looked around and rode away. Shortly afterwards the girl in the convertible drove back and dropped off the grinning guard.

'What did you do?' Yosif demanded, when his brother arrived at the rendezvous point.

Isaak held up a remote-control device.

'There's half a kilo of high explosive under the back seat of the target's car. All we have to do is get within five hundred yards and press the button.'

'Half a kilo?' I said.

'I didn't want any survivors.'

'Apparently.'

'The hookers come separately. We'll wait until there are no vehicles or people nearby.'

I looked at Yosif. 'It sounds good to me.'

The next day we followed the car into the Everglades. After half an hour we were in the wilds, an alligator's snout popping from the water near the road.

'The honour is yours,' I said, handing the remote to Isaak.

'I can see the car,' Yosif said, at the wheel. 'We're in range.'

There was a hell of a blast. On the way back to the highway, I debriefed them.

'Good work, Isaak,' I said. 'But there was – and

still is – a high degree of risk.'

'We might have been or might get spotted on this narrow track,' Yosif said. 'Getting away unnoticed and in one piece are not guaranteed.'

'That's right.' I clapped Isaak on the back.

'You knew,' he said, crestfallen. 'You both knew.'

'Don't worry,' I said. 'There's always risk attached to operations. I calculated that your planning was adequate.'

'Adequate?'

'Wait till we're back in Miami.'

We ditched the car, which Yosif had stolen, in the suburbs and took a taxi to the train station. We changed several times, picking up our own car in St Louis. This was in the years before Homeland Security. The deaths of the fascist-supporting drug runner and his bravos were put down to inter-gang rivalry.

I didn't care about the operation any more – it was in the past. The future belonged to my loyal and lethal sons.

THIRTY-THREE

Mavros called Nikos Kriaras when they were outside the museum.

'So now you're running the Greek Nazi Party?'

'How did you ... That fool Kalogirou talked.'

'Yes. I put a bomb in his office and locked him in.'

'What?'

'Don't worry, it was a fake. As you know, I don't kill people. Or haven't done yet.'

'Is that a threat?'

'You're fucking right it is. Tell me what's going on or I'll be outside your house tomorrow morning.'

'You don't know where I live.'

'That's what you think.'

'What do you mean "what's going on"? You're the smartarse investigator.'

Mavros took a deep breath. 'Let me make this simple for you. Why did Kalogirou call you last night?'

'I ... I knew nothing about his plan to abduct you.'

'Uh-huh.'

'Honestly.' Mavros swallowed a laugh – when operators like a police brigadier used such words you knew you were being pissed on. 'I suppose he got a bit nervous when he realised who you were.'

Mavros looked at Rachel, who was sitting on a low wall. 'He knew who I and my client were since the rally.'

'Well, if you must make a spectacle of yourselves on TV...'

'Is the Son involved in this?'

'The Son? Certainly not. I told you I would never bring that lunatic back.'

Mavros was almost convinced – a genuinely outraged tone was hard to pull off. 'So who firebombed the Fat Man's house?'

'I have no idea.'

Which may have been true. 'All right, what do you think I'm doing up here?'

'I know what you're doing.'

'At least you didn't try to feign innocence. Any comments?'

There was a pause. 'Beyond incomprehension that you're looking for a man who died sixty years ago?'

Mavros knew Kriaras was playing with him. 'There aren't many Jews left in Greece. But there are plenty of people – important people – descended from collaborators and black-marketeers, aren't there?'

Silence.

'What if Aron Samuel, or his descendants, are getting ready to take out prominent Thessaloniki citizens? I don't include that worm Kalogirou in that group.'

'What are you talking about? There have been no attacks.'

'Maybe they practised on Tareq Momani.'

'Who?'

'Don't play stupid. It's insulting.'

'The Jordanian? Why would they do that?'

'You're the hot-shot cop.'

'If you have any information about Aron Samuel or anyone else that might lead to the prevention of a major crime, it's your duty as a Greek citizen to report it.'

Mavros laughed. 'Don't talk to me about duty. Your colleagues here should have thrown Kalogirou and the rest of the Phoenix Rises into the old prison on the hill after they laid into those immigrants.'

'Look, I think it's time you spoke to the head of organised crime in Thessaloniki.'

'Why? You tell him what to do, don't you. The minister and the people who pull his chain use you as their bugler.'

Kriaras sighed. 'All right, have it your own way, but don't be surprised if you get taken in. This is all I can give you. There are indications that a Mossad death squad is operating in the co-capital. What we don't know is if this Aron Samuel has links to it.'

'And they took out Momani, leaving swastikas to frame the Nazis?'

'Possibly.'

Mavros watched Rachel as she picked up her laptop bag and walked away from the museum entrance.

'OK, leave it with me.'

'What do you mean?'

'You people can't do your jobs, so allow me to take over.' Mavros broke the connection. He had to have an in-depth conversation with Rachel Samuel.

They took a taxi back to the hotel. Going through museum security with a loaded pistol wasn't a good idea – he was now sure the weapon was real.

'What's the plan?' Rachel asked, as they passed the beige tower.

Mavros was looking out to sea. 'You've been playing me for a fool, haven't you?'

'What do you mean?'

He laughed emptily. 'How many jewellery executives know how to handle both themselves

291

and firearms?'

'You'd be surprised how rough some of the places I visit are.'

'Stop it, Rachel. You're playing at least a double game, though maybe your multiplication is even more advanced than that.'

She put her hand on his mouth lightly. 'Not here. Wait till we get to the hotel.'

'You think? It wouldn't surprise me if both our rooms are bugged.'

'All right, where then?'

Mavros told the driver to head to the Eptapyrgio. As the car went up the steep road to the upper city, he glanced at Rachel. She was looking out at the narrow streets and the battlements ahead. As usual her face was composed, the expression stern. He wondered what it would take to break down the barriers she had erected around herself.

They got out at the gate to the partially ruined citadel and looked over the city to the sea.

'This was the culmination of the Byzantine defensive walls,' Mavros said, remembering the visit he'd made with his brother. Andonis had explained to him about Gedi Koulé, as the old fort was known. It was still a prison when they'd been there, a place of pilgrimage where many Communists, men and women, had been executed.

'And the newer buildings?' Rachel asked, indicating the cream-coloured walls.

He told her briefly. It had suddenly struck him that Andonis might have been taken there later during the dictatorship, even though he'd disappeared near Athens. There was no rationale in the actions of tyrants.

'So this is a sad place for someone with your background,' Rachel said.

He nodded. 'But it's also appropriate for the conversation we're about to have, interrogation being a major part of the prison's heritage.'

She gave him a probing look and slipped her hand into the laptop bag. 'You're going to interrogate me?'

'As far as that's feasible, given the weapon you're currently fingering.' He smiled slackly. 'I don't suppose you'd like to tell me where you got the weapon? You didn't have it when we went through security at the airport in Athens.'

'Obviously not. What makes you think I have to tell you anything?'

'Because you need me, if only as an interpreter.'

'You haven't done much more than that, have you?'

Mavros shrugged. 'I worked with the materials available. When a client doesn't tell me everything, there's a limit to what I can achieve.'

'What do you think I and my father haven't told you?'

'Having only met your old man once, I prefer to keep him out of this. Besides, his health isn't very good, is it?'

'You're a funny man, Alex Mavros. What you're really saying is that if I don't talk, you'll walk away.'

'If you don't shoot me in the leg. I have, as you know, pressing reasons to go home.'

Rachel looked around the mélange of buildings. There was a cold breeze blowing and the place was desolate.

'All right,' he said. 'I'll make it easy. I ask, you answer, OK?'

She didn't respond.

'Ha! Question one: do you work for or with Mossad?'

Her eyebrows shot up. 'What?' she said, her voice high.

'They're suspected of killing the Jordanian, Tareq Momani.'

Rachel's hand was still in her bag. 'Is that what your policeman told you?'

'More or less. Plus, I saw you coming back late the night of the murder.'

'That's hardly something that would stand up in court.'

'You still haven't told me about the pistol.'

'I bought it here. How do you say ... under the counter? For personal protection. You should be grateful.'

He tried to catch her eye, but she looked away. It was possible to obtain weapons from dealers, although background checks were required. A bribe could make those disappear, and there were black-market suppliers – though how would a foreigner find out who they were?

Rachel turned back to him. 'You don't seriously imagine I'm a Mossad agent.'

'You'd hardly admit to being one, would you?'

'I came here – with you, don't forget – to find my great-uncle.'

He thought about that. 'Are you sure you didn't come to have a go at the Phoenix Rises? You were very keen to go to the rally.'

She raised her shoulders. 'Know your enemy.'

Mavros watched a small bird hopping around on the search for sustenance. He knew he was being manipulated by Kriaras, but there was nothing new in that and he could turn it to his advantage. He was also pretty sure he was being used by Rachel, but that was more complicated – together they'd uncovered aspects of her great-uncle's life that he was sure she hadn't known about. Something else was nagging him.

'All right,' he said. 'Here's how I see it. I'm off the case until you come clean.' He walked towards the gate.

Rachel didn't follow. He saw a taxi in the square behind the walls and hailed it. As he was getting in, the clouds parted and the weak November sun shone down on the hilltop. He didn't feel enlightened at all.

Mavros's first plan was to go back to the hotel, pick up his gear and head for the airport. That was encouraged by a call from his mother. She told him that Niki had just left.

'I don't want to interfere, dear–'

'Yes, you do.'

'Well, a bit. She's very upset, Alex. Are you ... are you sure you have to stay up there?'

'I'm considering it.'

'Good. Then there's Yiorgos, as well. Is he all right?'

'As far as I can tell. I presume you're still on full security.'

'Yes. Is that horrible man back?'

'He could be.' If the Son was involved, the case

would turn into the Gordian knot.

'How awful. I've a good mind to call Brigadier Kriaras–'

'No!' Mavros yelled, making the driver swerve and swear. 'Sorry, my friend. Look, Mother, don't phone anyone except Anna, OK? She'll keep you right. I'll be back when I can.' He rang off and thought about calling his sister. The last thing he needed was pressure from her. She knew the lockdown system well enough and would be careful.

He walked into the hotel and started to gather up his few possessions. If Rachel really wanted him to stay, she'd call. She didn't. Before he left, he sat at the window and looked down at the square. People were walking in all directions, some alone, some – teenage girls, in particular – hand in hand. Such were the people of Thessaloniki: the young unaware of what had happened to the Jews and the old not remembering. That made him feel bad.

Then the worm that had been wriggling in his subconscious surfaced, or rather the two worms: Allegra Harari and Shimon Raphael. The information they'd supplied about Aron Samuel had come in drip-feed fashion, almost as if it was organised to keep him and Rachel curious but not any closer to their target. They had been open enough about knowing each other, but hadn't admitted to pooling their resources. Surely they would have discussed the matter.

Mavros left his bag and ran downstairs. Shimon's office was only ten minutes' walk away. He got there in five.

'I'm ... I'm sorry,' said the black-haired young

woman at the nearest desk, taken aback by his damaged face. 'Mr Raphael's on a business trip.'

'When will he back?'

'I don't know.'

'Do you know where he is?'

'Yes.' She looked at one of her colleagues.

'Would you tell me, please? I'm a friend of Shimon's.'

'I'm sorry,' the woman said uneasily. 'I really can't say.'

'It wouldn't be Israel, by any chance?'

Her eyes widened. 'I ... I really can't say.'

Mavros smiled and left. He called Shimon's mobile, but it went to voicemail. He couldn't think of an appropriate message to leave.

He hailed a passing taxi and directed the driver to Allegra's building. He could have walked, but he suddenly had the feeling that time was essential.

Rachel watched Mavros leave the Eptapyrgio. She waited a few minutes before calling her contact, arranging to meet on the far side of the square. She checked that there was no surveillance.

A black Land Cruiser with darkened windows came towards her, the door swinging open. She got in before it came to a halt.

'What's going on?' asked the driver. He was unshaven, most of his thick curls under a cap.

'Mavros has walked.'

'Good riddance.'

'Unfortunately not. The order is to keep him on board.'

'Why? We can handle the job ourselves.'

'You think so?'

He glanced at her. 'What more can he find out?'

'I don't know. He has his own sources.'

'What about Allegra Harari?'

'I doubt he'll go back there.'

'I think we'd better make sure.'

Rachel raised her shoulders. 'You're probably right.'

The 4x4 shook as it went quickly down the narrow roads to the centre, forcing mothers with buggies and old ladies carrying shopping bags to the side. Then it turned a corner and was confronted by a removal van that took up all the space.

'Shit!' said the driver, looking over his shoulder. 'Reversing back up is going to take some time.'

'It isn't far,' Rachel said, picking up her laptop bag. 'I'll go on foot. Text me when you get there. Don't show yourself without confirmation.' She walked away at speed.

'Yes, sir,' the contact said sardonically.

THIRTY-FOUR

So we come to my return to Thessaloniki. I'd been back in Greece several times, my American passport attracting no attention. Or perhaps it did and the authorities either let me get on with what I was doing or failed to track me down. I took care to arrive and depart by boat, often small ones that served routes between Greece and Turkey.

1999 was the last time both Shlomo and Baruh joined me. Earlier in the decade the country had been in turmoil over the new state of Macedonia, as the former Yugoslavian republic wanted to call itself. Although the rabble-rousing Greek foreign minister was gone and the so-called socialists were back in power, the rumpus had brought several ultra-nationalist former Nazi collaborators out of their holes. The comrades wanted us to deal with one of them and we had no objection.

Christos Papakis was a few years older than me, in his late seventies. He had owned tobacco estates and cigarette factories in the north, and was thus responsible for many of his fellow citizens dying riddled with cancer. His son now ran the businesses and he had retired to a house on the coast near Kavala, about 145 kilometres east of my home city. We chartered a yacht in Piraeus from a company recommended by the comrades – even some purveyors of luxury goods have Communist sympathies. Yosif and Isaak sailed it northwards competently, without approaching land once we were beyond the islands near Attica. We anchored and came ashore about ten minutes' walk from Papakis's villa. The sun was going down behind Mount Athos – a spectacular site, I might say. Shlomo and Baruh were waiting for us in the latter's car.

We three old fighters embraced. Shlomo had

lost a lot of weight and breathed noisily.

'You don't have to come with us, my friend,' I said.

'That's what I've been telling him, but does he listen?' said Baruh. He was the same build as he'd always been and the wrinkles he'd acquired on his face when he was young were no deeper. They both shook hands enthusiastically with my sons.

'We must walk, not drive,' Yosif said.

'I know that,' Shlomo said gruffly. 'I can keep up.'

And he did, with Isaak's help. We walked along the water's edge, our footprints instantly disappearing. There were houses to our right, but no lights were on. It was a weekday in September and the properties were owned by the well-to-do of Kavala, who were back at work after the summer break. All except the retired Christos Papakis.

Isaak left Shlomo with us behind some tamarisk bushes, while he and Yosif reconnoitred. They came back a quarter of an hour later.

'They're on their own, the target and his wife,' Isaak said.

'Both on the front terrace,' added Yosif. 'There's a mobile phone on the table between them. If one of you could take it...'

'I'll do that,' Shlomo said eagerly.

I nodded. 'We need to get them inside and close the shutters. After that, events will take their usual course.'

There were some grim smiles, then we pulled down our balaclavas and moved slowly towards the house, following my sons. There was a moon, so the absence of lights in the vicinity didn't impede us.

Baruh demonstrated seniority by taking out his pistol with the suppressor and walking coolly on to the wooden terrace. 'Raise your hands,' he ordered. 'No noise.'

A few seconds later more guns were aimed at the couple. The woman was whimpering. Shlomo came up and reached for the phone, but it slipped from his grasp. He swore under his breath, then kicked Papakis viciously on the shin, provoking a yelp. We moved inside and secured the shutters.

'What is this?' Papakis demanded. 'A robbery?'

'No,' I said. 'You are the thief and it's time to pay what you owe.'

He stared at me, mouth gaping, while his wife started to cry.

'Take her upstairs and secure her to a bed,' I said to Isaak. 'Don't be too gentle. She knew about her husband's activities and fully supported them. Leave the door open so she can hear.'

I stood in front of Papakis and uncovered my face, as did all the others.

'No,' he gasped, looking down. 'I don't see you, I don't know you.'

'That doesn't matter, collaborator,' Shlomo said, spittle flying from his lips.

'What?' Papakis said feebly. 'What ... what is this?'

I took a thick file out of Isaak's backpack. 'As you are aware, though no doubt you've done

301

your best to forget, one thousand eight hundred Jews from Kavala were handed over to the Nazi allies the Bulgarians in 1943. Some of them were tobacco merchants. You bought their businesses and warehouses at ridiculously low prices, though no doubt it cost you something to pay off the enemy. What do you have to say?'

The old man raised his head. 'The Jews were gone. Someone would have taken their property. You can't steal from dead people.'

'That is a debatable point of law. In any case, you were a high-ranking member of the most anti-Semitic organization in Kavalla before the Jews were taken.'

'I was not.'

I showed him original documents that bore his name and signature.

'Tell us what you did when the few survivors returned to Kavala,' Baruh said, his pistol still aimed at the seated man.

'I did nothing.'

Baruh laughed. 'It is certainly true that you did nothing to help them. You wouldn't even give them jobs. But nothing is not throwing a seventeen-year-old girl who couldn't swim in the sea because she asked for a job, any job.'

'I ... I didn't know she couldn't swim.'

'Nor did you try to help her,' I said. 'In fact, when men who worked for you reached out their arms, you expressly forbade them to save her.'

'That's not true!'

I showed him a statement made by a witness. It had been removed from the police file.

'You paid this man off, yes?'

Papakis would not speak.

Shlomo hit him surprisingly hard on the side of the head. After that he was more eloquent. He eventually accepted all the charges laid against him.

'You realise there can be only one end to this conversation,' I said.

'No ... you can't...'

'Don't worry,' Baruh said. 'We'll help you.'

'What ... what do you mean?'

Isaak came up behind me. 'Shlomo's blow will leave a bruise. Hanging him isn't a good idea.'

'Yes, it is,' I replied quietly. 'We'll take the body, tie an anchor to it and dump it at sea. There's some kind of poetic justice in that – for the poor girl.'

He nodded. I could see Yosif in the sitting room. He'd taken the rope from his pack and tied it to the hook that supported the lamp. They usually held.

'Any last words?' Shlomo asked as Papakis was lifted on to a chair and the noose tightened round his neck.

'My sons... I want ... I want to talk to them.'

Baruh stared up at him. 'You think our people were allowed to make their farewells? Be thankful we don't force your wife to watch.'

'I'm ... I'm sorry,' the doomed man said.

'Too little, too late,' Shlomo said, pulling the chair away.

Papakis's hands had been tied behind his back and we stepped away from his kicking legs. Gradually the movements slowed and then stopped altogether. The sounds we'd grown used to over the decades got quieter. Baruh was looking at his watch.

'Twenty minutes,' he said.

Yosif cut the rope and Isaak lowered the body to the floor. I felt for a pulse.

'So die all collaborators,' I said.

An hour later we were back on the yacht. I'd said farewell to Baruh and Shlomo – it was to be the last time I saw the latter and we both knew that. They were driving to Alexandhroupolis, near the border with Turkey, for a few days of relaxation. Neither of them fancied a trip to Bulgaria.

Papakis's wife died a few weeks later, we were told. It was assumed that the rich man had been kidnapped for ransom, her story taken to be the babbling of an old woman in shock, and the lack of a ransom demand down to the kidnappers losing their nerve, having accidentally killed the old man. What's that? You think we were harsh to make her listen to her husband's demise? I don't agree. Marika Papaki's father was a notorious army officer, who tortured Communist prisoners during the Civil War. She herself supported Queen Frederica's children's camps – indoctrination centres, according to the party. But Papakis's wife went further. She established a home for the children of Communist fighters and ran it like a prison. She personally beat and starved the inmates, and may even have killed a small boy. Don't imagine we target innocents.

What about the women and children in Knaus's town? I've told you before, they were as guilty as any collaborator. Very few Germans were unstained by Nazism. The present pope was in the Hitler Jugend, was he not?

It's all right, leave him be. He can't understand. He isn't one of us.

THIRTY-FIVE

Mavros looked around as he got out of the taxi. There was no one loitering in the vicinity of Allegra Harari's apartment block, unless they were disguised as a lottery-ticket man or a bread-ring salesman. The ground-floor lobby was empty and the lift available. For once he took it, ribs still aching. Again, there was no one in the hallway. He went to Allegra's door and rang the bell.

'Alex, your face!' the researcher exclaimed, as she ushered him in.

'Courtesy of the Phoenix Rises.'

'The brutes. Are you all right? Sorry for the delay, I was in the bathroom. Sit down. What can I do for you?'

Mavros glanced around. All the doors were open and it seemed they were alone.

'I need the truth,' he said, staying on his feet.

'What do you mean?' Her eyes were on his. 'I've given you everything I know about Aron Samuel.'

'I doubt that, but you've certainly been leading us on. You and Shimon Raphael.'

'Shimon?'

'You know he's gone to Israel?'

'What? No, I didn't know that. I don't under-

305

stand what you're talking about, Alex. I don't work with Shimon.'

'Who do you work with, then, Allegra? Or rather, who do you work for?'

The tip of her tongue appeared between her lips. 'I...'

'What business is it of yours?'

Mavros turned to see a tall, heavily built young man a few metres behind him. He was wearing jeans and a matching jacket, and his hair was dark.

'Do you always creep up on people?' Mavros demanded, relieved that the other man wasn't carrying a weapon, though he looked like he could break bones without much effort.

'Only when they're annoying my aunt. Didn't you hear her? Sit down.'

'It's all right, Raul,' Allegra said. 'Alex isn't dangerous.'

'I saw him on TV, putting himself about in the Phoenix Rises rally.' The young man grinned. 'Not as much as the woman.'

Mavros's phone rang before he could reply.

'Alex!' came Rachel's voice. 'Are you at Allegra Harari's?'

He thought about denying it, then decided it would interesting to see them all together.

'Stay there!' she said, her voice even although she was breathing deeply. 'Give me a few minutes.'

Allegra raised an eyebrow.

'Rachel Samuel,' he said. 'She's on her way.' He glanced at Raul, who had sat down next to him on the sofa. 'So, how many of you and your

306

extended family work for Mossad?'

There was a pin-drop silence. Allegra's usually cheerful expression had curdled, while her nephew's fingernails were digging into the seams of his jeans.

'All of you?' hazarded Mavros.

'We don't joke about that agency,' Allegra said.

'I dare say. Do you report to it, though?'

'Aunt,' Raul warned.

Mavros shrugged. 'It doesn't matter. Rachel will clear everything up.' He risked a lie. 'She's already told me she's an agent.'

'What?' Allegra said, shocked. 'She couldn't.'

'Couldn't be an agent or couldn't tell me.'

'Both,' Raul said. 'They never come clean.'

'They? So you're not one.'

The young man shook his head.

'But you've had dealings with them.'

'Raul.' This time it was Allegra doing the cautioning.

Mavros turned his gaze on her. 'What about you? All the research you've done over the years – don't tell me some of it hasn't been passed to them.'

She stared at him, then looked down. 'I can't talk about it.'

Mavros glanced at his watch. Over five minutes had passed since Rachel's call. He went to one of the windows that faced the main street.

'Shit!' he exclaimed. 'Come on, Raul!'

They raced to the door, and then – the lift being elsewhere – down the stairs.

Rachel had sprinted down the narrow street,

slowing her pace as she reached Egnatias Street. She was about three hundred metres from Allegra's. Walking as quickly as she could through the crowd of people, she raised her phone.

'Where are you?' she asked her contact.

'Shouldn't be long. Three minutes at most.'

She rang off. The pavement suddenly cleared and she started to run. She moved her head from side to side, as she'd been trained. As she approached the building, she saw an old man selling lottery tickets and a younger one handing a bread-ring to a customer. Then she heard heavy steps behind her. Reaching into her bag, she gripped the pistol but it was too late. Heavy hands seized hers and another squeezed the back of her neck hard. Then she was propelled into the back of a van. Two men flattened her and she heard the doors close, then the engine roar.

'Jew cunt,' one of her captors said, in poorly accented English.

'Better, Jew asshole,' said another, laughing harshly.

Rachel's bag was pulled away, then ropes were tied round her wrists and ankles. Fingers delved into her pockets and her wallet and phone were taken. The latter rang, but wasn't answered. She inhaled calmly, as she had been taught. At least the fascists hadn't put her hands behind her back. She could work with that. 'Concentrate on the details,' her lead trainer had said. 'Concentrate on what you're going to do to them when you get free.'

She took a hard slap to the cheek and her head

bounced on the floor of the cargo compartment.

'You smile, bitch? Soon you cry.'

Rachel got herself into the zone. Preserve your energy. Observe. Prepare.

Mavros and Raul ran down the street after the white van.

'Get the number!' he said.

'I have it,' the young man said, slowing to a halt and taking out his phone.

Mavros stopped, put his hands above his knees and tried to get his breathing under control. He heard Raul give the number. Did he have a contact in the police? By the time he was upright again, the call was over.

'No good. The van was reported stolen this morning.'

'Fuck it. They were wearing caps so I couldn't see their heads. The boots and combat jackets make it clear they were Phoenix Rises.'

'Who else? I'd better get back to my aunt.' Raul turned away.

Mavros followed him. Just before he reached the building, a black 4x4 pulled up and a man in a black polo-neck and jeans came out and strode quickly towards him. His arm was grabbed in a steel grip.

'Where is she?' the man demanded, in English.

'The Phoenix Rises got her. White van heading east, but you won't catch it now.' He grimaced. 'Can I have my arm back?' The man stared at him, then let go.

'Maybe you should come upstairs,' Mavros said. 'We've been exchanging confidences.'

'I hope for your sake that's a bluff.'

His arm was clutched again, not quite so tightly, and he was walked inside. They took the lift.

The man spoke words Mavros didn't understand after he rang Allegra's door. It opened swiftly.

More words were exchanged, presumably in Hebrew. Allegra and Raul both shook the man's hand.

'I'm sorry,' Mavros said, in English. 'They were too quick, even for her.'

Allegra nodded. 'That's in the past. What we have to decide now is how we proceed.'

Mavros gave her a dubious look. 'We? Who exactly are we? I know who I am, but you three...'

More words in what he presumed was Hebrew were exchanged and the tall man went to Allegra's computer.

'So?' Mavros asked. 'Cards on the table time?'

'We have to wait. Dan's advising his controller.'

'So Dan's Mossad.'

She held his gaze. 'You could make that assumption.'

'What about you and Raul?'

Allegra sat down, signalling to him to do the same. 'No. But you must understand that our community has ties to the Israeli state – ties at all sorts of levels. For example, as you suggested, I provide my fellow researchers and historians with the fruits of my labours. Sometimes the secret agencies are interested.'

Mavros was about to ask her if she and Raul had been involved in the assassination of Tareq

Momani, but decided that wasn't a good idea. Dan looked like he was capable of anything.

'What about Aron Samuel?'

'I didn't lead you on. What I gave you is what I know.'

'And Shimon?'

'We haven't even spoken recently.'

Her tone, smooth and warm, was persuasive, but he didn't buy it – the best she was getting was the benefit of the doubt.

'So you don't know if Aron's in the city.'

'No. He could be. You know the evidence, such as it is.'

'Let's assume he is. Why would he come back after all these years?'

Allegra watched as Dan got up from the computer. 'Maybe it's nothing more complicated than that he wants to die where he was born.'

Mavros shrugged. Anything seemed possible.

'Right,' said Dan, standing by the sofa. 'I'll speak English for the benefit of our ... Scottish Greek.'

'Thanks, but I don't know if I want to hear it.'

Dan squatted down beside him. 'You're right to be cautious. But I'm going to appeal to your professionalism.'

Mavros sighed, thinking of Niki and the Fat Man. He should already have been on a plane. 'I'm listening.'

'We need a missing-persons expert with your experience in this country.' Dan shook his head. 'I was against Rachel employing you from the start, but she had her reasons. Now things have changed. Not only must you find Aron Samuel,

311

but you must help us find Rachel.'

'Must is a word I don't respond well to.'

Dan smiled, revealing white teeth and un-usually pointed incisors. 'Forgive me, English is my sixth language. Please help us find Rachel and Aron Samuel.'

'Why are you so interested in the old man?'

'Why do you want to know?'

Mavros laughed. 'As I was saying to Allegra, cards on the table. You know everything about me, but I know very little about you.'

'I will give you the information you need, but first you must agree to complete the case you took on. Your client has been lost on your watch.'

'My client's daughter.'

'Even worse. Surely your personal code of honour – what is it called in Greek?'

'"Philotimo",' said Allegra.

'As well as your professional standing, require you to get her back.'

Mavros was cornered. He wasn't sure whether they'd studied his past or divined his character from his recent actions, but he did feel at least partly responsible for Rachel, despite the fact that she hadn't been fully honest with him. And walking away from unclosed cases was something he never did.

'All right,' he said.

'A good decision,' said Dan. 'There will be a substantial bonus if you succeed.'

'Never mind that. Answer my questions.' He caught the agent's eye. 'Truthfully.'

The Israeli shrugged. 'I'm bound by my rules of service. If I am not allowed to answer, you must ... you will have to accept that.'

'I'll judge each question on its own merit.'

'Shall I bring coffee?' Allegra asked.

Mavros brushed away the offer.

'Why do you want Aron Samuel?' he asked Dan.

'I don't. He's Rachel's baby, so to speak. But it's felt that he should be found for his own good and for the good of the state.'

'OK.' Mavros gave him a grave look. 'Did you kill Tareq Momani?'

'Certainly not.'

'Did Rachel?'

Dan shook his head. 'She is not an assassin.'

'Do you know who killed him?'

The agent kept silent.

Mavros thought about that. People like Dan were trained to lie. He himself had learned how to tell when he was being told untruths. There was something not right about the Israeli's answers and his failure to answer. Then a thought struck him.

'Did Aron Samuel kill Momani?'

Another silence.

'Does Aron Samuel have people working for him?'

'Possibly. We know his sons have helped him in the past.'

Mavros turned to Raul, thinking of the man in the fish taverna with Baruh Natzari and the other one who had picked them up. 'Do they look like him?'

'They're not dissimilar, though more solidly built.'

Had Rachel known about them, Mavros wondered. And why would Aron's sons have met Baruh? Had they driven him to commit suicide? Or made his death look like suicide?

'Did you dispose of the fascists who tried to get in here?'

'That was me,' Raul volunteered.

'You've been well trained. Are you Mossad?'

'We use local contractors from time to time,' Dan said. 'Now, we must move. Rachel's in great danger.'

Mavros nodded and let the rest of his questions go for the time being. The truth was, he wanted to save her from the neo-Nazis and he wanted to find her great-uncle.

'You're the expert,' he said. 'What do you suggest?'

'Where would they have taken her?'

'Makis Kalogirou will be smarting after what we did to him this morning. He's a moron when it comes to history and ideology, but he's cunning. I doubt he's got her in any of his properties, personal or business, or known Phoenix Rises premises. Anyway, we haven't got time to check.'

'I don't suppose you took any photos of her abduction,' Dan said.

Mavros shook his head, then looked at Raul.

'Afraid not,' said the young man. 'No time.'

'Without evidence, diplomatic moves will be difficult.'

'Rachel's French,' Mavros pointed out.

'Among other things,' Dan said. 'It's too slow anyway. Any suggestions?'

'Yes.' Mavros took out his phone and called Nikos Kriaras.

Rachel was on her front on a narrow table. When the van had stopped, she'd been taken inside quickly, a hand over her eyes. Her hands and ankles had been untied, but she was held down with such force by the men whose faces were covered by black balaclavas that she couldn't make a move. She was spreadeagled, her wrists and ankles bound to the table legs. At least she was still wearing her clothes.

'Some ass,' said one of her captors, laughing lewdly.

There was a burst of Greek and he shut up.

Rachel took in her surroundings to the front. She was in a basement, she thought, the concrete walls unplastered. There was a shovel and a garden fork in the corner by the unpainted door. The floor was roughly finished. She inhaled damp and mustiness, and something else – was it liquid fuel?

Then the door opened. Two masked men came in, both wearing high boots and combat gear. They were followed by Makis Kalogirou, whose face was uncovered. Rachel's stomach clenched. If he was showing himself, that meant he didn't care that she could identify him. Did the piece of shit have the nerve to kill her?

'Mademoiselle Samuel,' he said, in oddly accented French. 'I suppose you thought locking me in with a bomb was very funny.'

'You're here, aren't you?'

He punched her on the side of her head.

315

'Yes, Jewish bitch, I am here. As are my men. I don't imagine you have experience of gang rape.'

She inhaled deeply.

'Don't worry, we're civilised. No good National Socialist would soil himself with a Jewish orifice.'

Rachel knew she had to play for time. 'I suppose you learned that, along with your execrable French, from Le Pen.'

She was hit again and heard a command in Greek. Sharp blades were applied to her clothes until she was naked.

Kalogirou lowered his head to the level of hers. 'We won't taint ourselves with you, Jew.' He grinned. 'Instead we'll use wooden stakes and iron rods like these.' He brandished the instruments of torture. 'Of course, if you give me the information I want, you'll escape the worst.'

Rachel resisted the temptation to spit in his face. She had to use her tongue in another way.

'What is it you want to know?' she said, with a sob.

Kalogirou smiled, as if he'd expected her to break so easily.

'Who do you work for?'

She paused and then told him.

The leader of the Phoenix Rises looked like he was about to faint.

THIRTY-SIX

My Gavriella died in March. No, it was a mercy. The cancer had been eating her for years and she was ready to go. The boys cried at her bedside when she was finally still - they have retained their humanity, as I hoped. I do not cry, have not since I joined the Sonderkommando. In fact, I smiled because I knew my darling was free of her pain and that of the world. She lost family members to the Nazis, though they were distant and she had never met them. I am proud that I protected her from the worst that men – and women – can do. She suspected I was doing terrible things – as she would have seen them – every summer, but she respected me enough not to ask. I never told her about the SK, confining myself to the loss of those close to me at Auschwitz.

But, for all my happiness, her death changed everything. My sons are married, have children and now live in different states. But I'm not talking about day-to-day changes. I have lived inside myself since before the Lager and I can't say that I missed my wife's presence. She had been through such a trial of strength in the last months. No, what changed was my ambition. I was no longer tied to our home for most of the year. My health was – and is – still good. I wanted to move on from shrivelled old Nazis and dry-hearted collaborators. I needed to make a state-

ment that all the world would see and understand. And I will make that statement in the city
of my birth.

What's that? Why was I on the sidewalk opposite the synagogue? Because my old comrade
Zvi's grandson was getting married and I wanted
to show my face, even briefly. Ah, Ester Broudo
saw me. So that's how you got on to me. No, I
won't tell you my plans yet. But you can be sure
what I will do is related to the story I have told
you. I want your agreement to participate. That
does not imply your approval, simply your
acknowledgement of the struggle against the evil
in humankind. Do not speak. I will leave you to
sleep for a few hours. I'm sorry I can't untie your
bonds. Close your eyes now.

THIRTY-SEVEN

'I don't know all Makis Kalogirou's properties,'
Nikos Kriaras said impatiently. 'Besides, he could
have taken the woman to some follower's place.'

'You can call him, can't you?' Mavros said.

There was a pause. 'I don't maintain that kind
of relationship with him.'

'Get a minion to do it.'

'And tell him what? "We hear you've kidnapped
a Jewish woman. Kindly let her go"?'

'Why not? It's an illegal act and you're the
police.'

'For God's sake, the Phoenix Rises is a legal

organisation. What proof have you got that they took the woman?'

Mavros looked at Dan. 'You do know who she works for.'

'Why should I?'

'Well, you were the one who told me there was a Mossad cell operating up here.'

'What? Your client's one of them?'

Mavros stayed silent.

'All right,' Kriaras said. 'I'll see what I can do.'

'Good move.'

'You realise that if I tell them that, they may become even more hostile towards her.'

'Do you really believe that?'

This time the brigadier didn't answer.

'Let me know what happens,' Mavros said, then terminated the call.

'Well?' Dan asked.

Mavros told them the gist of the conversation.

'How do they know there's a Mossad cell up here?' the agent asked.

'That's your people's department.' Mavros grinned. 'Maybe a Palestinian has infiltrated.'

Dan glared at him.

'So what are we going to do?' asked Raul. 'Just sit and wait? We should go and torch the fucking Phoenix's office.'

'I don't allow that sort of language in my home,' Allegra said sternly.

Mavros wondered if she meant the swear word or the neo-Nazi group's name.

'Calm down,' Dan said. 'We have no idea where they've taken her, so searching is futile. Provoking them is likely to be counter-productive.'

Mavros sat on the sofa and tried to get his thoughts in order. Kriaras's line of communication with Kalogirou wasn't news, though it disgusted him. At least it didn't seem that the brigadier had ordered the kidnapping. He considered what Dan had said about Rachel's hunt for her great-uncle. It was her affair, so why was he still in Thessaloniki? Did his organisation have other Arab targets lined up? That idea revolted him too. Whatever had happened to their people in the past, the Israelis weren't entitled to carry out assassinations in foreign countries any more than the Americans, the Russians or terrorist groups.

Then Dan's phone rang. Relief flooded his face. 'Where are you?' he said, in English, scribbling words on the pad Allegra handed him. 'I'm coming.' He showed what he'd written to the researcher. 'Where is this?'

'The Macedonia Pallas?' Allegra said. 'It's a big, ugly hotel on the seafront, not far beyond the White Tower.'

'I'll direct you,' volunteered Raul.

'I'm coming too,' said Mavros.

Ten minutes later Dan stopped the Jeep and Rachel got in the back.

'Are you all right?' Mavros asked, from the seat beside her. Her left ear was red and swollen.

'Nothing serious.'

'But they took your clothes.'

She was wearing an old overcoat several sizes too large, socks but no shoes and what looked like a cotton nightie. She was holding her laptop bag.

'Have you still got your weapon?' Dan asked, looking in the mirror.

'Yes. They removed the clip.'

'No problem.'

'No problem?' she shouted. 'They cut my clothes off with knives and threatened to sodomise me with bits of wood and metal.'

Mavros put his hand over hers and waited for her to calm down.

'Kalogirou was there, yes?' he asked in a low voice.

She nodded.

'Did he take any calls?'

'No.'

Mavros stared at her. 'How did you talk your way to freedom? I presume that's what you did.'

Rachel smiled tightly. 'I can be very persuasive.'

'I bet you can,' he said, with a grin.

As they were approaching the Electra Palace, his phone rang. It was Niki.

Dieter Jahnel looked out over the city of Thessaloniki from the penthouse apartment that had been rented for him on the seafront. The sea, the distant mountains, the sun lancing through grey clouds made a striking panorama, but he wasn't overly impressed. He was a Bavarian and glorious scenery was something he had grown up with – jagged mountain peaks, tree-lined lakes, woods that fed the soul. More to the point, he was a businessman, head of a consortium of manufacturers close to signing a deal with the Macedonian Development Council, backed by the Greek government and several state and private banks. All he was waiting for was agreement over some minor but significant details. The Development Minister, a Greek who had been educated in Germany and seemed more northern than southern European – apart from the bribes he expected – was already in Thessaloniki. The signing tomorrow afternoon should go ahead without any problems. There were jobs in it for the Greeks, as well as technical innovation; for the Germans, there was what any businessman lived and breathed – profit.

Jahnel dealt with a phone call from his secretary and then stripped naked. He had been neglecting his exercise regime because of his various work responsibilities – his family company manufactured telephone systems and he was also a non-executive director of two companies listed on the Xetra DAX. In recent weeks he had spent more time in the air than on the ground, not least because Jahnel Industries had taken over a failing American operation in Milwaukee. As he got back into the regime of squats and push-ups that he had kept going since his years on the university rowing team, he made himself focus on a single objective. Sometimes that would be one of his children: Erich, nineteen, was doing well at Heidelberg, Monika was in Grade 11 at gymnasium and fighting off the boys, while thirteen-year-old Max was a fully qualified assassin in several computer games. This time, though, Jahnel was thinking about his paternal grandfather, Helmut. He had set up the business in the hard years after the war and it was at exactly the right stage of development when

322

West Germany's US-supported economy really took off. Opa, though he preferred to be called Grossvater, was a strong-willed man, who regarded his own son, Jan, as little better than an average manager. He had seen promise in Dieter from an early age, watching with relish as he scythed the legs from opposition players on the football pitch. He had always confided in Dieter, and it was when he was fifteen that Opa told him he had been in northern Greece with the Waffen-SS in 1943, before his unit was sent to the Eastern Front. Almost all were killed there and Opa had lost a lung. He still smoked his pipe till the day he died, aged eighty-eight, only three years earlier.

Jahnel got up and stretched his arms as he got his breathing in check. He went to the window and looked down at the people on the pavements. Opa had never expanded on his activities in this country, but Dieter was a good student. He always did his research before planning deals and he knew what had happened in Thessaloniki, not only to the Jews but to the Christian residents, during the Axis occupation. None of the Greeks he had done business with had ever mentioned the war. Perhaps some of their families had been collaborators. More likely, they were ignorant, preferring to concentrate on increasing their fortunes. That was how the world worked.

On the way to the shower, Dieter Jahnel ran a hand over his close-cropped blond hair. It occurred to him that, in a uniform rather than a suit, he would have looked very similar to Opa in his wartime photos. Only he wasn't a Nazi; he wasn't even a Christian Democrat; he was one of the few members of the Greens to prosper in big business. His wife Greta's grandfather, a senior member of the Communist Party of Germany, had died in Dachau, and they had taken care to ensure their children were fully aware of their country's terrible history.

Why, then, did he feel ashamed to be staying in a luxurious apartment only a few hundred metres from the square that had hosted the first humiliation of Thessaloniki's Jews?

'Alex, this is your last chance,' Niki said. 'If you're not back tonight, we're finished.'

Mavros glanced at Rachel, then turned away. 'You're being unreasonable. Besides, there's every chance that I'll be on a plane by this evening.'

'My darling, that's wonderful news. Is everything finished up there?'

'No, but I've had enough. I'll tell you when I get back.'

Niki was crying and laughing at the same time. 'Thank you ... thank you, Alex. Call me ... call me when you land. I love you.'

'I love you too. Kisses.'

Raul, the only Greek-speaker in the Cherokee, gave no sign of having heard his words. Soon afterwards they were dropped off at the hotel, Dan telling Rachel that he'd be in touch.

'I need some clothes,' Rachel said, walking towards the shop.

'I'm going up,' Mavros said, unwilling to talk in public.

'Oh no you don't. I had to supervise your new wardrobe, so you can return the favour.'

'Haven't you got a change of clothes in your case?'

She smiled unusually widely. 'No, it's full of secret equipment.'

He wasn't sure how to read that. Was it an admission of her status as a Mossad agent? Asking her in a shop full of American tourists wasn't feasible. She held up blouses, pullovers and trousers, all dark-coloured, and he nodded unenthusiastically. Then she chose a leather blouson similar to the one she'd bought him.

'We'll look like twins,' she said, with a laugh.

They took the lift because of her numerous bags.

'I have to talk to you,' Mavros said.

'I know. Come to my room.'

He followed her down the corridor. Should he stay or should he go?

'Let's order room service,' Rachel said. 'I'm starving.'

She had a shower as they waited for the food. Mavros considered rifling through her things, but didn't have the energy. He'd had enough of the case, even if there was one – or at least one that he could do anything about.

The food appeared and they ate, Rachel in a robe with her hair in a towel.

'That's better,' she said. 'I must take some olives home.'

'Home? And where's that?'

'What do you mean?'

'I presume you have at least a pied-à-terre in

Tel Aviv.'

Rachel sat back. 'What's Dan been saying?'

'Nothing much. He did mention that you weren't only French.'

She raised her shoulders. 'So what? Dual nationality isn't a crime.'

'A foreigner carrying a firearm is, even in this Balkan balls-up of a country.'

She stared at him. 'I don't understand what your problem is.'

'Let me explain. You hired me to find your great-uncle Aron, aged eighty – if he's alive. He's such a ghost that now I'm begining to think Ester Broudo really was mistaken. All the other in-formation we turned up leads nowhere.'

'What about Baruh Natzari? He killed himself in front of that terrible photo.'

'Which proves only that your great-uncle was alive in the 50s.' He stood up. 'I'm sorry, I can't stay up here any longer. You haven't been honest with me and I have other priorities.'

She got up and gripped his arm tightly. 'Ask me anything.'

'All right. Do you really believe he's alive and in the city?'

'Yes,' she replied, without hesitating.

'Did you kill Tareq Momani?'

'No.'

He caught her gaze. 'Are you a member of Mossad?'

Like Dan, she kept silent.

'Goodbye,' he said, heading for the door.

At least Rachel didn't try to stop him. By phone he booked a seat on a flight departing at five in the afternoon and checked out. Instead of getting the hotel to order a cab, he walked down to the seafront. In the distance he could see the peninsula with the low buildings of Ayia Triadha. He had a flash of his brother Andonis on the beach there.

Then there was a screech of brakes and a black van stopped ahead of him. Two men in rolled-down balaclavas jumped out of the back and grabbed him. It was only a matter of seconds before the van moved forward. Then a sack or the like was pulled over his head and his hands tied behind his back.

'I'm sorry about the rough treatment, Mr Mavros,' came a voice from the front, speaking English with an American accent. 'I believe you've been looking for me.'

Mavros breathed in through the fabric over his mouth. It sounded like Aron Samuel was alive, well and in Thessaloniki after all.

THIRTY-EIGHT

'Wake up now, please.'

Mavros opened his eyes. The old man was sitting by the bed, as he had been when he told the story of his life.

'What time is it?'

'Six in the morning. Isaak is making your breakfast. Yosif will take you to the bathroom.'

The grip on his arms was vice-like, so he didn't

327

resist. After emptying his bladder and washing his face and hands, he looked in the cracked mirror. The bruising around his eyes was at its worst, but there were no new marks on his face. That made him ashamed. He should at least have struggled, if not fought back. But it was too late now.

On the way back he took in the room. It was in disrepair, the yellow paint on the walls faded and the wooden floors rough and uncovered. The shutters were closed and no light filtered through the slats. His ankles were bound and the rope secured to the end of the bed, while one of his wrists was tied to the bed frame, the old man pushing his chair out of range.

'It's miserable, I know, but my family used to live in this area,' Samuel said. 'In a finer house, I gather – not that I have any memory of it.'

Isaak came in with a tray. When Mavros finished eating and drinking – fresh bread and good filter coffee – his free arm was bound like the other one, while the chair was pulled closer.

'You will remember that I made you a proposition last night.'

Mavros stared at him. The skin on Aron Samuel's face was unusually tight for an eighty-year-old – surely he hadn't had plastic surgery? It was tanned and marked with liver spots, the long nose broken and misshapen. But the eyes were the main feature beneath the thick white hair. They were grey and cold, dimly lit as if by a star that had long been extinguished.

'I remember you wanted my agreement to participate in an unspecified action. Were you serious?'

'Deadly serious.' The old man's voice was low, making it all the more threatening. 'Why do you think I told you my story? To educate you? Yes. To elicit sympathy? No. To make you realise that some things cannot be allowed to pass? Very much so. These things are still flourishing. You must make a principled decision, Alex Mavros. As your father did many times in his life.'

'My father didn't kill people by the dozen.'

Samuel gave him a sad look. 'But can you be sure of that? He was undercover on Crete during the Axis occupation. How do you know he didn't kill the oppressors with his own hands? How do you know he didn't plan attacks?' He raised his still wide shoulders. 'You cannot have any certainty.'

'I don't believe that the party supplied you with targets.'

'Believe what you like. Consider me a liar as regards what I did myself. But you cannot deny the general truth of what I said. You have read too widely in the history of this country and the continent of which it is part. What the Nazis did was wrong. What their protectors – open and secret – did was also wrong. What their successors did and continue to do is wrong. I do not use the word "evil" because it suggests some external agency, either religious or ideological, that takes the focus away from men – and women, of course. Mankind. That is why I ask you to make a principled stand against those who do wrong. Can you refuse?'

'Do I have a choice?'

'Of course. I am not a savage. You will be left

here bound to the bed and, when the time is right, an anonymous call will be made to the authorities.'

'What happens if you and your sons are ... don't survive this great statement you're going to make?'

Aron Samuel looked over his shoulder to Yosif and smiled. 'The opposition will have to be very good to kill all three of us. Still, if they do you'll have to take your chances. This building is un-occupied and you will, of course, be gagged.'

'How am I supposed to eat and drink?'

'We will devise something with a bottle and a straw at the side of the gag. Though that won't keep you going for long.'

Mavros shook his head. 'You expect me to make a principled decision when the alternative is a slow and agonising death?'

'Yes. Principles stand above material consider-ations. Will you make a stand against people who treat others as dirt?'

Mavros thought about it. He couldn't argue with the old man's thinking, even though he sus-pected it would lead to problems later. Besides, he had to get out of captivity.

'All right,' he said. 'I agree to take a stand against people who treat others as dirt.'

'And count their lives as nothing.'

He repeated the words, seeing lines of old people and the disabled at Auschwitz railway station.

'That wasn't so difficult, was it?' Samuel said, touching his hand.

The skin was like greaseproof paper, more

manufactured than human.

'I know,' the old man said. 'Gavriella made me use moisturiser. Since she left us, I've given that up.'

'Are you going to untie me now?' Mavros demanded. 'And I want to call my partner in Athens. She was expecting me last night.'

'Not yet, as regards the first. We know about Niki because she called your phone many times. There are messages too.'

'I need to hear them.'

'And I need your mind to be clear. The battery has been removed from your phone. You'll get them both back later.'

Mavros shook his head. 'You aren't making it easy for me.'

'Don't you want to know what you've agreed to participate in?'

'I suppose so. But what about Rachel? Don't you have any desire to see her?'

Aron Samuel sat back in the rickety chair. 'My great-niece? I imagine she'll be in the vicinity today.'

Then he told Mavros what they were going to do.

THIRTY-NINE

Rachel had followed Mavros out of the Electra Palace in the hope of persuading him to stay on the case. She was puzzled when he didn't get straight into a taxi, but walked to the seafront. She ran towards the van when she saw what was happening, but wasn't quick enough to obstruct his kidnap. She got the registration number, though. Was it the Phoenix Rises? It was hard to believe they'd pick up her investigator after she'd put the fear of the agency into them. She called Dan and told him to trace the number. By the time she got back to her room, he had the information.

'It's a rental from a company on Egnatias Street. The name on the papers is Henry James Whitworth, American passport number 2964783946, credit card in that name, home address 1781 Sunset Avenue, Phoenix, Arizona. It's being checked now ... wait ... it's a fake.'

'What the hell?'

'Yeah. The credit card's been cloned.'

Rachel sat down on the bed. 'At least it isn't the neo-Nazis.'

'Those idiots? No, we're up against serious opposition now.'

'Tareq Momani's people?'

'Remember who was babysitting him.'

'Shit. The Russians.'

'I'd say they're the most likely candidates.'

'What do we do?'

'I've asked control.'

'You'd better get over here. We should stick together.'

'We should. Go into lockdown mode.'

'Right.' She broke the connection. Their phones were protected, but not against the kind of serious hardware the Russians would have.

Rachel checked the door locks, wedged a chair under the handle and drew the curtains. There was no point in her going on to the encrypted site since Dan was already in contact with their command team. She screwed a suppressor on to her pistol and sat in the dark, against the wall at right angles to the door.

Then she started to think. If the Russians, or any other major players, had taken Mavros, he would soon talk. That was manageable. He didn't know about the Momani hit, despite his suspicions that she and Dan were Mossad. If he passed on the latter, nobody would be surprised. The question was, did his capture compromise the next part of their mission? She suspected that control would judge it didn't. That left the issue of her great-uncle. She'd hoped they would have found him by now. There were records of his activities up to the previous year, but he and his sons, neither of whom was at home although their families were, had evaded border checks. They had probably crossed illicitly into Mexico.

A thought struck her. Was Henry James Whitworth the cover of Aron Samuel or one of his sons? Had they abducted Mavros? No, it was ridiculous. There was little he could tell them that they didn't already know.

Then she understood. Her great-uncle had taken Mavros to make a point to her. He knew she was after him and had made progress in tracking him down – so he'd removed her Greek expert. Which raised two issues. The first was family loyalty. It seemed obvious that he had no interest in meeting her – he could have approached her at any time over the last few days. But worse: he was planning one of his executions. If he succeeded while she was in the same city, her career in intelligence would explode like a pheasant hit by several simultaneous shots.

Makis Kalogirou was happier than he'd been a few minutes earlier. Confirmation of the final details of the deal with the German-led consortium had been accepted by the government. He had two reasons to celebrate. The family company was going to survive – even prosper – after foreign investment, and that would give the Phoenix Rises a solid financial base.

'Yiota!' he shouted.

His wife appeared, her expression even more curdled than usual. She had been badly frightened by the way the abduction of the Jew woman had ended and was taking it out on her husband.

'I want my best suit for tomorrow, the dark blue one.'

'It's in the wardrobe.'

Kalogirou gave her a sharp look. 'Make sure it's pressed. And I'll need a white shirt. Come on, hurry up!'

Yiota shared her husband's politics, but she didn't like the way women were kept in the background. They had no children and she wasn't interested in either cakes or the kitchen.

'I have work of my own to do,' she said, turning on her heel. She was a lawyer and her earnings had kept both the family and the party going as Kalogirou SA plunged ever deeper into debt. She was surprised that foreigners would invest in such a company – the furniture factory and equipment were in poor condition and the ceramics off-shoot had never made money.

Her husband pounded after her and grabbed her arm.

'Don't!' she said, jabbing her pen at his eye, but not making contact.

He fell backwards in a heap.

'Woman, you can't treat me like that,' he said, struggling to his feet.

'You may be the führer of the party, but you don't order me about,' she said, walking away. 'You don't frighten me either.'

Kalogirou went back to his study and eyed the picture of Hitler behind his desk.

'You never allowed Eva to talk to you like that, did you?' he said, picking up the baseball bat he kept in the umbrella stand.

On his way downstairs he smiled. When Yiota woke up, she'd be spread-eagled on the bed, arse up like the Jewish bitch. She might even enjoy it – not that he cared.

Yiorgos Pandazopoulos picked up his mobile phone with a groan. He was sitting in an uncomfortable chair in Apostolos's spartan flat and his burns were still painful. The comrade's wife had gone to stay with her sister, so he was welcome, at least for a short time.

'This is Niki.'

The Fat Man steeled himself. 'How are you?' he asked, preparing for the storm.

'It's Alex. Have you heard from him?'

'Not since ... when was it? Yesterday morning. What about you?'

'Yesterday afternoon. He told me he was on his way home.'

'Good.'

'No, it's not good. He hasn't arrived.'

Yiorgos's considerable abdomen clenched. 'What?'

'I've been calling him since yesterday evening. His phone goes straight to voice mail. I must have left twenty messages.'

'What the hell? Have you called the hotel?'

'He checked out yesterday at 1.35 in the afternoon.'

'That's ... worrying.'

The word set Niki off. Her sobs were long and loud.

'Calm down,' the Fat Man said, completely out of his emotional depth. 'There's bound to be a logical explanation.'

'Yes ... he's been grabbed by ... the Phoenix Rises...'

'I doubt it,' he lied. 'They're pathetic cowards.'

'They ... they may have been ... the ones who burned down your ... house.'

That was true. Yiorgos was still bothered by the

336

young man who had taken him to hospital. Why was he familiar?

'What ... what are we going to do?'

He didn't like the sound of 'we' at all. 'Have you spoken to Alex's family?'

'His mother ... and his sister haven't ... haven't heard from him either...'

He let her howl for a bit longer, considering his options. Shimon Raphael. He would be able to help.

'Listen, Niki ... take a deep breath ... and another one... All right, I've got a contact in Thessaloniki. I'll call him and see what he says. I'll be in touch.' He broke the connection. He felt sorry for Niki, despite his general dislike of her. Alex had been playing hard ball with her over this case.

The Fat Man found Shimon's office number. He was told that Mr Raphael was abroad, so he used the mobile number he had.

'*Shalom aleichem.*'

'What? Shimon, this is Yiorgos.'

'Yiorgos Pandazopoulos? How are you, my friend? Out of hospital?'

'Yes. What did you say before?'

'Oh, that was Hebrew. I'm in Tel Aviv.'

'Shit.'

'Actually, it's not that bad. I'm visiting family.'

'No, I mean I hoped you were in the co-capital?'

'Why?'

'Alex Mavros seems to have fallen off the radar.'

'What?'

The Fat Man explained.

337

'Well, he was all right when I last saw him,' Shimon said. 'Though he managed to get the Phoenix Rises on his back.'

'That's what I was wondering. Could they have grabbed him?'

'It's possible. I don't know what we can do about it.'

'I do. *Shalom.*' Yiorgos cut the connection and took out his wallet. It had been in his back pocket and had survived the fire. He kept a card with essential numbers on it.

'Yes?' Nikos Kriaras said brusquely.

'This is Yiorgos Pandazopoulos.'

'Who?'

'Alex Mavros's partner.'

'Oh, the Fat... What do you want?'

Again, Yiorgos explained.

'So?' the brigadier said. 'What do you want me to do?'

'Alex told me you had a link to Makis Kalogirou. Tell the wanker to let him go.'

'Why?'

The Fat Man laughed. 'I know all about you. The independent press and the comrades would be very interested.'

There was a silence. 'I don't take well to threats.'

'Me neither. If anything happens to me, a file is automatically sent to three national newspapers. As well as to the comrades, of course.'

'You're taking a big risk,' Kriaras said. 'I'll call you back.'

Yiorgos sat back and wiped his brow. One day he really had to get round to writing up everything Alex had told him about the brigadier.

338

Ten minutes later, Kriaras rang back.

'They don't have him.'

'Are you sure?'

'Don't push your luck.' The brigadier hung up.

Now the Fat Man felt seriously lost. Shimon was out of the country, the most likely suspects were out of the equation and Alex was still not answering his phone – he'd rung and left a message of his own.

'Niki?'

'Did you get anywhere?'

'In a sense.' A very negative one, Yiorgos thought. 'Listen, leave it with me. I've got leads I can follow.'

'I've … I've been thinking … about going to Thessaloniki.'

'Bad idea. I said leave it with me, Niki. All right?'

She agreed reluctantly.

The Fat Man broke the connection and called the airport. Three minutes later he had a booking on the plane that left for the co-capital in two hours. Despite the sting of his burns and the worry about Alex, he felt good. He was the heavy cavalry, riding to save the day.

While Rachel was in the shower, Dan accessed the encrypted site. She had already received information for their mission in the evening and shared it with him. He had personal instructions to confirm. As he waited for control to respond, he kept an ear directed towards the bathroom. Water was still running.

He'd had doubts about their partnership from

the beginning. Not because of Rachel as an agent. He'd worked with her before and she'd proved herself to be capable and committed. The problem was the dual nature of this operation. Dealing with Tareq Momani had been both justified and straightforward. True, they'd potentially kicked open a Russian hornets' nest, but the blame for that had been put at another door. No, the problem was the issue of Rachel's great-uncle. He'd read the old man's file. It was an amazing document. Dan had plenty of hits to his name, but Aron Samuel made him look like a babe in arms. The Auschwitz survivor was a stone killer and a genuine hero. Eighty years old and still taking the bad guys down – it was remarkable. But also sad. Was that how he was going to end up, Dan thought. Killing with a colostomy bag and a catheter?

He shrugged. Why not? It would be better than playing golf with a bunch of wrinkled old farts in Florida. Only that wasn't how it worked. Stone killers didn't die in their beds. It was against their natures – he could understand that.

The water in the bathroom had stopped. Dan looked at the screen, ready to log out. He heard Rachel brushing her teeth, then confirmation came through. It was as he had expected.

FORTY

Dieter Jahnel had asked his German colleagues to come to his apartment before three o'clock. The sheik's security detail duly arrived at that hour and carried out both a technical and hands-on check of the place and its occupants. Given the amount of money that was coming from the Gulf, the businessmen and women were prepared to submit to that minor invasion of their privacy. Muhammed bin Zayed arrived with his two bodyguards when the all-clear was given.

Dieter went to meet him at the door, bowing as he shook his hand. The sheik was in white robes, his thick black curls almost reaching his shoulders and his sleek beard making him look more like a rock star than one of the world's shrewdest investors – and he was only thirty-five. The only significant blemish on his reputation – who cared about gambling and rumours of high-end call girls? – was his secret funding of Islamic clerics with suspected links to Al-Qaeda cells, some of which had been active recently. A woman from the secret service had visited him at his office in Munich and informed him that the sheik was out of favour with the Americans, even though they allowed him to conduct business in New York without hindrance. The BND file was submitted to the Minister of Economic Cooperation and Development, who approved the consortium's involvement with the sheik.

'Dieter,' said the Arab, in English, taking his hand, 'how very good to see you again. I do apologise for this rigmarole. One can never be too careful.'

The sheik had been educated at public school and Oxford, but seemed to have learned his English from the works of P.G. Wodehouse. Fortunately Wodehouse was one of Dieter's favourite authors, an addiction he had picked up on an exchange visit to a college in Gloucestershire.

'You don't mind if I have a cigar? I know you don't partake.'

'Be my guest,' the German replied, with a liberal gesture. His wife would have been unimpressed. Smoking was banned in their home.

Shortly afterwards, the Greek contingent arrived. The Development Minister dispensed handshakes and smiles with his usual aplomb, while the businessmen did their best to disguise their excitement. Several had already told the press that Thessaloniki and the surrounding area would be economically transformed by the deal. Local MPs and politicians crowded in, at a loss over how to address the sheik. Dieter found most of them boorish and grasping. They made local politicians in Germany seem like models of probity. There was only one person missing.

'At least that idiot Kalogirou hasn't shown up,' the Minister said to Dieter, hand shielding his mouth. 'He's an embarrassment to both us and your delegation.'

The German wasn't going to make a fuss an hour before the signing of the agreement, but he wanted to ask what the leader of the Phoenix Rises had to do with his team of business people.

Ursula, Dieter's hyper-efficient assistant, came over and told him it was time to start moving to the town hall, where the ceremony would take place. The cars were waiting below. He went over to the sheik.

'The signing hour is almost upon us.'

'Very good,' said the Arab. 'No witching hours around here, at least.' He laughed. 'At least I hope not.'

Dieter Jahnel watched as the security personnel gathered around the sheik in a human shield. He was glad he had no need of such protection. Then again, he was worth about a thousandth of the man. He glanced out of the window as he went to chivvy the Greeks along. Mount Olympus and its snowy cap glinted in the distance. Not even Zeus could have matched the wealth of the Gulf states. But Zeus's thunderbolts could level all people, rich and poor.

'No!' Yiota Kalogirou shrieked. 'Let me go!'

The man in the balaclava punched her in the face, sending her flying through the hall. Her head hit the parquet floor hard and she lay still.

'What ... what have you done?' her husband said.

'Gag her,' the second man said, in heavily accented Greek. 'But you, we want you to talk.' He pushed the Greek into the sitting room and told him to pull the blinds down, pistol aimed at his midriff.

'Now, Mr Kalogirou, come and sit beside me.'

The second man's teeth were visible in the gap in his balaclava. They were grey.

'What ... what are you going to do to me?'

'Fascists,' the man said over his shoulder. 'Have you ever met one who isn't a coward?'

'There was that Bulgarian.'

'Oh yes. Shooting him in the balls made him squeal like the others, though.'

Kalogirou whimpered. The pistol's muzzle was jammed into his side.

'You'll notice I'm not worried about making a noise. What does that tell you, leader of the neo-Nazi Phoenix Rises?'

'That ... that you don't care who hears.'

'Correct. So talk.'

'What ... what about?'

'You hear that, Sergei?'

'I hear it.'

'Give me your knife.'

Sergei handed over the weapon, a combat model with a well-honed edge, then rammed his own pistol into the nape of the Greek's neck. His colleague ran the knife over Kalogirou's leg.

'Talk!'

'I don't understand. Please! Ach!'

The Russian had sliced into the flesh of his left thigh.

'Tareq Momani. Your group of pathetic nationalists shot him, yes?'

'No. We were ... we were framed.'

The man with the knife laughed. 'Someone else sprayed swastika on the dead man and gate? Who?'

'I don't ... I don't know... Please!'

'Don't know is no good.' The blade cut deeper.

'I ... aaaah! Maybe ... maybe Israelis ...'

The Russian laughed. 'You think Mossad come to Thessaloniki? You have the dreams of a madman.'

'Whoever ... whoever it was ... made fools out of you. Aaaah!'

'How you learn that?'

'Senior ... senior police. Tasers...'

'Mossad kill us, not use Tasers, fool. Last chance. Who did it?'

'I don't ... honestly ... I don't ... know.'

'What do you think, Sergei?'

'Judging from the stink, he's telling the truth.'

'Nazi shits himself. Most unusual. So, we move to next stage.'

'What ... what's that?' said Kalogirou.

The man with the knife looked at the portrait of Hitler. 'I take it you like swastikas.'

'I...'

'Yes or no?' the Russian yelled.

'Ye ... yes.'

'Good. How many would you like?'

'What?'

'Three, I think. Forehead and both cheeks. Hold him down, Sergei.'

He went to work with the combat knife.

Mavros had been in the back of the van with Yosif for a long time. Initially it had moved around, stopping and starting as if rounds were being made. For some time it had been stationary.

'Why do you do this?' he asked.

'What?'

'Aid and abet a murderer.'

'You heard his story. There are things that cannot be allowed to happen unavenged.'

'Sixty years have passed. Eventually the world has to move on.'

Yosif gave him a sharp look. 'The world moved on many years ago. That's the problem. In Germany, by the mid-50s former Nazis were back in their jobs as judges, teachers, businessmen... And look what's been happening in Austria with the far right.'

'None of that justifies murder. Your father is no better than the people he's persecuted. But you and your brother, you're still young. You don't have to do this.'

'He hasn't indoctrinated us, if that's what you're implying. We made our choices freely and we can stop any time.'

'So stop now. He has a death wish, I can see it in his eyes.'

Yosif laughed. 'You have experience of death wishes, no doubt.'

'Unfortunately, yes. But I sometimes think this whole country has a collective death wish, letting politicians do what they want in the mistaken belief that selling their votes will benefit them in the long run, maxing out half a dozen credit cards, destroying the environment...'

'I'm not letting my father down and neither will Isaak.'

Mavros picked up the flicker of doubt.

'What happened to Baruh Natzari?'

'You saw him. He hanged himself.'

'But why? What did Isaak say to him in the taverna?'

'Nothing. At least, nothing that would have driven him to that.'

'I don't believe you.'

'Who cares what you believe?' Yosif paused. 'Isaak told me he thought Baruh was only just holding on psychologically.'

Mavros thought back to the meeting he and Rachel had with the old man. If anything, he'd been agile, both mentally and physically.

'Isaak must have said something that got to him.'

Yosif shrugged. 'He told him that my father was back and wanted him to take part in one last operation.'

'But no one is to be killed.'

'He was told that. He was shocked and thought the old man had gone soft.'

'So you're saying Baruh committed suicide because he was disillusioned by your father?'

'Maybe everything got too much for him. He was an Auschwitz survivor, after all, and many of them kill themselves sooner or later.'

Mavros sat back and looked at the American. They were both wearing Greek police uniforms. He felt like a traitor to his father and brother when he'd put the dark blue dress uniform on, but he didn't have much choice. The plan outlined to him by Aron Samuel was non-violent and their holsters contained fake pistols. But what if he'd been tricked and only his was a toy?

The engine started and the van moved off. Yosif was checking his uniform. It looked like zero hour was imminent.

Rachel and Dan had left the hotel separately, having gone over the details of their mission for the last time. The Town Hall was nearby, but she would not approach it until a few minutes before the group of VIPs came out to face the press. Dan had reconnoitred his position earlier. It was still unoccupied; if that was no longer the case, he was perfectly capable of overcoming any resistance.

She walked down to the seafront and looked out across the water. There were several ships at anchor, one of them a rusty old freighter. She found herself thinking of her family – her father would have been smuggled out of Greece on a ship like that; Aron had no doubt made many trips by sea over the years. Would she really see him at last today? Control was certain he and his sons would be at the press conference outside the Town Hail, without stating their source. Could one of her cousins be a traitor? But who was he betraying? A man who had murdered more people than all but the most psychotic Nazis. The time for revenge was long gone.

As for their target, she had no qualms. The man was a disgrace to humankind and his death would do only good. The people he funded had killed women and children in Afghanistan, Iraq and Yemen. Then it struck her that she was thinking like her great-uncle. Enemies had to be struck down – there could be no middle way, no attempt at reconciliation or understanding. She shivered as the north wind blew past her and over the choppy water. What was the name Mavros had told her? And where was the missing-persons

348

specialist? She couldn't help thinking that he would have a part to play in the denouement.

'Excuse me,' said a large man, in execrable English. 'I am Yiorgos Pandazopoulos. You are Rachel, yes?'

She stared at him in amazement, not just because of his corpulent form. 'How did you find me?'

He held up printed sheets, some with her photograph on them. 'Internet. You know where is Alex?'

She raised her shoulders. 'Somebody took him.'

'This I understand for myself. Who?'

'I'm not sure. I'm sorry, I have to go.'

The Fat Man moved with surprising speed, securing a handcuff to her wrist. The other was on one of his. 'We find out together, yes?'

Rachel looked around, considering her options. Despite the presence of several people, she could shoot Mavros's partner, not necessarily fatally, retrieve the key and run for it.

'See,' he said, tossing a small key into the water when she turned to him. 'Other one not here.'

Rachel swore in several languages, which made her captor laugh heartily.

Yiota Kalogirou came round and scrambled to her feet, reaching out for the wall. She pulled off her gag and called her husband's name, at first in a low voice and then in a scream.

'Here,' he said. It sounded like he'd spat at her.

She tumbled into his office, clutching her shattered nose, and shrieked. Makis was tied to a chair, a curtain of blood covering his face.

'What … what have they done … to you?' Yiota said, extending a hand.

'Don't touch me!' he squealed.

She went closer, smelling the voiding of his bowels, and stared at him. Beneath the blood she could see the angular shapes that had been cut into his skin.

'Oh my God,' she whispered.

'There is … no God,' he hissed. 'Only the Führer. I bear his mark with pride.'

Despite her broken nose and searing headache, Yiota Kalogirou laughed. Only a madman could rejoice in the carnage that had been wrought on his face. She had just seen the light.

FORTY-ONE

Dan looked down from the fifth-floor window in the block opposite the Town Hall. The shutters were closed, but he had removed two of the slats and could see clearly. It was a curious building to house the city's administration, a great block on Venizelou Street that had apparently originally been built as a hotel and was still known as the Karavan Saraï. Next to it was the Hamza Bey mosque, dating from the fifteenth century but more recently a cinema. The grey dome and dirty red tiles surmounted a building in serious need of reconstruction. Still, it gave the scene a Middle Eastern feel that southern Greek cities didn't possess. That was appropriate, considering what

350

he was about to do.

He wondered if he'd get the shot. The police had already blocked off the road and there were many of them present, including some from the riot squad. So far no demonstrators had turned up. Dan couldn't see why they would. The agreement would bring much-needed investment to the city and region. No one seemed to care that the consortium was primarily German – the Second World War was ancient history as far as the Greeks were concerned, even though the city had suffered during the Axis occupation. As for funding from a Muslim state in the Persian Gulf, people were unconcerned. That would soon change.

Dan looked at the watch he had set up next to the SR-99 sniper's rifle. The Israel Military Industries weapon wasn't his favourite, but it was perfectly serviceable. It also had specific relevance to this mission, including the part Rachel wasn't aware of. It wasn't time for her to arrive, so he wasn't concerned by her absence. She was very precise about everything. He wondered how she would react when he carried out the secret order. Practically, it made no difference as their exit routes were different, but for an instant he felt sorry for her.

People started moving across the space between the barriers, many of them festooned with TV cameras and concomitant equipment. More police had arrived too, including a pair of officers in full-dress uniform that he recognised. So that was how they were gaining access. Good thinking. But where were the other two? He panned around with the scope. No sign of them. Had they hidden inside the Town Hall earlier? That could make the scenario even more interesting.

Dan started to inhale deeply. He'd carried out the routine so often that it was almost second nature, but he made sure he never got complacent. It was easy, as the execution of Tareq Momani had been. Think of your sister, she who died in the bus bomb. Think of your brother, he who was killed on the Lebanon border. Strike to avenge them. Strike again and again.

'I have to go to the toilet,' Rachel said.

The Fat Man grunted. 'Old ... how say ... trick?'

'It may be old, but I'm desperate. I'm going back to the hotel. Or do you want me to start screaming?'

'Do it and I stand on your toes.'

She tried to pull away.

'Exact. You not walking for many months. All right, lead way.'

They barrelled into the lobby of the Electra Palace like a pair of extremely ill-matched lovers holding hands.

'You'll have to let me go,' Rachel whined. 'I can't wait.'

'No key.'

'Of course you have a key. What were you going to do when we're finished? Tear the cuffs off with your bare hands?'

'Could do.'

She groaned. 'Please.'

Yiorgos walked her over to the toilets, then took a key from his shoe and freed her. 'Two minutes then I coming in.'

'Thank you,' she said, moving quickly away.

Two minutes passed. The Fat Man shook his head and walked into the Ladies, provoking a squeak from an elderly woman with blue hair on her way out.

'Where are you?' he shouted, looking below the cubicle doors.

'Here,' Rachel said, bringing down her right hand in a rabbit punch that she only slightly pulled. Yiorgos collapsed like a bull stunned by a bolt gun. She turned and left, briefly hoping he wasn't too badly injured.

On the walk to the Town Hall, she took the foreign press ID from her pocket and hung it round her neck. Her weapons were in her bra, which was a larger size than she usually wore. Men on the street looked at her differently.

'*Le Figaro*,' she said to the policeman at the barrier by the old mosque. Control had checked that the French paper wasn't sending a reporter. It was late afternoon now and the streetlights were coming on. There were extra lights around the platform where the VIPs would appear, as well as a lectern bearing the logos of Thessaloniki and the Development Ministry in Greek and English.

Edging her way through the journalists, she got to the front, only a couple of metres from the lectern. It was amazing what a smile and a large bosom could do. Then she started to look around. Was her great-uncle here? Control had assumed that the combined presence of Germans, some of whom had Nazi forebears, and Greeks with collaborators in their families would be too tempting for him to miss. She shared that opinion, but she had seen no sign of either him or his sons. Their disguise must be effective – unless they were going for long shots like Dan. She glanced up at the building on the other side of the road. The balconies were all devoid of people because of the early evening chill. Then again, a decent sniper would be concealed. She wasn't convinced. In all the kills attributed to Aron Samuel, he got close to his victims. It was hard to see him changing his modus operandi so late in life.

Then she saw a familiar face and blinked in astonishment.

'Remember,' Yosif said, 'do nothing to disrupt proceedings and you'll be home and free.' He gave Mavros the eye. 'Try to intervene and I'll cut your liver out.' He pointed to the haft of the knife in his belt under the uniform jacket.

'All right. But if anything happens that I haven't been told about, my agreement with your father is null and void.'

The van stopped and the front door slammed shut.

Yosif went to the rear doors. He motioned Mavros towards him and put on his own police cap, before winding the investigator's long hair up and jamming the hat over it.

'Pity you didn't have a shave this morning.'

'Your fault.'

'It's not important. Nobody will be paying attention to us.'

He opened the doors and they got down. They were outside the mosque, the Town Hall visible behind. The driver had already disappeared.

'Come on,' Yosif said. 'I'll be one step behind you.'

Mavros headed for the end of the barrier. There was a plastic name tag – Athanasopoulos – on his right breast pocket. He wondered if it would get him through. He could raise the alarm, but he was sure Yosif would carry out his threat. His eyes weren't as dead as his father's, but they would be soon.

The officer at the barrier waved them past and they walked at regular pace to the platform, as Mavros had been told they would do earlier. The air was full of the gossip and laughter of media people, a cloud of cigarette smoke rising in the lights. Mavros suddenly thought of the last remains of the death-camp victims as they blew away in black clouds. It was then that Aron Samuel's plan made complete sense. He almost wished he had a functioning pistol.

The main doors of the Town Hall opened and security men came out, their eyes studying the crowd. Then the Development Minister, the Mayor and the Minister of Macedonia and Thrace came forward, a group of business people behind them. In the middle of that, surrounded by men who were considerably taller than him, walked a man in Arab costume, his white robe reaching what looked like very expensive black shoes, and a red and gold turban on his head.

Yosif nudged him and climbed up on to the platform, nudging officers of lower rank aside.

None of them objected. They were on the right of the lectern, only a few metres from the Development Minister, who had started to speak.

Then Mavros saw Rachel. She was right below the platform, with an identification tag round her neck. It was resting on her chest, which was larger than it had been when he'd last seen her. She was staring at him, in control as ever, but clearly puzzled. He moved his eyes to the speaker and waited.

The Development Minister, a relative of the Prime Minister, was extolling the virtues of northern Greece, in particular Macedonia, whose name the neighbouring country had no right to use. He gave thanks to his colleagues, smiling crookedly at the Minister for Macedonia and Thrace. Mavros knew they hated each other and presumed the ceremony wasn't taking place at the more imposing building that housed the other man's ministry because he'd lost the power struggle. The Mayor seemed happy about that, smirking in the background. The speech droned on and the smiles of the foreign visitors became more forced, while the Greek businessmen, used to such affairs, stood to sullen attention. At last the minister finished and invited Dieter Jahnel, head of the investment consortium, to speak a few words.

Clearly at ease, the German congratulated his hosts in unaccented English. He started to outline the virtues of the agreement but, as the first of the ash began to fall, he lost concentration.

Mavros looked up. Aron Samuel's plan was working like a Swiss clock, even though he wouldn't approve of that simile.

Then the banners unfurled from the balconies on the third floor of the Town Hall and mayhem duly broke out.

Aron was on the third floor, looking at the sudden chaos below. It had been a masterstroke to involve the local anarchists in his plan. The young men had even washed their hair and cut off their beards so they would look like convincing cleaning staff, the real ones having been paid off. The women had baulked at the gaudy yellow coats, but had soon seen sense. This was going to be the most talked-about display of opposition to the government and big business in decades. They weren't particularly interested in the story of Thessaloniki's Jews – their older relatives had either kept silent or didn't know about it – but they liked the idea of throwing ashes over the podium. The ashes themselves were a mixture of the residue of log fires and human remains that had been bought from a crematorium in Bulgaria. Aron wanted the VIPs to experience the real thing, at least in part.

People started looking up as the flow of ash increased – there were anarchists up on the fourth floor too, with Isaak overseeing. They released the banners, which unrolled smoothly, their lower ends a couple of metres above the heads of those on the podium. There were five banners, each with a large colour image of the subject, their family background and crimes printed in large red letters below. The Development Minister's father had made his fortune from former Jewish-owned leather factories bought cheaply; the Mayor's grandfather had been a senior Thessaloniki police officer, who had enthusiastically taken part in the persecution of the Jews; the leader of the German consortium, Dieter Jahnel, had a grandfather in the Waffen-SS, who had killed many Greeks, including Jews; another of the German investors was related to Max Merten, the wartime civilian commandant of the city, whose arrest in the late 50s had caused an international scandal; and Makis Kalogirou, businessman and neo-Nazi, grandson of a collaborator and soon to be one of the recipients of the consortium's largesse – though it appeared he wasn't present.

All the cameras were pointed at the façade of the Town Hall. Aron nodded to the anarchist coordinator and leaflets giving more details of the five men's tainted backgrounds were thrown out, many of them floating beyond the podium to the media scrum.

The old man smiled. His plan was almost complete. There was just one more element, the final act of remembrance.

Mavros brushed the grey dust from his jacket. When he touched it, he realised some was grittier than the rest. He caught a glimpse of Aron Samuel on a third-floor balcony as the banners unfurled. The Greeks on the podium started shouting and shaking their fists, while the German who had been speaking looked up in astonishment. The press mob grabbed leaflets like hungry hyenas, mobile phones clamped to their ears. This was going to be a huge story. Then Yosif pushed past him and made for the lectern, throwing away his police cap. Calm amid the chaos, he pushed the German away and began to read out a list of names and ages. First were members of the Samuel family, then others who had perished on the way to or at Auschwitz. The electricity was cut, but Yosif kept going, projecting like an ancient orator. Every camera was on him. Mavros unexpectedly felt proud of what Aron's son was doing.

Then he looked to the front and saw Rachel climbing on to the platform. The police line had broken now, as officers ran into the building to seize the demonstrators. The man in Arab dress had initially been hustled towards the Town Hall doors, but when it became clear that the action wasn't directed at him – the Development Minister was talking to him desperately, almost clawing his robes – he stepped forward, the security men rapidly regrouping around him.

Rachel had both hands down her top. When they emerged, there was a black object in each one. Jesus, Mavros thought, moving forward, is she going to shoot him? There were two cracks in the general clamour and the bodyguards in front of the sheik went down, their arms and legs jerking. Tasers. Then the Arab's head exploded in a mist of reddish grey, the sound of a shot following immediately. Now serious pandemonium broke out. Mavros followed Rachel as she reached the far end of the podium and pushed through the crowd, all of whose members were staring at the heap of bloodied white. She got to the northern barrier and dealt the policeman there a blow that laid him out, before hurdling the wooden horizontal. Mavros was about twenty metres behind her.

Then a second shot ran out. Rachel turned. Mavros looked over his shoulder to see a body falling and then hitting the platform in front of the first dead man. Aron Samuel's blood-spattered face was recognisable above the heads of the spectators.

'No!' Rachel screamed. 'No!'

Mavros caught up and put his arms round her. She fought him, but he pinned her arms to her body.

'No,' she moaned, as he pushed her up the street. 'That wasn't part of the ... mission.' She tugged away from him. 'That fucker Dan...'

Mavros went after her. 'Leave him. If he can kill your great-uncle, he can do the same to you. Where are you supposed to be?'

She stared at him blankly and then came back to herself. 'Corner of Baltadhorou and Venizelou Streets. I know the way.'

Looking over his shoulder, Mavros saw that some of the press were still gathered around the podium. Given the fact that a sniper – Dan, if Rachel was to be believed – was in the vicinity, he reckoned that proved the media's representatives were either devoted to their duty or crazy. Or both. He caught a glimpse of Yosif, his police jacket off, heading down a Street on the other side of the road, another man with him. He hoped it was Isaak and that they would get away. They'd done the right thing to leave their father

360

behind. His long life of vengeance was over. Perhaps Aron would have enjoyed the irony – that he had been killed at the only peaceful mission he'd carried out.

Mavros had to run hard to keep up with Rachel. His lungs were straining by the time she stopped before the corner.

'So this ... is it?' he said, panting. 'Your bosses in Tel Aviv ... will be pleased that the sheik's down. I presume ... he was some kind of terrorist.'

Rachel looked him in the eye and then laughed. 'I'm not Mossad, you idiot. Dan and I are CIA, though you'll never be able to prove it.'

The driver of the large 4x4 on the road ahead honked his horn.

'And your great-uncle?'

'My father and I were genuinely trying to find him. Obviously my superiors wanted rid of him on foreign soil.'

'So I've been working for the bastards who ran Greece for decades?'

'Indirectly. But my father's paying you.' She grabbed his arm. 'And he doesn't know about my second job.'

'I don't want his money.'

'Take it.' She smiled with some warmth. 'You'll need it when the baby comes.'

Then she kissed him on the cheek, ran to the open door and got into the vehicle. It drove into the night at speed.

FORTY-TWO

The Fat Man was lying in a room with two other men. He'd come round half an hour earlier, his head thundering as if a herd of mammoths was loose.

'Don't worry,' a chirpy nurse said. 'You'll be all right. The doctor was worried your upper spine was injured, but it isn't.'

'Feels ... like ... it is.'

'What happened?' Her lips twitched. 'You were found in the Ladies' Room of the Electra Palace Hotel.'

'Was I?' He thought about that. 'Oh, yes.'

'Oh yes, what?'

'Someone hit me ... from behind.'

'In the Ladies' Room? Come on, Mr Pandazo-poulo. Don't you remember anything else? Such as, what you were doing there.'

'Er, no.' But he did. That cow Rachel must have hit him with a fire extinguisher, but he wasn't going to own up to that.

'And what about these burns? You've been in the wars recently.'

He closed his eyes and pretended to nod off. Shouts from the other patients made him open them again.

'What a disgrace!'

'Those fucking anarchists!'

'Wait, that Arab was shot.'

362

Yiorgos sat up and tried to focus on the small TV. He saw a large building with banners hanging from it, a crowd of people round the platform in front.

'The second shooting victim has not yet been identified. Police have dismissed suggestions that Sheik bin Zayed's assassination is related to the murder of the Jordanian Tareq Momani earlier in the week in Thessaloniki. Over twenty people have been arrested and are being held at police headquarters, though no one armed has yet been found.'

'What's going on?' the Fat Man asked.

He was told, three voices vying to inform and comment.

'So,' he said, holding a hand up, 'a group of protesters poured ash over the VIPs, dropped banners and leaflets proclaiming the collaborationist and Nazi pasts of some of them–'

'Though that lunatic Kalogirou wasn't there.'

'What do you mean lunatic? Makis is a good man.'

Yiorgos sighed. If Mavros hadn't been in the vicinity, he would be very surprised. The Jewish angle, with the man shouting out names and ages, proved that. He picked up his phone from the bedside table where it had been put and called his friend's mobile. It went to voice mail. He left a message, saying where he was.

The argument had got louder, with the youngest of the men raising his arm in a Nazi salute.

'Fuck this,' the Fat Man said, under his breath. He got up, clutching the back of his head, and looked in the wardrobe. His clothes were there. It took him several minutes to get dressed, his vision clouding and his legs unsteady.

'Where are you going?' said one of the arguers.

'Out of this shit hole.' Yiorgos looked at the youngest patient. 'Come over here and do that salute, you cretin. I'll break your fucking arm.'

The air went out of the loudmouth and he sat down on his bed.

'That's more like it, Nazi jackass.'

He managed to get down the passage without being spotted. He was on the first floor, so he avoided the lift and took the stairs slowly. Then he was outside, the chill air making him button his coat. Now what?

Back to the Electra Palace. Maybe Rachel tough girl Samuel was still there, though he knew it was a long shot. It was even less likely that Mavros would be there, but it was the only lead he had.

The Fat Man hailed a cab and almost fell over after extending his arm. Maybe getting out of bed hadn't been such a good idea after all.

Mavros was wrestling with his options. They were few. He was in a back street near the hotel, but he didn't want to show his face there again. He was cold, dressed in a fake police uniform, without the jacket and cap, and without his own clothes, phone and wallet – they'd all been taken from him by Aron Samuel. So buying new clothes and phone, and changing his flight were out of the question. There was also the point that he was a wanted man – or would be soon, when the police started going through the videos and CCTV of the disastrous publicity event. That wasn't even the worst of it. Dan was probably still on the loose and likely to be gunning for him. If he really was CIA, Mavros's involvement with Rachel and his knowledge, limited as it was, of what had gone on would be embarrassing for the agency. He huddled further into the darkness, then made up his mind.

There was a police station up the road from the hotel. He put his head down and walked quickly towards it.

The officer at the door looked at his incomplete uniform. 'Who are you?' he demanded.

'I need to talk to the man in charge of the Town Hall investigation – or rather, he needs to talk to me.'

'And why's that?'

'Because I know who the shooter was.'

After that, the wheels turned quickly. A quarter of an hour later, Mavros was in an interrogation room in the police headquarters building. An inspector had taken his personal details, then left him alone, declining his request for a phone call. Mavros was worried about Niki, as well as his family. He'd been out of touch for well over a day now.

The door opened and Nikos Kriaras walked in.

'What the hell are you doing here?' Mavros asked.

'The same goes for you.' The brigadier, wearing a black suit, leaned over the table. 'It had better be good.'

'Are you in charge of the investigation into the shootings?'

Kriaras sat down and eyed him dubiously. 'I'm in charge of anything the minister wants. His colleagues who were at the scene are squabbling about who has jurisdiction. Let's say I'm neutral. That appeals to the top men in Athens.'

'Neutral?' Mavros said, an eyebrow arching. 'You're the establishment's pet Alsatian.'

The policeman shrugged. 'And you're its pet hate. Start talking.'

Mavros did as he was told, skimping only on Aron Samuel's back story and his and Rachel's discovery of Baruh Natzari's body – it really did seem to have been suicide.

'You realise that impersonating a police officer is a serious offence,' the brigadier said.

'So arrest me. But it won't get you anywhere. I was forced into it and Yosif Samuel had a knife at my back all the time.' Mavros looked at the hood-eyed cop. 'Have you caught him and his brother?'

'Would what you know of their abilities suggest that we have?'

'No. What about Rachel and Dan? Are you going up against the CIA?'

Nikos Kriaras was picking his nails. 'Surely you didn't believe her. Agency operatives don't go around telling civilians who they are.'

Mavros thought about that. 'So they were Mossad after all?'

'Maybe.'

Kriaras had a better poker face than most, but Mavros reckoned Rachel had told him the truth.

'Tell me this, Alex. Did you have any idea that the sheik was going to be attacked?'

'I didn't even know there was a sheik involved

366

until I saw him. Who was he, anyway?'

'Mohammed bin Zayed, one of the Emirates' richest men.'

'Why would anyone want to shoot him? Don't tell me. He was funding terrorist groups. Both the CIA and Mossad would have wanted him dead.'

'Especially in another country.'

'Did he have anything to do with Tareq Momani?'

'Not that we know of. I doubt he'd have come if he had.'

'True. Then again, rich men can't resist the perfume of profit.'

'You're a fucking aphorist now?'

'And the five men on the banners?'

'They all have the backgrounds that Aron Samuel dug up.'

'The German who was speaking when it all started looked pretty shocked.'

Kriaras grinned. 'Dieter Jahnel? Yes, his grand-dad was a piece of shit, but he seems to be a decent man. The sins of the fathers, eh?'

Mavros had reached the stage of every conversation with Kriaras when his outrage could no longer be controlled.

'You and your squalid friends sat back and let this happen, didn't you? It suits the government and its backers for terrorists like Momani to be killed on Greek soil; they look good in the eyes of the so called civilised West. You wanted Aron Samuel dead as well. The Americans were applying pressure. They didn't want to kill him in their own country because of the Jewish lobby, whereas Jews here are nothing.'

Nikos Kriaras, as ever at such times, wore a look suggesting his personal honour had been impugned. 'We couldn't have guessed what he was going to do or that there was a killer on his tail. You said yourself that Rachel didn't know.'

'Of course she didn't know. They, you, all the corrupt fuckers in the world used her like I was used.'

'Rachel Samuel is no innocent. The indications are that she and the agent called Dan killed Momani. Not only that, they Tasered the Russians that were protecting him.'

'Russians? You're kidding. What is this, Cold War Number Two Central?'

'The weather is getting wintery. By the way, Makis Kalogirou is in hospital. Someone carved swastikas all over his face. I don't suppose you know anything about that.'

'You don't suppose correctly. Though that piece of shit deserves all he gets.' Mavros stood up. 'Which reminds me. Who burned the Fat Man's house down?'

'Why are you asking me?'

The silence that ensued was not golden.

'All right. We think the Athens branch of the Phoenix Rises did it.'

'To get me out of Thessaloniki?'

Kriaras shrugged. 'Who knows how those people's minds work?'

'You.'

Again, the brigadier looked insulted. 'Oh, by the way, you do know that your overgrown friend is up here?'

'What?'

'He called me this morning, convinced Kalogirou had you. I was able to tell him that wasn't the case.'

'You and your little Nazi friend.'

'Grow up. Anyway, I had a tag put on Pandazopoulos's name and, lo and behold, he was on a flight that landed in the early afternoon. Obviously you haven't seen him.'

'No. Can I call Niki? She'll be going out of her mind.'

'I thought she already had.'

'Fuck you.'

'I don't know why I help you,' Kriaras said, sliding his phone across the table.

'Because you couldn't do your job without me.'

Kriaras showed no sign of getting up, so Mavros called Niki in front of him.

The Fat Man had been refused entry to the Electra Palace by a pair of granite-faced doormen.

'Lackeys of the rich!' he shouted from the square. 'Oppressors of the people!'

'Gut bucket of a pervert!' one of them called back. 'Dress up in drag the next time you want to use the Ladies.'

Yiorgos felt his balance go and staggered to a bench. He sat there for some time, feeling far from well. Then his phone rang. 'It's me. I hear you're in Thessaloniki.'

'Alex? Are you ... all right?'

'Apart from having just been forcibly put in a police car going to the airport, yes.'

'Can you pick ... pick me up?'

'You sound awful.'

The Fat Man heard partially muffled talking.

'Where are you?'

'Outside that hotel you were staying in.'

Mavros relayed the location. 'What are you doing there?'

'I ... I don't know.'

'Christ, Yiorgo, you're scaring me. Do you need an ambulance?'

'No! No ... I just want to meet up ... with you and go home go back to Athens.'

'We'll be there in a few minutes.'

The Fat Man started to inhale deeply. He stood up, holding on to the top of the bench, then forced himself to walk to the road. Sweat bloomed all over his body and he wiped his face with a handkerchief. It felt like steel fingers were squeezing the back of his neck.

An unmarked car pulled up and the back door opened. Yiorgos stumbled over and almost fell on top of Mavros. He was pushed gently into an upright position.

'You shouldn't have travelled,' Mavros said. 'It was too soon.'

'No ... I ate a bad pizza.'

'Only one?'

'Very ... funny. What happened ... to your face? Quite an improvement.'

'I hope he isn't going to throw up,' said the plain-clothed officer in the passenger seat.

'I'll be ... OK.' The Fat Man glared at his friend. 'What are you doing in a cop uniform?'

'The rest of my clothes, not to mention my phone and wallet, are casualties of war. I tried to

370

talk Kriaras into buying me a new outfit, but all he did was give me this jacket. Are you sure...'

'I'm ... fine.'

'In that case, give me your phone.'

'Pocket nearest you.'

Mavros took out the device and pressed buttons.

'Niki? I'm sorry I couldn't talk much before. What is it? Don't cry, my love. It's true, what I told you. I'm on the way to the airport now. We'll be back in a couple of hours. We? Yiorgos and I. Yes, he came to find me. Touching, don't you think? Yes, I'll call you when we land. Love you.'

'Screw touching,' the Fat Man said. 'You're paying me by the hour.'

Mavros laughed, then called his mother to tell her he was fine. Half an hour later they were at the boarding gate, the pair of Thessaloniki cops waiting to see that they got on the plane. They were wasting their time. He'd had enough of the co-capital. He wanted to be back in Athens with Niki.

Maria Orfanou was sitting on the sofa with her arm round Niki, who was crying.

'Come on, darling. He's on his way. The case is over.' They had seen the TV news. Although Mavros's name wasn't mentioned, they were both sure he'd been involved in some way with the events at the Town Hall. 'Cheer up, dearest. You might even get pregnant tonight.'

Niki buried her face into her friend's chest, then sat up. 'I can't ... take it,' she whispered.

371

'What do you mean?'

'Alex disappearing all the time ... running out on me ... ignoring me.'

Maria looked at her. 'Niki, get a grip. I'm not Alex's biggest admirer, but what you're saying isn't fair and you know it. It's not as if he gets involved with other women or drinks or does drugs.'

'How do you know?'

Maria groaned. 'You're not yourself. Go and have a shower and tidy up. Your man's coming home. You know he loves you.'

Niki wiped her face with her sleeve. 'Do I?'

'Get in the shower,' Maria said firmly. 'If he sees you like this, he really will hit the road.'

'You're right,' Niki said, after a long pause. 'He deserves to see me at my best.'

Maria watched her walk away. Not for the first time, she thought her friend needed therapy from a psychiatrist rather than a fertility specialist.

FORTY-THREE

Mavros was at the window. The plane wasn't full so there was a seat between him and the Fat Man who, unusually, had passed up the opportunity to buy food at the airport shop. His friend's abdomen was giving the seat belt some trouble and his face was drenched in sweat as they took off.

'You don't look at all well.'

'Another brilliant observation ... from Greece's

foremost dick,' Yiorgos wheezed.

'Sorry I care.' Mavros turned to the window and looked down. It was a clear night and the lights of the peninsula below shone brightly. He made out the road that led to Ayia Triadha and then the resort itself. That made him think of Baruh Natzari's trip to the taverna there. The old man hadn't struck him as a potential suicide, but Aron Samuel's plan must have been the last straw.

Then he had a flash of his brother – Andonis sprinting across the sand like a bronzed ancient athlete. The trip to Thessaloniki had brought him back more vividly than for some time. Was that good or bad? Mavros wasn't sure.

The Fat Man groaned as the aircraft hit turbulence off the eastern flank of Mount Olympus. Mavros didn't like the look of him at all – his face was sallow under the runnels of sweat and one hand was supporting his head as if it might roll off. He would have said something, but he didn't want to be snapped at again.

Besides, he was still trying to tie together elements of the case. Aron Samuel had devoted several hours to telling his story. Why was that? Did he want Mavros to get it out to the world? Surely that was his sons' job. Then again, he might have been concerned that they wouldn't live long enough to do so. Would they carry on with Aron's work? Mavros hoped not. He wasn't going to put any more of the old man's story into the statement Kriaras would take from him in Athens. That meant Yosif and Isaak would be in the clear at least as regards earlier executions –

though the CIA might well have them in their sights. If the sheik had been funding terrorists, his assassination was understandable enough. But what about Aron's? Had the Americans finally had enough of the old man's renegade actions? They'd agreed to give him citizenship back in the 50s. Perhaps they'd only recently discovered his links with the Communists.

Then Mavros thought of Rachel. She'd been betrayed by her controllers, whichever agency she was working for. He wondered if she would leave, or even go after Dan. She was a strange woman and he had never succeeded in breaking her armoured carapace. Maybe Kriaras had been right – maybe she and Dan were working for Mossad all along. The world of espionage didn't provide easy answers, only shadows, mirrors and stabbings in the back. Who had cut Makis Kalogirou's face? Was that Dan? Could it have been Rachel? Or maybe there really were other players. It was hard to believe the Russians were involved too, but anything was possible – especially in the city that had once been the melting-pot of the Balkans.

He sat back as the plane began its approach to Athens airport. Aron Samuel. He hadn't always lived the black life, but he had been swallowed up by it far too young. Who could say how they themselves would react in similar circumstances? Except that wasn't right. The overwhelming majority of death-camp survivors lived ordinary, if troubled, lives after liberation. And it wasn't just the experience of the Sonderkommando; Samuel had become a killer even before he left his home city – the killer of another Jew. There was something harder than titanium in him. It had kept him alive, but had consumed his soul. Mavros remembered how he had no particular desire to meet his great-niece, and had never been in touch with his nephew. Still, despite all the horror Aron had been responsible for, Mavros couldn't help respecting him. He had made a stand against an evil much greater than himself and refused to let it prevail. He had also brought the issue of collaboration, long dormant in Greece, to the fore, though that was a lesser achievement. There would be a period of recrimination and accusations, then the media that were controlled by the special interests would start to bury the story. At least the foreign press would have taken note. Aron Samuel's last mission had not been in vain, even if the killing of the Arab would steal some of his glory. As for the investment consortium, how likely was it that its members – mostly German – would feel like going ahead after they'd been symbolically sprinkled by the ashes of their ancestors' victims?

Yiorgos clutched the arm rest with his free hand until the plane stopped taxiing. There was the usual stampede for the exit and they waited till it abated.

'Let's go,' Mavros said, undoing his friend's seat belt.

The Fat Man looked up at him, eyes initially unfocused. Then he got up with difficulty and moved down the aisle. Mavros followed, asking for his phone as they went into the terminal.

'Niki, we've landed. I'll see you in about an hour.'

'Alex, I'm so happy,' she said. 'Hurry back, I've got a surprise for you.'

'Is that right? It wouldn't have anything to do with lingerie, would it?'

'Might.'

'Hold me back.'

'I love you.'

Mavros looked at Yiorgos, who was lumbering along, his breathing heavy.

'Love you, too. Bye.' He put the phone in his pocket and took the Fat Man's arm. 'You'd better sit down for a minute.' He led him to a seat. 'Why are you propping up your head? I don't remember hearing that you'd injured it in the fire.'

'I ... didn't.'

'So what happened?'

'That bitch ... client of yours. She ... she hit me from behind.'

'Rachel hit you?' Mavros looked at the back of Yiorgos's head. There was bruising below his neck.

'I was trying ... to get her ... to find you.' Then the Fat Man passed out and keeled over, nearly sending Mavros to the floor under him.

'Help!' He waved to a uniformed woman. 'My friend's in trouble.'

The airport personnel were efficient and swift – it was run by a German company. Within a quarter of an hour, Mavros and Yiorgos were in an ambulance, heading for the KAT hospital in the northern suburb of Kifissia. It was motorway all the way and the paramedics radioed ahead with a report on the patient's condition. Emergency staff were waiting for the ambulance. A junior doctor took the Fat Man's details from Mavros and pointed to the waiting area.

In the rush it was an hour before Mavros remembered to call.

'It's all right, Alex, I understand,' Niki said. 'Take as long as you need. At least find out what they're going to do for the lump of lard.'

'Charming.'

She laughed. 'I won't take off what I'm wearing till you arrive. But I'm going to bed now, all right?'

'The very thought's making me salivate.'

'Careful, they'll diagnose you with rabies.'

'What makes you think I'm not rabid for you?' He paused. 'Niki, we will have a baby. I promise.'

'Thank you, my love. But for that to happen, there's something you have to do.'

'Don't worry, I will. Several times.'

'Promises, promises.'

'Kisses on the mouth and elsewhere.'

Niki laughed as if all the cares had been lifted from her and vanished on the wind.

It was after three when a white-coated doctor arrived and told Mavros not to worry. Yiorgos was stable, his neck in a brace. He'd been lucky. The strain of holding his head up had caused a hairline crack in his second cervical vertebra and could have led to permanent nerve damage, but they'd been able to pre-empt that. The patient would be on his back for some time. He was asleep, so Mavros could go.

'Can I see him?'

'Just for a few moments and don't wake him.'

Mavros had an ulterior motive, though the sight of the Fat Man in a large brace, his hands attached to the side of the bed, was disturbing. He opened the wardrobe and removed his friend's wallet from his trouser pocket. Arriving home and having to ask Niki to pay the taxi would somewhat shatter the romantic dream. He touched Yiorgos's hand lightly and left.

In the taxi Mavros considered calling ahead, but decided to let Niki sleep. The roads were clear and he was on the slopes of Lykavittos forty minutes later.

The politician's guard was asleep in his box, not for the first time. Mavros considered banging on the glass, but couldn't be bothered. If someone wanted to sneak in and hammer on the money-grabbing pig's door, all the better. He was going to take the stairs, but his legs ached even from the three steps to the hall. Sleep deprivation was beginning to overwhelm the lengthy adrenaline rush that had kept him going. The lift smelled of perfume and cigar smoke.

On the fifth floor, all was quiet. He tapped on the numerical pad outside their door, then inserted his key. It struck him the Niki might have put on the chain without thinking and he'd have to wake her anyway. Thankfully she hadn't.

The light was on in the living room. Maybe she was on the sofa under a blanket. Mavros took off the ill-fitting black shoes Aron Samuel's sons had given him and padded inside.

The first thing he saw as he went towards the

end of the hall was a broken vase, roses spread around the pool of water like dead goldfish. Then he saw a chair from the dining table on its side.

Acid gushing into his stomach, Mavros went on. He gasped and stepped towards Niki's hanging form. She was in red and white underwear, her toes pointing to the floor. He wrapped his arms round her thighs and looked up. Her head was to the side, a large knot by her upper ear and the other end of the rope on the ceiling hook from which the lamp was suspended. He felt for a pulse in her wrist.

Then he became aware that he was saying her name over and over. Leaving her for a few seconds he dragged the coffee table closer and stepped on to it. He held on to her, hand now touching her throat. The tip of her tongue extended from blue lips, drops of blood on her chin.

Eventually, when the pain in his chest became too great, Mavros let his lover go and called the police. He wanted to cut her down, but the apartment was potentially a crime scene and he shouldn't touch anything else. Then he saw a photograph on the floor by the chair. It showed him and Rachel at the restaurant in the Electra Palace, both of them laughing.

Alex Mavros had stared into the abyss of the twentieth century's greatest crime, without realising how great a price there would be to pay. He squatted in a corner and felt his life turn everlastingly, indelibly black.

The publishers hope that this book has given you enjoyable reading. Large Print Books are especially designed to be as easy to see and hold as possible. If you wish a complete list of our books please ask at your local library or write directly to:

Magna Large Print Books
Magna House, Long Preston,
Skipton, North Yorkshire.
BD23 4ND

This Large Print Book for the partially sighted, who cannot read normal print, is published under the auspices of

THE ULVERSCROFT FOUNDATION